PROTOCOL

The Maggie O'Malley Mystery Series
by Kathleen Valenti

PROTOCOL (#1)

A MAGGIE O'MALLEY MYSTERY

PROTOCOL

KATHLEEN VALENTI

HENERY PRESS

PROTOCOL
A Maggie O'Malley Mystery
Part of the Henery Press Mystery Collection

First Edition | September 2017

Henery Press, LLC
www.henerypress.com

Trade Paperback ISBN-13: 978-1-63511-239-9
Digital epub ISBN-13: 978-1-63511-240-5
Kindle ISBN-13: 978-1-63511-241-2
Hardcover ISBN-13: 978-1-63511-242-9

Printed in the United States of America

To Alan, my partner in crime writing.

ACKNOWLEDGMENTS

It's been said that writing is a solitary act. For me it's felt like one great big group hug.

I've been lucky enough to experience the embrace of encouragement from friends and family, from that first "Hey, I think I'll write a book" to the moment I held *Protocol* in my hands. It may take a village to raise a child, but it takes a small nation of experts, readers and grammatical doulas to birth a book.

I have a million thanks, but not nearly as many pages, so I'll keep my words of gratitude brief-ish.

First, my many thanks to my family: my husband, Alan, who believed in me when I didn't; my children, who tolerated overly detailed updates on imaginary people; my mom, who was my first teacher of love and loss; my dad, who always encouraged me to reach higher; my mother-in-law, Molly, for her close-reading and rum cake baking; my kind and talented cousin-in-law, Tara, for reading and cheering me on; John for serving as a beta reader; and Phyllis for her meticulous proofreading.

I'm also grateful to those who are like family for offering endless support and tireless beta reading: Valerie, dear friend and browbeater-in-chief; Nancy, best friend, Jazzercise compatriot and writing inspiration; Tenley, Georell and Lisa, former coworkers, forever friends and happy hour companions; Randy, faithful reader and flying buddy; and Ed and Martin, amazing humans and cherished friends.

I also benefited from the incomparable expertise of industry and category mavens. My greatest debt of gratitude in this regard is to Jim, who provided unflagging pharmaceutical counsel and never once suggested that I gave that whole "there are no dumb questions" adage a run for its money. I am also deeply grateful to Vince for his technological expertise, and to Kristen, who made my manuscript drop and give her twenty.

Of course, this book would never have seen the light of day if Jordan at Literary Counsel hadn't said, "I do" when I asked him to be my agent and if the amazing team at Henery Press hadn't welcomed me into their feathery fold. The Hen House is home to some of the kindest, most gracious people I've ever known, and I feel especially blessed to have Rachel as my editor and ally, as well as Erin, Kendel and the rest of Henery's crack editorial team.

This book may have my name on the cover, but it belongs to all those who helped me create it and to all those who choose *Protocol* to grace their nightstands. To all who have helped and all who read, I am truly grateful. The only things for which I can claim 100 percent credit are any errors; those are mine alone.

Prologue

It wasn't until she was five blocks from home, well past the newsstand but before the buckling sidewalk in front of the old library, that Elsa Henderson knew she was being followed.

She'd left the office late, her desk a maze of notes and lipstick-stained paper coffee cups, and headed into the starless night with her briefcase empty and her head full of the work that would be waiting in the morning. She didn't worry about walking alone at night. This was Collinsburg, for God's sake. Safe. Charming. The Goldilocks of the Midwest. Not *too* anything. Except maybe hot.

Then...a feeling. A tingle at the base of her neck. The sensation of being watched.

She turned, casually flipping salon-blown hair, and looked behind her.

The street was empty.

She sighed and shook her head. Laughed her signature throaty laugh. Work was getting to her. Maybe the protests, too, although those were daytime affairs and more nuisance than worry. She needed a glass of wine, a hot bath and an hour of mindless television. Maybe *Dancing with the Stars* or—

Elsa stopped. The hair at the back of her neck stood at attention as if an icy hand trailed a finger along her spine. A feeling of unseen eyes crawled over her.

She spun quickly this time, eyes darting from the streetlight to the blue US Mail drop box to the doorways where darkness clotted.

The street was still vacant.

Hadn't she heard something? A whisper of fabric? The slip of rubber soles on a pebble? Or was it all in her head, a figment of her imagination—or what her coworkers insisted was increasing paranoia over unseen and undefined danger?

She squinted as if trying to read the street. A half-block away, in the doorway of her favorite smoothie shop, the shadows seemed darker. Denser. Man-shaped.

Elsa's heart thudded sickly in her chest. She quickened her pace, the clap-clap-clap of her heels in time with her heart. Telegraphing her growing dread.

Hurry up. Stop.

Get home. Stop.

Don't look back. Stop.

She wanted to run, but didn't. That would've been rude. What if she was overreacting? What if she *was* being paranoid? Maybe the man (the shadow?) was simply walking the same way. She hadn't even seen him—seen anyone, for that matter. Even if she had, there was no proof of pursuit beyond a sound, a feeling.

And yet...

Elsa Henderson broke into a light jog. A bead of sweat snaked beneath her arm, settling at the waistband of the Spanx she had yanked on that morning. Unable to resist, she chanced a look behind her.

A pair of headlights suddenly swung into view.

There was no man, no silhouette. Just sleek steel, shiny chrome and hungry, churning tires.

The headlights grew larger. The tires squealed, eating pavement as the car sped toward her, shuddering with each gear shift, nosing aside a rubber garbage can wheeled to the curb for tomorrow's collection.

"But—" she said.

The car struck her, tossing her into the air like a crash-test dummy without the car. Her head collided with the windshield, creating a pebble-sized ding in the glass and a spider web fracture in her skull.

The car sped on, pushing Elsa toward the roof rack until she rolled off, hitting the asphalt with a wet splat. She watched the red taillights recede into the darkness through the haze of blood now streaming down her face. The lights stopped. Then flashed to white.

The car backed up. Rolled over her. Then did it again.

Wash. Rinse. Repeat.

Bones ground to dust. Blood bloomed from her head. Her heart, with nothing left to pump, stopped.

Then everything became shadow.

Chapter 1

Maggie affixed what she hoped was a believable smile on her face. An arrhythmia-inducing techno beat thrummed through her body as a band called The Florid Drunks performed relentlessly a few feet away. Three women with long hair and short skirts danced toward the low stage, shoulders dipping and hips rolling, trying to catch the eye of the lead singer, who strummed the microphone cord in front of his crotch.

Whoever said it took more muscles to frown than smile had never been to The Office Bar & Grille.

"Isn't this great?" Zartar shouted, her kohl-lined eyes squinting against the bar's colored strobe lights.

Maggie widened the pasted-on smile and nodded. "Oh, yes," she yelled back. "Fantastic."

She had felt a ripple of panic when her two new coworkers had invited her out for a drink at the pharmaceutical crowd's favorite watering hole. Sure, her new lab partners were nice, but Maggie didn't friend easily. Outside of Constantine, she had, what? Two, maybe three friends?

But today was the beginning of a new chapter, her first day at her first real job. What better time to do something different, *be* something different, to define her life instead of the other way around?

She just had to get through the evening without losing her hearing. Or making a fool of herself.

Zartar glanced at Maggie's drink and raised her hand to catch the waiter's attention. She held three fingers aloft, the international sign for another round of the same. "Let's turn up the fun, shall we?" she trilled.

Before Maggie could protest, the waiter trotted off toward a black walnut bar crammed with twenty-somethings. Maggie shifted in her seat, trying to scoot farther into the tiny booth that threatened to disgorge her and her new coworkers/maybe-friends.

Her mouth ached with muscle fatigue. She licked her lips and took a sip of water.

The band ended its set and the musicians fist-bumped their way to the bar. Maggie's ears still rung with their cover of "Crazy Train."

"Finally," Zartar said, pulling her peasant blouse lower as the guitarist walked by. "Now we can hear about your first day."

"Yeah," Roselyn said, lining up her mozzarella sticks like tiny jets readying for takeoff, then blotting them with a napkin. "How was it?"

"Good," Maggie said, smiling genuinely for the first time. "Great, actually."

And why wouldn't it be? The position had been a real coup, not just because she'd bested a hundred and forty other applicants, but because she'd found something in her field with a company on the rise. The economy had left most new grads scrambling for the crumbs that fell from the corporate table. She was damn lucky, especially now that her father needed her. Plus, she was trying new things, like tonight.

The drinks arrived, white wine for Roselyn, margarita for Zartar, and vodka Collins for Maggie. Maggie took a long drag on her drink, savoring the sensation as the alcohol burned a path from her lips to her belly. "So how many years have you logged at Rxcellance?" she asked.

"Rx," Zartar corrected. "That's what everyone calls it. Rozzie's been there two years, I've been there three. Nearly four."

"You like it?"

"Something like that," Zartar said.

Maggie grabbed a jalapeno popper and stole a look at Zartar's face. Not a crack in the pore-minimizing foundation. She glanced at Roselyn. She was busy squirting hand sanitizer from a trial size bottle onto her hands. "Trouble in paradise?" Maggie asked.

Zartar downed her drink in two gulps, then sucked her teeth. "Not really. I just grew up to be someone different than I thought I'd be."

Maggie was trying to find a nice way to ask what *that* was supposed to mean when her phone chimed, its cheery bicycle bell warbling through the thin fabric of her nylon purse.

She plunged her hand into the bag, batted aside a billfold, a wad of Post-it notes and a half-eaten Luna bar, then pulled it free. She looked at the screen, sure it was her father checking in after her first day of work—a.k.a. Day One as the Human Life Raft.

A photo of a middle-aged woman with a designer haircut framing model-perfect cheekbones smiled back.

Zartar peered over her shoulder. "Who's the hottie?"

Maggie stared at the tiny screen. "I don't know," she answered. "I've never seen her before." Maggie tapped the phone's screen. A phrase appeared beneath the woman's photo:

MEETING REMINDER

TIME: 9 p.m. – 11 p.m.

Maggie frowned and tapped the screen again, hoping a name, contact information, something helpful, would materialize.

Nothing happened.

"If you've never seen her before," Zartar asked, reading the text, "then why do you have a meeting with her?"

"I don't," Maggie said. "I mean, it says we're scheduled to meet, but I've never seen her before, and I definitely didn't arrange any meeting." She shrugged, deleted the photo and dropped her phone back into her purse. "Must be some kind of glitch. I just got this phone a couple of days ago."

Maggie made a mental note to ask Constantine about the phone.

Maggie stayed longer—and drank more—than she intended. After she hit the bottom of her third drink and second serving of nachos, which had arrived at the table with a tiny Mexican flag as if the nation had conquered mountains of chips and cheese, she checked her watch, a dainty rhinestone affair that had once belonged to her mother.

Ten fifteen. How had the time gone so quickly?

She stood, peeling the backs of her sweaty knees from the leather seat. "I've gotta go. It's getting late."

"Late?" Zartar choked on her margarita. "What are you, ten years old?"

"Careful, or I won't share my candy necklace with you." Maggie folded some bills and slipped them under her glass. "I have to catch up on a couple of journal articles tonight, get up early for a run and—"

"Prepare your speech for The World's Most Boring Twenty-Five-Year-Old," Zartar finished. She pulled a tube and compact from her clutch purse and reapplied lip gloss. "I'm kidding. I mean, I prefer my exercise between the sheets, but whatever floats your boat. See you tomorrow."

"Bye," Roselyn said, bouncing up to give Maggie a quick hug. "I'm so glad you came out with us."

Maggie gave her a small squeeze back. She was glad, too. Despite the crowds and the noise, it had been a good evening. Fun, even. And she was starting to like her new coworkers. Maybe this doing-something-new thing would pan out.

Maggie excuse-me'd and pardon-me'd her way toward The Office's entrance. She glanced up at the enormous TV near the door. Someone had changed the channel from football to the news. A "BREAKING STORY" banner bleated from the top of the screen. Maggie read as she dragged her hand through her purse, trolling for keys.

Post Reporter Killed in Hit-and-Run

It wasn't the words that made her breath catch in her throat. It was the image that accompanied them.

The photo was a classic promotional shot, dated but professional. It featured a woman with long straight hair, fuchsia-colored blush and oversized eyeglasses. Maggie had never seen the photo before, but the woman's features, her self-assured gaze, were unmistakably familiar.

Maggie felt something stir deep in her belly, a feeling of disquiet that yawned and stretched and awakened. She swallowed.

It was the woman from the strange meeting reminder. Maggie was sure of it. She plucked her phone from her purse and scrolled.

No photo. No meeting reminder. Nothing to prove that the woman whose face was splashed across the TV screen was the same woman who had appeared on Maggie's phone a couple of hours earlier.

Right. Because she had deleted it. Genius.

She cleared her throat. The bartender, who looked as if he moonlighted as a Swedish tennis star, looked at her. "Can you turn that up?" she asked.

He gave a toothpaste commercial smile, grabbed the remote from beside the cash register and stabbed the volume button.

A hair-helmeted woman in a nipped-in navy blue jacket looked earnestly into the camera. "Tragedy tonight as award-winning journalist Elsa Henderson was killed in a hit-and-run in the heart of the city. Henderson, who worked for *The Post*, is remembered by friends and colleagues for her talent, professionalism and determination to get the story."

The camera cut away from the news anchor to archival footage of the woman who had been on Maggie's phone. Elsa Henderson receiving awards. Elsa Henderson being interviewed. Elsa Henderson looking cool and professional. And alive.

Maggie took a moment to marvel at how quickly the station had pulled together footage. It made sense. Elsa was print and they were TV, but as a journalist, she was one of their own.

The story was long on sentiment but short on answers. There were no eyewitnesses. No security camera footage. Just the reporter's description of Elsa Henderson's body lying in the street, arms outstretched in the equal sign that formed the crosswalk.

Maggie tapped a finger against her mouth. The more she watched the footage, the more she was certain that it was the same woman from the appointment reminder. The woman who had been killed within hours of appearing on Maggie's phone.

A chill scuttled up Maggie's back. She rubbed her arms briskly to scrub away the goose bumps that had sprung on her skin. She had a sudden and intense urge to get out of The Office, to escape the TV screen and whatever the strange coincidence meant.

And that's exactly what it was. A coincidence.

What else could it be?

Chapter 2

Maggie rubbed her eyes and craned her neck. A sea of brake lights stretched out beneath the morning sky. It had been a long night of sleep fractured by images of the woman on her phone. Now it looked like it was going to be a long morning.

Maggie opened her car door and stepped out to see why traffic had stopped. A long line of vehicles stretched out before her. She squinted. In the distance, she saw picket signs bouncing up and down. She and her fellow commuters were adrift in the latest wave of demonstrations.

Maggie was surprised that she was surprised.

Even before she'd moved to the big city, news of increasing disquiet had traveled from Greenville to Collinsburg with breathless alacrity, bringing reports of pockets of unrest that spread like prickly heat across the blistering city.

Maggie just didn't think she'd find herself in the middle of it. On the way to her second day of work.

She checked the dashboard clock. 7:48. Twelve minutes to get there.

A tightness traversed her chest. This was supposed to be the honeymoon phase of employment, where she wowed management and coworkers with her dedication, competency and work ethic.

Pretty much the opposite of showing up late on the second day.

She thought about her father. The restaurant with its peeling paint and empty parking lot. A surge of bile threatened to climb up her throat.

Come on, come on, come on, she pleaded silently to the line of cars. *Move.*

As if in response to her plea, brake lights blinked off ahead of her. The line of cars crept forward, a reception line moving toward the union of two busy intersections.

Progress. Slow, yes. But at least it surpassed glacial.

Maggie slumped against her seat as she idled forward. The traffic jam had a silver lining: now she had plenty of time to relive the embarrassment of the night before.

Spurred by a desire to escape the unnerving newscast she'd just witnessed, Maggie had charged toward The Office's entrance. The moment she'd reached the pub's rough-hewn door, however, it swung open to admit a new stream of after-work revelers.

Maggie lost her balance and pitched forward. She stumbled, ankles turning in new sling-backs, and fell clumsily against a man. She had tried to right herself, hands scrabbling for purchase, then slipped again, pulling the man's pants down with her.

"Whoa." The man grabbed the waistband of his khakis as they slid down his hips. He took Maggie by the elbows and righted her against the door.

Nearby patrons looked at her like she'd grown another head. Across the bar, she could see Zartar and Roselyn pausing mid-drink to take in the scene, their mouths tiny Os of shock.

"Are you okay?" the man had asked.

Maggie widened her stance to regain her balance and stared at him. The man smiled, his broad mouth revealing two crooked eye teeth. She wanted to look away, to answer his question. It would be the polite thing to do. The *normal* thing to do. But she felt stunned, as if an electric jolt had coursed through her body.

His grin broadened, dimples sprouting on cheeks. "I've had women fall for me, but never quite like this."

She had opened her mouth, closed it, opened it again, trying to find her voice, trying to find something witty—or anything at all—to say. Then the crowd surged forward and swept the man into the warm embrace of the bar as he smiled and waved at her.

Now trapped in morning gridlock, Maggie felt her face grow hot with the memory. She gave herself an inner eye-roll and mental face-palm. Another tick in the column for Maggie, Queen of the Socially Awkward.

But it wasn't like she was going to see Captain Handsome again. She was free to move on to other uncomfortable thoughts. Like the woman who had appeared on her phone then ended up dead.

Maggie couldn't imagine why she had received a reminder for a meeting with Elsa Henderson. She didn't know her. She hadn't even set up any appointments in the app. Maybe the reminder was intended for someone else. Or maybe it was a preview of coming attractions, an electronic crystal ball that offered a glimpse into the future.

Maggie knew that was ridiculous, but her stomach hadn't gotten the message. It flip-flopped in her belly, sending a surge of acid into her esophagus. She opened the glove box and shook out two antacids from an old film canister.

She chewed slowly.

There had to be a rational explanation, and she'd find it. She was a woman of science, after all. The fact that the same stranger who'd appeared on her phone was now lying in the morgue was just some strange quirk of fate, a technological glitch or both.

Or maybe it was—

Suddenly a man lunged from the sidewalk and pounded on her passenger window. "Death to capitalist pigs!" he yelled.

Somewhere in her brain she registered the lack of originality of his rallying cry, and it irritated her. *At least make an effort.*

But there were no catchy catchphrases or rousing songs to accompany these protests. What had begun as a peaceful Occupy Main Street demonstration to decry a proposed salary freeze for government employees had devolved into a me-too movement that attracted the generally-disgruntled as well as the directly affected. Tempers matched temperatures for heat and intensity. There wasn't much room for creativity. Or kindness for drivers on their way to work.

Maggie flinched at the angry voice, her arm accidentally hitting the horn.

The man's face purpled, his mouth twisting first in surprise, then in rage. He heaved his sign over his head and brought it down on Maggie's windshield. An image of Porky Pig dressed as Uncle Sam crashed against the glass. Maggie ducked as if the sign had struck her head.

The man raised the sign and swung again. The traffic light turned green. Maggie put the car in gear and stood on the gas pedal. The car bucked, throwing Maggie back in her seat, then lurched forward, knocking the man's sign from his hand. He stumbled and fell to the ground.

Maggie sped away. At a whopping eight miles per hour.

She glanced into her rearview mirror. The man gave her a one-fingered salute but didn't seem interested in pursuing her.

Fecking ass, she thought, using the Irish-ized version of the F-bomb her father, and therefore Maggie, had always preferred. She flipped the man off in her head, hoping she'd magically developed a Carrie-like telekinesis that would jab him in some secret lobe of his brain, then concentrated on the matter at hand: getting to work on time.

Her mind wandered back to the woman on her phone.

Could her death somehow be a result of the protests? Was the hit-and-run driver a protester who was angry about the media coverage? Someone exacting revenge for an unflattering portrayal of the conflict? The protests had been the top story for weeks, especially after sanitation and transportation employees had joined the fray, leaving the city still and reeking like a corpse rotting in the sun. Maybe frustration had boiled over, sweeping Elsa Henderson away in its frothy rage.

Maggie shook the thoughts from her mind. Her theories were pure conjecture, made out of whole cloth and half-assed ideas. She was getting caught up in emotion. And there was no time for that.

Maggie willed her pulse to slow, concentrating on loosening the muscles that banded her stomach like steel ropes. Six minutes later, Maggie arrived at the company parking lot.

She took a deep breath and looked up at her new professional home.

Ensconced in a hulking steel monolith, Rxcellance loomed over its neighbors like an officious landlord.

A spinoff of Dulton Pharmaceuticals, Rxcellance played Apple to Pfizer's IBM. Small. Agile. Innovative. With one miracle drug under its belt and rumors of more in the queue, Rxcellance was on the tipping point of greatness. Whispers of an IPO, once met with derisive snorts, had risen to the unmistakable rumble of the inevitable.

Rxcellance was going to be big, and Maggie was going to be a part of it.

Maggie parked and checked her teeth in the rearview mirror. That poppy seed bagel had been a mistake.

Maggie took a tiny flathead screwdriver from the glove box and gently wedged it between the seed and her right canine tooth. The poppy seed went flying. She grinned to the mirror in satisfaction. *And Pop wonders why I'm single.*

Maggie climbed out of the car and examined the hood. No damage from the jerk who'd assaulted her vehicle. She rubbed the fender. "My faithful chariot," she whispered.

The 1960 Studebaker was cherried out. Custard exterior, crimson interior. Original everything, including three-on-the-tree manual transmission. Maggie and her dad had restored it the summer she turned twelve. The summer cancer had planted a flag in her mother's liver and colonized her body until there was no room for a heartbeat.

She clicked across the parking lot, rode the elevator to the third floor and deposited herself in a cubicle covered in a tan fuzzy fabric that rivaled particle board for shade and luster.

Her stomach had gone back to churning. A metallic taste had seeped into her mouth, replacing the bitter taste of bile. Either her adrenaline was still in overdrive, or she was on the brink of a serious illness. Maggie resisted the temptation to palpate her glands, which she was sure were swollen. She figured she was coming down with something because of the stress of the morning. Like the flu. Or the bubonic plague.

Maggie logged on and waited for the computer's applications to load. Her eyes roved the cubicle, which was furnished with an ergonomic chair, a set of wire mesh in and out boxes, a desk phone and a small flowering plant desperately in need of a drink.

She stretched and yawned. Despite her jangled nerves, she was tired from what qualified as a late night in Maggie World. She needed caffeinated fortification, stat. She just hoped her sour stomach wouldn't rebel.

Maggie took the stairs down to the second floor and headed to a small kitchen she'd been introduced to on her official Day One tour. The tiny room housed an industrial-sized coffeepot and a small microwave and refrigerator. The wall to the left of the refrigerator was papered with company memos, Bureau of Labor and Industries notifications and a poster that told her to Keep Calm and Research On. Maggie's eyes zeroed in on the coffeepot. Empty. She groaned.

It was going to be *that* kind of day.

She opened a white Formica cupboard above the microwave, retrieved a box of coffee filters and studied the coffee options: regular and decaf. Judging by the labels and a startling lack of reference to actual coffee beans, Maggie was pretty sure they'd both taste like topsoil. But any port in a storm, right? She scooped regular coffee into the machine and waited.

"I love the smell of napalm in the morning." The man who Maggie had crashed into at The Office Bar & Grille leaned against the doorjamb, thumb in his pants pocket, a crooked grin lighting his face.

The mortification from last night's spectacular stumble returned. Evidently Captain Handsome wasn't a one-time run-in. Maggie felt her cheeks grow hot and prayed she wasn't blushing as ferociously as she felt she was. Unlike other gingers who pinked charmingly beneath a dusting of freckles, Maggie turned the approximate shade of a rutabaga.

Not exactly Jane Austen material.

Bar Guy took a deep breath of the room's acrid aroma, choked, then dissolved into a paroxysm of coughing. He crossed the room and ran the tap into the "Chemists Are Worth Their Weight in Au" mug in his hand and drank deeply. He wiped his mouth with the back of his hand. "Good stuff," he wheezed.

He was funny. Funny was good. And he was more gorgeous than Maggie had remembered. Maybe today she'd do more than stare and open and close her mouth like a cod.

Captain Handsome, a.k.a. Bar Guy, extended his hand. "I'm Ethan Clark. I think we met yesterday. Bumped into each other is more like it."

Maggie forced herself to look nonchalant, as if the memory of their brief encounter was slowly coming to mind. "The bar last night, right? I'm Maggie O'Malley." They shook hands.

"I know. I hear you're working with Jon's crew," he said.

Maggie was surprised. "Word travels fast."

Ethan tapped the ID badge hanging from his lanyard. "We management types know everything."

Management? So much for a good first impression.

Maggie wanted the earth to swallow her up. When that didn't happen, she tried for casual. "So what do you manage?"

"To stay out of trouble, mostly. And I head up Bioanalytics."

"Lots of great work being done in that sector these days. Real innovations. You must be out there on the bleeding edge."

"We're making some pretty exciting advances, especially lately." He checked his TAG Heuer watch. "Damn. I'm late. Well, back to the salt mines. It was nice to officially meet you, Maggie."

He thrust out his hand again. Maggie extended her own, then realized she was still holding the carafe and placed it back on the coffeemaker. "And it was...officially nice to meet you," Maggie stammered, her cheeks flaming again.

She watched him round the corner, catching a glimpse of herself in the reflection of the glossy refrigerator door. A giant coffee stain squatted in the center of her company issue button-down shirt like a fat spider.

Nice.

Maggie's phone chirped. She looked at the display. Constantine.

"Miss me yet?" he asked when she answered.

"Yes, I'm in the final stages of Constantine withdrawal," she said, a smile spreading across her face.

"Well, I am pretty addictive."

Maggie walked to the stairwell and began climbing to the third floor. "I'm glad you called. I mean, other than the fact I get to hear your voice."

Constantine affected a deep baritone. "Really?"

"Yeah, there's something weird going on with my phone. Did you get my text?"

"Something about a reminder?"

She emerged from the stairwell and crossed the hall to her desk. She waved to a couple of colleagues whose names she had learned but couldn't quite remember. "Yeah, I got this weird reminder on an app I didn't know I had for a meeting I never scheduled with someone I've never met."

"I'd say that qualifies as weird."

She thought about mentioning the dead woman. The fact that she was killed so soon after she appeared on Maggie's phone definitely dialed up the weird-o-meter. But was it anything more than strange timing? She didn't see how it could be.

"I'm wondering if you could take a look at it when I'm at Pop's this weekend to get the last of my stuff," she said. She paused, tried for nonchalant. "How is he?"

"You mean in the seventy-two and a half hours since you last saw him? Grouchy and foul-mouthed. You know, the usual."

Maggie remembered how her father had looked the last time she'd seen him. Hollows nestling beneath his cheekbones. Angles announcing bones at the shoulder and elbow. It took time and pressure to change the land. Could the geography of the body be much different?

Maggie suddenly realized Constantine had asked her a question. "I'm sorry, what was that?"

"I was asking about the new job. Have you made any friends? Cured any diseases?"

"No to the second, yes-ish on the first. I actually went out for drinks with a couple of coworkers last night."

Constantine whistled. "Drinks with coworkers on the first day? Sounds like you've loosened your policy on new relationships. What's next, vegetables with dinner?"

"French fries count, right?"

"Absolutely. See you Saturday?"

Maggie closed her eyes and pictured her father's wide, weathered face. "I'll be there."

Chapter 3

They were squatting in her mind again. Charlene could feel them moving around in the whorls and folds of her brain. Whispering. Cursing. Giving greasy, ruinous advice.

The doctors said she was sick, that something was wrong with the way her neurotransmitters talked to each other. But with all the voices in her head (and there were five now), she was pretty sure her brain didn't have a problem making conversation.

Charlene crouched beside a dumpster, looking over her rounded shoulder into the blackness that pooled in the shadows of sleeping buildings. She drew up her slack jaw, her cracked lips disappearing into a thin line.

She would not submit to the mind control of her doctors, the charlatans who sold the snake oil that made her calves twitch beneath the black plastic bags she wore over her stained clothes. Things were changing. She was changing.

She scratched her shoulder blades against the dumpster's rusty, ragged edge. "My wings are sprouting. Angel wings," she said, hugging herself. "Just as he promised."

A cone of light bore into the inky night. Charlene shielded her eyes. The line of her mouth twitched, rose at the corners. He had come.

Maggie arrived at Rx early the next morning and took the elevator to the second floor, emerging onto a long hallway carpeted with practicality in mind. The corridor was studded with photographs that marked the timeline of pharmaceutical advancement. Maggie studied the men in the pictures—men because there was not a woman among them until the late 1970s—who alternately held up test tubes to the light or peered into microscopes, shirtsleeves rolled up to show they meant business.

Forearms = Successful Corporation

Maggie's lab stood at the corridor's terminus. She opened the large glass door and peered inside, feeling the same little thrill as the first time she saw the lab.

The laboratory was at once spare and impressive: one thousand square feet of white walls, white vinyl and black counters, banked with workstations stocked with scanning electron microscopes, microplate readers, isolators and an extended family of vitreous containers. The center of the room was dominated by a centrifuge and HPLC.

Six pairs of eyes, all clad in plastic safety glasses, watched her walk in.

Zartar lifted her chin in a silent "what's up." Roselyn chirped "Maggie!" and waved energetically.

Jon Baumgartner, a balding man with a beaklike nose who was the senior project manager for her lab group, rose from his stool. "Maggie, I'm glad you're here. I want you to meet some people."

He stepped out from behind the counter. His right leg was twisted like the gnarled trunk of a windblown tree. He leaned heavily on a cane.

He had told her that he'd had polio as a child (she hadn't asked), that his Christian Scientist parents believed God would cure him. Evidently, God was busy that week.

"We've been doing some human resource reallocation," he said, clasping his hands behind his back.

Maggie swallowed. Somehow this did not sound like the beginning of good news.

"Don't worry, don't worry," Jon said, reading her face. "You still have a job." Maggie released the breath she hadn't realized she was holding. "We're just moving teams around, a shuffling of the deck chairs, if you will. Tommy, a lead statistician, will be joining us."

A man with bleached surfer-dude hair grinned and nodded. "Hey there." Maggie smiled and stopped herself from quoting a line from *Tommy Boy.*

"Miles, one of the company's star biochemists, has also been reassigned to our team."

Maggie offered her hand.

Miles stared at her unblinkingly from behind safety glasses, arms stiffly at his sides. He was short with a rhomboid bodybuilder's physique. Thick shoulders and a veined neck supported a tiny square head with an equally square jaw. He was impeccably groomed with a tailored lab coat. Aloof and handsome in a country club gym rat kind of way.

Miles finally extended a gloved hand and grasped hers, giving it a single pump.

"Nice to meet you," Maggie said.

Miles held her hand another moment, tightening his grip. Her fingers pressed uncomfortably against her ring, a simple circle of turquoise-embellished silver, a gift from her mother. Maggie could feel Miles watching her face, his eyes hooded by a Dodgers ball cap that struggled to hide thinning hair and failed. "Same," he finally replied, releasing his grip.

Maggie pulled her hand back uncertainly. Miles smiled at her. Her finger throbbed where her ring had cut into flesh. He was clearly a graduate of the School of Firm and Manly Handshakes.

Jon made his way back behind the counter and consulted a notebook. "This new team will work on the development of an acne drug."

Maggie's heart sank. Jon's team was known for its work in developing therapies to attack cancer cells. She was thrilled to learn he was her project manager and hoped she'd be invited to join the crusade. After all, it was the vendetta against her mother's killer that had driven her to pharmaceuticals in the first place, the steady drumbeat of grief that had provided the soundtrack of her ambitious climb from mediocre student to scholarship winner.

The old feeling rose again. Maggie mentally clamped down, but it was too late. Wisps of memory seeped around the stoppers she'd so carefully positioned.

The cool smoothness of her mother's hand on Maggie's face.

The smell of Neutrogena lotion on her mother's skin as she tucked Maggie in.

The half-full commode near her mother's bed.

The piles of vitamins and dishes of organic food when the chemo and radiation had stopped working.

And perhaps worst of all, the excessive niceness from her friends' moms. The compliments about what a good daughter she was, the promises that her mother was watching her from heaven, the comments about how brave she was to take care of her dad—as if she had a choice.

They had always been sweet. Concerned. Caring.

No matter how much of a shit she was being.

The school counselors had called her mother's death *transition*. The word sickened Maggie in its impotence. It was so passive, so clinical, so unlike the monstrous grief that seemed to be eating her from the inside out.

They could keep their transition. To Maggie the loss would always feel like eating broken glass.

Jon went over the discovery parameters and gave Maggie some homework: reviewing the pharmaceutical company's previous work in developing a herpes treatment. Some researchers believed that the compounds developed for herpes had properties conducive to ameliorating other skin conditions, he told her. He doubted it would affect acne, but didn't want to leave any stone—or compound—unturned.

Tommy and Miles retreated to their desks, giving Maggie a chance to better familiarize herself with Rx's equipment and procedures. Roselyn jumped at the chance to play teacher and seemed to relish showing Maggie where to find extra gloves, which unguator worked best and how to order additional test supplies. Maggie usually hated when people helped her. She could figure things out on her own, thank-you-very-much. But Roselyn's enthusiasm quelled Maggie's knee-jerk "no" to any offer of help.

Zartar, on the other hand, hid behind the autoclave, occasionally reappearing to retrieve or replace tools, her nude-lipsticked mouth set in a hard straight line.

"Is she okay?" Maggie whispered to Roselyn, nodding at Zartar.

Roselyn chanced a glance in Zartar's direction. Zartar had moved from the autoclave to the counter and was fiddling with the sifting deck, her dark hair a curtain that obscured her face. "I don't think she's happy about the new research assignment," Roselyn whispered back.

That makes two of us, Maggie thought reflexively, then silently chastised herself.

She was happy, damn it. Happy and grateful for the job, now more than ever. Who cared if she didn't save the world? At least she could save what was left of her family.

Chapter 4

The days were long, but the week was short. Maggie racked up hour after hour in the lab, breaking for a lunchtime shopping trip with Zartar and Roselyn only once and leaving at dark every night, begging off invitations to happy hour at The Office with excuses about piles of paperwork that rivaled the Himalayas.

Saturday morning, Maggie rose early. She grabbed her keys and stood at the door, surveying her apartment, calculating which of the remaining belongings waiting for her at her father's restaurant would fit in her small one-bedroom flat.

She sighed deeply. Her apartment had all the appeal of a Department of Motor Vehicles lobby.

In the process of converting the gracious (albeit timeworn) Victorian home into six individual apartments, the landlord had spared no expense to make each space as nondescript as possible. Neutral walls dissolved into neutral floors. Drapes drooped under the weight of stiff, institutional fabric. The smell of disinfectant floated through the air.

Yep, home sweet home.

The sun was still low on the horizon as Maggie eased the Studebaker onto the street, the hilltops pinking as if embarrassed by the sun's lingering touch. Traffic was thin, the streets nearly deserted save for the occasional lone jogger and the thickets of coffee-seekers clustered outside the Starbucks that seemed to sprout on every corner.

Clumps of industrial complexes and chain restaurants gave way to bus benches and low-slung strip malls. Soon the rolling hills of concrete and steel flattened into a vast prairie of green and brown.

Ninety minutes later, Maggie pulled into O'Malley's parking lot.

She walked to the mint-colored building, then pulled open a rusted metal door. O'Malley's Pizzeria was exactly as Maggie had left it: garlic-scented and unapologetically dated.

The restaurant was fifteen hundred square feet of battered wood flooring with a brass rail bar, well-worn tables and mismatched chairs. A chalkboard sign with a handwritten menu of daily specials (linguica-stuffed calzone and Emerald Isle cheesy bread) stood beside a display case that showcased desserts that appeared to be from the Carter Administration. A mural of St. Patrick streaked the wall above the men's bathroom.

She spotted Constantine behind the bar introducing a tray of pint glasses to a tap of Guinness. "Gus!" Maggie cried.

It was a common nickname for Constantine, an etymological jaunt from Konstantinos (the Greek form of the name) to Kostas to Gus, and the name of the crankily funny patriarch in *My Big Fat Greek Wedding*. But only Maggie was allowed to use it.

Constantine whooped, then set down the tray and jumped over the counter, his six-foot frame neatly clearing the napkin holders and parmesan shakers. He wrapped Maggie in a bear hug, his whiskers prickling her cheek. "Aren't you a sight for sore eyes."

Maggie and Constantine had been best friends since seventh grade when they met in the cafeteria line loading chicken or fish (it was impossible to say which) onto their plates. He was the new kid at St. Cecilia's, the sole Papadopoulos in a sea of Murphys, Rossis and Hernandezes. Different. Alone. The proverbial square peg. Just like Maggie who always felt different, awkward, half-orphaned not just by death but her peers' accidental indifference.

They were immediately joined at the hip. Even during college, they'd never been apart for more than a week. Maggie often thought about those studies documenting twins separated at birth. Divided by ocean or land, they remained tethered by an invisible umbilicus, choosing the same career path, marrying partners with identical names, hurting when the other fell. Sometimes it was hard to tell where she ended and he began.

She hugged him tightly around the neck. "It feels like I've been gone for a month."

"Well, you know what they say. Time flies when you miss

someone so much you feel like your arm's been sawed off and you've been beaten with it. Or something like that."

Maggie dropped onto a bar stool and looked around. "So where's Pop?"

Constantine inclined his head toward the office upstairs. "On some kind of conference call with Fiona."

Maggie's stomach clenched. "Oh."

Constantine didn't seem to notice the crack in her voice or the sudden vigor with which she began trimming her cuticles with her incisor. Just as he didn't seem to notice her father's gaunt face and worried eyes. Was he clueless or in denial?

"Anyways," he said, throwing a bar towel over his shoulder, "tell me everything. How was your first week?"

Maggie took her pinky out of her mouth and stuffed it into her pocket. "Good. I was asked to help administer a trial for a new acne drug."

"Saving the world from zits. Noble, Maggie. Very noble."

"Ha, ha, very funny." Maggie hopped off her stool and skirted the bar. She grabbed a pint glass from a cupboard and filled it with a stout from an Oregon microbrewery. "Before you give me a scene by scene description of the fifty *Dr. Who* episodes you watched since I've been gone, can we please talk about my phone? I hold you responsible since you gave it to me."

He had given her the phone the day before she left in typical Constantine fashion: a practical joke wrapped in relentless goofiness.

He'd hidden it in a box of Cap'n Crunch, then placed the cereal box inside one of her moving crates. She was unloading crates from her car when he called the phone. After pawing through several crates to find the source of the ringing, Maggie dug the slim black device from a nest of corn syrup-laden puffs and answered it.

"Hello, gorgeous," he'd said.

"Constantine. What is this?"

"It's called a phone. You use it to make and receive calls. And do important stuff like play Cat Piano. I slipped it in while I was helping you pack. I picked the *Rockford Files* ringtone. You've always reminded me of James Garner. I figured you needed the gear to go with the career."

She recalled being unexpectedly, unreasonably moved by the gesture. There had been a sudden tightness in her throat, the warning pinprick in her eyes that came before the tears. She blinked rapidly, ramming her emotions back where they belonged. Away.

She was an accomplished feeling-stuffer, and she'd be damned if she was going to go all mushy over a stupid phone. "You can't afford this," she had said, trying to sound practical. "You're unemployed."

"*Under*employed. I work for your dad, remember? And not to worry. I bought it secondhand from an old coworker who gave me a great deal. Consider it your housewarming gift. Plus the Cap'n Crunch. That's the real gift, actually. The phone's just gravy."

Now she watched Constantine's face as he formulated his thoughts. She could practically hear the gears turning. "I see a few possibilities for the reminder," he said. "The most logical is that your phone wasn't adequately wiped."

"Um, ew," Maggie said.

"What I mean is that since I bought your phone used, it had a previous life that left all kinds of digital breadcrumbs in its proverbial couch cushions. Phone numbers, texts, personal information. That kind of thing."

He walked the tray of pint glasses to a booth upholstered in green pleather and distributed the glasses to three men who looked as if they'd been there since the restaurant had opened thirteen years ago. He pivoted, spun the tray, Globetrotters-style on his forefinger, then plunked down beside Maggie.

"You're supposed to be able to erase all that stuff when you sell your phone," he continued, "but sometimes people forget to wipe the internal memory. And even when they use built-in tools to erase it, remnants can be left behind." He shrugged. "It's more common than people realize."

Maggie took a swig of beer. "There's something else." Constantine looked at her, eyebrows rising until they resembled a bushy McDonald's logo. "The woman who I supposedly had a meeting with died less than an hour after I got the reminder."

The eyebrows arched even higher. "What?"

Maggie nodded. "I saw it on the news. She'd been killed in a hit-and-run not long after her picture showed up on my phone."

Constantine stared then grabbed Maggie's beer and took a sip. "Seems kind of fast to announce the name of the victim, doesn't it?"

"She's in the media, a sister in arms. Plus the murder of a big wheel—even a *reporter* big wheel—means a big story. They must have been able to confirm her identity, reach next-of-kin and put together enough content to run with it. Anything for the scoop."

Constantine handed the beer back. "You're sure? I mean, like, *sure*-sure."

Maggie took another sip of beer, trying to push down the uneasiness that seemed to be crawling up her throat. "I'm positive. Well, almost positive. I had already deleted the reminder, so I couldn't double check. But I'm 99 percent sure."

Constantine grabbed a towel from the bar and threw it over his shoulder. "That is beyond bizarre."

"Think it's just a coincidence?" Maggie watched him beneath her lashes.

"Absolutely. I'll give you that it's seriously strange. Maybe even creepy. But it's not like you have the Grim Reaper on speed dial or something."

Maggie laughed reflexively. Inside, she felt far from gleeful. As ridiculous as it sounded, she couldn't help but feel that something more than chance was at play. "What am I supposed to do about it?"

Before he could answer, a voice boomed above them. "There she is. Rxcellance's newest clinical researcher."

Her father stood on the stairway's landing, arms outstretched. The Pope in a golf shirt. He lumbered down the remaining stairs and gave his daughter a kiss on the cheek.

"*Associate*, Pop. Clinical research *associate*. It'll be a while before I make researcher."

He waved her off. "Associate. Researcher. What's the difference? I'm surprised a company like Rxcellance would hire you, but I'm proud, sweetheart. Real proud."

The compliment sandwich. Nobody made them like Jack O'Malley.

Maggie's Aunt Fiona sailed down the stairs clad in high-waisted pink polyester slacks and a filmy floral blouse, a wake of organza and Jean Naté billowing behind her. She gave Maggie a hug, then looked at her over the top of her bifocals, studying her face for signs of sleep deprivation, poor nutrition or illness. Satisfied that Maggie's greatest affliction was the intermittent application of sunscreen, she smiled. "It's wonderful to see you, dear. You'll stay for dinner?"

"Aunt Fiona, it's not even lunchtime. It's barely *brunch*time."

Fiona waved off Maggie's logic. "It'll be dinnertime before you know it. You'll stay. I'll make something special."

Maggie shook her head. "I've got to head back. It's crazy busy at work."

Jack put his arm around Maggie. "Oh, come now. You don't want to rush back just to eat a TV dinner. Stay. I promise you'll be home before bedtime."

"Well." Maggie looked back and forth between Jack and Fiona. Fiona gave a subtle head flick toward Jack and cleared her throat. "Okay. I'll stay. After all, it's only..." She checked her watch. "Eight and a half hours away."

Maggie's father clapped his hands together with an explosive laugh of delight. He twirled Maggie around, his blue eyes sparkling in his wide red face.

He was right about the microwave entrée that awaited her at the apartment. Truth was, she missed him, them, the noise and bustle of the pizzeria, no matter how many times she told herself she didn't.

Fiona made good on her prediction. The day sped by and dinnertime arrived before Maggie knew it. Fiona prepared lamb stew and the four of them gobbled up conversation right along with the food, each hungry to know what had gone on in the short time they'd been apart.

Once the plates had been cleared and the kitchen tidied, they headed to Jack's office. They unearthed the odds and ends Maggie had kept at the restaurant, which had been like a second home for the better part of a decade.

Fiona eyed a carton perched on Maggie's hip. "Take this box, Jack," she called out to him as he headed for the door. "It's too heavy for Maggie. She'll tip her uterus."

Jack pivoted and retrieved the cardboard cube. He disappeared with it through the pizzeria's double doors.

"What's in there?" Fiona asked Maggie. "More jeans and t-shirts?"

Maggie nodded. "Plus my formal sweats. You know, for special occasions."

Fiona sighed in exasperation. "I'm only trying to help, you know. Your mother would have wanted that. She was always so beautiful. So elegant." She looked meaningfully at Maggie's cutoff denim shorts. "Not a rivet in sight." Fiona took Maggie's elbow and led her away from the door. "I want to talk to you about your father."

Maggie didn't respond. In Maggie's experience, *I want to talk to you about* was a phrase never followed by something positive.

Silence settled into the empty spaces between their words like cloud cover. Maggie could feel herself slipping behind it, disappearing into the fog. Her personal Penn & Teller act performed in hopes that she could make her emotions disappear.

"What's up?" Maggie heard herself say. Her own voice sounded small, far away.

"It looks like he might lose the restaurant."

Maggie sagged against the bar as if she'd been hit in the gut. "I thought things were going better, that he wouldn't have to close it if I started sending home money."

"I'm not talking about closing the restaurant, dear. I'm talking about *losing* it, building and all, to the bank."

Maggie's mind refused to process this. "What do you mean?"

"Your father took out another loan. Just until things picked up. He'd already borrowed against the house, so he had to use the restaurant as collateral." She shook her head, then grabbed a paper napkin out of the dispenser and blew her nose.

Maggie bit her lip. Of course he had used the restaurant as collateral. He'd mortgaged the house when her mother had gotten sick, when hospital bills started tiling the counters. Borrowed again to send Maggie to the college of her dreams to land the job of her dreams. What else did he have left to leverage?

Fact was, the restaurant had become her father's whole life. Built in the shadow of her mother's death, it had been a tombstone marking not just her passing, but the loss of his job when he'd missed too many days of work caring for his dying wife. It was dated and kitschy with three-star food and two-star service, but it was his.

It was *him.*

Fiona sighed. "We just got off the phone with the bank. They're going to foreclose. It's all but done."

Maggie straightened her back. She'd already lost one parent. She sure as hell wasn't going to let another one fade away, bled dry by loan payments and late notices and worry. "No," she said. "I'm not going to let that happen."

"But what can we do, dear? The bank wants him to start making payments immediately. Your father doesn't have the money."

"I'll take over the payments," Maggie said.

Fiona clicked her tongue dismissively. "Don't be silly, Magnolia."

Maggie mentally cringed at the sound of her full name. Her father had wanted her to be a traditional Margaret, but her mother's South Carolina roots won out. Maggie knew she'd never live up to the name's Southern gentility.

"I'm serious," Maggie said. "My salary's good at Rxcellance, and my rent isn't much."

"But what about food?" Fiona protested. "Electricity? Besides, you're brand new at your job. Who knows how long you'll keep it."

"Thanks for the vote of confidence, Fiona. But I'm doing well. Maybe I'll even get a promotion, a raise. I'm doing this, Aunt Fiona. Just don't tell Pop I'm covering all the payments. Say the restaurant is doing better and leave it at that."

Maggie grabbed her purse off the counter and rummaged around for her checkbook. After forcing Fiona to tell her the amount, she made out the check and pressed it into Fiona's hand.

Fiona hesitated. "I don't know..."

"I do," Maggie said. "*Please.*" She folded Fiona's hands around the rectangle of paper. "For Pop."

Jack reappeared, brushing imaginary dust from his hands. "Guess that's the last of it. No need for long goodbyes. It's not like you're moving across the country."

Maggie could see her father calculating the distance between Greenville and Collinsburg. He smiled. It slipped. Then returned too brightly.

She knew how much he missed her mother. How alone he felt.

A week after her mother died, Maggie thought about swallowing bottle after bottle of pills until everything—the pain, the guilt, the regret—had been numbed away. But she didn't. Part of her worried she'd go to Hell. The rest of her felt she had no right.

Her grief wasn't big enough, important enough, to warrant suicide. If anyone had been entitled, it would have been her father. He was the clear winner of loss. Haunted. Empty. A ghost dosing himself with equal parts of Bushmills and boxing as he sat in his harvest gold recliner, reeking with the unspoken suggestion that her grief was smaller like the "less than" alligator facing the larger number.

You hardly remember her.

You didn't know her like I did.

We had a life of our own before you came into the world.

So Maggie put the pills away. She found new and improved ways to tranquilize the monster that fed on her insides. She applied a carefully made tourniquet to her heart, tight enough that no messy emotions would leak out, loose enough that she wouldn't lose all feeling. Then crammed a batting of witty repartee and myopic ambition down her throat to stanch any leftover tears.

She escaped into movies. Into running. Into school. Into a career that would one day allow her to kill the cancer that had stolen both mother and wife. She'd bide her time, work her way up the pharmaceutical ladder. Then cut out the tumor of grief that had sunk its greedy tentacles into her life.

That was the idea.

She gave her father a hug, holding him tightly for a moment. Then she kissed Fiona on the cheek. Her skin was cool and papery, a leaf at summer's end. Maggie gave Fiona's arm an extra squeeze and looked into her eyes. Fiona nodded her secret assent.

"I'll be back again soon, I promise," Maggie said.

The three of them stood there awkwardly, committing the moment to memory. Marking the removal of all of her possessions, the last seconds Maggie would call this place home. Trying to decide how much to make it matter.

Constantine cleared his throat and sidled up to the trio. "I'll walk you out, Mags. I'm trying to get in three minutes of exercise every day anyway."

Maggie blew Jack and Fiona a kiss and pushed through the green door pocked with flaking paint. She looked up at the small office perched above the restaurant, suddenly wistful for the life and the people she was leaving behind.

She had already moved. Had over a week on her own under her belt. Getting the last of her boxes just seemed so...permanent.

She slid behind the wheel of the Studebaker and cranked the window down, then grabbed Constantine's hand through the open window. "I don't want to leave," she said softly.

He crouched down and put his chin on the window's rubber seal. "Of course you do. You have a great new job with one of the hottest companies in the industry. You're probably on your way to your first ulcer right now. It's fantastic."

"I know, but...but..." Maggie floundered, trying to identify what she was feeling. "But what about you?"

"Me? Oh, I'm excellent. I'm glad I got laid off from Zeitgeist IT. The downtime has given me time to reevaluate my career goals. Besides, your father needs me. He likes witnesses when he shouts at the TV."

Maggie squeezed his hand tighter. "You'll call? Help me with my phone thing? Make sure I don't get lonely or forget the best lines from *The Godfather*?"

Constantine smiled, chocolate eyes crinkling into half-moons. "I love to enable your cinematic Tourette's. Your inability to stop yourself from blurting out movie quotes has its own special charm."

Maggie grinned and pulled Constantine's head through the window. She hugged his neck tightly. "I think I'll miss you most of all, Scarecrow."

He hugged her back. "Thanks, Dorothy, but I won't give you a chance to."

Maggie turned the key and the engine came to life. She gave a final wave to Constantine and to Jack and Fiona, who stood motionless in the doorway, their silhouettes cardboard cutouts against the restaurant's neon glow.

Chapter 5

Maggie peered at her computer screen and groaned. She'd only been in her Thursday check-in meeting for an hour and already her inbox was clogged with fifty-eight new emails, not counting an invitation to enlarge her penis and a notice that Russian brides wanted to meet her.

It had been a good week. A great week. She'd been awarded the PrePharma Foundation award, one of the highest honors for pharmaceutical grads, and word had spread quickly through the company. Her boss was impressed. Jon gave her new responsibilities, and she'd made a breakthrough on the acne drug. Yet more responsibility meant more hours. Maggie was exhausted.

Maggie sighed and grabbed the chipped mug she'd brought from Pop's. Maybe caffeine would help stave off the fatigue tugging at her brain.

Maggie walked into the deserted second-floor mini kitchen and filled her cup to the two-thirds mark. She wandered around for a few minutes, picking through the shelf-safe non-dairy creamers, skimming posted memos, half-heartedly scrubbing an unidentifiable stain in the microwave with a paper towel, then glanced at the door.

No sign of Bar Guy Ethan.

She had crossed paths with him a few times earlier in the week, running into him twice in that very kitchen and once in the hall. He'd even stopped by her desk on his way to her supervisor's office to ask if she needed anything, making her feel like she had a seat at the cool kids' table.

There had been no sign of him today. Maybe he'd taken off early for the weekend?

Maggie silently cursed herself for trying to engineer an accidental meeting. Sure, their conversations had grown warmer, his hand alighting on her forearm, barely touching and gone within seconds, as he talked and laughed. But he was just being friendly, trying to make her feel welcome. Mistaking his friendly overtures as flirting was pathetic.

Maggie dumped two pods of hazelnut creamer into her cup and trudged up the stairs back to her floor, feeling hot and sweaty and annoyed with herself. She wound her hair into a topknot and stuck a pencil through it, determined to get down to business.

Her phone chimed. A bicycle bell. Maggie slid it out of her old nylon purse. She looked at the display. Frowned. An icon she'd never noticed before was illuminated, a tiny "1" next to it.

Maggie squinted. The icon was shaped like a Post-it note. "Reminder" was printed in faux pencil across the top.

The meeting reminder app? She certainly didn't remember any icon with her first reminder. She wasn't exactly focused on those kinds of details when a stranger showed up on her phone.

A sense of foreboding settled in the center of Maggie's chest. Hunkered down. Squeezed. Her heart began to hammer.

She told herself she was being silly.

So what if she had another reminder? It was just an artifact from her unwiped phone.

No. Big. Deal.

Except last time, the person she was supposed to meet ended up meeting with death.

Maggie tapped the icon.

A man's smiling face filled the display. Maggie felt her hands grow cold and moist with fear. Another reminder for a meeting she didn't schedule with someone she didn't know.

The reminder appeared to have come in late last night after she'd turned off her phone. It wasn't something she typically did, but she didn't need her phone robbing her of much-needed sleep with alerts of new Facebook posts or incoming emails.

Maggie flexed her hand to get the blood flowing then lightly rubbed her thumb across the face of her phone, smudging the man's laughing face with the whorls and ridges of skin newly slicked with sweat. He was early thirties with smiling eyes, skin the color of burnished mahogany and a shaved head. Not skinhead shaved or desperately-trying-to-hide-male-patterned-baldness shaved. Cool guy shaved. Mr.-Clean-getting-his-groove-on shaved.

She tapped the screen.

MEETING REMINDER

TIME: Friday, 1:30 a.m. – 3:30 a.m.

It was the same as before: No name. No contact information. No meeting place.

Maggie set the phone down and tapped her fingers.

Same as before. Same as before. Same as before. The thought drummed through her head, keeping time with her fingers and heart.

Suddenly there was a knock on the faux walls of her cubicle. She started, then looked up at the man who had arrived at her cubicle as if by *Star Trek* transporter.

Roy Hubbins, Lead Supervisor. Her boss Jon's boss.

Fiftyish with a compact muscular build and sensible Supercuts hair, Roy looked like a TV dad. Dependable. Wise. Sweater-vested, even in a heat wave. He wore a broad grin and a red-checked shirt. Maggie thought he could double as a picnic table.

"Hey, Maggie," Roy said, a Southern accent rounding his vowels. "Are you getting all settled in, learning the ropes?"

"I sure am." She thought about the state-of-the-art equipment. The warm welcome she'd received. The friendships that seemed to be blossoming. "Everything is going great." She pointed to the stack of papers Roy held in his hands. "Is that for the project I'm working on?"

"Actually, no. I found this on the printer. Plans for the rollout of Pollonexe, the new antiallergen." Roy's smile was intact. The accent homespun and down-to-earth. But his gaze was direct. Penetrating. "Didn't realize you were working on that."

Maggie was confused. "I'm not."

"No?" Roy's brows knit as if he were trying to diagram a sentence. "Not sure why you'd trouble yourself to print it out then. Printer indicated that it came from your machine right there. Seems strange you'd be accessing and printing out documents for a project you're not working on." The drawl was long, deliberate. Maggie felt like she was in an episode of *Matlock*.

"Roy, I have no idea—"

"You're new here, so it's not your fault you didn't know. At Rxcellance we pride ourselves on keeping confidential information *confidential*. We work on our own projects and mind our own business." He flashed white teeth, the thousand-watt smile not quite touching his eyes. "That's not going to be a problem for you, is it?"

Maggie opened her mouth to defend herself, then thought better of it. She swallowed hard, pushing down the acrid taste that had seeped into the back of her throat. "No. No problem."

Roy looked at her for a moment, then clapped her amiably on the shoulder. "Didn't think so." He turned on his heel and walked down the hall to his office. She heard his office door slam shut.

Maggie stared at her computer screen. How could she have printed something she'd never even seen and didn't even know about? She checked her printer log. It showed that *PollonexePlan1.doc* had indeed been printed from her computer. Maggie stood and peered over the wall of her cubicle. Her coworkers were a paragon of industriousness, fingers tapping keyboards, heads bowed over reports.

Maggie sank back into her chair and rubbed her shoulders. It didn't make any sense. How could this have happened? And oh, God, what did Roy think of her now?

Maggie grabbed her purse, rummaged around and produced the film canister that served as her portable medicine cabinet. She popped it open and threw a couple of Advil into her mouth. She swallowed with lukewarm coffee.

She felt like the walls were closing in. She had to get out. Get some air. Distract herself from the strange encounter with Roy and the feeling of dread that had lodged in her throat after the second meeting reminder.

Maggie shoved her feet in her running shoes, took the elevator to the first floor and headed out the door.

The hot, sodden air of midday Collinsburg wrapped itself around her like a living thing. Maggie rewound her hair into a higher, tighter bun and surveyed her surroundings. She spotted a dirt path at the perimeter of the pharmaceutical property.

The trail was longer than she had expected, paralleling great swaths of chain-link fence and dipping into little grottos of untamed vegetation. Overhead, clouds, sullen in their lack of productivity, drifted aimlessly over a patchwork of grass, cement and brick that blanketed the Rxcellance campus.

Maggie walked briskly. Within ten minutes, her cotton blouse clung to the small of her back and beneath her arms. Maggie pulled the damp fabric away from her sweat-slicked skin, silently chastising herself for not bringing exercise clothes. She needed to cool off before she was drenched.

Maggie spied a tree stump shaded by the boughs of an old silver maple and made her way to the makeshift bench. She sat on the rough wood and palpated the front of her right knee, her forefinger tracing the scar of the ACL reconstruction she'd undergone four years earlier. She took a long drink from the water bottle, then closed her eyes, relishing the solitude, drinking in a quiet interrupted only by cicadas droning from watchtowers of aspen and pine.

Her phone chimed. She reached into her pocket and pulled out the device. A text from Constantine.

We never finished talking about your phone. Chat over lunch tomorrow? I'll be in town.

Relief washed over Maggie. She'd not only get to see her best friend, she could tell him about the latest reminder and hopefully get some answers. Or at least get the reminders to stop.

She texted back: *Perfect. There's been a new development. Pick me up?*

Her phone pinged with Constantine's reply. *New development? Curiouser and curiouser. See you at noon.*

Maggie was about to text her goodbye when a shadow fell across her phone.

"Hi," a gravelly voice said.

Maggie started and looked up. Miles stood over her.

"Oh, hey." Maggie stuffed the phone in her pocket. "I didn't know you were there."

Miles smiled. "I'm sneaky that way." He doffed his baseball cap to swat at a wasp, exposing a naked patch of scalp that looked like a pink yarmulke. He replaced the cap, pulling it low to hood his eyes.

"Out for some exercise?" she asked.

"Actually, I wanted to talk to you."

"Oh?"

"I feel like we didn't get off on the right foot last week," he said. "I wanted to offer you a proper welcome."

Her first impression of him as a snob had been dead wrong. He was probably just shy. She could understand that. She was fluent in introversion. "That's so nice. I really appreciate that, Miles."

Miles crouched to the right of Maggie's makeshift seat. "So tell me about yourself."

"Um, not much to tell, really. Grew up in Greenville, just graduated from the U with a master's, more of a dog person than a cat person."

Miles laughed. "Yeah, me, too." He squinted across the campus yard. "This is great, isn't it? Us talking together." He turned to her, his eyes locking onto hers. "I really hope we can get to know each other better."

Maggie shifted on the log and gave a half-smile. "Uh, yeah. Me, too."

"Great. How about drinks after work?"

Maggie blinked. "Drinks?"

"Don't tell me you don't drink." He tut-tutted. "I saw you a couple of weeks ago at The Office with Zartar and that other girl. The fat one who wears brown."

Maggie could feel her cheeks flame. The fat one? "Hey, now—"

Miles cut her off. "Three vodka Collins in two hours. Impressive."

Maggie's mouth hung open. He'd watched her? Made notes on what she consumed? Maggie felt her mental warning flag unfurl. "Oh, I don't date coworkers," she said lightly.

"Every rule has an exception," Miles said. His thin lips spread into a grin. Calculating. Hungry. Almost predatory. "Besides, who said anything about a date? I distinctly remember saying 'drinks.'"

Maggie licked her lips. The office suddenly seemed very far away. Miles stood, his wide form blocking her view of Rxcellance. The mental warning flag fluttered. Her heart thudded thickly in her chest. Maggie pulled her phone from her pocket and gave an exaggerated look at the time. "Oh, man. I'm going to be late. I'll see you later, okay?" She brushed brusquely past Miles, giving him a wide berth, and walked quickly toward the building. "Talk to you in the lab," she said over her shoulder.

Miles called after her or shouted. She couldn't tell which. She turned her head and saw him step from the little green alcove, fists balled against his legs. He called to her again, but she couldn't make out the words, couldn't hear anything over the *thwap thwap* of the warning flag. *Get out, get out, get out* it seemed to whisper in the wind. She bit her lip, forcing herself not to turn around again.

Walking became speed-walking. She burst through the entrance, her heart hammering wildly in her chest. Flushed, sweaty and shaking, Maggie darted into the ladies' room.

She ran the faucet and splashed her face with water, then pressed brown paper towels against her face, imagining what Fiona would say about scratchy paper products and the delicate skin beneath her eyes. Maggie leaned against a diaper changing station that looked like a tiny Murphy bed.

She took two deep, cleansing breaths. What was wrong with her? She'd run away from Miles like he was an axe murderer. He didn't do anything except act a bit weird. A little pushy.

But another, quieter voice, the one that came from some ancient part of her brain, told her that she was right to get away from Miles. Right to run.

Maggie dampened a few paper towels and patted beneath her arms. She looked in the mirror and released her hair from its makeshift bun, then dragged her fingers through it. Satisfied she looked normal, or normalish, she exited the restroom to join the flight pattern of workers en route to labs, cubicles or lunch.

Maggie headed toward her desk. She wondered where Miles sat, whether she'd run into him as she made her way through the cubicle farm. Her stomach went oily. He was probably harmless, but she didn't need any more awkward encounters. She'd just try to stay out of his way when she could—and pivot and cajole and pretend it didn't bother her when she couldn't. She'd find a way to get along. She had to.

She plopped into her chair and guzzled water then cold coffee.

"That doesn't look like a very balanced lunch."

Zartar stood outside her cubicle, nodding at Maggie's cup. Roselyn stood beside her, her hair blending into the cubicle's beige fabric.

Maggie smiled. "It goes with the peanut butter sandwich I

brought from home." Maggie opened the paisley tote Fiona had given her as a graduation gift and produced a plastic-wrapped sandwich as evidence. It looked like a tan hockey puck. "Oh. I guess it got squished under my running shoes."

"We came by to see if you wanted to have lunch with us in the cafeteria," Zartar said. She looked at the crushed sandwich. "Looks like all signs point to yes."

Maggie opened her mouth to decline because that's what she did. Turn down dates. Say no to concerts. Beg off dinner parties. Then she stopped herself.

Right. New job. New life. New outlook. Besides, the walk hadn't exactly calmed her nerves. Maybe a dose of camaraderie would. "Sounds great," she said.

The three trekked to the company cafeteria, a large butter-colored room flanked by floor-to-ceiling windows and two buffets complete with plastic sneeze guards. The room was polka-dotted with dozens of round plastic tables and smelled of French fries, fried fish and industrial cleaner.

Zartar found a table in the corner opposite the entrance. Roselyn shrugged out of her lab coat, revealing a shirt in a shade of brown that Maggie thought could only be called old Band-Aid, and opened a soft-sided black lunch bag. She extracted a cloth napkin and an assortment of Tupperware containers, which she began arranging by size.

Maggie was so mesmerized by the organizational process she didn't realize Roselyn was talking to her. "And she was folding the clothes *over* the clothesline and *then* pinning them," Roselyn said as she uncapped a cylinder of melon balls. "Can you imagine? Everything had *creases.*"

Zartar gave Maggie a look. Maggie covered her smile with a hand.

"This is my first time here," Maggie said. She looked across the room, eyeing a pile of sandwiches lying helplessly on mountains of ice chips. "Is the food here good?"

"Define 'good,'" Roselyn said.

"Define 'food,'" Zartar said, popping open a can of Diet Coke.

Maggie weighed hunger against a slab of meat that leered at her from the deli case. She pushed herself back from the table and stood. "How bad can it be?"

Twenty minutes later, the orange Joe Joe's and defeated club sandwich she had consumed sat in her stomach like a brick. "Ugh. I'd get some more exercise, but I don't think I have time."

"How was your walk?" Zartar said "walk" the way most people say "hemorrhoid."

Maggie hesitated then cleared her throat. "It was fine."

Zartar arched a brow. "Doesn't sound very fine."

"Well, I...I ran into Miles on the trail." Maggie put her hands in her lap so they wouldn't notice them shaking. "He's kind of...um...different, isn't he?"

The two women exchanged a look. Zartar folded her arms. "You could say that, yeah."

"What's his deal?" Maggie allowed one hand to escape, grabbed her water bottle and drank deeply, hoping to drown the feeling of unease that churned with the fried potatoes in her belly.

"His deal," said Roselyn, "is that his father is Mr. James Montgomery, president of Rxcellance."

Maggie choked on her water. "His dad is the *president* of Rx?"

"Yep," Roselyn said, "and he has a serious case of affluenza. Ironically, the nepotism is sort of a double-edged sword. Daddy Big Bucks treats Junior like absolute crap. He can't do anything right. His work is never good enough." She shook her head. "Poor guy."

"Poor us." Zartar examined a long crimson nail on her right hand, rubbed an imaginary bit of dust from its mirror-like surface. "My advice to you: watch your ass. He'll certainly be watching it."

Roselyn pulled at Zartar. "It's almost one thirty. We'd better get to the lab."

Zartar rolled her eyes. "Yes, we wouldn't want management to give us a tardy, would we?" She looked at Maggie. "You coming?"

Maggie coughed into her elbow. "You guys go ahead. I'll be right there."

"Okay," Zartar said. "See you in Hell—a.k.a Lab 3."

Maggie watched the women disappear through the cafeteria door, then sank into her chair.

So Miles was the son of the company's president. Fantastic. Now she'd have to double up on the kid gloves when she turned down overtures. She had a feeling Miles wasn't used to hearing no.

She pulled her phone from her pocket. She could do a quick check-in with Pop before she headed to the lab. In her peripheral vision, she saw something flicker on the tiny screen. A tiny shift of shadow and light. A reflection. She turned.

Miles stood at the cafeteria door, staring at her. Maggie's breath caught. How long had he been standing there? How much had he heard?

Miles grinned at her, teeth glistening beneath the cafeteria's fluorescent glow. He wriggled his fingers at her in a childlike wave, then stepped back through the door. Disappearing as if swallowed whole.

Chapter 6

The van door slid open and Charlene climbed in, her long, tattered shirt billowing commodiously around her stooped frame. The backseats had been excised like rotted teeth, a stack of moving blankets acting as seating stand-ins. Charlene plunked down on the pile of scratchy blue blankets and stared out the window into the nothingness of night and the somethingness of her own reflection.

Charlene considered her image in the window. Smiled to see if it would smile back. It did. That seemed like a good sign.

She closed her eyes. It felt good to sit. Luxurious even after years on the streets spent standing or walking or lying or squatting. But Charlene knew that the extravagance of sitting would soon be replaced by the freedom of flying.

Her shoulder blades were tingling again. The wings would be growing fast now, fueled by elixirs the archangels had given her over the past few months.

It was providence, the way they had found her. Clad in the star-white purity of the highest order of heavenly hosts, they had come while she was sleeping. God had already been talking to her, His mighty voice rising above the din of the squabbles that filled her head. And when the archangels appeared in their bright-white chariot, promising transformation and everlastingness, she knew His prophecies were coming to pass. It was time for her destiny to be fulfilled.

The van door screamed shut. Charlene started at the noise, but kept her eyes closed. She felt a presence at her side, the sensation of eyes watching as she meditated. A smooth, gloved hand touched her forearm. Reassuring yet insistent. Charlene opened her mouth and emptied her mind. Communion was about to begin.

* * *

The next morning's reveille was the ring of Maggie's phone. She turned over, pulling her new sheet, still stiff and scratchy, over her head. The phone stopped ringing. Then began again. Maggie yanked the sheet down to her chin and squinted at the Scooby-Doo clock her dad had given her for her eighth birthday. Seven forty-five a.m. *Crap.*

Maggie reached across the mountain of unfolded laundry that occupied the other half of her queen-size bed, plucked the phone from the nightstand and checked the screen. Fiona.

"Oh, hello, dear." Fiona sounded surprised, as if Maggie had called *her.* "How are you?"

Maggie threw back the sheets and ran to the bathroom. "I'm actually running late." She kicked off her shorts and slid deodorant under each arm. She stopped. "Is everything okay? This is early for you, isn't it?"

A pause. "Oh, everything's fine, dear. Sounds like you need to run. I'll call you tonight."

Maggie pulled on a cream-colored skirt and shimmied into a sleeveless silk button-up that Zartar insisted she buy during their lunchtime shopping excursion.

"You're sure everything's okay?"

"Yes, everything's great. I'll talk to you later."

Fiona signed off. Maggie had the distinct feeling she was lying. She'd have to think about that later. Right now, she barely had time to breathe.

Maggie splashed her face with cold water, showed her teeth the toothbrush, then raked her hair into a ponytail. She flew out the door and into the Studebaker and cranked the ignition, feeling the same panic that clawed at her when she was stuck in traffic.

She couldn't be late. She couldn't screw this up.

Her floor was deserted when she arrived. She checked the clock on her phone. 8:05. Where was everybody?

She walked slowly to her cubicle and snatched the note that had been affixed to her computer monitor.

Maggie—

Where are you? The chief called a big meeting. All hands on deck. Get your ass (and whatever else you want to bring) to the cafeteria.

— *Zartar*

Maggie rummaged through her desk drawer and retrieved her iPad. She pounded on the elevator's down button and spent the journey to the first floor trying to mop up the sweat accumulating under her arms, between her breasts and behind her knees. The building was air conditioned; her endocrine system didn't seem to notice.

The elevator door slid open. She emerged slowly and walked to the cafeteria on tiptoe.

The entire staff of Rx was seated at small round tables, coffees growing cold on plastic slabs that usually supported insulated lunch sacks and cardboard fry baskets. A man stood at the center of the room, his arms jutting spasmodically from his jacket. His face was beet-red, his white hair an untidy corona that danced with each gesture.

James Montgomery, president of Rxcellance. It was the first time she'd seen the company's leader in person. Clad entirely in gray wool gabardine, he reminded Maggie of the great white in *Jaws*.

You're gonna need a bigger boat.

Maggie tried to slide in behind Roselyn, who was seated near the entrance. She bumped the display of individual cereal boxes perched beside the cash register with her iPad and watched in horror as tiny boxes of Special K and Honey Smacks cascaded onto the floor.

All heads turned toward her with marching band unison. James Montgomery glowered, the bones beneath his jowls sliding as he ground his teeth. Maggie sank beside Roselyn and pretended to look at something interesting on her pants.

James Montgomery had wound himself back up into speech mode. "As I was saying..." He looked pointedly at Maggie. "...Rxcellance is on the brink of greatness. We've had tremendous success with landmark developments, such as our pneumonia and herpes drugs. They've not only bettered our position in the market, they've bettered the world." He paused for effect. "And we have new miracles in the queue. We're developing something revolutionary that will eradicate disease and save millions of lives."

A murmur of surprise and excitement rippled through the room. James Montgomery held up a meaty palm. "Now, I'm not going to reveal that development today," he said over the muffled voices. "But I will tell you the reason I've brought you here." The room went still. Montgomery smiled. "I'm pleased to announce that Rxcellance, Inc. has filed a registration statement with the Securities and Exchange Commission for an IPO—and we're giving each employee stock in the company."

The room exploded in applause. People high-fived. Roselyn hugged Maggie's shoulders. Maggie spotted Miles sitting toward the front of the room. He crossed his arms over his chest and leaned back, a look of self-satisfaction crawling across his face like a New York Stock Exchange ticker.

James Montgomery raised his hand for attention and the room quieted again. "We haven't set terms for the IPO yet. But we do believe that performance for the shares will be *impressive*. Naturally, all this depends on our ability to raise the funds to carry this plan through. It's essential that we continue to do the best work we can and keep our endeavors confidential."

He turned, rocking back on his heels like a Weeble-Wobble, and paced slowly from table to table. "We've had some problems recently, some lapses in confidentiality." The light caught silver tufts of hair that peeped out from his nose and ears. He scowled at the pale faces that turned toward him like a hundred tiny moons. "We don't take the precautions we take, we don't work the hours we work, to give our compounds to the competition. So I remind you: be ever vigilant against the specter of corporate espionage."

The Pollonexe report that had been printed from her computer leapt to her mind. Roy's words about confidentiality and minding her own business rang in her ears. Was *she* the breach Montgomery was talking about? Had Roy reported her? She couldn't afford to lose this job. The future of her family—what was left of it—was in her hands.

Montgomery rocked back and forth on his heels, his eyes roaming the room. His gaze settled on Maggie, his piercing eyes holding hers. "I thank you for your attention, and I congratulate you on this exciting new journey we're about to embark on."

He looked around the room expectantly, as if waiting for the pop of camera flashes. When none materialized, he gave a Nixonesque wave, then left the room with the self-generated fanfare and glad-handing of a presidential candidate.

Maggie got to her feet and looked at Roselyn. "Corporate espionage?" Maggie imagined men in trench coats handcuffed to briefcases containing the recipe for Coca-Cola. "That's a problem here?"

Roselyn stood, pushing in her chair with a knee. "It could be. I mean, think about it. It costs, what, $800 million to bring a drug to market? And that's just the average. Not to mention years of research—sometimes decades. With enough financial motivation, I could see someone leaking data to the competition." She shrugged. "We could have a spy right here and not even know it."

Roy Hubbins' face swam before her. Maggie swallowed. "Yeah. That would be awful."

Roselyn gathered her things and hugged them against her chest. "Beyond awful. Anyway, I'm taking off. My mom's having oral surgery. I'm her designated driver today and Lifetime movie companion tomorrow until I escape for the company gala. See you then?"

"You know it." Maggie said good-bye and made her way back to her desk. The knot that had snarled in her stomach yesterday returned, tightened, going from slip-knot to hangman's noose. She wiggled her computer mouse and logged on. As she waited for her computer to warm up, she reached for her phone and brought it to life with the touch of her finger.

The icon for the meeting reminder app seemed to look back, mocking her. There was no number, no new message. But a feeling of disquiet filled her. Again she remembered the woman who had appeared in the same way on her phone, what had happened to her. She thought about the new stranger on her phone and what might happen to him.

On impulse, she wiggled her computer mouse, opened an internet browser and typed the URL of the local news station in the search bar.

She watched as regional stories rotated through the carousel.

Student Advances to National Spelling Bee.

Mayor to Speak at Benefit.

Annexation Planned.

Then finally: *Local Man Killed in Auto Wreck.*

Maggie felt her scalp tingle. She clicked. The photo of the man on her phone took center stage on her computer screen. He mugged for the invisible photographer, laugh lines bracketing brown eyes, fist propped under a goateed chin in a mock *GQ* pose.

The feeling of recognition was overwhelming. Almost as overwhelming as the sense of déjà vu. Another appointment reminder with a stranger. Another death reported in the news.

She began to scroll.

Suddenly there was a pair of hands on her shoulders, squeezing, massaging. Maggie tried to turn around, to see whose hands were on her body. The grip tightened. She felt warm air against her ear.

"Just relax," Miles whispered, his lips an inch from her ear. "I'm really good at this."

Maggie shrugged off his hands and spun around, her heart pounding, her body on high alert.

Miles smiled. The expression looked like an afterthought, something donned for the situation, like a tie for work. "Didn't mean to startle you. You just looked tense."

"Oh." Maggie wanted to rub her shoulders briskly, to wipe off the feeling of Miles' hands. Instead she put on her own smile. She was the new girl. He was the big boss's son. She had to play nice. "Nope, not tense. Just busy."

Miles looked at her computer monitor. "You don't look busy. You look like you're surfing the Net."

Whoops.

"Oh this?" Maggie poured on the nonchalance. "I have the local news set as my home page. I was just about to log onto *Bioconjugate Chemistry.*"

Miles nodded slowly. He'd forgotten about his smile, and it slid off his face. He put it back on. "I thought you were going to update your online dating profile or something. You're probably into the kinky stuff." The smile broadened, turned wicked. "The quiet ones always are."

Maggie's stomach turned. "No online dating," she said evenly, continuing her act of indifference "Just work." She began to turn around. "Speaking of..."

Miles stared at her a moment. "I'll let you get back to it. Just remember, these..." He wriggled his fingers. "...are always available." Miles backed out of her cubicle then popped his head back in. "Oh, and don't forget about that drink invitation. It's always open." Then he was gone.

Maggie closed her eyes and let out the breath she didn't know she was holding. What the hell was that? Was Miles just socially tone-deaf? Trying to be funny? Or was he the king of creeps?

Given their earlier encounter on the trail and the ease with which Miles put his hands on her, Maggie's money was on the latter. And it wasn't like she could do anything about it. A friendly massage. Some office banter. He's just trying to be nice, she'd be told. Don't take it too seriously, she'd be advised. It was a song she'd heard before, a tune she guessed most women were familiar with. And right now, she couldn't afford to make waves.

Maggie turned her attention back to her computer monitor. Right. The reminder. The death. She looked over her shoulder then continued scrolling.

The article was short, terse:

Collinsburg resident Carson Parks was pronounced dead at the scene of an accident on Ridgecrest Drive at approximately 2:20 this morning. The car collided with a concrete noise abatement wall that bordered the neighborhood of Ridgecrest Heights, resulting in fatal head trauma, a police spokesperson said. No other vehicles were involved. An open bottle of Smirnoff Vodka was recovered from Mr. Park's car.

Mr. Parks served as a social worker at New Horizons, one of the area's three homeless shelters. A memorial service will be held next Sunday, August 9 at Restful Waters Memorial Gardens at 10:30 a.m.

An inset photo showed paramedics working to pry apart what had once been a door in the twisted ball of metal. Maggie held her phone next to her computer screen, reconciling the man on her screen with the corpse in the car.

Two reminders. Two deaths. One an accident. One a wrong-place-wrong-time scenario. Nothing to tie them together.

Nothing except the phone in Maggie's hand.

Chapter 7

"Maggie?"

Maggie flinched. For a moment, she thought Miles had returned. Then she realized the voice was female.

Zartar peered around the corner of Maggie's cubicle. "Sorry. Didn't mean to startle you. I was down on the first floor and saw a cute guy asking for you at Reception. You have a secret boyfriend or something?"

"I don't have a boyfriend," Maggie said, her mind on two dead strangers and the phone that connected them.

Zartar crossed her arms in front of her chest. "Well, there's a guy waiting for you downstairs. He says he's taking you to lunch?"

Maggie looked at her watch. Had she been so preoccupied by the reminder that she sleepwalked through her entire morning?

"So who's the mystery man?" Zartar pressed.

Maggie opened the phone's gallery app, clicked on a picture of Constantine and turned the screen toward Zartar. "This guy?"

Zartar grabbed the phone, pursing her mouth into duck lips as she examined the photograph. "Yes and yum. What's the story?"

Maggie shrugged. "Just a friend."

"Friend with benefits?"

Maggie grabbed the phone back. "A friend-friend. My best friend, actually. Since middle school."

"Whatever you say, you lucky, lucky girl," Zartar said, sashaying off.

Maggie found Constantine seated on an austere chair in the lobby. He was pretending to read a biogenetics journal.

He wore a dark blue vintage shirt and tan shorts. His olive skin was peppered with new beard growth and his eyes were a warm brown beneath thick, dark lashes. Maggie had never thought of Constantine as handsome, although objectively she knew it was true. He'd always had female admirers in high school and college, but he never seemed interested in seeing how many notches he could add to his bedpost. He seemed to prefer hanging out with Maggie and quoting Monty Python.

They trotted out to the company parking lot and Maggie folded herself into Constantine's 1977 Datsun B210. She slammed the door, then palpated her neck. Her lymph nodes weren't swollen, but she was certain she could feel something coming on. She grabbed the film canister and popped three Vitamin C tablets into her mouth. She swallowed without water.

Constantine watched her as he started the car. "How's that chronic hypochondriasis coming along? You know, I gave to the Hypochondriacs' Association last year in your honor." He put a fist to his lips and stifled a fake sob. "Until there's a cure for things that need no cure."

"You're going to feel terrible when I die from some horrible disease."

Constantine eased the car from the parking lot to the street. "Can I go ahead and feel terrible now? I hate to procrastinate."

Maggie rubbed her tongue against the roof of her mouth in a futile effort to scrape off the chalky vitamin residue. "I'm under a lot of stress, okay? I'm sort of freaking out."

Constantine turned to look at her. She could see the concern in his eyes. "What's wrong?"

Maggie took a deep breath. "Things just got weirder with my phone. Last night, I got another appointment reminder for a meeting I didn't schedule with someone I don't know."

"*Another* reminder?"

"Except that's not the weird part. Or not the really weird part. The guy who showed up on my reminder is dead, killed in a single-car accident. I just read the article online."

"What?" He pulled into a parking space in front of Sensei's Sushi Shack and killed the engine. He stared at her, something like fear behind his look of incredulity. "Please tell me you're kidding."

Maggie produced her phone, showed him the meeting reminder, then logged onto the internet and showed him the article.

"Shit," he said under his breath.

"My thoughts exactly."

They got out of the car and walked toward the restaurant in silence. The sign at the entrance told them to seat themselves. They took a booth beside a conveyor belt carrying tiny payloads of tuna rolls and salmon sashimi. Constantine took two blue plates from the conveyor belt and began mixing wasabi and soy sauce.

He loaded sushi into his mouth and chewed. "Let me get this straight. You've got two appointment reminders and two deaths. Basically, you're batting a thousand."

"Problem is, I don't know what I'm playing. Or who's playing with me."

The waitress came and took their drink orders. She returned thirty seconds later and deposited a large plastic glass of Dr. Pepper in front of Maggie and a cup of coffee in front of Constantine.

Maggie looked at Constantine. "Coffee with sushi?"

Constantine grinned and took a sip. "It sounded good."

Maggie rolled her eyes and drowned her sushi in a lake of wasabi-laden soy sauce. "Do you think I should call the police?"

Constantine dragged a paper napkin across his mouth. "And tell them what—you have a direct line to Death? The whole thing is weird. Maybe very weird. But the fact is, both deaths were accidental, and there's no reason to believe they had anything to do with each other—or your phone."

Maggie set her chopsticks down. "But don't you think it's odd that people I don't know appear on my phone one day and are dead the next? Doesn't that give you pause?"

"Hell yes it gives me pause. It gives me stop and rewind, too. But it's not evidence of anything criminal. You need *actual* for-reals evidence, some kind of information beyond 'hey, this is freaky' before calling the cops."

Maggie took a long drag on her Dr. Pepper, then sighed. "I guess you're right. But I can't just sit here and do nothing. I mean, what if the reminders don't stop?" Maggie looked at her plate. "What if people keep dying?"

The last word died in a whisper. Tears pricked the backs of her eyelids. She blinked rapidly and took another sip of her drink.

Constantine waved his hand in a get-outta-here gesture. "That's not going to happen. Let me take a look at your phone and see what I can do about these reminders." He grabbed another napkin and wiped his hands. "Meanwhile, you can say hello to my little friend."

Maggie put her hands on her hips. "You'd better be channeling *Scarface.*"

"Guess again."

"Tell me you didn't."

"I can't do that because I did." Constantine dropped the crumpled napkin on the table and reached into his pocket. He produced a hamster, like a rabbit out of a hat. "I couldn't leave poor Miss Vanilla at home."

"Put that thing away before you get us both thrown out," she whisper-shouted.

"She is not some 'thing,'" he said indignantly. He lifted the caramel-hued animal out of his pocket and put her small pink nose to his slightly crooked one. "Miss Vanilla and I will pretend we didn't hear that, won't we?" The hamster's whiskers twitched. "She hasn't been out at all today. It's good for her to see people. Besides, I bring her into your dad's restaurant all the time. He doesn't seem to mind."

"That's because he doesn't know. Or he *pretends* not to know."

"Oh. Well, Miss Vanilla was lonely. I could see it in her eyes."

"You're probably violating a whole book of health codes. At least put her back in your pocket."

"No one understands, do they, Miss Vanilla?" Constantine cooed to the hamster. He sighed and tucked her back in his pocket.

"Can you please be serious for five seconds?" Maggie said.

"Okay, okay." Constantine extended his hand. "The phone, please."

Maggie placed the phone on Constantine's palm. He flipped it over as if trying to ascertain its sex, then turned it over and entered the password Maggie gave him.

Before majoring in computer science, Constantine had been pre-med. When he told his parents about his new major, they reacted like he'd told them he was going to clown college. They eventually came around and supported his career plan, lobbing only a few passive-aggressive remarks at family gatherings.

Maggie watched in silence as he poked and prodded her phone. "Uh-huh," he said to himself. "Yep." He tapped and pinched and swiped the screen. "Okay."

"I hate to interrupt this scintillating conversation with yourself, but *what*?"

Constantine turned the screen toward Maggie. "I accessed your calendar. It looks like whoever had this phone before you installed a custom app that's configured to talk to the cloud." He opened the app and showed her the settings. "It's linked to the previous owner's other calendars, which means that whenever Outlook or Google or whatever are updated to add a meeting or appointment, the data is transmitted to that person's various devices: laptop, tablet, phone."

"Which goes back to your theory of the incomplete wipe?"

Constantine nodded. "Right. If the internal memory on this secondhand phone wasn't adequately wiped, it could still be syncing to the previous owner's calendar."

They were both quiet for a moment. "So someone's calendar is syncing with my new phone—which is their *old* phone?" Maggie asked. "And now we're both getting reminders?"

"Seems like it."

Maggie furrowed her brow. "Does this other person know I'm getting reminders?"

"I doubt it. Since the phone ended up at a phone recycler, the previous owner probably thinks it's in a million pieces or has been wiped of any data. I don't think this kind of thing would be on anyone's radar." He watched Maggie twirl her hair, then chew on her straw. "Don't stress out or anything. I can't seem to hack in to see whose phone this was, but I know the guy who sold me the phone. If you're that worried about it, maybe he can help us."

"Friend of yours?"

"Friendish. We worked together at Zeitgeist IT. After we got laid off, he started selling used smartphones out of a hole-in-the-wall shop in midtown. I'll give him a call."

Constantine returned Maggie's phone, brought out his own and dialed. He waited, then rolled his eyes. "Voicemail," he said. "Totally boring, too." This from a man who considered voicemail performance art. Constantine left a message for his friend to call him or Maggie, slowly reciting their numbers.

"Done. And done."

Maggie grabbed a crab roll from the sushi conveyor belt and shoved the whole thing into her mouth. "I don't know about that," she said with her mouth semi-full.

Constantine looked at her blankly. "Don't know about what?"

She swallowed. "That we're done. I mean, we can't just sit around waiting for another reminder. And another...death."

"There's still no proof the two are related," Constantine said.

"But you know the chances of this being mere coincidence are about nil."

Constantine was silent.

"We have to do something, Gus. We have to figure out what's going on. Find some sort of explanation beyond coincidence."

He spread his hands wide. "Okay. What do you suggest?"

Maggie tapped her nails on the counter. "Well...I have an idea, but you'll have to be my date."

"Ooh."

"To a funeral."

"Oh."

"The funeral for the guy who died in the crash is a week from Sunday. Maybe we'll learn something more about him or even the original owner of my phone."

"You want to crash a funeral of someone you don't know on the off chance you might, possibly, maybe find out what's going on with your phone or who owned it?" Maggie nodded.

Constantine sighed. "Fine. Just don't make me steal a hearse."

Chapter 8

Maggie had nearly forgotten about Saturday night's gala.

No biggie.

It was only the most important event Rxcellance had ever hosted.

Fortunately, Zartar called to see what she was wearing. When Maggie described the sensible, versatile shift dress she'd bought on sale three years ago at J. C. Penney, Zartar showed up at her apartment ten minutes later insisting Maggie borrow a slinky gray dress with a halter top and beaded waist.

Now clad in Zartar's dress and her own black cashmere wrap, Maggie walked into Rxcellance on the balls of her feet in an effort to keep her cute but loud peep-toe pumps from heralding her arrival. She hated being in the spotlight, even if it was just coworkers checking out her outfit.

Maggie cracked the heavy door of the cafeteria and peered inside. The place had been transformed from pharmaceutical boring to invitation-only elegance.

Ivory gauze masked fluorescent lights. Temporary sconces bordered reproduction paintings. Linen-lined tables replaced plastic cafeteria furniture.

Maggie yanked at the neckline of the borrowed dress and walked the perimeter of the room searching for a table. Zartar caught her eye and motioned to the seat between her and Roselyn.

Zartar handed Maggie a glass of champagne and studied her. "You clean up pretty good, Maggie Mae," she said. "With practically zero makeup, no less. You drink virgins' blood or something?"

Maggie snorted loudly. Two people at a nearby table turned to look at her. She covered her mouth. "What did I miss?" she whispered.

"Not much. They're just kicking off the Rx love fest with an overview of how awesome the company's been to the developing world."

Maggie followed her friend's gaze to a simple wooden podium. A small man wearing the traditional turban of a Sikh clicked the button on a wireless remote. His PowerPoint advanced to the next slide: a photograph of a young girl.

It was the kind of shot that inspired donations from people told they could "adopt" a starving child for the price of an Egg McMuffin a day. The girl was alone, sitting on a rough brown blanket beside the bowl in which she prepared what passed as food on most days. She stared down the barrel of the camera lens, molten black eyes lit by a fire within. Her mouth was expressionless, a line that bisected the hemispheres of her face.

She was skeletal. Maggie had expected that. Bones tenting up skin gray with dehydration and malnutrition was the norm. What she didn't expect was for the left quarter of her face to be gone. The skin that covered the girl's cheeks and ear had eroded. Chewed away by a necrotizing lesion that fed on flesh and hungered for more. The area was in varying degrees of decay. Red-pink crater. Desiccated skin. White bone gleaming from the depths. Soon, the lesion would spread across her face into a death mask.

The man adjusted his glasses and clicked his Mac to advance to the next horrific photo: a man, flesh of his tibia putrefying to the point of near liquefaction, begging in a crowded marketplace.

"A viral neglected tropical disease, Ghana necrosis is the developing world's latest scourge," he said. "It is now found in twenty-five of the world's most impoverished nations. And it is spreading, a fire that consumes and turns lives into ashes."

Click. A baby. Click. An old woman. Click. Girls playing in the dirt, wounds weeping down coltish limbs.

Maggie shifted in her chair. The room had grown unbearably hot. She fanned her face with the paper program she'd found propped on her plate. Nausea crawled slowly, teasingly, up her throat. She guzzled the champagne hoping the cool, sweet liquid would settle her stomach and quiet her mind. Then poured herself another glass.

What is wrong with me? I've seen worse in college.

But that wasn't true. Not really. Cadaver lab and disease studies were one thing. Human disintegration multiplied over an entire continent was something far different and far worse.

"Ghana necrosis can create disability, cause blindness and result in death," the speaker continued. "The most at-risk are women, not because of morbidity." He paused for emphasis. "But because of the cultural implications of disfigurement."

Click. A woman was stooping to lean into the window of a battered Jeep, her short animal print skirt hiking up spindly brown legs. "They become unmarriageable. Untouchable. Reduced to begging and prostitution—with all of the attendant risks."

Click. A bloody sheet covered the unmistakable form of a casualty of violence. Hot pink nails peeping out like Chiclets on blood-leached toes.

The house lights came up. The audience blinked in an attempt to adjust their eyes and clear their memory banks. "Ghana necrosis is the latest plague against humanity," the speaker said. "A holocaust blazing before our eyes. If it weren't for Project Collaboration and Rxcellance's continued leadership in the battle against neglected tropical diseases like Ghana necrosis, these people would have no hope. No advocates. And for this, we can thank Mr. James Montgomery."

James Montgomery materialized from nowhere. Magic. Maggie wondered if he'd now select someone from the audience to saw in half.

"Project Collaboration is pleased to recognize Mr. Montgomery and Rxcellance as Partner of the Year for the company's exemplary contributions." He faced James Montgomery and handed him something square and Lucite. "It is a pleasure to work with a company so young yet so committed to the betterment of humanity. It is with companies like Rxcellance that we can win the wars that kill millions each year. You are truly changing the world. We look forward to seeing what Rxcellance will do next and joining you in these valiant efforts."

The men shook hands and applause echoed through the auditorium. Montgomery grinned and continued shaking the small man's hand, turning slightly so that the flashing cameras, manned by the company's social media sycophants, could get his best side.

The men returned to their seats, Montgomery pressing the flesh of any well-heeled guest within five feet of his path.

"Wow, that was amazing," Maggie said, sipping her drink. "I knew Rxcellance was involved in the fight against neglected tropical diseases, but I had no idea they were doing so much."

"Don't wet yourself, Maggie," Zartar said. "That Lucite paperweight from Dr. Sharma doesn't mean a lot."

Roselyn blotted colorless lips on her cloth napkin. Her lank brown hair blended perfectly with her sagging brown shirtdress. "I know it was a lot of chest-beating," she said, "but Rx is doing good things by participating in this consortium. Not all pharms are stepping up to the plate, not even the big players. Less than 10 percent of research funds are devoted to the health needs of 90 percent of the world's population. They're not called 'neglected' diseases for nothing."

Zartar's face was stony. "The timing seems convenient, that's all. Montgomery announces the IPO and, bam, Rx wins a prestigious humanitarian award in front of the city's biggest movers and shakers. What are these 'exemplary contributions' Rx has made? Must be donations, because it certainly ain't research. Not anymore."

Roselyn looked surprised. "I had no idea you were this passionate about NTDs."

Zartar looked away. "If you think it looks bad through a camera, try it up close and personal."

Now it was Maggie's turn to look surprised. "You have personal experience with NTDs?"

She smiled tightly. "I wasn't always a heartless bitch, Maggie. I did a stint with a relief program in Angola before grad school. Sort of like the Peace Corps without the love beads. What you don't realize is that pictures are just what you *see*. They can't capture the crushing heat of the savannah. Or the taste of water from a stagnant river where people wash. Or the smell. Did you know hopelessness has a smell?" Zartar wiped her nose on a napkin. "And here we are, working to create drugs to help mitigate herpes symptoms and help teenagers go to prom zit-free, all while watching fat cats like Montgomery collect his awards and line his pockets and take people off work that matters." She stood. "I, for one, need a drink. This evening is leaving a bad taste in my mouth."

Chapter 9

Maggie watched Zartar amble toward the portable bar, then looked at Roselyn, whose face had blanched.

"She's pointing at the shot glasses," Roselyn said, her eyes trailing Zartar. "When Zartar does shots, she shoots off her mouth."

Maggie put her hand on Roselyn's, which now clutched a napkin that resembled a strangled goose. "Don't worry," she said, grabbing her purse. "I'll talk to her."

Maggie got to her feet and slalomed around guests standing in gossipy clumps. She got halfway across the room when a cold hand clamped down on her bare shoulder. She flinched and turned to see who was attached to the hand.

"Maggie," James Montgomery said. "I've been looking for you."

Maggie spun around. Montgomery looked even larger than she had remembered, as if the upcoming IPO and the evening's events had inflated his body along with his ego. "Mr. Montgomery. Congratulations on the award. What an honor."

"It is an honor," Montgomery agreed, "but it's an even greater honor to advance medicine and serve our human family." Montgomery closed his eyes for a moment, as if meditating. The moment stretched toward a minute. Maggie wondered if he'd forgotten she was standing there. His eyes snapped back open and he fixed them on Maggie. "I'd like to introduce you to some people, show off my brightest new star to potential investors. Do you have a few moments?"

"Of course." Maggie felt her heart rate quicken. Personal introductions to industry heavy-hitters? This was good. Maybe very, very good.

Montgomery ushered Maggie from table to table, the pair island-hopping across the transformed cafeteria. She smiled, shook hands, laughed politely and blushed whenever Montgomery bragged about her achievements.

Bar Guy Ethan caught her eye as Montgomery introduced her to a city council member. She could feel his gaze travel up and down her body as he took in the dress, the simple jewelry and her hair, which she had braided then piled high. He raised his eyebrows, then his glass. A toast to her. She returned the gesture, feeling a flush of embarrassment, pleasure and pride.

When Montgomery had reached the end of his political tour, he removed a handkerchief from his breast pocket, mopped his forehead and upper lip, then stuffed the moist cloth back into its small square hole. He watched Maggie watching him.

"I like you, Ms. O'Malley," he said finally. "You work hard. You're obviously smart. And you look..." He gave her an appraising gaze. "Responsible. I'd like you to be my administrator for the Rxcellance Foundation. It's the charitable wing of the company that helps fund the fight against neglected tropical diseases. Part of our commitment to this NTD consortium and the main reason we've been recognized for our work in this arena. Miles used to manage it, but he's been *relieved* of his duties." Montgomery snorted in disgust, nostril hair waving in the tiny breeze. "He's made some mistakes lately. Had some indiscretions. I need someone I can count on."

Maggie stifled the urge to perform an end zone dance. "I'd be honored, sir," she answered calmly. "Thank you so much."

"Excellent," he boomed. "It's nothing too taxing. Deposit funds from contributors, reconcile statements. That kind of thing. I'll have someone get in touch with you about the details." He took her hand, gave it a paternal pat. "It's nice to know I finally have someone I can trust."

Montgomery's cell phone rang. He removed it from the inner folds of his jacket and checked the display. His mouth turned down at the corners, a horseshoe with all the luck running out. He glanced quickly around the room, then at Maggie. "Excuse me."

Maggie nodded solemnly and waited until he'd turned his back before doing a little jump. It wasn't a promotion. Not exactly. But it was an increase in responsibility, an outward indication of her trustworthiness and value, doled out by the president of the company himself. Maggie hugged herself. Maybe she'd save Pop's restaurant and have her dream career.

"The old man seems to like you," a voice near her ear said.

Maggie turned.

Ethan, looking more handsome than usual.

Maggie felt her face flush rutabaga red. "Oh, Mr. Montgomery? He was just introducing me to some people."

Ethan broke into a broad smile. "Word around the water cooler is that you're blowing management's socks off."

Maggie sensed the flush climbing up her skin like a rash. She scratched her neck. "Really?"

Ethan moved closer. They were inches apart, almost touching. He was taller than she had remembered. Maggie's heart started hammering wildly in her chest. "Face it, Maggie. You're a rock star." He raised an eyebrow. "Which I guess makes me a groupie."

He made fake crowd noises, then waved an imaginary lighter to a make-believe song. Maggie laughed. "Very convincing. What's your second act?"

"Wouldn't you like to know?" His crooked grin broadened, then he looked around the room. "Well, I suppose I should do the compulsory mix and mingle." He held her eyes for a moment. "Great seeing you, Maggie."

Maggie watched him stride into the crowd. Maggie blinked. What just happened? Was that friendly coworker repartee, or was he *actually* flirting?

She thought about his eyes, the cool blue of the Caribbean. The full lips that always seemed ready to break into a smile. He probably had dozens of women chasing him. Not that it mattered. The truth was, she was okay basking in the glow of his attention, even if it was just friendship. She loved the way she felt around him. Interesting. Intelligent. And, for the first time in her life, attractive. It was enough. And she had a lot of practice being happy with enough.

She heard a loud cackle from the bar and then remembered. Zartar.

Feck.

Maggie turned quickly to find her friend, who she imagined was already doing body shots, and instead slammed straight into a man busy inhaling a plate of hors d'oeuvres.

Crab cakes leapt into the air. Sauces splattered and splashed.

"Oh my God," Maggie gasped, mortified at what she'd done. "I am so sorry." She looked into the face of the man whose powder blue sports jacket now looked like a Jackson Pollock painting. She tilted her head and looked at the man more closely. "Dan?"

The man returned her gaze with a mixture of surprise and bewilderment. "Maggie? What on earth are you doing here?"

Maggie's face broke into a smile. "I work here," she said. "What are *you* doing here?"

Dan's gape of astonishment morphed into an impish smile. "Didn't expect to see your old professor at such a posh event, eh?"

Maggie laughed. "I admit I usually picture you in the lab with a test tube in your hand, but I guess it's a small pharmaceutical world after all. How have you been? Looks like life outside the ivied walls of academia agrees with you. I mean, aside from the cocktail sauce."

Dan laughed and replaced his hat, straightened the lapels of his too-small jacket and stroked his Magnum, P.I. mustache. "I suppose I've traded my mad scientist mystique for bureaucratic BS, but I can't complain. No office hours. No lectures." He smiled. "The money's still terrible, but now that I'm with the FDA, I get to hang out with industry bigwigs like James Montgomery—and now you." He gave a small bow. "Congratulations."

Maggie ducked her head.

"Thanks. I feel very fortunate."

He summoned a waitress who refilled Maggie's glass. "You've got the job, the salary and the chance to better the world. And that's why we're in this business, right? To save the world." He smiled a funny little smile and lifted his glass. "Here's to bright futures and rewarding careers."

Maggie raised her glass and clinked it against his.

Dan checked his watch and winced. "I've gotta run. Don't want to miss my curfew. The wife will have my hide."

Maggie nodded. She knew Dan's wife, an unapologetic gold digger who'd picked the wrong man to mine. Despite expensive vacations and a diamond ring that could summon spacecraft from distant galaxies, she was always stopping by his office, haranguing him about what she lacked—or more specifically, how *his* lack caused hers.

"It was great to see you, Maggie," Dan said warmly. "Keep in touch, will you? I'd love to hear how my favorite former pupil's doing."

"I will," Maggie promised. They hugged the sort of hug typically reserved for great-aunts on Thanksgiving. Brief, minimal contact, accompanied by rapid back pats. Then Maggie watched Dan sail out of the door, a fedora on his head, his powder blue pants bunching awkwardly around his buttocks. Maggie placed her glass on an adjacent table and scanned the area by the bar. It was empty except for Ryan from marketing, who was attempting to impress the female bartender with his ability to vacuum peanuts off the bar with two straws thrust up his nostrils.

Maggie's eyes darted from table to table, corner to corner, as she searched for Zartar. Finally, she spotted her near the windows, a cell phone at her ear. Her friend's free hand gesticulated wildly, pointing, thrusting, chopping. Then her hand came to her mouth, where it rested against her trembling lips. Zartar closed her eyes and shook her head again and again. Then she threw the phone at the Linoleum floor. It exploded in a shower of plastic.

No one flinched. The room's hundred-plus heads didn't turn, Rockettes-style, to identify the source of the commotion. Fueled by alcohol and excitement, the crowd had grown too loud to hear the anguish of one woman. It was as if Zartar's actions were part of a silent movie playing only for Maggie.

Maggie watched in horror as her friend fled the room. "Zartar," she called. "Zartar, wait!"

She jogged down the hall again, motion-sensitive lights awakening to illuminate her path. She caught a glimpse of a gauzy black scarf around the corner and picked up speed. She rounded the corner and headed down a new corridor. Her ankle turned in her slingback heels. Maggie's phone shrilled from her purse. She yanked it from her bag and checked the display. Feck.

"Fiona? I'm so sorry, but can I call you back?"

A pause. "Yes, dear. I just wondered when you'd be sending along...you know." A conspiratorial whisper. "I know it's early, but we're already running short on funds..."

"No problem." Maggie looked around, trying to get her bearings. The unfamiliar hallway dead-ended at a door. "I'll send a check tomorrow. Okay? Gotta go."

"Thank you, dear. I—"

Maggie clicked off and dropped the phone back into her bag. She looked at the door before her and opened it. A flight of stairs led down into a black abyss.

She placed her right foot on the top step and peered into the darkness below. The stairs were steep, carpeted with a thin, padless runner that ran down the center like a skunk's stripe. "Zartar?" Maggie called uncertainly. Her own voice echoed back.

Maggie took off her heels and tucked them beneath her left arm. She began to make her way quickly down the steps. The door slammed behind her, plunging Maggie into inky blackness.

Maggie thrust her hand inside her purse. She pulled her phone free and activated the flashlight app. A small beam of light trickled from the back of the phone. Maggie shone the anemic light down the stairs and followed its path to the landing at the bottom. There was no carpet at the base of the stairs, just a wide swath of dilapidated vinyl that ruptured into blisters of worn, dirty plastic that snagged the bottom of her stockings.

Maggie wrinkled her nose. While her lab smelled like chemicals engineered for germicide, this section of the building smelled dank and oily. The walls and floors were slicked with a thin layer of grime.

She paused, listening intently. A soft, indiscriminate sound emanated from a hallway that snaked to the left. Maggie turned and followed it down the narrow corridor, stockinged feet padding on filthy vinyl. Although the stairs were unlit, the hallway was lit by the feeble glow of dim bulbs held captive by wire cages.

This must be an older part of the building, she thought. *Maybe even the original structure.* She remembered reading that Rx had converted an old factory into its new headquarters.

Maggie turned off the flashlight app and dropped her phone into her purse. She walked on, her hand trailing along a brick wall, which felt cool and chalky and filthy beneath her touch.

Maggie squinted. Ahead, a sliver of light sliced through shadows, a tiny lighthouse beckoning her on. It leaked from beneath a door.

Maggie approached the door slowly. She heard voices from the other side. She moved closer to hear if Zartar's was among them.

The sound of Maggie's phone, with its old-fashioned Jim Rockford ring, punctured the hallway's silence.

Shit, shit, shit. Maggie tore open her purse, her hand grasping frantically for her phone.

Wallet. Sunglasses. ChapStick. Luna bar. Finally her fingers found the thin plastic slab. She clutched it and yanked it from the bag.

She tried to hit the silence button but hit SPEAKER instead.

"Hello?" a voice boomed.

Maggie fumbled with the phone, trying to turn off the speaker. She found the right button then pressed the phone against her ear. "Hello?" she whispered, not entirely sure why she was whispering.

"Is this Maggie O'Malley?"

At that moment, the sliver of light beneath the door blast into the hall, ensnaring Maggie in its cool fluorescent glare.

Maggie froze. Her pupils retreated, contracting into tiny pinpoints. For a moment, she couldn't see anything. She heard the low rumble of surprised voices. A heavy door swung shut.

"Ms. O'Malley?" said the voice at the door.

"Maggie O'Malley?" said the voice in the phone.

"Uhh," said Maggie, not sure which voice to answer first.

She blinked, her eyes still adjusting. A rotund form crossed stubby arms across a barrel chest. White hair caught the light.

"Mr. Montgomery?"

"Yes?" he replied.

"Just a second," she mumbled into the phone.

"Can I help you with something?" Montgomery asked.

"I, um," Maggie stammered, putting the phone behind her back. "I seem to have gotten myself turned around. Too much champagne, I guess." She laughed. Montgomery did not. She started talking, faster now. "I was trying to find my friend Zartar, and the next thing I know, here I am. Which is kind of cool, because I got to see a historic part of the building. It's very interesting. Almost institutional."

Maggie knew she had started blathering, but it was as if she were running down a hill. No matter how hard she tried, she couldn't stop herself. "Not in a bad way. Just, you know, architecturally."

An awkward silence rolled in like thunderheads.

Maggie cleared her throat. "Is this part of the building still in use? I mean, I guess it is because you're here, ha ha."

Montgomery looked at her, then at the shoes under her arm. A frown formed between his shaggy eyebrows. "It's used for storage now," he finally said.

"Oh."

The silence thickened.

"Well," Maggie said. "I'd better get back to the party. Mix and mingle and stuff." She mentally slapped herself for sounding like she was on her way to third period algebra.

Montgomery opened the door and slid halfway inside. He smiled at Maggie. "Enjoy the rest of your evening, Ms. O'Malley. I hope you find Zartar."

"Thanks, Mr. Montgomery," she said cheerfully. "I'll see you—"

He disappeared into the room and the door clicked shut.

"Tomorrow."

Chapter 10

"Hello? Hello?" A voice, thin and tinny, called from the phone behind Maggie's back.

Feck.

Maggie put the phone to her ear and ran down the hall. She wanted to get away. Away from the strange old part of the building. Away from the anxiety worming its way into her mind. Away from the tangle of thoughts that snarled in her head.

What if Montgomery thought I was sneaking around? What if he thought I was spying? What if he doesn't let me act as administrator for his charity? What if I lose my job? Please, God, don't let me lose my job.

"Yes, hi," she whispered into the phone as she scrambled up the stairs. "I'm here." She hoped she was speaking clearly. She couldn't hear her own voice over the thundering torrent of blood rushing through her ears.

"This is Travis from Reincarnated Phones. I'm calling for Maggie O'Malley?"

Maggie ran through the main hallway and opened the door to the cafeteria. "Reincarnated Phones?" The blood continued to roar through her ears, drowning out everything but her own thoughts.

She couldn't hear over the din of the party, over the loud voices that competed with her internal voice, which was getting more hysterical by the moment. She grabbed her wrap from the back of her chair and darted back into the deserted hall.

Maggie closed her eyes. In the still of the empty corridor, clarity climbed above panic and confusion. "Reincar—oh, right. You're Constantine's friend? He bought my phone from you?"

The voice on the other end chuckled. "Right. I thought for a second I had the wrong number."

Maggie dropped her shoes and slid her feet into the pumps. Right number. Wrong time. But at least it was someone who might be able to give her some answers.

She concentrated on slowing her heart, on concentrating. "I'm your gal. Constantine told you about the problems I've been having?"

"Yeah. Something about getting someone else's messages?"

"More like someone else's calendar updates. Constantine thinks the phone may not have been wiped completely and is still connecting to the cloud. So when the previous owner syncs his calendar with his devices, my phone gets updated, too."

"Uh-huh."

Maggie opened the front door of the building and walked toward her car. Night had descended during the party. Shadows huddled in doorways, beneath the entrance's decorative benches, in spaces left empty by neglect and design.

Maggie squinted, eyes adjusting to the darkness. "I was hoping you could put me in touch with the phone's previous owner so I can let them know I—" *see dead people on my phone* "—have been receiving their updates."

"Uh-huh," Travis said again. "Well..." Long pause. "I don't know that I can do that."

Maggie stopped walking. "What?"

"I like to keep my customers' information confidential. I don't think he'd appreciate a call from a random girl."

"Random girl?" Maggie felt her face flush. "Look—"

"But what I can do is this." He spoke as if she hadn't said anything. "I can get you a better phone, one with all the latest bells and whistles."

"I don't want a better phone," Maggie said tightly.

"It's my bestselling phone," he continued in full sales guy monologue. "And because you're a friend of a friend, I can give it to you for only $60 more."

Maggie felt a blood vessel in her temple begin to pulse. "Like I said, I don't want a better phone. I don't even want a new phone. I want to talk to the guy who had *this* phone."

Travis made a sound that sounded like a yawn mated with a sigh. "Man, I really wish I could help you out, but it's company policy."

"Don't you own the company?" Maggie retorted hotly.

She heard an audible click in her ear. Then nothing.

"Hello? Travis?"

Nothing. *He hung up. The jerk actually hung up.*

Maggie walked to her car, shoulders slumping under the weight of worry that had returned heavier and more oppressive than ever. She shoved her phone back into her purse and fished out her car keys, dropping her cashmere wrap into a puddle in the process.

Awesome. Montgomery thinks I'm a spy. I'm no closer to finding out who owned my phone. And now I've ruined the only nice thing I own.

Maggie crouched down to retrieve the garment and heard a scrape of gravel behind her.

She turned. Miles stood watching her, his arms folded over his chest as if evaluating her form. The Russian judge gives a 6.7.

"Hi, Miles," she said, returning to a standing position.

"Hi, Maggie," he replied. "Nice time at the party?"

"Yeah. It was great. Very cool about your dad."

He acted as if he hadn't heard her. "Saw you drinking with some people."

What? "Not really. Just a couple of glasses of champagne with Zartar, Roselyn and an old professor from the U."

"You'll have a drink with them but not me?" he asked. His mouth stretched into a plastic smile that didn't touch his eyes. He wagged his finger. "I've invited you twice now. Even gave you one of my very special massages. And you keep blowing me off. That doesn't seem very nice."

Miles listed sideways against the car. Maggie could smell the pungent odor of alcohol on his breath. He was sweating Tanqueray.

"I haven't blown you off," Maggie said. "Besides, looks like you've had a few yourself."

"You're very perceptive," he said in a singsong voice. The wagging finger approached her nose. Grazed it. "Yes, I've had a couple of..." He paused searching for the word. "*Libations.* With my three best buddies: me, myself and I. Some of us have to drink alone."

He cackled. Stopped. The evening had gone strangely silent. Nobody in the parking lot. No cars driving by.

Miles took a step toward Maggie, backing her against the Studebaker's fender. "You should be careful walking out here all alone. You never know what kind of weirdoes are around."

Maggie's throat tightened.

Miles took another step closer, his thigh brushing hers. "You think you're pretty special, don't you?" Miles whispered.

"What? No, I—" Maggie tensed her body, ready to strike with her keys or bolt from the car. But where would she run? The building seemed far away and the jumble of woods that surrounded the property looked like it had the power to ensnare rather than deliver.

"Miss Popularity. The pharmaceutical superstar Jon keeps bragging about. The new foundation administrator."

How did he know about that?

She could feel him studying her, his eyes crawling across her face, which she felt paling beneath the blue-white slash of the security light overhead. He was close to her now. She wondered if he could sense her fear. Smell it growing inside her. He smiled as if reading her mind.

"You think you're so special," he continued. He thrust his face toward hers, engulfing Maggie in his alcohol aura. "You think you're better than everyone else. Smarter. More capable. Not to mention more attractive. And you are attractive, Maggie. In fact, you look good enough to eat."

Her previous encounters with Miles came crashing back. The way he squeezed her hand when they met. The meeting in the grove on her lunchtime walk. The unwanted chair massage and implication that she frequented kinky dating sites.

Miles extended a muscled arm, brushed a lock of hair from Maggie's forehead. Maggie shrank from the touch, revulsion festering in her belly, heart thrashing against bone. She felt her insides liquefy. Maggie clenched her hand around her keys, considered her targets. Which first? Eyes or groin?

Then the sound of approaching footsteps.

She turned to see Ethan emerge around the corner, his footfalls ringing against the asphalt. He waved and walked toward them. "I thought I heard voices," he called.

Miles stood, swaying slightly, and looked at Ethan with disdain. "Sucking up to the boss, eh, Clark?"

Ethan laughed good-naturedly. "It's my night off." He looked from Miles to Maggie. Maggie was shaking. Miles looked infuriated, a lion interrupted before it had a chance to taste its kill. Ethan looked at Maggie again and mouthed, "Are you okay?" She didn't move.

Ethan's face darkened. He turned to Miles. "Some kind of problem here?"

Miles put his hands up. "No problem. I don't see any problem." He made a show of looking under the car, behind him, in his armpit. "Do you see a problem, Maggie?"

Maggie looked down, saying nothing.

Ethan's face was stony. "Okay. Well, I'll just wait here to make sure your car starts, Maggie." He turned toward Miles, eyeing the stains on the front of Miles' yellow Ralph Lauren polo shirt and his teetering stance. "Why don't you go back to your office and sleep it off, Montgomery. You smell like a distillery."

"Screw you," Miles said.

Ethan acted as if he hadn't heard him. "What'll it be, Miles? Are you going to rack it here at Rx HQ? Or should I go inside and ask your daddy to take you home?"

Miles expanded, a puffer fish in country club casual. He swayed dangerously, flexing his hands open and closed. He opened his mouth to say something, then changed his mind and lumbered toward the crouching behemoth of Rxcellance, a string of obscenities in his wake.

Maggie waited until his hulking form disappeared into the metal mandibles that jutted out from the entrance before turning to Ethan. "I didn't need you to rescue me," she said tightly.

Ethan looked hurt, confused, then embarrassed. "I'm sorry if I stepped in when I shouldn't have."

Maggie was suddenly filled with regret. Ethan had been nothing but sweet and kind and helpful, and now she was snapping at him. What was the matter with her?

"No," she said softly. "I'm the one who should apologize. I didn't mean to sound so ungrateful. I am glad you showed up when you did." She gave a small laugh. "I didn't want to have to kick Miles's ass."

Ethan began pacing in front of the Studebaker, kicking gravel that skittered with a metallic giggle across the parking lot. "That son of a bitch," he said under his breath. "That entitled—" Ethan stopped. He looked at the ground, then up at the dark sky above. He seemed to be waging some internal war. He shook his head, the battle lost. When he spoke again, his voice was measured. "Don't worry about Miles. I'll make sure he doesn't bother you again."

Maggie was tempted to say she could take care of her own problems, remind him that she didn't need a knight in shining armor. Instead she simply said, "Thanks."

Ethan opened the Studebaker door and held it as Maggie slid across the bench seat. Their hands brushed as she grasped the door for balance. She felt that same electric jolt run through her. Maggie chanced a glance to see if Ethan felt it, too. He was looking at her, his face filled with worry and something she couldn't quite identify.

He put his face near hers, almost as if for a kiss. "Goodnight, Maggie," he said as he began to close her door. "See you Monday."

The door clicked shut, enclosing Maggie in a cocoon of aged leather and vanilla-scented air freshener. Dazed, Maggie started her car, put it into gear and drove into the night. As she pulled out of the parking lot, she looked into her rearview mirror.

Ethan was still watching her.

Chapter 11

Charlene shuffled from garbage can to dumpster to recycle bin and back again. Getting dinner at this time of night was the worst. Anything good had already been snatched up. The light was pathetic, a sorry stream dribbling from an anemic streetlamp. And you never knew who you'd run into. Who was watching.

Charlene picked a bag of Sara Lee bagels from the dumpster and sniffed. Something was starting to turn, the yeasty smell becoming sugary and ripe. She tore open the plastic bag and pulled three bagels free. She held each to her eye, tilting to maximize the feeble light. Mold on two of the bagels. Threads of rot through the third. She let them fall to the ground and pocketed the remaining three, which looked relatively unblemished—although those "raisins" could really be anything.

She turned heavily and gazed the length of the alley. The streetlamp cast funhouse shadows, long and crooked and reaching, against the concrete foothills of the mountainous buildings around her. Where now? East toward the maze of alleys that burrowed into homeless camps? Or west toward more prosperous, although less welcoming, prospects?

Charlene pulled her hand from the pocket of a tattered men's overcoat. It was time to consult The Thumb.

The Thumb used to be the resting place of the Antichrist who had taunted and tortured her with evil thoughts. She had cast him out, gouging her thumb with a screwdriver she'd found at a construction site, working it back and forth to be sure to get the root. He had tried to come back, pulsing a code through her thumb to infect her brain with more evil thoughts.

Then the angel appeared. He cleaned The Thumb and made her pure. Now The Thumb was a tiny tabernacle where the holy of holies resided.

Now it was her guide to righteousness.

She brought The Thumb up to her nose and sniffed. She flicked out her tongue and touched the stump's shiny puckered top. Held it aloft. A tiny breeze cooled its left side.

East. She should go east, just like the Magi seeking the newborn King. It made perfect sense.

She turned toward the maze of alleys, making her way toward the warren of homeless camps.

Then she heard something. A mewling voice. A hand-patting voice.

She stopped, let her head fall to one shoulder and listened, focusing on the sound beneath the voices that were always bickering in her head.

"Who is it?" she hissed. "Show yourself, you little pricks. I'm on a mission from God."

Last week's copy of *Us* fluttered in the recycle bin beside her, turning a Kristen Stewart story into a flipbook of open-mouthed gazes and frowny pouts. Next to it, she spied a bulging Hefty bag, leaking something orange and putrid from its seams. Maybe there was something good in there, too. The prize in the Cracker Jack box.

She reached for the bag.

The mewl. The hand-pat. The outside voices again.

Charlene followed the building to its corner, then peered around. She gasped. An angel like the one who had exiled the Antichrist, like the one who would give her wings. Garbed in white, he bent over a woman who was puddling in her own tears.

Charlene frowned. The woman had no concept of propriety. When to "let it be done to me," like Mary said to Gabriel. She'd learn, though. Soon enough, the woman would learn the only way to salvation was to let the angel purify her.

The shakes had started right after she pulled out of the Rx parking lot. She wasn't afraid, she told herself, but her skin felt as if it were crawling with thousands of wriggling insects. Maggie drove a mile and a half, then pulled over on the side of the road and called Constantine. She listened as the phone rang. She wasn't sure what she was going to tell him if he answered. That she had nearly been attacked? That the guy she liked at work had leapt to her rescue, leaving her feeling both resentful and grateful? That she wanted to hear her best friend's voice, to talk over something she could trust only him to understand?

It didn't matter because he didn't answer.

Maggie drove home, feeling as if the tether that had bound her and Constantine had frayed and broken.

He hadn't known she needed him. He hadn't felt her pain. He hadn't even answered the damn phone.

She knew she was being irrational. She didn't care.

Maggie parked in front of the apartment house and dragged herself through her door, locking it behind her. She fell into bed without brushing her teeth or washing her face, her mind and body exhausted.

Sleep came in broken bits and pieces. At nine o'clock, Maggie dragged herself out of bed and headed to a small coffeehouse to meet Roselyn and Zartar. It was the last thing she felt like doing, but they'd already planned it and she was sure they were waiting for her.

She'd just have to shake off last night and move on.

That was her specialty, wasn't it? Pretend she didn't feel anything, and if she did, cram down those feelings with whatever was handy. School. Work. Runs. Movies. Constantine.

Maybe not Constantine. He hadn't even returned her voicemail.

Roselyn and Zartar were already seated with tiny cups in hand when Maggie arrived. Maggie waved, ordered at the counter, then dropped onto an old comfortable sofa.

Zartar wore skinny jeans, a shrunken tee that lived up to its name and red wedges. She wiped lipstick from the lip of her cup. "Glad you're here, Mags. We thought you might ditch us like last night."

Maggie sputtered with indignation. "I didn't ditch you."

Zartar arched a perfectly groomed brow. "Well, you certainly left quickly. And without telling anyone." She sipped her latte, wiped the cup, shrugged. "It just seemed... surprising."

"What about you?" Maggie could hear the defensiveness in her voice. "Last time I saw you, you were playing Bounce the Cell Phone. It exploded into about a million pieces, then you ran from the room." She raised her own eyebrow. "I think you may have been crying."

"I wasn't crying," Zartar said, her voice growing louder. "I was just upset." Her eyes slid to Maggie, then to Roselyn. She bit her lip. "About my brother."

"*Quelle surprise*," Roselyn said under her breath.

"What?" Maggie said.

"That's French for 'I think your brother's a dumbass,'" Zartar said, looking pointedly at Roselyn. "Ari's had some trouble in the past, which has hurt his popularity with some of my friends. Drugs, mostly. You name it, he's smoked, snorted, injected or swallowed it. So, yeah, I'm worried about him, real worried." She stopped, bit her lip again. Harder. The soft skin blanched where an eyetooth pressed. Her eyes met Maggie's. They were red-rimmed and shiny. Zartar blinked rapidly, took a sip of coffee. "Back to you. You take off early for a hot date with your cute just-friend or something?"

Maggie hesitated.

"Come on," Roselyn wheedled. "You can tell us."

Maggie looked into the faces of her two new friends. She wanted a second opinion on what had happened with Miles.

Or in this case, a third opinion.

When Constantine hadn't returned her call, she had called Fiona, who had insisted she go to HR to report him for harassment. In the light of day, Maggie wondered how her complaint would go over with Rxcellance's testosterone-laden management team, especially since the star of her grievance was the spawn of the company's head honcho.

Zartar crossed her arms across her generous bosom. "Out with it, Maggie. Something's clearly bothering you."

Maggie cleared her throat. "Something happened after I left the party. Out in the parking lot."

Roselyn and Zartar leaned in.

"What?" Roselyn asked.

"Well, I kind of had a run-in with Miles."

Zartar laughed, a harsh, bitter bark. "A run-in, huh? As in he wanted to run his dick into your vagina?"

"Zartar!" Roselyn gasped, aghast.

Zartar jutted her chin out.

"Am I right, Maggie? Junior try to test the limits of nepotism?"

Maggie could feel emotion swelling up, threatening to spill over. She grabbed her coffee cup and took a long swig, thankful it had already cooled, hopeful the caffeine could quell her feelings the same way baking soda got out wine stains.

She nodded. "He didn't get far because Ethan showed up." She folded her arms. "Not that I needed him to rescue me," she added.

Zartar's mouth twisted into a smile. "How chivalrous. Did he challenge Miles to a duel?"

"No, but he sort of chased him away."

Zartar considered this. "Interesting." She looked into her coffee, then at Maggie. "Miles has been harassing women since the day he trailed in on his daddy's coattails. But the girls are either too afraid to say something or they just—" Zartar made her hands into fireworks. "Poof. Disappear. Someone needs to stand up to that asshole, report him for what he really is: a predator."

Roselyn shifted in her seat. Crossed her legs. Then recrossed them. "I don't know," she said, pulling at the floppy bow around her neck. "I mean, couldn't she get in trouble? I don't want Maggie to get in trouble." Roselyn looked like she wanted to recede into the wall behind her.

"Why would she get in trouble?" Zartar snapped. "She didn't do anything. Miles is the criminal here."

"Well, I don't know if he's done anything *criminal*..." Roselyn began.

Zartar turned on her, eyes blazing. Roselyn shrank back even farther. "That's right, Roz. You don't. You don't know shit about what Miles has or hasn't done." She turned back to Maggie. Smoothed her hair and her composure. "But let's leave it up to Maggie. It was her 'run-in.' It's her choice. You do what you want." She assessed Maggie, coolly calculating her mettle. "No judgment from us. But if you decide to file a complaint, I'd go to Roy first. HR has been historically useless."

Maggie wondered how Zartar knew that.

She worried that she was right.

*   *   *

On Monday morning, Maggie stationed herself near Roy's office.

She patted the low chignon she had secured with one of her mother's vintage combs and checked the clock on her phone. She'd been waiting nearly ten minutes for Roy to emerge from his office, pretending to get documents from the printer, getting a drink from the water cooler.

She was running out of reasons to hover near his door.

Maybe I should forget the whole thing. I can't afford to cause trouble. Besides, Miles didn't really do *anything. I'm probably blowing this way out of proportion.*

Maggie turned to go. Roy's door swung wide, revealing a crowded trophy wall and an empty desktop. He strode out, stainless steel coffee cup in hand.

"Hey, Maggie," he said jovially. "You look as nervous as a rooster on Sunday."

"Oh," she laughed uneasily. "I'm fine. I was just wondering..." She paused to clutch at the courage that seemed to be seeping away. "I was wondering if I could talk with you for a minute."

He gave a surreptitious look at his watch, shut his door and began walking again. "Sure, if you can manage a walk and talk. I'm late for a meeting."

A sexual harassment allegation in the hall. Not exactly ideal.

"Maybe we should talk in your office?" she asked his retreating form. "It'll just take a second."

"No time," he called over his shoulder. "If you've got something to say, just say it."

Maggie trotted after him. "Well, I've..." She cleared her throat and lowered her voice. "I've been having some problems with another employee."

"Oh?" Roy furrowed his brow thoughtfully, going full-on TV dad. "What kind of problems?"

Maggie swallowed hard. "With Miles Montgomery. I guess I'd call it sexual harassment—"

Roy stopped short. Maggie almost ran into him. "Whoa, whoa, whoa." He waved his hands, an umpire telling the batter he was outta there. "I thought you were going to tell me about a *real* problem. Someone not pulling his weight. Safety issues. Not some sandbox squabble about an off-color joke or a compliment about your hair."

"But—" Maggie closed her mouth. Opened it again. She felt like a ventriloquist's doll. Her mouth moved. Roy's words came out.

"I don't cotton to people who make trouble or create drama or fail to solve problems on their own," he was saying. "I hope there isn't an aspect about your job that you can't handle."

Maggie stood frozen, her mouth stuck in the open position. "No, not at all," she finally managed.

He hitched up his pants. "Good," he said. "Because that would be a damn shame." He gave her a pointed look, then chewed the inside of his cheek. "I will say something to Miles, though. Let him know that he made you...uncomfortable."

Roy talking to Miles suddenly seemed like a terrible idea.

"Oh. No, Mr. Hubbins, that won't be necessary. I—"

Roy turned on his heel and retreated into the bunker of Conference Room B at the end of the hall. Maggie heard a hail of greetings emanate from within. Then the door closed.

Maggie slunk back to her desk and collapsed into her chair. She pressed the heels of her hands against her eyes, ignoring Fiona's voice in her head warning of ruined eye makeup and premature wrinkles.

Maggie barely registered a quiet thump, but then her elbow brushed against something. She took her hands from her eyes and saw a large manila envelope on her desk. She stood and peered over the cubicle wall to see who had delivered it. Her coworkers were all seated, working quietly at their desks.

She returned her attention to the envelope. She picked it up, turning it over in her hands. It was thick, bulging in the middle, the corners turned down as if in protest against its bloated midsection.

She opened the envelope and shook out a plain brown folder. She paged slowly through the contents.

Target identification. Compound assays. Toxicity.

There were reams of data related to drug discovery, yet nothing to identify what was being developed. No compound number. No memos. No reports. No notes.

Strange.

Yet there was something familiar about the data, something that resonated like the echo of a bell rung long ago. She just couldn't put her finger on it.

Maggie's phone chimed. Another meeting reminder.

Maggie's stomach cramped. A feeling of unease wrapped around her heart, squeezed. She took a deep breath, picked up the phone and tapped the screen. The photo of another stranger appeared.

Bad lighting, gray backdrop and an awkward pose suggested that the image was used for a photo ID. The woman pictured was in her mid-thirties, clad in a body-conscious gray blazer and a ruffled blouse so voluminous it threatened to eat her head. She had ash blonde hair, hazel eyes and fine features frozen in an expression of cool self-reliance. The vibe was intellectual, studious. A trifecta of brains, beauty and bottle blonde.

Maggie tapped the screen again. Beneath the photo, the familiar text appeared:

MEETING REMINDER

TIME: Monday, 9:00 p.m. – 11 p.m.

Maggie felt as if her blood had grown cold. "Please be alive," Maggie whispered to the woman in her phone. "Please be alive and stay that way."

The soft swish of the elevator door heralded the entrance of someone to the floor. In her peripheral vision, Maggie saw a woman step onto the landing and extend her hand. James Montgomery stepped into view, took the woman's hand and pumped it vigorously. The woman glanced Maggie's way and smiled.

Maggie stared, her mouth half-open, her mind working frantically to connect fuzzy dots. The dots suddenly converged.

The woman with Montgomery was the same woman Maggie had just seen on her phone.

Chapter 12

Maggie wanted to stand, to talk to the woman, to warn her that her phone had told her something terrible was going to happen. But she sat immobile and mute. Her nervous system had gone on a coffee break.

Then as quickly as she'd frozen, Maggie thawed. She sprang to her feet, desperate to talk to the woman. Her hand bumped her mug of coffee. Black-brown liquid sloshed onto her desk. A mini Exxon Valdez.

Maggie ripped open her desk drawer and began sopping up the liquid with cafeteria napkins. The woman looked at Maggie, wrinkled her forehead in puzzlement, then swaggered down the hallway.

Maggie groaned and continued the mop-up. With the spill finally contained, she peeked around the corner of her cubicle wall.

The woman walked toward the room Roy had entered moments before. The door opened. James Montgomery appeared. Maggie squinted, trying to make out the details of the room's beige interior. She saw a carafe of water, a tray of muffins, a hat perched on the polished conference table, a couple of suit jackets thrown over the backs of chairs. Montgomery ushered the woman in with gallant flair, then closed the door.

Maggie exited her work area and walked toward the conference room. She stopped at the water cooler, picked a paper cup from its plastic tree and filled it to the brim. She drank slowly, straining to catch any scrap of conversation that might slip beneath the door. She was becoming an expert at loitering.

She heard the rabble-rabble of muffled voices. One voice was high-pitched, presumably the woman from the reminder app. Two others had lower timbres. One of the male voices was surely

Montgomery's. Big, booming. The other was also male but quieter, more subdued. And somehow familiar.

Roy? She couldn't detect a Southern accent. Then again, she was separated by a slab of cherry wood. If only she could make out the words or hear more clearly, she could—

"Hey, Maggie." Tommy from her lab group brushed by her. His arms hugged a stack of three-ring binders.

Maggie choked on her water, drooling onto her shirt. "Hey, Tommy," she said cheerfully after her fit of coughing had passed.

"Heading down to the lab?" Tommy asked.

"Yep. I'll be right there. Just pausing for some liquid refreshment." She hoisted the now-empty paper cup. Exhibit A. She tried to mop up the drool on her shirt with one hand.

"Cool. See ya there," he said as he walked to the elevator.

Maggie waited until he was out of sight, then edged back toward the door. She listened. The voices were quieter now. She couldn't hear anything other than the soft hum of fluorescent lights.

The door to the conference room yawned open. Maggie hurried back to her cubicle, disappearing behind the wheat-colored partition just as the blonde woman emerged from Montgomery's office alone, traipsing out on impossibly high heels, her knees conjoined by a very tight black pencil skirt. Maggie thought for a moment. Then followed her.

"Um, miss? Ma'am?" Maggie said softly. "Excuse me?" she said, louder this time.

She didn't know what she was going to say, but she knew she couldn't stay silent. In the pit of her stomach, she felt with a terrible certainty that unless she warned this woman, she'd end up dead like the others who'd appeared on her reminder.

The woman walked down the hall, rounded the corner and disappeared into the ladies' room. Maggie followed.

The air in the women's restroom was thick with Glade air freshener. Six stalls lined the wall to Maggie's right. The one at the end appeared to be occupied.

Maggie stood at the sink and washed her hands long enough to scrub in for surgery. She dug into her pockets, hoping to busy herself with an activity that would explain her prolonged presence. A few seconds of rooting around produced a partially melted tube of ChapStick and a retractable comb. Maggie applied a generous waxy coat of lubricant to her lips, then attempted to smooth her hair, which she knew was hopeless.

The muted sound of a toilet paper roll unspooling from the last stall drifted from beneath the door. Then a flush. The woman emerged from the stall, straightened her skirt and bumped the faucet on with a narrow, rhinestone-encrusted wrist. Maggie turned toward the woman.

Don't sound crazy, don't sound crazy, don't sound crazy, she told herself.

"Excuse me," she said. "But the strangest thing just happened."

The woman regarded Maggie in the mirror. "Oh?"

Maggie laughed. "You see, I've got this app on my phone that sends meeting reminders with a photo of the person I'm supposed to have a meeting with. And a few minutes ago, I got a reminder with your picture."

There. Totally not crazy.

The woman pulled a wad of paper towels into her hands. Dried. Folded her arms across her chest. "You don't say."

"Yes. And, um..." Maggie opened her purse and fished for her phone. "Hang on, I'll show you—aw, dammit."

Maggie dropped the phone. It skipped noisily across the tile. Maggie bent to retrieve it, talking faster in a race to finish before she lost her audience. "Anyway, the reminders I'm getting are actually for someone else because my phone wasn't adequately wiped."

She glanced at the woman, whose eyebrows were so high they'd almost disappeared into her scalp. "It's kind of a long story, but the point is, whenever I get these reminders, the person whose photo appears on my phone ends up..."

A long pause.

"Yes?" the woman prompted impatiently.

"Well, the person ends up...dead."

And...totally crazy.

"Dead?" Shock rippled across the woman's lineless face. "Your phone shows you who's going to die?"

"Well, yes. I mean, no. Sort of."

Maggie felt her powers of rational explanation ebb away. It was like drowning in quicksand. The more she struggled to explain, the deeper she sank.

The shock on the woman's face was replaced with a look of annoyance.

"You were staring at me when I got off the elevator, weren't you?" she asked. The woman swore under her breath. "God, why do I always attract the nut jobs?"

She looked Maggie in the eye, her expression hard. "Listen, I don't care about your psychic phone or your crystal ball app that shows who's going to die, okay? I have somewhere to be five minutes ago. Now if you'll excuse me." She tucked a red patent leather clutch under a taut, tanned arm and reached for the door.

Maggie leapt in front of her. "I'm only telling you this because your life could be in danger," Maggie said. She knew her desperation was making her sound even more irrational, but she couldn't help herself. She had to make her understand. "Please. Just listen. I know this must sound crazy—"

The woman pushed past Maggie and out into the hall. "You think?" she said.

"But the fact that you appeared on my phone..."

"Goes to show that you're a hallucinating lunatic." The woman huffed toward the elevators.

"Wait," Maggie cried, as she jogged behind her. "*Please.* I think something bad is going happen to you."

"It couldn't be worse than this conversation." She stepped into the elevator and jabbed a button repeatedly. "Ta-ta," she said to Maggie, stepping into the car. "Oh, and say hi to Elvis, will you? That is, if your psychic phone's plan includes calls to the afterlife."

She waved at Maggie with French-tipped fingers. The elevator doors embraced, enclosing the woman in its metallic crypt.

Maggie watched helplessly as the elevator lights counted down to the first floor. In her mind's eye, she saw the woman exit the building and get hit by a mail truck. Or gunned down by a sniper. Or dive-bombed by a drone from Amazon.com. There were a thousand ways for her to die. Maggie couldn't prevent a single one.

Or could she?

Maggie hurried to her cubicle, Googled the Collinsburg Police

Department's contact information and dialed the non-emergency number.

"Collinsburg Police Department," a female voice said.

"Yes," Maggie said. "I'm calling about a crime that is about to happen."

"A crime that's happened?"

"No, *about* to happen."

"Are you going to commit a crime, ma'am?" The woman's tone was at once annoyed and wary.

"No!" Maggie practically shouted. "No," she said more softly. "It's, um..." Maggie twirled a strand of hair, considering the best approach. "I have a meeting reminder app on my phone that shows pictures of people I'm scheduled to have meetings with. But the people who appear on the reminders always end up dead."

Silence.

"I don't know the people in the reminders," Maggie pressed on. "I'm actually receiving someone else's reminders because I have a used phone that still has some of the previous owner's data."

Louder silence. Maggie barreled ahead.

"I'd gotten two of these reminders before, and in both cases, the people on my phone ended up dead. I wanted to call you after the second one, but I didn't want to sound crazy."

"Right," the dispatcher said with the careful casualness of someone talking to someone crazy. "What is the name of the person on your...*reminder*?" She said the word as if it were especially repugnant, like a contagious disease or tapered jeans.

"I don't know."

"But you got a reminder that you were going to meet with him?"

"Her. Yes. But like I just said..." Maggie stopped herself. *Stay calm.* "Like I said, the reminders are intended for someone else. I don't actually know her."

"But you want us to save her. From something that *might* happen."

"Well, something that will happen. Um, probably."

A long sigh. "I don't know if you're aware of this, but the city is practically under siege by protesters." Before Maggie could answer, the woman pressed on, her civic-centric soliloquy already gaining momentum. "There are daily demonstrations. Riots in some parts of the city. Our resources are stretched very thin. We were understaffed before, and now everyone's working overtime. *On actual threats to public safety.* I don't know if this is some kind of joke or an actual problem, but the best I can do is pass you along to our cybercrime division. No one's there right now, but you can leave a voicemail."

Before Maggie could say anything else, she heard a chorus of chirps and beeps, then an automated invitation to leave a message. Maggie complied, trying to be as specific yet uncomplicated as possible, over-articulating her phone number. She hung up and put her head in her hands.

Maggie: 0

Bad day: 4

She scrubbed her face with her hands, trying to wipe away the dread growing fat on her fear. The fear that she'd be frozen out for being a company snoop and whiner. That she'd be fired, leaving her father destitute. That the meeting reminders would keep coming, one after another, like a trailer for a movie she didn't want to see.

She stared at her desktop, trying to think what to do next. Then she saw it. Or rather, didn't see it. The envelope that had been delivered to her desk was gone.

Chapter 13

Maggie trudged up the steps to her apartment door, her legs leaden with fatigue. The evening seemed darker than usual, the inkiness of night blotting out everything but the glow of windows freckling insomniac houses.

Then again, maybe it was her mood that had cast the shadow.

The rest of the day had been a blur. She had searched for the missing folder. Sliding open drawers. Peering into the desk's built-in filing cabinet. Dragging a hand through her purse. She came up empty each time. It was like playing hide-and-seek with David Copperfield.

It was probably a simple mistake. Wrong file delivered to the wrong desk, then redelivered to the intended recipient—most likely while she was cornering that woman in the bathroom.

But something told her it was more than that. For Maggie, the era of coincidences had ended.

She had called Constantine from the bank drive-through, waiting to make her first deposit into Rx's charitable fund. She wanted to tell him about the new appointment reminder, imagining what he'd say about the woman who showed up on her phone walking through her office, Maggie's call to the police, the strange envelope. She also wanted to make sure they were still on for the funeral of Carson Parks, the man who'd trespassed into her phone and now her thoughts. But Constantine didn't answer. Again. She felt her anger bubble up as she listened to his voicemail message featuring a very bad Jamaican accent accompanied by steel drums. She asked him to call her back.

It seemed that he was never there when she needed him these days.

Not that she needed anyone.

Now she squinted, trying to locate the correct key on a ring that would rival a school janitor's. It was full dark now. She could barely see her hand.

Maggie looked up. The light bulb that stood guard at her front door was out.

Odd.

She pulled her phone from her purse, turned it on with a flick of her thumb and activated the flashlight app, as she had when she pursued Zartar in the bowels of Rxcellance. She aimed the stream of light at the door, then breathed in sharply. The bulb adjacent to the doorframe wasn't out. It was gone. Someone had removed it from the fixture.

Maggie's mouth went dry. The fear that had been sleeping charged out, battering her heart and sending it into a flutter of rapid, irregular beats.

A gust of wind blew her hair across her eyes. The cloying scent of musk, spice and citrus wafted to her nose. Maggie's stomach contracted involuntarily, a primitive part of her brain cataloging the scent as Miles's putrid and overpowering cologne.

She spun around, expecting Miles's hulking figure to tower over her. But the porch was empty. The street naked.

She turned back to the door, a chill climbing her spine. A small bundle was crammed against the hinges. Silhouette against shadow.

Maggie shone her phone's flashlight on the bundle. It was soft and furry and indistinct. Even with the flashlight's beam, she couldn't quite make it out. Was it some kind of animal? A rabbit or a kitten, curled up (dead?) against her door? She swallowed hard and reached out, her hand hesitating over the fluffy object.

She stroked it with a finger. It collapsed into a heap. It wasn't an animal; it was her cashmere wrap, the one she'd worn to the company gala.

It had been impaled by a giant safety pin. Maggie exhaled, momentarily relieved. Then she saw the note affixed to the safety pin.

You left this in the parking lot.

— Miles

The memory of what had happened that night flooded back. Dropping her wrap as she dug for her car keys. Miles behind her, sizing up the possibilities. Them inches apart, Miles fingering a lock of her hair.

A shudder slithered through her body. She shook it off, her hands ruffling beneath her hair to rid herself of the feeling that something alive and dangerous was scuttling up her back.

She plucked up the wrap from its filthy nest and gave it a gentle shake. Miles's cologne escaped into the night air. It was as if it had been poured on every inch of her sweater, marking his territory.

She hoped she wouldn't be next.

Maggie unlocked the door, dropped her purse on the floor, then locked the door behind her. Her phone rang and she jumped, almost dropping it.

"You rang?" said Constantine, doing his best Lurch impression.

"About time." She aimed for breezy. She missed.

"Aw, sorry, Mags." Constantine sounded suitably chastised. "It's been a crazy couple of days. Job interviews all over the region, including weekend wining and dining. I forgot to bring a phone charger, which, as it turns out, isn't available in the hotel vending machine. The good news is I got a job right here in Collinsburg. One with a paycheck and everything. You're talking to Quatra Corp's new IT manager."

Maggie swallowed her anger and tried to be happy for him. "That's great. Congratulations."

"Thanks. I was hoping to get a call back from the FBI for a computer and information systems manager gig I applied for. But I guess I'll just have to play Jack Ryan on weekends."

"Isn't Jack Ryan CIA?"

"Close enough. What's up? You tried to contact me with everything but carrier pigeon and sandwich boards. Something wrong?"

Maggie paused. She could hear the distinctive, musical tinkle of cereal being poured into a bowl. Probably Lucky Charms.

Suddenly, she didn't feel like telling Constantine about Miles anymore. It wasn't just anxiety over talking about it, reopening a wound she was trying to close. It was more than that.

Resentment had seeped into her. Bitterness about the missed text and phone call. The Lucky Charms and the easy jokes and the emerging feeling that Constantine didn't take anything seriously. Constantine didn't seem to notice the strain in her voice. The hurt and fear she was sure bled through. Maybe he didn't care.

She knew she was being irrational and selfish and small. She knew she could be just as flip as Constantine. But that was different. *She* was different. And now she didn't feel like rewarding Constantine with this new secret piece of her life.

"I got another meeting reminder and the woman whose photo appeared on my phone walked right by my desk," she said smoothly.

"Seriously?"

"Yep."

"Did you talk to her?"

"I tried. I followed her to the ladies' room, but she didn't seem to enjoy my company. Or my warning that my phone is the harbinger of her imminent death."

"Some people are so sensitive," Constantine said.

Maggie dropped her purse in the foyer and walked to her bedroom. She flopped on the bed and put her feet on the headboard. "I also called the police."

"Wait, you called the *cops*?"

"Well, I didn't 911 call the cops, but yes, I called the station to tell them about the reminders and the other deaths so they could do something. I can't just sit around waiting for this woman to be murdered."

"And how did that go over?"

"Like a lead zeppelin. They acted like I was A, wasting their time and B, a total lunatic. They said they'd pass it along to cybercrime or something, but I'm not holding my breath." She examined her big toe. The nail was torn. She picked at it with her thumb and forefinger until it came off in one thin strip. "Oh, and I also got a call from that friend of yours who sold you the phone. He's the mayor of Assville. He wouldn't give me any information about who had this phone before me, then tried to talk me into upgrading to a more expensive model."

Constantine crunched his cereal. "He's always been kind of a tool." He paused, slurped something. "Don't worry about it. We'll go pay him a visit in person. The closer you get, the less sleazy he is."

"Okay." Maggie swung her legs off her headboard and sat on the edge of the bed. "Let me know when. And we're still on for the funeral for Carson Parks on Sunday?"

"I'll turn on the Constantine charm."

"The panties will fly. Pick me up at ten?"

"I'll be there with bells on. No, really. I will. It's a little game Miss Vanilla and I play."

"Goodbye, Constantine."

They hung up and Maggie padded to the kitchen. She made macaroni and cheese, ate from the pot, then streamed *It Happened One Night* on her laptop. For Maggie, nothing beat the classics. She fell asleep in bed without brushing her teeth.

An electronic beep jolted her back into consciousness. Maggie rolled over and looked at her phone, which she'd propped against her Goodwill table lamp.

It wasn't a meeting reminder. Thank God. But it didn't sound like a text or email alert either.

She reached for the phone and brought it to eyes bleary from sleep.

There was a tiny "1" next to an icon she didn't recognize.

She clicked to open it.

You have 1 ZipLip message, it cheerfully informed her.

Huh?

ZipLip was the latest iteration in time-limited messaging apps, used to send photos, videos or messages that could be viewed for up to ten seconds, then disappear from both the mobile device and the ZipLip servers forever. This message will self-destruct in ten seconds.

Maggie had never received a ZipLip. She didn't even realize she had the app on her phone. She tapped the app. It opened to reveal a still frame of a video. Curious, she tapped the play icon.

A woman moved through a darkened landscape. She strode up to the window of a restaurant and peered intently at something on the glass—a menu? The restaurant's hours?—then tucked a lock of artfully messy hair behind her ear.

Maggie squinted. The woman seemed familiar. She almost looked like the woman who had appeared on her phone and then at work.

Maggie felt as if her blood had turned to ice. A cold hand gripped her heart. Squeezed.

Maggie heard a moan, eddied by wind and mingled with street noise. It sounded as if it came from whoever was taking the video. The woman in the video started, as if she heard it, too. Her head snapped around, trying to determine the direction of the sound. She peered into the darkness, taking in the abandoned street.

The voice of the camera/phone operator called louder. "Help. Please help."

The woman began to approach, her form growing larger in the camera phone's lens. "Hello?" she called. A soft keening, more animal than human, came from the person taking the video.

The woman grew larger on Maggie's screen. The groaning from the cameraperson intensified.

"No," Maggie whispered, knowledge dawning.

The woman ran forward, heels splashing through dirty puddles from afternoon rain. "Oh my God," the woman said. "What happened? Are you hurt?"

Abruptly, a hand snaked out and clamped on the woman's wrist. She fell to the ground, scraping against the alley's jagged asphalt.

A giant hand suddenly covered the lens then disappeared as the phone was placed on the ground.

From the lens' new vantage point, Maggie could see two people in the frame: the young woman she'd seen looking in the restaurant window and an old woman in a black coat.

The old woman touched the top of her head and pulled. A wig slid to the ground like a snake shedding its skin, revealing the man who'd been hiding beneath.

Maggie's heart slammed against her chest. "Run." Maggie whispered at the phone. "*Run.*"

But the young woman didn't run. She lay motionless on the gravel.

The man straddled the woman, arms cantilevered to make the most of the laws of physics. Maggie watched helplessly as the man tightened his hands around the woman's windpipe, whipping her head against abraded asphalt. Maggie could feel the terror boiling up. "Oh, no. Oh, God." She imagined the woman's flesh yielding beneath the pressure of his fingers. Maggie felt her own throat close up. She gulped for air.

The man kept squeezing. The woman kept living.

The man released his grip and pulled a knife from the folds of his housedress. The blade flashed, then plunged into the woman again and again. Light. Dark. Light. Dark. Until the brightness of the blade was coated in red-black blood.

Maggie screamed. Or at least she thought she did.

She couldn't hear anything over the hammering of her own heart and the wounded, terrified cries of the woman as her blood streamed from her body and mingled with the muddy rainwater of the puddle beneath her.

Chapter 14

Sleep was elusive, dreams fractured by images of a shadowed alleyway, a crouching woman and a knife that glinted and plunged and let loose a torrent of red.

She had called the police, fingers shaking and sloppy as they fumbled over the keypad. Maggie's near hysteria was complemented by the placid response of a dispatcher who sounded as if he was taking her order at the drive-through.

Let's see, we have witnessing a homicide and a freaky phone. Would you like fries with that?

Morning came. Maggie dressed slowly, feeling as if the color had seeped out of everything during the night.

The detective was already waiting for her when she arrived at work.

Maggie felt a stabbing pain in her chest when Connie, the receptionist, told her a policeman was waiting for her in Conference Room A.

Talking to the police during work hours wasn't exactly the professionalism she was hoping to project. Why hadn't the police waited to take her statement at the station, as they'd discussed on the phone? Why interrupt her here, now?

Maggie pushed open the door of the conference room with her arm already extended. "I'm Maggie O'Malley," she said as calmly as she could.

The man stood and shook her hand briskly. "Detective Nyberg."

He was early fifties with a deeply tanned face and dishwater blond hair threaded with gray. Salt substitute and pepper. He had made himself comfortable, folders and pads of paper scattered across the conference room table.

He gestured to the chair across the table with his notebook. Maggie sat and folded her hands in front of her as if she were ready to say grace.

Nyberg took his chair. He sat back, relaxed, almost reclining, with knees apart. Two people having a friendly chat.

"I understand you have some information about the murder that took place near Le Petit Chou last night," he began.

"That's a restaurant, right?"

"Yep." The detective tossed his notebook on the table and opened the folder that sat before him. He leafed through the loose papers, then plucked out a photograph and slid it across the table to Maggie. "This might help."

Maggie scrutinized the building's honey-hued limestone exterior, rough-hewn rock accents and beveled diagonal panes on large glass windows. "That's it," she said softly. "That's the same place I saw on my phone. At least, I think it was. It was dark. Everything happened so fast."

Nyberg returned the photograph to the folder and pulled out a paper. He scratched his neck. "Right, so..." He scanned the page. "You said you saw the murder in a video you played on your phone. And someone sent you this video?"

"Yes, it was a ZipLip."

"A ZipLip," he repeated. He wrote in his notebook then underlined with gusto. "And what exactly does that mean?"

"It's a kind of messaging system. You can send a note, a picture or a video. But after you see it, it disappears forever. Really forever."

"Uh-huh." Nyberg frowned, lines becoming subduction zones that carved deep ravines into leathery skin. "So it's a message that only you saw and that can never be retrieved or seen by anyone else?"

Maggie shifted in her chair.

"Right."

"Who sent you this ZipLip?"

"I don't know. There was no name in the 'from' box, no email address. Nothing."

"Uh-huh," he said again. Nyberg tapped his pen on the sheet of paper, making tiny dots and dashes on what had already been written. A nervous tic morphed into Morse code. "Tell me what happened."

Maggie's mouth seemed very dry. She ran her tongue across her chapped lips, but it felt shriveled and clumsy. "I got a ZipLip message last night," she began. "I'm not sure what time it was. Maybe ten? Ten thirty? I'd never gotten one before, and it didn't say who it was from. And I'd been having, um, problems with my phone, so even though it was strange...it wasn't."

Nyberg stopped tapping and scanned the sheet of paper again. "Says here you reported getting reminders for meetings you've never scheduled with people you don't know."

"People who end up dead," Maggie said more loudly than she'd intended. "They show up on my phone and then they end up dead."

"And you find out about the deaths how?"

"The news. The first time on TV, the second time online. I bought a used phone and its data wasn't cleared completely, so whoever had it before is transmitting to his old phone, which is my new phone. Well, my new-to-*me* phone. I called the police about it. I was worried something was going to happen to the last woman on my meeting reminder. She was also in the office. The police didn't seem interested at the time and transferred me to the cybercrime division where I left a voicemail. But I'm pretty sure it's the same woman I saw in that video. Actually, I'm almost positive."

Nyberg's brows furrowed more deeply, but he said nothing. The tapping resumed.

Maggie rushed to fill the dead air. "I'm trying to find out who owned the phone before me. Get some answers. Maybe talk to people who knew the people on my reminder app."

"Right." He was writing quickly in his notebook now, tall, looping letters that looked like the longest doctor's signature she'd ever seen. She said a silent prayer that he'd be able to read his own handwriting. "Okay. And what did you see on this..." He referred to his notes. "...this ZipLip?"

Maggie tried to swallow. It felt like someone had stuffed sand into her mouth. "There was a woman. She was standing outside of a restaurant. Then there was a sound. It sounded like it was coming from whoever was videoing her. Like a moan." Maggie paused. "I saw her turn her head toward the alley, toward the sound, I guess. The moans kept getting louder. Then I could definitely tell it was from the person taking the video. The woman walked toward the screen, the lens. She was getting bigger, but I couldn't see her that well because it was dark. Then whoever was holding the phone put it on the ground but kept recording. The woman ran over to help this person, this old woman she thought was in trouble. Then the old woman took off a wig and I could see it was really a man. And he started to...he had a knife and he..."

Maggie's throat closed. She tried the useless swallowing again and choked, starting an avalanche of coughs.

"That must have been very upsetting," he said without emotion. He lifted a sleek stainless steel carafe from the table and poured a glass of water. He passed the glass to Maggie wordlessly, then flipped through his folder again. He held up a large color photograph. "This is the woman you saw in the video?"

A woman, her face solemn and pale and still in death, looked back with unseeing eyes. Maggie's stomach dipped. "I—think so. It all happened so fast, and like I said, it was pretty dark."

Nyberg looked at her sharply. "And you said she was also in the office, is that right?"

"Yes. She went into a meeting with Mr. Montgomery."

"Mr. Montgomery." His voice was calm, almost flat.

"Yes, the president of Rxcellance."

Nyberg made a note. "How did you know her?"

"I didn't. I'd never seen her before she showed up on my phone."

"And you'd never seen her at Rxcellance before?"

His questions were coming fast now. Each one felt dangerous.

"No," Maggie said carefully. "But I just started working here."

"Did you talk to her?"

"I followed her to the ladies' room to tell her that she had shown up on my meeting reminder. She thought I was a fruitcake."

Nyberg made no comment. "Do you still have that meeting reminder?"

Maggie brought her phone out of her pocket and pulled up the app. She passed the phone to Nyberg.

Nyberg compared the images, his eyes flitting back and forth between them. He scrolled to Carson's photo from the previous meeting reminder. "Is this someone else who showed up on your phone, then died?" he asked.

Maggie nodded.

Nyberg returned her phone. He closed his folder, continued drumming on the folder's cover. He looked at Maggie. "I met Mr. Montgomery in the front lobby when I was waiting to be shown to the conference room. I told him why I was here, showed him the picture of the dead girl. He didn't recognize her. Can you explain that?"

"What? No, I—"

"As far as we can determine, nobody had seen her after she'd left her office on the morning of her death. Except you."

"But what about the video of her murder? Someone had to take it."

He closed the notepad, capped his pen and began corralling the items that had escaped onto the other half of the table. "Are you talking about the video no one else has seen or can see again?" he asked evenly.

Maggie gritted her teeth and focused on sounding reasonable. "Can't the guys in cybercrime hack it? Can't they somehow retrieve the video so you can see who killed her?"

Nyberg leaned back. "Maybe. They're smart guys. We'd just need your phone."

"My phone?" Her phone held all of her friends' phone numbers, showed all of her upcoming meetings, was her sole source of communication, other than her ancient laptop, outside of work. She picked it up and grasped it protectively in her hand. "How long would you need it?"

He shrugged. "Let's just say we haven't installed an express lane yet."

He stood, pulling a business card from his breast pocket. "You can keep your phone for now. I'll see when the boys in cybercrime can take a look, then you can bring it in. Meanwhile, call anytime if you remember something. Just don't leave town. We may have some follow-up questions."

Maggie's heart thudded sickly. "Follow-up questions?"

Nyberg stood and gathered the rest of his things. Some went into a briefcase, others under his arm. "Sure. You were the last person to see Ms. Rennick. You know details about the crime that we haven't made public yet." He ticked off items like a to-do list. "That the murder took place in an alleyway near a French restaurant. That the victim died of multiple stab wounds. That a woman's wig was found at the scene."

He glanced at her red hair. "You don't wear a wig, do you?" He laughed. The congenial, low-key, let's-hang-out-and-shoot-the-shit guy had returned. "No? Well...I'm sure some questions may arise. I have a feeling you'll be just the one to answer them."

He turned on his heel and reached the door in two long strides. He paused with his hand on the doorknob. "Have a nice day, Ms. O'Malley."

Chapter 15

Maggie walked to the lab in a daze. Her lab partners were in a meeting, so she'd have the room to herself. Perfect, since she didn't know how to feel or act.

There were no pamphlets on appropriate behavior after witnessing a murder. No how-to books at Costco or life hacks on YouTube. Should she tell anyone? Not tell anyone? What did her superiors know? Did Montgomery simply fail to recognize the police's photo of the woman who was killed? Or was he lying? And if he was lying, to what end?

Maggie stood with her hand on the lab door, dizzied by the questions buzzing in her head. She had to call Constantine. It was suddenly, vitally important that she talk to him, tell him what happened. This time, he'd be there for her. She could just feel it.

She spun around to find someplace private to talk, the employee lounge or some lonely corridor.

She nearly collided with Ethan.

He pinwheeled his arms, regaining balance. "Hey, this is like our first meeting," he said. "Except this time I'm falling for *you*."

Maggie felt her cheeks get hot. Partly in embarrassment for another near collision. Partly at the suggestion that Ethan might actually fall for her.

"I'm glad I ran into you," he continued. "I wanted to make sure you were okay. After, you know, the gala and Miles and..." His voice trailed off. He searched her face, his eyes filled with concern.

Maggie lifted her chin, reflexive defiance at his worry, his protectiveness. "I'm fine."

She thought about telling him that she'd gone to Roy with her complaint, that he'd promised—threatened?—to confront Miles about it. But somehow her complaint to Roy felt like criticism of Ethan's ability to handle Miles. She said nothing.

"You're sure?" he asked, eyes still searching, probing.

"Positive." Maggie smiled, hoped it looked natural.

Ethan returned a tentative smile. "Okay, good. Let me know if...if you have any more problems, okay?"

Maggie nodded. She thought of the woman's body lying in the alley. Wondered if he knew a detective had been in the office to question her about it. She shifted to one foot, then the other.

"Welp." Ethan clapped his hands together. "I should get back to work." He made no move to do so. He cleared his throat. "Actually, there's another reason I'm glad I ran into you. I was wondering if you'd want to go out sometime."

Maggie almost asked him to repeat himself. Surely Ethan with the smiling blue eyes, Ethan with the witty repartee, Ethan with the promising career, wasn't asking her out on a date. "To talk over a new research project?"

Ethan flashed his trademark dazzling smile. "Yeah, I'm researching everything I can about Maggie O'Malley. What she likes. Who she is. What makes her tick."

Maggie could feel her face purpling. "Oh, I, uh..."

"How about dinner Friday night? Pick you up at seven?"

Maggie opened her mouth. Closed it. Her old codfish routine. She managed a breathy "Sounds great." She was nearly hypoxic from forgetting to breathe.

"Perfect," he said. "See you then."

Maggie watched him walk down the hall to another laboratory and disappear inside. She hugged herself and did a little dance. Ethan liked her. *Liked* liked her.

For once, she wasn't just the brainy classmate or hardworking coworker or funny friend of a friend. For once, she was pretty enough, interesting enough, *whatever* enough to be more.

Maggie began a mental walkthrough of her closet for date-appropriate attire when her phone chirped.

"Constantine, thank God."

"Wow, that's quite the greeting. Have you finally realized the depth of my awesomeness?"

Maggie walked to the end of the hall and installed herself in an alcove near a window. "No," she whispered, "but I know what it's like to watch someone being murdered."

Maggie told him about the ZipLip message and her meeting with the detective.

"My God," Constantine said when she'd finished. "Do you think it's the same woman you saw at your office, the one who was on your phone?"

"Absolutely."

"Hang on. I'm emailing you something. Okay, should be there."

"Okay." Maggie tapped the Home icon, then opened the email app on her phone. She clicked the link in Constantine's email, then watched as pixels transformed into a digital photo.

The star attraction: the woman whose murder she'd witnessed.

The headline: *Woman Killed in Mugging.*

Maggie scrolled. Maggie learned Mia Rennick was killed in a mugging in downtown Collinsburg. That she had worked as a financial advisor at Capital Ideas Investments. That she had been found at six fifteen Tuesday morning by an elderly woman walking her dog.

What Maggie didn't know was what Mia had for breakfast. If she liked the toilet paper to roll over or under. Whether she was lonely or happy or loved or in love. A thousand ordinary, poignant details that meant nothing and everything.

Maggie exited the internet and opened the phone app. "That's her," she said quietly.

Constantine let out a big breath. "Remind me: how did the other people who showed up on your phone die?"

"Elsa, the first woman, was killed in a hit-and-run. Carson, the second reminder, was killed in a single-car accident, supposedly driving drunk—"

"And now the third person on your reminder—"

"Mia—"

"Right, Mia, was murdered."

Neither of them said anything. Finally, Maggie said, "Everyone who's shown up on my reminder has died within a few hours of the time we're scheduled to meet. It's feeling less like a meeting reminder and more like..."

"An appointment with death?" Constantine finished.

"Right. Like..." She searched for the right words. "Like a digital hit list."

"Oh my God."

They fell into silence again.

"But why the video of Mia's murder?" Maggie asked. "That wasn't a 'go kill this person.' That was a 'look what I've done.'"

"Bragging?"

"Maybe. Or maybe it's a warning, something to be documented and used to persuade."

"Persuade who?"

"Whoever's not falling into line. Maybe I'm seeing it because it was uploaded to the cloud." Maggie's voice caught in her throat. "Or maybe it was intended for me."

"You're being paranoid."

"You don't think I have a right to be?"

There was a pause. "You do. I just don't think that's what's going on here. I think it's a proof of death or, like you said, something to be used as a warning. But not for you. They don't even know about you."

Maggie swallowed. "I hope you're right."

"Whatever it is, I think you should talk to the police. Tell them what's going on with your phone. With everything."

"I tried that. They wouldn't believe me. In fact, because of this video, the police think I had something to do with Mia Rennick's murder."

"You're joking."

"Do I sound like I'm laughing?"

A lab door to Maggie's right opened. A tall man with an Abraham Lincoln beard emerged. He glanced at Maggie, nodded and headed for the elevator, head down as he studied his clipboard. Maggie lowered her voice to a shade above a whisper. "The detective who showed up— here at work, I might add—didn't accuse me outright, but the implication was clear: I wasn't just a witness; I was suspicious."

"But if you just explained things—"

"They'll figure out what's going on? Ride to my rescue?" Maggie snapped. She closed her eyes, fought for calm. "I've tried explaining things to the police. They already have their minds made up. At best, I'm crazy. At worst, I'm a murderer. Remember, the video no longer exists outside of my memory. All I have to show for it is knowledge of a crime that only the perpetrator should have."

Constantine released another gust of air. "So now what?"

"I say we go visit your friend at Reincarnated Phones. See if he'll give us the name of my cell's previous owner."

"Sounds like a plan." Maggie could hear Constantine changing ears, pictured him cradling the phone with his shoulder and chin. "How about Friday? I was going to surprise you and take you out anyway. We could do a telephonic pre-function."

"Friday?"

"Right. The one between Thursday and Saturday? I scored two tickets to a concert featuring that horrible woman who cries and pretends it's singing that you love so much. Show is at eight, and I figured we could go out to Zorba's before so I can make myself into the cliché I've always dreamed of."

"I'm so sorry, Constantine, but I can't go. I sort of have...plans."

"Plans? What plans? What could possibly depose me from the top of your *People I Want to Spend Friday Night With* list?"

"I guess I...I think I have a date."

A pause. Then, "Oh."

"Yeah, it's this guy from work. Nice, funny, doesn't say 'supposably.' You'd like him."

"Sounds like just my type." Constantine's voice had gone quiet. "Is he any better than that rodeo clown you dated?"

"He was a *bull rider*."

"Oh, right. What was his name again? Austin...Austin Tatious?"

"He only wore rhinestones during the rodeo. He was a great guy, by the way."

"If you go for that whole tall and handsome thing." Constantine sighed. "So, you're going on a date." She heard him tapping something. Anyone else and she would have guessed a pen. With Constantine, it was probably a Yoda PEZ dispenser. "I'm glad you found someone, Maggie. Someone worth dating." He paused again. "That's awesome."

Maggie felt something tighten in her chest. "You don't sound like you think it's awesome. You sound like you're waiting for a root canal or watching Canadian parliament on C-SPAN."

Nothing.

"Constantine?"

"I'm here. And I am excited for you. It's just...it's been a long day."

Tell me about it, Maggie thought. "Still picking me up for the funeral Sunday morning?"

"Yep." A pause. "Have a good time on your date."

Chapter 16

Detective Nyberg called her twice the next day. Maggie snuck into the hall and covered the mouthpiece when she took his calls, as if she were hiding an affair. The conversations were brief, perfunctory, questions already asked posed again in shiny new ways.

Maggie's story stayed the same, simply because there was no "story."

She began to worry that her coworkers knew about her interview with Nyberg. She imagined furtive glances by coworkers, conversations that stopped as soon as she approached and whispers around the water cooler as innuendo oozed under doors and around cubicle walls.

If word did get out, it would be enough to knock her rising star out of the sky. She decided to work harder, longer, more diligently, to counter any possible damage to her reputation and her job, whether or not the threat was real. The corporate anti-venom was always the same. Relentless workaholism.

Fortunately, Maggie had been in training for that her whole life.

Maggie spent her days sitting in meetings, racking up long hours in the lab, poring over files at her desk and occasionally flirting with Ethan at the coffeemaker.

At home, when the apartment and her mind were quiet, kaleidoscope images of Mia Rennick, Elsa Henderson and Carson Parks rolled through her mind, followed by Nyberg's blank face and her father's empty restaurant.

She tamped down fear, anxiety, the feeling that people suspected she was somehow involved in the death of the woman whose name and broken body flashed across TV screens throughout the city. Some nights she escaped her haunted thoughts. Other nights, she wondered again and again why she was sent the video. Had she accidentally intercepted an upload to the cloud, similar to the meeting reminders? Was it a warning for someone getting too close to the reason behind the deaths or the person responsible? Could it have been intended for her?

The questions were relentless, the fear exhausting.

When date night with Ethan finally arrived, Maggie was ready for a distraction. She was excited—almost as excited as Roselyn, who'd offered to help her get ready.

Within an hour of arriving, Roselyn had organized Maggie's closet by color, style, sleeve length and fabric and was ironing Maggie's selected ensemble with military precision.

"Is there anything else you'd like me to press for you?" Roselyn asked hopefully. "Your curtains look mussed. And I'd be happy to take care of any tablecloths, napkins, sheets or—"

"Sheets?" Maggie said. "You iron sheets?"

"Doesn't everyone?" Roselyn asked.

"You scare me sometimes, Roz. You really do."

Maggie rummaged through her jewelry box and selected a pair of slender gold hoops and a pendant of amethyst briolettes. She held them up for Roselyn's inspection. "What do you think?"

"I think you're going to be more gorgeous than usual, which I find completely depressing, by the way." She tossed a purple raw silk slip dress to Maggie.

Maggie shimmied out of her t-shirt and a pair of shorts she'd created with pinking shears and slipped the dress over her head. The dress, the nicest she owned, was tighter than at graduation, when long hours of studying—and forgetting to eat—had trimmed pounds off her muscular frame. Now the dress hugged her breasts and hips. Maggie pulled it down past her knees and tried to stand up straight like her mother had told her.

"Well?" Maggie asked uncertainly.

"Let the heartbreaking begin," Roselyn said.

Ethan squired Maggie to an intimate trattoria in his Audi A4, chivalrously opening and closing her door. It was the first time anyone had done that since Junior Prom. Normally, she had a thing against German-built cars (chalking it up to her father's insistence on American steel), but the Audi's smooth ride and surplus of creature comforts made her a temporary convert.

They were seated by an old Italian woman clad entirely in black whose silver bun was pulled so tight that her widow's peak rode high like a headband. She handed the menus to them gravely, as if ordering an entrée was an undertaking that required soul-searching contemplation. Then she waited.

Maggie stole a glance at Ethan, who was trying not to smile. She felt the corners of her own mouth turn up and suddenly felt like she did during eighth grade history class, stifling a howl of laughter when her cousin Anne would provide golf tournament-style commentary on their teacher's every move.

Now she's walking to the chalkboard. No, she's turned around now. Okay, she's getting more chalk from her desk.

Ethan cleared his throat and asked the server if there was a special.

"Everything here is special," she said in a heavy Italian accent. Offended, she crossed her arms over the precipice of her pendulous bosom. Ethan pursed his lips in an attempt to hide his widening grin. Soon both of them were shaking in silent laughter behind the wine list.

"I'll come back," the woman said dourly.

The food was as good as their server had threatened. Large servings of pasta, meat and cheese in various combinations. Rustic loaves of bread made spongy by repeated dips into olive oil. A bottle of Sangiovese, with a second up for consideration.

Maggie was thrilled she hadn't spilled ravioli onto her dress, and Ethan seemed pleased—or perhaps stunned—by her hearty appetite. It was hard to tell between bites.

"But enough about me," he said. "What about you? What do you think of me?"

She laughed. "Bette Midler quote. I like it."

"I also do impersonations," he said. "Want to hear my Pacino?"

"Hey, I've been working on Pacino, too." She rolled her shoulders and assumed a threatening stance. "'Don't ever take sides with anyone against the Family again.'"

He winced. "My God. That has got to be the worst impression I've ever heard."

Maggie laughed. "You don't know a good impression when you hear one, but at least you have good taste in movies."

"And in women," Ethan said, his eyes holding hers. Maggie looked away, a flush creeping up her neck. For once it was pleasure rather than embarrassment.

After dinner they headed to the movies, settling in their seats just as the previews began to roll.

Maggie felt that familiar sensation every time a movie was about to begin. Anticipation, yes, but not only for the story to begin or the stars to appear but for the heady feeling of escape. For ninety-two minutes, Maggie could shake off the shackles of reality. She could live another life, be another person.

She and Constantine had begun going to the repertory theater together weeks after they met, when they realized they had more in common than a love for *Mad Magazine*.

Movies became their magic tree house. The place where they shared secrets and hid from the world. In the movies, schoolyard bullies got their comeuppance. Overbearing parents got lessons in letting go. The homely boy got the gorgeous girl. And orphans got a second chance at happiness. Everything was sterilized and sanitized and wrapped up with a sparkly ribbon and a host of merchandising opportunities.

Maggie sank down in her chair. Her cell phone was silenced, along with worries of would-be rapists and dead strangers. She was ready to be enveloped in the popcorn-scented anonymity of the theater and forget.

Except she couldn't.

Sitting next to Ethan, their elbows touching on the shared armrest, the heat from his arm penetrating hers, Maggie felt the tug of guilt. Movies were what she did with Constantine. It was their special thing, just as their constant movie-quoting was their private language. Being there with Ethan felt like cheating. Yes, she'd been annoyed at Constantine. Angry, even. But he was still her emotional twin. Nothing could change that.

She concentrated on relaxing, and thirty minutes into the movie, her body complied. When the house lights came up, they squeezed their way out of the crowded theater and made their way to Ethan's car.

On the drive to Maggie's house, she learned that Ethan was a Virgo, had lived in Rome for two years working as an artist and volunteered weekly at two different organizations. He also didn't know how to swim, but he did know how to cook.

Maggie decided he was the ideal man.

Ethan walked Maggie to her door. She had replaced the porch light with an eco-friendly variety, and Ethan's face was masked by shadow, giving him a Sam Spade vibe.

He leaned in and gave Maggie a kiss. On the cheek. She turned her lips toward his. An invitation. He hovered above her mouth, their breath mingling in the hot evening air, then brought his lips to hers. They were soft and tender. And gone within a second. She had felt passion beneath the soft graze of his mouth, a building heat that seemed to emanate from him, but he'd held back. Pulled away.

"I'd like to see you again," he said. "I mean, apart from hanging around the coffeemaker at work."

"I'd like that, too." She thought of her dad, stooped and frail. Then of Montgomery, large and gray. "But aren't there rules against fraternizing?"

Ethan took a step toward her and traced her cheek with his finger. The heat had returned, stronger this time. "Is that what we're doing?" he asked softly. "Fraternizing?" Before she could answer, he gave a small chuckle. "It's okay. I promise. We'll keep it on the QT."

He gave her another quick kiss, then walked away. Ethan had been a perfect gentleman.

Maggie wasn't so sure she liked that.

Chapter 17

Maggie woke early and filled her day with Saturday chores she'd put off for weeks. Vacuuming. Sweeping. The last of the unpacking. She even cooked, which involved a can opener, a box of Ritz crackers and some cheese.

At seven o'clock, despite unfinished chores and unread pharmaceutical journals, Maggie pulled on running clothes, soft and faded from too much washing. She locked the handle of her front door and headed toward the neighborhood park that marked the head of her favorite footpath.

Damn the to-do list. She needed a little me-time.

The park was deserted. The last of the afternoon's sun glinted off stout trees, making the light look granulated, touchable.

Maggie placed her foot on the base of a tree and stretched her hamstrings and calves. She switched sides, her mind already down the wooded trail, the steady rhythm of each footfall scouring her mind clean of everything but the slant of light, the whisper of wind, the rock on the path to avoid.

Movement by a low bench near the park's entrance caught her eye. Maggie raised her right hand to shield her eyes from the low sun. A car idled by on the street that skirted the park's perimeter. A bird stalked worms at the foot of the bench. Eddies of wind lifted part of a fruit snack package into a tiny tornado, then spit it out. Situation: normal.

Maggie shook out her arms and rotated both ankles. Then she saw it again from her peripheral vision. A wink of sunlight. The sway of a branch.

Maggie walked slowly toward the bench. A few precocious leaves, too eager to wait for autumn, listed against her foot. She put her hand on the bench, moved a low-hanging branch that scraped against its weathered wooden back and peered into a small grove that stood sentry at the park's entrance. A squirrel bounded down the branch, shooting past Maggie's arm and across the top of the bench.

Maggie put her hand to her chest, gasped, then laughed. Stupid squirrel.

Maggie squinted at the entrance. Deserted. Even the worm-hunting bird had left.

She returned to her stretching tree near the wooded footpath. The trail suddenly seemed friendlier than the wide open of the park. Safer for all its dark, shady greenery. She took a deep breath and plunged down the trail and into the shelter of the woods.

An hour later, she emerged red, sweaty, exhausted and happy. She bounced up the steep, wide stairs of the apartment house and let herself in with the key she hid under the mat for the times she didn't feel like carrying anything during a run.

She peeled off her Lycra tank and running shorts as she made her way from the front door to the apartment's single bathroom, leaving a line of wrinkled, sweaty clothes behind her. Maggie rinsed off under a blast of icy water, then slid into an old t-shirt and pair of cutoff sweatpants she'd rescued from Fiona's Goodwill pile.

Dinner was a can of ravioli and a half loaf of bread, toasted and slathered with butter, consumed while sitting cross-legged on the couch in front of the TV. She scraped the bottom of her chipped ceramic dish with a spoon, set the dish on the coffee table, then flopped back on the couch's cream and orange paisley cushions.

She loved her couch. Worn, stained and sporting a psychedelic flowered print, it had been her father's most interesting piece of furniture. "Take it. Take it," he had insisted. "Your mother and I picked it out together."

Jack O'Malley rarely talked about his dead wife. The small revelation about furniture shopping made Maggie feel like she'd walked in on him in the shower.

Maggie lay dozing on the riotous pattern, her t-shirt laden with bread crumbs and butter, before finally succumbing to sleep just before midnight.

The whistle of her phone dragged her from the depths of sleep. A text message. Groggily, Maggie reached for the device, certain it was Constantine.

It was from a phone number she didn't recognize. Maggie clicked to read.

Want to play?

Maggie blinked and rubbed her eyes. Another text appeared: *How much?*

How much for what? she texted back.

How much for a date?

Maggie stared at the message, trying to process what she was seeing.

U looked very $$$exy in your pic, the texter continued. *All sweaty and wet in your shorts and tank top. U do what I say & I can B very generous.*

Maggie felt a surge of fear and revulsion. First the reminders. Then the video. Now this. Her phone seemed to be a portal to evil. And she seemed to be a magnet for torment.

Maggie deleted the message and dropped the phone on the couch as if it were alive. With a shaking hand, she shoved it away from herself.

It beeped again. Another text. And then another.

I pay whatever you want.

Lots of $$$ for playtime.

Don't you want to play?

She snatched the phone from the flowered couch cushions and turned it off. She got up, crossed the room and put the phone in a kitchen drawer next to her mismatched set of silverware, hoping the drawer was strong enough to contain whatever malevolence lurked within.

Chapter 18

There were eight of them when she woke up.

Eight new text messages from eight different people, each asking her how much for a night. For a blowjob. For letting someone do whatever he wanted with her for an hour. Maybe two, if the price was right.

Some asked for additional photos. Others for a meetup time and place. All made her feel as if a hundred different hands had clawed at her clothes and pawed at her body.

She took a shower. It was too hot. She didn't care, and it didn't help.

Constantine knocked at the door three minutes after she'd toweled off. She yanked on a pair of cutoff sweatpants and an old Led Zeppelin "Houses of the Holy" t-shirt and opened the door. He stood there with arms thrown wide in a pose that said "just look at this deliciousness."

He wore baggy pants, shiny, pointed shoes and a white shirt overrun by black pianos.

"Wow," Maggie said. "I didn't realize I would be escorted by Liberace."

Constantine took in her attire. "Wait, wait. Don't tell me." He held up a finger. "*Duck Dynasty? Daisy Duke's British Invasion? Project Run Away?*"

"Very funny. I'm running late. You can come in while I change."

Constantine followed her from the front door into her bedroom. Maggie spun him around and pushed him back into the hall. "Nice try. Now go keep my TV company while I make myself beautiful. I think *Casablanca* is on."

"A movie about unrequited love. Perfect."

"What?"

"Nothing,'" Constantine replied, hopping onto the couch. "Go do whatever it is you do."

Maggie emerged five minutes later in black trousers and her logo-ed white company button-down. She'd put a black bowtie at the collar. Constantine smirked.

Maggie put up her hand. "Save the Charlie Chaplin comments. I'm behind on laundry, and it's the only suitable thing I had. Even this is only spot-cleaned since I wore the top to work on my first day."

"Can I ask about today's specials?"

"No."

"Soup du jour?

"Let's go."

Since the Studebaker's air conditioning consisted of hand-cranking the windows, they opted for Constantine's Datsun. Christened "Nellie" when Constantine drove her off the used lot five years ago, the car sported lime green fuzzy dice on its rearview mirror and a plastic hula dancer that undulated reluctantly on the dashboard.

"Everything copacetic?" Constantine asked as he started the engine. "You don't look so good."

"Thanks."

"No, I'm serious. You look—I dunno—green around the gills or something. Pale."

Maggie pulled the elastic that encircled her wrist and dragged her long hair into a ponytail. "Wasn't it you who told me my legs looked like they were dipped in Wite-Out? Which I haven't recovered from, by the way. It's probably proof of some kind of terrible condition—and don't say being Irish."

"So are you going to answer my question or not?" Constantine's eyebrows bunched over his long, straight nose.

"Yes, if you'd let me get a word in edgewise." She knew she sounded irritable, but didn't she have a right to be? She'd gotten exactly two hours of sleep and couldn't shake the feeling of hidden eyes crawling over her. "Something weird happened last night."

Constantine glanced over at her, concern growing in his eyes. "Another reminder?"

"No, but it does involve the phone. I got a text message asking how much I cost. More like a dozen text messages."

Constantine looked at her full on. "How much you *cost?*"

Maggie nodded. "Yeah, for a whole smorgasbord of sex acts." Maggie freed a tendril from her ponytail and twirled a strand of hair. "I have no idea who it was or how these guys found me, but it totally creeped me out. It almost sounded like they were looking at a picture of me taken during one of my runs."

Like the one last night.

"I turned off my phone and shoved it in my kitchen drawer," she continued. "I didn't want it anywhere near me. I thought that was the end of it. That it was a wrong number. Whatever. But when I turned on my phone this morning, there were more texts. All from different people. All asking how much."

"Holy shit."

"You're telling me. So what do you think?"

Constantine edged the Datsun onto the freeway and shifted into fourth gear. He scratched his head with his free hand. "Well, it could have something to do with the previous owner of the phone, just like the reminders. Maybe the original owner was a prostitute and you're getting her texts, too. But if that were true, I'd think you'd have been getting texts from day one."

Maggie shrugged. "Maybe she got pinched by the cops and just got out."

"True. But I tend to agree with your first assessment: wrong number."

Maggie looked dubious. "Everyone has my wrong number?"

"They do if there was a typo in an ad for escort services."

"What, like a phonebook?"

"Like craigslist."

Maggie sucked on the strand she was twirling, then spit it out. "I guess they do have an adult section, don't they?" She swiped her phone on and tapped open her browser and pulled up craigslist. She scanned the ads promoting full-release massage, evenings of cuddling and promises of unfettered shoe-sniffing. She found the ad with her phone number almost immediately.

The ad contained a single photograph of Maggie stretching after her run, fingertips touching the ground, backside toward the camera. She looked closer, taking in the running shorts, the tree to her right.

It was taken last night.

She thought of the movement at the edge of the playground. The feeling that she was being watched. Gooseflesh crawled up her spine.

Beneath her photograph the ad's headline asked, *Want to play?*

Maggie flagged the ad, trying not to see the ad copy inviting prospects to "super sexy private time," then collapsed against her seat.

"Bad?" Constantine asked.

"Very." She turned off her phone and shoved it into her purse. "And it's not a typo. It has a picture of me in my running clothes—taken last night."

"You're sure?"

"I own a mirror, Constantine. I know what I look like. What I don't know is why someone would do this."

"Maybe you pissed someone off?"

Maggie stared at him. "What do you mean?"

"Haven't you heard? Cyber-revenge is all the rage these days. Your girlfriend breaks up with you, you post naked pictures of her on Facebook. Or have your friends text-bomb her with messages to kill herself. Or..." He looked at her meaningfully. "You post fake ads on craigslist with her phone number."

Maggie thought about who would hate her enough to do such a thing. Miles was the obvious choice. Maggie had thwarted him personally and overshadowed him professionally. But would he go to such lengths to seek revenge, to punish her? Maggie shuddered despite the heat. She wondered what he was capable of.

Constantine glanced over at her, concern in his eyes. "Sorry, Mags. Didn't mean to freak you out. It's probably someone playing a stupid joke."

Maggie looked out the window at the anthill of cars teeming in the distance. She had a feeling that whoever had taken her photo and set up the craigslist ad wasn't the joking type.

They were the last to arrive at the memorial. The assembly squeezed together on a square of grass cordoned off by white velvet ropes, as if the lines of demarcation could contain not just the grievers, but their unanswerable grief as well.

The graveside service was well attended. The bereaved—family members, coworkers, friends and about a dozen homeless men and women—were numerous and subdued. Maggie and Constantine hung at the back of the group behind a man who looked to be wearing all his clothes at once and an older man sporting a parka made from a Hefty bag. Maggie couldn't imagine how hot they must be.

The men turned and looked at them briefly, then refocused their attention on the minister, who seemed more emcee than man of the cloth. An a cappella rendition of "Amazing Grace" floated from the front of the crowd, and Maggie and Constantine joined in, getting every second or third word right.

The crowd thinned, began to straggle out to the parking lot. Constantine gave an almost imperceptible nod toward the woman walking past them from Carson's grave. Maggie intercepted the woman as she stuffed a tissue up her sleeve.

"Such a tragedy," Maggie said softly to the woman.

The woman looked at Maggie, confusion flitting through her eyes as she tried to match face to name. "Yes," she said softly. "It is." The woman was young. Early twenties, tops. Her fishtail braided hair was secured by a leather thong. "Did you know Carson well?"

"More acquaintances than friends," Maggie said.

The woman sniffed. "I don't care what the cops say. He didn't drive drunk. Booze wasn't his bag. He was into *herbal* supplements." She pantomimed smoking a joint. "But he never touched a drop of alcohol." She reached into her sleeve, which evidently doubled as a dispenser, and produced a tissue which she used to mop up a tear teetering at the edge of her nose. Then she stuffed the tissue back in.

"You worked together?" Maggie asked.

She nodded. "At the homeless shelter, nearly three years now. He was *real*, you know? No bullshit. He cared about the residents. 'The Forgotten,' as he called them. He tried to get work for them. Housing. Health care. Medication. Whatever they needed." She dispensed the tissue from her sleeve again, blew her nose. "I can't believe he's gone."

"Me neither. It's terrible." Maggie paused and reached into her purse. "You know, I think Carson and I had a mutual friend."

Maggie pulled up Elsa Henderson's obituary photo from the newspaper's online site, expanding it so the woman couldn't see the context of the article. She handed her phone to the woman.

The woman studied the photograph, then handed the phone back to Maggie. "Yep, he knew her. Not sure about the friends part, though."

"They weren't on good terms?"

"No, that wasn't it. I mean, it was more like a professional relationship. She'd stop by the shelter. The conversations were always real short. No clue what about. He'd kind of tense up when he talked to her. Get real short with me afterwards." She shrugged. "Hope they were on good terms when he died. It would suck if there was unfinished business between you and someone who died."

Maggie paused, remembering the preteen, hormone-laden years that had preceded her mother's death. The arguments. The long, cold silences. In the quiet of the night, Maggie often wondered what could be sown with tears, what would grow in a field plowed by pain and strife. Whether her mother had inhaled the poisoned air of Maggie's adolescent angst and had gotten sick. And then sicker.

"Yeah, that would suck," Maggie finally said. "Thanks for your help. I'm very sorry for your loss."

The woman teared up and nodded. She walked away, her shoulders rounded into a question mark that sought answers to the inexplicable.

"Who's she?" Constantine asked when Maggie returned to his side.

"A friend of Carson's. I didn't get a name. She says there's no way Carson drove drunk. And she recognized Elsa, the woman from my first appointment reminder. She said Elsa would come to the shelter to talk to Carson. That means two of the people from my phone reminders knew each other."

"Yeah, I think...um...I think..." Constantine stopped, his mouth hanging open. His eyes were fixated on the entrance to the cemetery, a combination of horror, disbelief and amusement marching across his face. He nodded toward a shrieking woman barreling toward Maggie. "Friend of yours?"

The woman had picked up speed. Her arms swung wildly as she ran, her round face, purple from exertion, bounced like a bobber tethered to a large, overly caffeinated fish. She was in mid-conversation with herself when she reached them.

She stopped in front of Maggie and put a scant inch or two between them. The woman stared at Maggie, her thin mouth disappearing into a lopsided grimace. She reached up and touched the crest on Maggie's shirt. She scraped the embroidery with a dirt-encrusted fingernail, then peered into Maggie's face. "I'm trying very hard not to say the secrets," she whispered, her eyes pleading. "But when I sleep, they grow in my hair and look at my brain."

Maggie knew she should draw away, extricate herself from the strange woman and her even stranger words. But a part of her was fascinated.

Maggie put the woman at sixty, maybe sixty-five. But it was hard to be sure. Her skin was embroidered by wrinkles as sharp as knife pleats, the fat pockets beneath her cheeks doing little to buttress her sagging skin. Her hair was long, thin enough to expose an ashen cranium. But it was surprisingly tidy. Neatly combed despite the grease and dirt that bound each strand. Remnants of pride and perhaps long-buried beauty.

The woman extended a fat finger capped by a jagged nail from her other hand and tapped Maggie's sternum. "You bear the mark. I've seen it before on those who transform the living into the immortal and the heretics into demons."

The woman drew her ruined clothes around her short, squat frame and pulled on Maggie's shirt to bring her face even closer to Maggie's. A cloudy eye rolled in its socket before stopping to focus on Maggie's chin. The other eye was sharp with inquisitive intelligence. "I can't tell if you're seraphim or human. But no matter. I'm ready for the final Trials." She cocked her head coquettishly. "You'll see." She drew herself up and pointed to her chest. "Charlene is strong. Charlene is obedient." She winked at Maggie. "Charlene won't end up breathless like the others."

She flicked her finger at Maggie's collar, bumping her in the neck. Then the woman half-ran, half-scampered away, her bent form melting into the shrubbery that surrounded the cemetery.

"She seems nice," Constantine said.

Chapter 19

Constantine pulled up in front of Maggie's apartment and they got out of the Datsun. Constantine stretched. "Well, thanks for an interesting morning."

"I'm nothing if not a magnet for interesting."

They walked up the front stairs to Maggie's apartment house. Desiccated daisies languished in the flower beds. Blades of grass browned beneath sprinkler tractors that looked like they should be up on blocks.

"What do you think that was all about?" Constantine asked.

"The homeless woman? I have no idea, other than I possibly bear the mark of the beast."

He nodded sagely. "That's always been a suspicion of mine. But you did find out that Carson knew Elsa, so that's something." Constantine wrapped Maggie in his strong, warm arms. "You want to hang out tonight? Watch *The Jerk*, maybe get chili from a pump at 7-Eleven?"

Maggie smiled. "Can't. I've got a mile-long list of work catch-up, not to mention some sleep catch-up."

"Just as well. I need to finish unpacking in my new tenement, I mean apartment. It's quite lovely. Very few rats. And lots of room for my Teenage Mutant Ninja Turtles collection." Constantine bounded back down the stairs and opened the driver's door. "You sure you're okay? You're not worried about more creepy texts? Or..." He let the other terrible possibilities—more reminders, more videos, someone following her—die on his lips.

Maggie forced a smile. "I'm fine. Really." For a moment, she hoped he didn't know her as well as he did, that he would buy her false bravery.

Constantine frowned. He wasn't buying anything. "Maybe I should stay. Or at least come back."

Maggie sighed in mock irritation. "I'm a big girl, Gus. I can take care of myself. Plus, I have tons to do. We'll hang out soon, I promise."

Constantine looked at her for a moment. "Okay." He folded himself into the Datsun. "Call me later and we'll figure out a time to go visit Travis, my sort-of friend from Reincarnated Phones." He tooted the horn as he drove away.

Maggie went inside and dropped her purse by the door, then headed into her bedroom where her laptop computer sat charging on the desk her father had made for her.

She gathered her hair into a high ponytail, booted up the computer and opened her Chrome browser window. Her phone rang. Maggie ran back to the hall and fumbled for it in her purse. Fiona.

"Did you do it?" Fiona asked.

"Do what?"

Fiona sighed in exasperation. "Turn in that scoundrel that tried to take advantage of you. I've been absolutely sick with worry."

Maggie cringed. *Feck.* She'd forgotten to call back. Or send a check. *Double feck.* She made a mental note.

"Oh. Right. Actually, I did talk with my boss."

"And?" Fiona demanded. Maggie could practically see her aunt tapping her foot.

"And he, um, he said he'd talk to the guy."

"*Talk* to him?" Fiona harrumphed. It sounded like a whale mating.

Maggie waited for the remonstrations, the rants, the homily that Maggie needed to do more, but Fiona had pulled away from the phone. There was the muffled sound of a hand being placed over the receiver. Then Fiona said into the phone: "Your father's picking up the extension in the office. He wants to say hello." She paused, then added quietly, "I didn't say anything to him about what happened with that awful man or your help with the you-know-what."

There was a click. "Maggie," he boomed heartily. "How's my best girl?"

"Great, Pop. I'm doing great." Maggie imagined her father in his office, entombed within the mess.

"That sister of mine says you're working too hard. Burning the midnight oil. You're not going to make yourself sick with too much work, are you?"

Maggie silently cursed Fiona for worrying her father. In addition to acting as a human news ticker, Fiona was president of the Pessimist's Club, always looking for the downside. The worse things were, the happier she seemed.

"I'm great, Pop," Maggie repeated. "Long hours are a side effect of pharmaceuticals, but it's no worse than school."

"Did you tell her about the message?" Fiona interrupted on the extension.

Her father cursed exuberantly. "I'm getting to it, Fi. I'm getting to it. Maggie, someone called looking for you. Said he was an old high school friend. Something about updating student records for the next reunion. I gave him your new address so he could send an invitation. He said to tell you he'll see you very soon. Wanted to make sure you got the message."

Alarm rang through Maggie. "You gave out my address? Who was it? Did you get a name?"

"I don't think he mentioned his name, come to think of it," Fiona interrupted. "But he sounded real nice. Handsome, too."

"You can hear handsome over the phone?"

"It's an art, dear. Maybe if you tried it, you'd have a boyfriend."

Maggie's eyes ached from rolling. "Thanks, Aunt Fiona. I'll keep that in mind."

"Come visit us, will you?" Jack said. "I know you haven't been gone long, but it sure is quiet around here without you."

"I'll come home soon," she said, knowing she wouldn't. Being busy was only part of it. She didn't want to see how much her father missed her, couldn't stand the thought of him holding her chin in his hand, his eyes growing soft as he looked into her face. She knew he never really saw her. He saw her mother.

Maggie wondered if that made her a ghost.

Maggie spent Monday morning Googling the strangers who had disappeared from the earth as quickly as they had appeared on her phone.

Work wasn't the ideal place to conduct this sort of research, but the city workers who had replaced those on strike had inadvertently cut the cable line that connected her entire block to the internet. Constantine hadn't gotten around to getting his internet hooked up yet. "The cobbler's children have no shoes," he'd said when she called about it. "And the IT geek's home office has no internet. Not yet."

Maggie wasn't worried. She was always one of the first to arrive at work. She'd have the place to herself to research Elsa, Carson and Mia in peace.

A search for "Carson Parks" had yielded a pittance of data: an eight-year-old college graduation photo, a bio on the staff page of the homeless shelter where he worked and the obligatory obit that highlighted his life and glossed over his death.

Elsa Henderson and Mia Rennick, on the other hand, did not seem to embrace the concept of low-profile.

A mountaineer of capitalism's highest peaks, Mia Rennick had scaled Microsoft, GE and Dean Witter before summiting financial planning house, Capital Ideas. She had been the topic of reams of press releases covering mergers, IPOs and mega-estate management. In her spare time, she adorned the arms of older men at museum openings and art galas. Her hair was coiffed. Her taut body was buffed and bronzed. Her eyes were cold, appraising with the precision of a ten-key calculator. Together, the articles formed a mosaic of a Mia who was smart, calculating and ambitious.

Information about Elsa Henderson was as voluminous, yet decidedly warmer. Elsa had amassed an impressive stockpile of ego-stroking articles proclaiming her expertise at *Getting the Story*. She'd won a Sigma Delta Chi Award for her undercover work in human trafficking and had been nominated for an Edward R. Murrow Award for an exposé on a senator's proclivity for underage aides. The way the newserati saw it, Elsa Henderson was bigger than the Second Coming. With better hair.

The search engine's indiscriminate datamongering also disgorged such important details as Ms. Henderson's marital status (recently divorced), hobbies (playing vintner with a friend at a jointly owned Napa vineyard) and humanitarian efforts (on the board of a women's shelter called Saving Grace). And finally, a breathless teaser on what would have been her final story: an exclusive that promised corporate conspiracy, government bribery and crimes against society's most vulnerable. The exposé was slated to hit newsstands August 30. She died in a hit-and-run on July 23.

Maggie stood and stretched, her eyes scanning rows of cubicles for prairie-dogging workers who might pop up at any moment. She saw no one. Maggie sat back down and printed out the information she'd found on the victims. She rose and walked quickly toward the printer.

"Hey, Maggie." Roselyn jumped in front of Maggie like a jack-in-the-box. "Oh my God," Roselyn trilled. "What a morning. I got here early, but someone had misfiled the psoriasis study yesterday, so I had to..."

Maggie licked her lips and glanced over Roselyn's padded shoulder at the printer. No pages had printed. Yet.

"Then Susan from accounting shows up wanting to know why we ordered additional binders," Roselyn continued.

"Uh-huh," Maggie said, nodding. "Wow, that's a bummer." She watched the first page emerge from the printer's inner workings.

"Can you believe that?" Roselyn showed no signs of slowing down. Maggie kept her eyes fixed on the printer. Paper began collecting onto its tray.

Maggie's nods became faster. "Right," she said. "Man, sounds like you're off to a rough start. Hey, let's talk about this tonight at The Office."

"The Office?" Roselyn considered the idea. Slowly. "I don't know. I've been going out a lot. I should really be saving my money. Plus all the calories..."

The door on the elevator parted, expelling a half-dozen early birds. The printer became obscured by a flurry of white coats and corporate casual, then reemerged. From where she stood, Maggie could see Elsa's photograph on the top of the machine.

"My treat," Maggie said quickly. "We can see if Zartar can join us." Maggie jogged lightly toward the printer, trying to look like she was infusing exercise into her busy day.

"Zartar just left. I just saw her walk out the door with Ethan."

Maggie stopped. She spun to face Roselyn. "Zartar left with Ethan?"

Small red circles blossomed on Roselyn's cheeks and spread. "Well, uh, I'm not sure they left *together*. Maybe they just left at the same time."

Maggie stared, immobilized. As if trying to work out a bizarre math problem.

Zartar plus Ethan. Carry the one...

"I did hear them say something about taking Ethan's car," Roselyn blurted out into the silence. "But they were carrying files, so I guess she's working offsite. With Ethan. For the rest of the day. And night, maybe?" Maggie said nothing. "Um, I need to go. I'll see you later, okay? Um, bye."

Roselyn turned on her sensible ballet flats and headed for the door, her relief palpable.

Maggie shook her head, trying to clear the jumble of images that jumped through her brain like snow on an untuned television. Then she remembered.

Oh, God. The printouts. She ran toward the printer. Stopped. Voices drifted from down the hall. Rising. Falling. Quilted conversation of a man and woman snarling from behind a closed door.

She knew she should grab the printouts and hightail it back to her desk, but she felt herself pulled toward the voices. Felt the sense of something familiar and terrible.

Maggie padded down the hall and found herself in front of three small conference rooms. Two were vacant and sterile, striped with vacuum tracks and scented with cleaner. The third had its door buttoned shut.

Zartar's voice, shrill and slicing, drifted from behind the door. Maggie froze. What was Zartar still doing here? Didn't she leave with Ethan?

"Who the hell do you think you are?" Zartar demanded.

"I'm just doing my job," the man replied.

"Bullshit," Zartar retorted. "You're enjoying this. You're getting off on every second. And I'm sick of it. Sick of the lies, the secrets. I'm done. Got it, meathead? Finished. Finito."

Maggie glanced over her shoulder to see if anyone else overheard the conversation. Coworkers milled around in the cube farm, oblivious to what was happening out of earshot.

"No one likes a quitter, Zartar," the man said. "And there are incentives to consider. I'm told I can be very persuasive."

The conference door swung wide and Miles stepped into the hallway. Who else? Maggie couldn't believe she hadn't recognized the ever-present sneer in his voice.

He spotted Maggie staring at him, kissed the air with his full, almost feminine mouth, then strode down the hall, arms bent in a permanent bicep curl.

Zartar burst from the room, her face streaked with tears and reddened by fury.

"Oh my God. What happened? I thought you left with Ethan."

Zartar wiped her eyes with the back of her hand. "I was on my way out when Montgomery Junior insisted on an impromptu meeting. And nothing happened. Nothing other than not being able to buy back my soul from the devil." She looked up at the acoustic ceiling tiles and fanned her eyes in a futile attempt to stem the flow of navy blue mascara. "Turns out there are no refunds."

Zartar bolted for the ladies' room. Maggie watched, her heart thudding sickly in her chest. She swiveled around to find Miles.

He was standing at the end of the hall, one hand behind his back, his face turned up in a smug grin.

She was on him in seconds, her anger building with each step. Her heart was jack-hammering now, threatening to break through her sternum. She felt an overwhelming desire to bash Miles's head against the door.

"You stay away from her," Maggie growled. Her face was so close to his she could see every pore in his skin. His breath smelled like rotting meat.

Surprise flitted through Miles's eyes, but was quickly replaced by something malignant. He pulled himself to his full height, expanding as if he were filled with helium. "Who's gonna make me?"

Maggie felt something give way in the back of her mind, a dam bursting, flooding her with emotions she'd always carefully kept in check. Her fear of Miles was drowned beneath a red-hot river of rage.

Rage over his unwanted advances. Rage over the craigslist ad she was almost certain he was behind. Most of all, rage over his treatment of Zartar. Maggie had only a few friends. She'd be damned if she was going to let Miles push any of them around.

Maggie moved even closer. At this distance, she could see that Miles's face had taken on a mushy quality, his muscles running to fat beneath his skin. "Me," she whispered. "I'm going to make you."

Miles hesitated. Confusion flashed across his face, illuminating his dawning realization that a woman—a small young woman—was daring to challenge him.

He recovered. Smiled. "I'd like to see that." He took his arm from behind his back. "Oh. I almost forgot. I found these on the printer after my conversation with Zartar." Miles waggled a thin pile of papers between stumpy fingers. "Header says they came from your machine. Tracking printouts is part of management's efforts to monitor communications." He leaned close and whispered in her ear. "We have a mole, you know."

Maggie could feel a vein in her head throbbing. A handful of thumbtacks seemed to be making their way down her throat.

Maggie extended her hand. "Thank you."

Miles rifled through the stack, making a show of giving each page a thorough review. She watched him pause on a page emblazoned with Elsa Henderson's photo, her bio trailing beneath it like a long cape of text. Miles's eyes cut to hers. "Looks interesting."

"Thank you," she repeated through gritted teeth.

Miles held the papers out, his eyes locked onto hers. The sweet-sick scent of musky cologne wafted from his polo shirt. She grabbed the stack and pulled. Miles held on, a child's game of keep-away, before relinquishing his prize.

"Take Elm Boulevard to *The Post*," he said. "Traffic can be a real bitch."

Chapter 20

Anger bled away from Maggie as if she'd opened a vein. She leaned against the wall as dread, cold and thick, chugged through her body like embalming fluid.

She didn't need to make an even bigger enemy of the president's son. Miles was already unpredictable and frightening. And she couldn't afford to rock the employment boat. For the moment, though, it felt worth it, even if the confrontation had scratched an epitaph upon her future.

Here lies Magnolia O'Malley's career.

Of course, none of that mattered compared with what was going on with Zartar.

Which was *what* exactly?

There was no love lost between Miles and Zartar, that much was clear. But it was more than garden-variety hatred. Miles was trying to get Zartar to do something. Or pressuring her into *continuing* what she was doing.

Maggie walked to the ladies' room. She stared at the door. She knew how Zartar would respond if she followed her inside and tried to comfort her. She'd tell Maggie where to go and what to do with herself when she got there.

Maggie recognized the stubborn self-sufficiency in herself. Wasn't that why she lived alone? Insisted on doing 100 percent of car repair and maintenance on her own? Hadn't cried (until recently) since Mrs. Maloney handed her a tuna noodle hot dish at her mother's wake?

Maggie returned to her desk and slumped in her chair. She began sifting through emails and found she couldn't concentrate.

She opened a web browser, searched and found the news story

about Mia's death. She was rereading her short biography when a pair of hands landed on her shoulders.

"Surfing the internet on company time?" asked a voice inches from her ear.

Maggie jumped and spun around, memories of Miles sending adrenaline into her bloodstream.

Ethan grinned. "That's a serious infraction, you know."

Maggie gave an internal sigh of relief. "Does this mean you're going to turn me in to HR?"

Ethan folded his arms across his chest and stroked his chin thoughtfully. "Well, I'd hate for it to go into your permanent record. I'd better put together an action plan to get you back on track."

He looked around to make sure no one was watching, then spun her ergo-chair until it faced him and crouched in front of her, his large hands clasping the armrests. "Step one: dinner with me at my place. We could watch a movie, have Red Vines for dessert."

"I thought you were gone," she said casually. "Roselyn mentioned seeing you leave with Zartar."

She watched Ethan's face, waiting for a change in his expression, something that indicated knowledge or duplicity or guilt.

Ethan spread his arms wide. "Nope. Still here. And now I've done all my chores and can go to the ball."

No reaction to the report of him leaving with Zartar. No explanation of where they were going or why or what had changed their plan. No indication of a guilty conscience.

She stared into his eyes and saw her own reflection swimming in the sea blue of his irises. He smiled, his eyeteeth akimbo. She knew she should feel guarded because of Ethan's lack of candor. But the explanation was most likely very simple. Besides, escape felt good. Someone paying attention to her felt good. And reveling in a feeling that lay in the hinterlands between crush and infatuation felt great.

"You had me at Red Vines," she finally said.

"My place, eight o'clock? I'll text you the address."

"Can't wait," Maggie said.

He peered over her shoulder. "What's so interesting? Did they find Jimmy Hoffa's body again?"

Maggie froze, suddenly wondering which part of the news story was visible. The screeching headline? The photo of a sheet drawn over Mia's lifeless body, hospital corners at her heels and head? "A story about a woman who was killed in a mugging," she said casually.

Ethan made a face. "There are all kinds of maniacs out there these days. Something to do with the protests?"

"Doesn't seem like it." She spun around and grabbed her computer mouse to close the browser. Then stopped herself. "Actually, I'm wondering if you might know her."

"Who?"

"The woman who was killed in the mugging."

"Really?"

"I saw her in the building the other day. She had a meeting with Mr. Montgomery. And I...I chatted with her."

Harassed. Chatted. Whatever.

"I thought maybe you'd recognize her." Maggie scrolled up the page to the woman's photograph—the same photograph that had popped onto her phone days earlier—and rolled clear of her computer screen. She nodded at the monitor. "Anyone you know?"

Ethan squinted, studying the image. Mia, challenging and confident and beautiful, seemed to reach back, severing the curtain between living and dead.

A tiny muscle in his jaw twitched. Ethan clicked the red X and Mia disappeared. His face had grown dark.

"I've never seen her before."

Chapter 21

Maggie stood in front of the vending machine.

Corn Nuts or a Rice Krispies bar? Or maybe a Coke?

She dug in her pocket, jingled the change. She couldn't concentrate at her desk and hoped a trip to the kitchen would clear her mind of the morning's events.

"Health food, eh?" Dan, her old college mentor, appeared in the doorway.

"Dan." A wide smile spread across Maggie's face. Maggie extended her arms and they shared a side hug. "What are you doing here?"

"Reviewing some data on a drug Rx is hot to trot out." He smiled. "If they're willing to pay, we're willing to make house calls."

Maggie chuckled. "Ah, yes. The power of the Prescription Drug User Fee Act."

"It's a beautiful thing. Less red tape. Faster approvals. Treatments into the marketplace where they're needed more quickly than ever. Plus, the fees help keep the FDA going strong, despite the fact we're understaffed and underfinanced." He pointed to his yellow polo shirt, which was fraying at collar and cuff. "We government types don't get paid like you guys do."

"Well, Rx isn't exactly perfect, either."

Dan's brow sank toward his nose. "You're not happy here?"

Maggie paused, weighing her words. "Let's just say it's been a rough start."

Dan nodded. "I didn't want to say anything to you at the benefit gala, but Rx has a reputation for...being a difficult place to work."

"It feels more than just difficult. It feels poisoned."

Dan sighed. "I know this is a great job, a strong start to your career, but I also know what it's like to be unhappy at work. I have a new boss who thinks his real job is to look up my butt with a microscope. It's a living hell." Dan took out a handkerchief and mopped up the sweat that had sprung up on his face like morning dew. "Take it from an old man: you want to love where you work, to feel good about being there fifty or sixty hours a week. At Rxcellance, you'll be swinging with the big boys. And they don't pull any punches."

"But I need this job." Her father's broad, craggy face floated to the front of her mind. She'd just sent a check. Another would be needed soon. And then another. Endless responsibilities stretched out before her. "I appreciate the concern, but I'm going to stick it out as long as I can." Maggie fumbled in her pocket and put two quarters into the machine. She punched the combination of keys that would spring Snap, Crackle and Pop from their coiled prison. "Jack O'Malley didn't raise a quitter."

Dan smiled. "No, he certainly did not."

They both watched the Rice Krispies treat travel to the end of the mechanical arm. The coil spiraled, then stopped, leaving the treat in a metallic limbo. Maggie smacked the machine with the heel of her hand. The cookie dropped into the tray. She reached to retrieve it.

"Dan." Blond hair helmeted with hairspray popped through the doorway, followed by Roy's face and body. "I've been looking for you." He nodded at Maggie, flashed capped teeth. "Hi, Maggie. You're not really eating that, are you? I'd wager it's older than you are." He laughed a giant "Ho!"—Santa phoning it in.

Before Maggie could answer, another head appeared. Miles. His eyes narrowed beneath the bill of his cap. He licked his lips, but said nothing.

"Dan," Roy said, "could you join us for a quick consult?"

"Sure. Be glad to." He looked at Maggie. "Just think about what I said, Maggie. Life's too short."

Dan and Roy turned on their heels and left. Miles pointed a finger gun at Maggie and squeezed the imaginary trigger. He blew on his finger, seductively rounding his lips, then followed the other men.

The familiar sick feeling returned to Maggie's stomach. She stuffed her uneaten Rice Krispies into her pocket and made the march up the stairs to her desk.

She found Constantine playing Asteroids at her computer.

She had to smile. "Only you would turn my work area into an eighties arcade."

"Oh, good. You're here. I'm almost out of tokens." Constantine rolled himself away from the desk and spun around to face her.

"How'd you get in here?"

"I got a hall pass." He flashed his visitor's badge. "The receptionist knows me. Miss Vanilla, too, since I brought her along for Take Your Hamster to Your Best Friend's Work Day last time I was here. Actually, quite a few people got to know her."

Maggie rolled her eyes. "I'll bet they did. What are you doing here?"

"Had a break in my day, thought I'd pop by and see if there was any phone drama, text or otherwise."

Maggie ushered Constantine from her chair with her hands. "No, I haven't gotten any more appointment reminders or texts. The offending craigslist ad has been taken down, and I blocked all the numbers that texted me for my services. Maybe whoever started that little game got tired of it." She thought of Miles and his finger-gun. "Besides, I've been dealing with my own drama here."

He looked at her expectantly.

"I'll tell you about it later," she said, lowering her voice. "I researched the people from the appointment reminders, but nothing earth-shattering."

"Why don't we test that two-heads-are-better-than-one thing? I'll take you out for a nice dinner at Arby's, then we can head back to your place, watch old movies and talk about murder. It's the perfect evening."

Maggie swallowed. She could feel her cheeks purple. "Well, I sort of have..."

"I got us a couple of options." Ethan bounded around the corner of the cubicle, two Blu-rays in hand. "Oops. Sorry. Didn't know you had company."

Maggie watched the men size each other up. She cleared her throat.

"Um, Ethan, this is my friend, Constantine. Constantine, this is my, um, this is Ethan."

Ethan extended his hand. Constantine put his out slowly. The men clasped, shook.

"Constantine, nice to meet you."

"Heard a lot about you, Ethan."

Both smiled toothy, TV news anchor smiles, said nothing. It was like Maxwell Smart's Cone of Silence had descended over Maggie's cubicle.

Constantine bobbed his head toward the disks in Ethan's hands. "Film buff?"

"Oh, yes and no. I mostly like modern films—especially foreign pictures. But Maggie likes the oldies, so I got..." He turned the boxes over. "Let's see...*An Affair to Remember* and *How Green Was My Valley.*"

"How uplifting. Remember to put away sharp objects before watching." Constantine turned to Maggie. "Well, we'll have to save the world another day."

"I'll talk to you later." Maggie reached up, kissed Constantine on the cheek, then hugged him tightly around his neck.

He hugged her back, then let her go and held out his hand to Ethan. "Nice to meet you."

Ethan extended a manicured hand. "You, too, man." Ethan watched Constantine stride down the hall, then turned to Maggie. "You two...work together before or something?"

"No. He's a friend. My best friend, actually."

"Lucky guy," he said, his eyes still trained on Constantine's back.

Chapter 22

Maggie arrived at Ethan's with red lips, loose limbs, a bottle of Oregon Pinot Noir and "Make 'Em Laugh" running through her brain.

After making a deposit for Rx's charitable fund (being the fund's administrator was proving to be ridiculously easy) and another into her own account to cover the next check for Fiona, she went for a run, showered, moisturized and dressed in front of Gene Kelly, who was splashing and singing and dancing in the rain on her ancient television. She was glad to be free—no matter how temporarily—from worries about work, her father, death and whether Detective Nyberg would visit her with a pair of handcuffs.

She approached Ethan's front door and used the doorknocker, an ornate, carved Rococo reproduction that reminded her of a scene from *Young Frankenstein*. Great knockers. The door opened, spilling light onto the landing's polished tiles.

Ethan was shirtless, his shorts on but unbuttoned. A towel was draped across one shoulder.

"Hi, you," he said, pulling her close. "I'm glad you're here." They kissed. Maggie felt that same electric pulse every time their skin touched.

"Me, too," she said.

Maggie slid past him and carried the wine to the kitchen. The room looked like an "after" on the kind of HGTV shows Fiona watched. Amber pendant lights dangled gracefully from exposed beams. Copper-colored silica gleamed from granite peninsulas. A wine refrigerator, nestled in a small rough-hewn cave of rock, hummed quietly.

"Wow."

Maggie looked at her wine bottle, suddenly unsure of her

selection. She was glad she'd decided against a box of Franzia. He took the bottle from her and examined the label. "Pinot Noir. Very nice. You know, Pinot Noir is very difficult to cultivate. It takes patience to bring it to its full potential." He placed the bottle on the counter and gathered Maggie into his arms again.

"Think you can bring me to my full potential?" she teased.

"Dunno, but trying sure sounds fun." He kissed her. His lips were warm, soft, insistent. It had been a long time since she had been kissed like that. She could hear the *Love, American Style* theme song playing over and over again in her mind as Ethan's teeth grazed her earlobe.

Ethan walked her to a couch and eased her back onto the plush pillows. He kissed her neck, murmuring words she couldn't hear, didn't care about. Then he slipped a hand inside her blouse. "Would you care to join me in ze nudity?"

Maggie laughed, moving her hands over the wiry hair on his chest. "That is the worst French accent I've ever heard."

"It was Belgian."

"Even worse." Maggie straightened her blouse. "Besides, I only go topless on Thursdays."

"Until next Thursday then." He walked toward the stairs. "I'll go slip into something less comfortable."

"Don't be long."

Ethan flashed a grin and disappeared up a gleaming cherry wood staircase. Maggie heard a door click closed. She rose and spun around the room, casting an appraising eye on her surroundings.

It was an open floor plan with the kitchen and living room blending almost seamlessly. To the left of the great room, a pair of French doors announced a study garnished by Persian rugs and lined with old hardcover volumes.

Ethan had left two glasses of Cabernet Sauvignon to breathe. Maggie plucked one, bolted half of it and wandered into the study to the left of the kitchen. She padded over the thick white carpet, then sank into an oversized suede chair. She closed her eyes, breathing in the scent of leather and Endust and flowers and Ethan.

The luxurious house was a far cry from the empty anonymity of her own apartment or the bare-bones modesty of her childhood home. The O'Malleys had nice things when she was growing up: furniture covered in plastic, tables she wasn't allowed to put her Pepsi on. But they eventually faded away, disappearing beneath bottles and bills. Just as her mother had.

Maggie felt something tug at the edge of her joy. A sense of unraveling. Maggie put her hand to her chest and took another drink of wine. And then another. There was a sharp pain above her heart, but that was nothing new. She learned long ago the world was full of pain that doctors couldn't do anything about. She pushed it aside and concentrated on the beauty of the space.

Suddenly, Men at Work's "Who Can It Be Now?" blared somewhere to the left of her ear.

Maggie tried to jump out of the chair, but struggled against the quicksand of its deep folds. It was like being trapped in the skin of a giant Shar Pei.

She wrenched free of the furniture's cavernous creases and placed her glass on a polished black entry table. She followed the sound to the song's source. Ethan's messenger bag.

A cell phone stuffed into one of the side pockets along with piles of stapled pages illuminated with the beat of the ringtone. *"Who can it beee now?"*

She was instantly curious. And jealous. Who was calling Ethan? Work? Zartar? The tinge of jealousy flashed larger. Where had Ethan and Zartar been going when their plans were thwarted? What were they going to do?

Maggie looked toward the staircase. Deserted. Maggie turned toward the phone again. *Probably should let it go to voicemail.*

But the phone was insistent. *"Who can it be knocking at my door?"*

Maggie glanced at the staircase. Still empty. She stepped toward the bag and tried to see the phone's display. She could only see the top of the phone's shiny case.

Maybe it was important. Maybe it was a work emergency. Maybe Ethan had a sick aunt (or mother) who had fallen and needed his help.

Maggie took another step toward the bag, glanced toward the stairs. She should probably at least see who it was so she could tell Ethan. Maggie parted the heavy canvas of the messenger bag, revealing the phone in its entirety.

Zartar's face smiled at her from the display.

The pain in her chest exploded into a tight, burning ball, as though her heart were turning itself inside out. What was going on between Zartar and Ethan?

She let her hand fall away from the bag. The black material snapped back into position, shielding the phone's screen from view. Maggie turned away.

So Zartar's calling Ethan, she argued to herself. *So what? It doesn't mean—*

Maggie stopped, pivoted quickly toward the bag again. She felt memory, the petulant attention-seeker that it was, grabbing at her. There was something strange here. Something familiar.

Her hand darted into the bag, pushed the phone out of the way. Behind the phone, behind the takeout menu from Chan's, behind a crumpled quarterly 401(k) statement, lay a document that looked surprisingly familiar, although it had spent only a moment in Maggie's hands.

The report that had been delivered to her desk the day Mia Rennick came to the office. The report with the coffee stain Maggie had created by knocking her cup over in alarm at seeing the woman from her appointment reminder appear in the flesh. The report that had disappeared when Maggie questioned Mia Rennick in the ladies' room.

Maggie heard the door at the top of the stairs bump against a doorstop. Ethan was whistling.

She wanted to see the contents of the report, to see if something might strike a chord. But she couldn't exactly do that now.

Oh, hi, Ethan. Just rummaging through your personal belongings and found something that had been stolen from my desk. You don't mind if I review it for the next hour or so, do you?

Ethan's footsteps skipped lightly down the polished wood. Maggie glanced over her shoulder. She could see his feet, bare, then his legs, then his knees, enter her line of sight.

She pulled the report from the bag and stuffed it under the cushion of the mega-chair before sitting down on top of it. The report made a crunching noise like dry leaves beneath the suede-encased foam.

"Miss me?" he asked.

Maggie stretched in what she hoped was a seductive way and prayed the paper wouldn't rustle again. "Terribly," she said.

"Good. Let's eat. I'm starved out of my mind." Ethan extended his hand to help her up. Maggie looked at his smooth palm with a growing sense of panic. What if the report fell out when she stood up?

"I think my feet are asleep," she said with a laugh. "Talk about a comfy chair. Let me just get my circulation going."

"Are you trying to trick me into massaging your feet? I have an advanced degree in Little Piggy Relaxation, you know." He reached for her feet.

"No!" Maggie said. Ethan looked at her quizzically. "I mean, not right now. As soon as I get the blood flowing, I'll join you in the kitchen." She twirled her ankle. "This little piggy had roast beef…"

"Chicken biryani, actually," he said. "Which I do need to check on." He walked toward the kitchen. "Come help me with the rice when you're ready," he called over his shoulder. "I'll show you what I can do with my saffron."

"Is that what the kids are calling it nowadays?"

Maggie waited until Ethan's head disappeared into the oversized refrigerator, then slid her hand beneath the cushion. Her fingers pinched the report's edge and she pulled. There was a ripping sound. Maggie coughed loudly and peered into the kitchen. The refrigerator door was still open, the clink of rearrangement audible through the appliance's stainless steel exoskeleton.

Maggie stood and yanked the pages from beneath the cushion. She had torn the cover, but the rest of the document appeared to be intact. Maybe she should put it back. Maybe he wouldn't notice the torn cover. On the other hand, she wanted to see what was in the report—and why Ethan might have taken it from her desk.

Maggie considered the options and consequences for one terrifying and seemingly interminable moment. Then she rolled up the document and grabbed the purse she'd tossed onto the base of the hallway coat rack. She tucked the report beneath old wrappers, dried-out pens, her wallet and phone. Then she zipped Ethan's messenger bag and her purse shut.

Chapter 23

The rest of dinner was excruciating, even more excruciating than the gut bombs Rx tried to pass off as nachos every other Friday. Maggie was sure she'd been in her aerobic zone throughout the meal. Perspiration sprouted like a fine mustache onto her upper lip, and she dabbed daintily with a napkin that twisted in her trembling hands beneath the table.

She couldn't stop thinking about the report. Or rather, she couldn't stop thinking about why it had been in Ethan's bag. He must have taken it from her desk. But why?

After pushing the food around her plate for an hour, Maggie claimed a migraine, put on a brave face when Ethan asked if it was a bad one and asked for a rain check to make up for the truncated date.

As Ethan walked her to the door, his cell phone had begun ringing.

"Who could it be now?"

Maggie flinched. Ethan glanced in the direction of his messenger bag, craning his neck to see the display. Maggie's pulse hammered at her throat. She felt like the narrator in Poe's "Tell-Tale Heart." Would Ethan be able to hear the blood tearing through her veins? Hear guilt thundering wild and unchecked through each heartbeat and see the crime of her theft and, worse, her treachery?

The phone continued to ring. "Probably a solicitation," he said, taking her into his arms. "I'll let it go to voicemail."

She let him kiss her, but kept part of herself back. She could feel herself hiding behind the old layers that had kept her from getting too close, too involved. She felt off-balance, not sure what to think or believe.

Fifteen minutes later Maggie stumbled up the steps to her apartment, breathless and shaking from adrenaline. The key to the front door was like a live thing, dancing and bumping around the lock, and she had to use two hands to guide it into the keyhole. Once inside the apartment, she threw the bolt and leaned against the door.

Maggie unsnapped her purse and retrieved the report. She flicked on the overhead light, which illuminated grudgingly from the heart of its eco-friendly bulb, and headed for the kitchen.

She had eaten little at Ethan's and, despite the mounting nausea, was ravenous. She opened the refrigerator and surveyed the plastic cityscape of bottles, cartons and cans before deciding on frozen burritos with sour cream, guacamole and ketchup.

She opened the report slowly, careful to keep the sloppy mess that was her dinner away from the pages. She intended to see what the hell was in this report and why Ethan had it.

As she was turning to page forty-six, the doorbell rang.

Maggie glanced at her watch. 10:20 pm. Pretty late for an unannounced visitor.

The bell rang again, this time longer. Someone was leaning on the buzzer. She imagined Miles with his fat finger pressed against the doorbell. Maggie swallowed hard and plucked her purse off the counter. She fished out her phone, finger poised to dial people who were paid to care if she were being murdered, and walked cautiously toward the door.

Three sharp raps ricocheted from the other side. Maggie heard herself yelp.

"Maggie?" Constantine called through the door. "It's me. Hurry up, will ya? Your porch is one mosquito bite shy of a bloodbath."

Maggie belched out a lungful of air and threw open the door. "What are you doing here?"

Constantine darted inside and slammed the door shut. "My God, it's like a horror movie out there. *Attack of the Killer Mosquitos.* I think one of them had a recipe book."

"Do you know what time it is?" Maggie demanded. "You scared the daylights out of me."

"Is that more or less than the bejesus? I think it's one and a half daylights for every bejesus, but I've forgotten the conversion."

He gave her a kiss on the cheek and strode into the kitchen, where he examined the plate on the table. He sniffed deeply at the moist, steaming heap. "Mmm...Burrito Surprise. You shouldn't have." He sat and shoveled a forkful into his mouth. "You know, I'm going to tell your dad about your ketchup fetish. It's an unseemly condiment, especially with your, your..." He gestured with his fork. "Epicurean background. But I'm here on official business."

"What kind of 'official business'? And why so late?"

He patted his throat. "Do you have anything to wash this down with? Something in the beerish neighborhood?" He turned in his chair, opened the fridge and plucked out a dark bottle. "Perfect. As I was saying, I'm here to let you know..." He stopped, looking at the stack of paper he was about to use as a coaster. "I'm not interrupting anything, am I?"

Maggie sighed. "Well, sort of."

Constantine raised his eyebrows and jerked his head toward her bedroom. "Right. Your date. I forgot. Did you bring Aaron here?" He lowered his voice to a stage whisper. "Is that why you cooked this marvelous meal?"

"Ethan, and no,'" Maggie said indignantly. "I was reviewing something."

"Something...?" He fingered the pages on the table before him.

"Something...I sort of took from Ethan's bag."

"Ah, examining ill-gotten gains. How romantic." He took a long pull on the beer. "So tell me about your detour from romantic date into life of crime. You know the risks, don't you? Jail time. Paper cuts."

"I didn't *steal* it," Maggie said hotly. "It was mine to begin with. Well, sort of. It was delivered to my desk, I'm not sure who did it or why, but then it went missing when I chased Mia Rennick into the ladies' room."

"What's so special about it? Looks pretty unspecial to me." Constantine scratched his forearm. "Dammit. Do you see this? I must have twenty bites here." He pushed up a sleeve and rotated skin dotted with a constellation of bumps. "I'm like human bubble wrap. Here, feel this."

Maggie sighed in exasperation. "Just tell me why you're here."

"Right after you tell me why this document is so damn important.

I mean, it's gotta be for you to jeopardize...whatever it is you have with international film buff and man about town, Ian."

"It's *Ethan*," Maggie said sitting at the table. "And I *do* think it's important. I'm just not 100 percent sure why."

"Take a guess. I'm good at bouncing things off of. Minored in it, actually."

She picked up the small stack of papers and leafed through the document. "Okay, here's the deal. At first glance, I thought this was a typical 'proof of concept' report. Basically, a document that says the drug being developed is affecting the intended target—or disease mechanism—in the intended way. But something's strange."

She rummaged through an aptly named junk drawer and grabbed a pen dented with tooth marks. She made a wide circle in the center of the page and tapped at it. "See this? This says the biologic—that's the compound that they hope will become the approved drug—bonded to and modulated the target in a way that altered the disease."

"That's good, right? I mean, that's the whole idea. Get Compound A to affect Disease B."

"Right. But get this." Maggie flipped toward the front of the document and sat next to Constantine. "The target here, on page thirty-two, isn't the initial target indicated for proof of concept."

"You lost me," Constantine said.

"This is what I saw when the report was first delivered to my desk, although I didn't know that's what I saw."

"Still lost. Lost-er, really."

Maggie scooted closer to Constantine and creased the report open. "In a nutshell, the compound is showing a positive impact on a target. But that target isn't the one the drug is supposed to alter."

"Which means the drug-to-be can cure a disease—just not the disease it's supposed to?"

"Exactly."

Constantine ripped a paper towel from the roll at the center of the table and wiped his mouth. "Well, that's not *bad*, is it? I mean, don't you get extra credit if you cure a disease you didn't even set out to eradicate?"

"You'd think so. But someone tried to bury this report—or this section of it." Maggie turned to the last page. "The recommendation in the conclusion states that the company should pursue the development of the biologic on the intended target but 'forgo any additional assays into the efficacy—or lack thereof—of the secondary reaction identified during discovery.'"

"Translation?"

"They're saying to ignore whatever it is the drug is curing because it's a side effect, not the intended purpose, of the biologic."

"But why would they do that? And what's the disease?"

"Good questions." Maggie got to her feet and began scrolling through her phone. "I'm going to see if I can find out."

Matt picked up on the first ring. "Maggie, how are ya?"

"I'm great, thanks to your inside tip about the job at Rx, Matt."

Matt was Maggie's former lab partner. Tall with white-blond hair, icy eyes and pale skin, he looked like he hadn't seen daylight in years. Between his commitment to science and video games, Maggie had often wondered if that were true.

"It's one of the perks of being head dude at Rx's favorite contract lab. So to what do I owe the pleasure? Sending some stuff my way?"

"Actually, I was wondering if you could do me a favor."

"Anything for the girl who helped me get through clinical pharmacokinetics. Wait. Anything that doesn't involve spiders or me dressing up like Cher. I had a really bad Halloween in '09."

"I'd like you to do some research." She paused. "Sort of on the sly."

There was a pause. "Okay. What do you have in mind?"

"I'm going to scan something and email it to you. I want you to tell me if you've ever done any work with the biologic indicated, if your records detail what disease it's associated with and who ordered the workup."

"You got it."

"And Matt?"

"Yeah?"

"Don't tell anyone."

"Don't worry. And I'll get right back to you. I don't have anything else to do. Well, besides work."

Maggie ended the call. She felt a gnawing in her chest, anxiety trying to eat its way out. Surely she could trust Matt to be discreet. Couldn't she? Her chest cramped harder.

Maggie got up and scanned three pages from the report with the multifunction printer on her desk and emailed a zipped file to Matt. Then she grabbed Constantine's arm and dragged him toward her pimp-print couch.

"While we're waiting to hear from Matt, why don't you tell me about your official business? You know, the reason you interrupted my very busy evening?"

"Prepare to be impressed," he said.

"I always am."

"First of all, I finally connected with Travis at Reincarnated Phones. We can come by basically anytime this week."

"Good. And?"

"And I've been thinking that if Travis can't tell us who owned the phone before you, he could at least help us recover phone numbers called and received, texts, emails, et cetera. If not in their entirety, maybe partially."

"That sounds promising."

"But wait, there's more. I've been thinking that if we figure out the email address of the person who had the phone, we could email a fake spam message to that address. When he opens it, we'll know which IP he uses. And once I know that, I can call in a couple of favors and get someone to tell me who the account is registered to. You like?"

"I love. What kind of spam do you have in mind?"

Before he could answer, her phone rang. "Matt. What's the good word?"

"Well, not a lot in the good word department," Matt said. "I accessed some files through the company extranet, and I have bad news, more bad news and a side of okay news. What do you want first?"

Maggie groaned. "Guess I'll go with the okay news."

"I do have a name for the person who ordered the diagnostics. A Zartar...um...Nazarian?"

Maggie got to her feet. She felt something catch in her chest. "Zartar Nazarian? Are you sure?"

"Yep. But the work was later canceled by Miles Montgomery. Much easier to pronounce."

Maggie chewed her lip and started walking a small circuit around the cramped living room. "Miles Montgomery. Got it." Her mind began knitting and purling connections. "What's the bad news and the other bad news?"

"The bad news is that all of the accompanying data, things we typically keep on file, is gone."

"Gone?"

"Yep. Which is not only strange, but also means I don't know what the target or the biologic are. That's the other bad news."

Maggie was silent, thinking.

"Maggie? You there?"

"Yeah, Matt. I'm here. Thanks for all of your help."

"No problem."

Maggie stopped pacing and ended the call. She looked at Constantine.

"Get all that?"

"Sounds like a bunch of dead ends."

She nodded and flopped onto the couch. "Actually, it sounds like Rx is hiding something, and Zartar and Miles are involved. Explains the blowup at work, I guess."

"Blowup?"

Maggie recounted the fight she overheard.

"Someone's tired of keeping secrets," Constantine said. "Question is, what are they?"

Maggie was quiet for a moment. "One way to find out. I'll ask her."

He gave her an *oh-come-on* look. "You seriously think she'll spill the beans, just like that? Doesn't seem like they're eager to send out a press release on whatever it is they're doing."

"No," Maggie agreed, "but it sure sounded like Zartar was ready to move on. I mean, that was the whole tone of the conversation. Maybe she needs another reason—or some help—to get out of whatever she's in."

Constantine scratched his five o'clock shadow. "Hope springs eternal."

"I'll talk to Zartar in the morning, see what she's willing to tell me. In the meantime, what do you think about concocting our fake email?"

"Ready when you are."

They spent thirty minutes crafting an email featuring a fake deal for a Hawaiian vacation. Maggie looked at their handiwork, complete with color photos, a "buy now" button and a link to unsubscribe. "Looks totally legit."

"Yep. Now all we need is that email address, and we're in business."

"We make a good team, Gus. Partners forever?" She extended her pinkie. He wrapped his around it and squeezed.

Constantine rubbed his eyes. The skin below his eyes was tinged with blue thumbprints. "It's late," she said, "and you look exhausted. Why don't you pull up some couch and stay the night?"

Constantine crossed his arms and legs. "Don't you think your boyfriend might have a problem with me bunking here?"

Maggie rolled her eyes. "He's not my boyfriend. Even if he were, he knows you're just a friend."

Constantine scratched his head and looked at the ceiling. "That's me. The just-a-friend."

Maggie walked to a small closet that functioned as both linen closet and pantry. Behind the peanut butter and cans of chili, she found a pillow, pillowcase and lightweight blanket. "Here." She threw the linens to Constantine. "Sweet dreams."

"What, no mint?"

"I think I'm sweet enough."

"That you are, Mags."

Chapter 24

Constantine was gone when Maggie woke at five thirty, the house quiet and still. On the kitchen table, he'd left a smiley face made out of Cheerios and a note to call if "something interesting" happened.

Maggie made a cup of instant coffee, swallowed it in three gulps and dressed quickly, choosing a Kelly-green silk halter and slim-fitting gray pants. When she arrived at Rx just after six thirty, the place was a ghost town. The cubicles, a facsimile of shuttered mercantiles and abandoned saloons, made her feel like the planet's last survivor.

She walked to Zartar's cubicle, sure her friend wouldn't be there so early, and was surprised to find her organizing papers, drinking a Diet Mountain Dew and talking on her cell phone. Maggie stared at her, hands on hips.

Zartar swiveled around to face Maggie. She covered the phone with her hand. "What's up, buttercup?" she asked.

Maggie tossed the file she had taken from Ethan's bag onto Zartar's desk. "Tell me about the cure."

Zartar set down her Diet Dew, opened the folder with a blue-tipped nail and scanned the documents. Her eyebrows drew together in a perfectly groomed line. "I'll call you back," she muttered into the phone.

Zartar placed her phone on the table and took a deep pull on her Mountain Dew. "Where did you get this?"

"Someone delivered it to my desk."

Zartar arched a brow impossibly higher.

"And then took it from my desk," Maggie continued. "Last night, I found it in Ethan's bag."

Zartar's expression hardened. "Well, isn't that cozy?"

"What's going on, Zartar? What's Rx involved in? What are *you* involved in?"

"Nothing," Zartar said, "unless you count flushing a treatment for Ghana necrosis down the john."

"Ghana necrosis?"

"Shhh!" Zartar said, bangles jangling as she waved her hands for quiet. "No need to broadcast to the entire world, Anderson Cooper."

"Rx discovered a cure for Ghana necrosis?" Maggie whisper-shouted.

Zartar stood and looked over the wall of her cubicle to ensure they were alone. "We didn't cure it, but we sure as hell came close."

Maggie's forehead wrinkled. "But why—why would you hide that?"

Zartar sat back down and crossed her legs, then her arms. "It wasn't my choice, Maggie. It came from the top. We didn't even *mean* to find it. We were working on a gen-2 drug for Herpex, the company's oh-so-successful herpes simplex drug, and I stumbled across it. Unlike, say, Buruli ulcer or some other God-awful neglected tropical disease that's bacterial, Ghana necrosis is viral. My antiviral investigations led me to a key for unlocking a treatment for GN." She shrugged. "Dumb luck more than anything."

"That's why the data looked familiar," Maggie said more to herself than to Zartar. "Jon introduced me to the herpes studies before he put me on acne duty."

"And I'm guessing Jon is the one who delivered the file to your desk."

"Jon? Why would he do that?"

"Only a few of us knew about the Ghana necrosis breakthrough. Those in charge had ways of making us comply, but there was resistance. Maybe Jon saw you as an ally. A whistleblower they didn't have any leverage over. At least not yet. Jon was always interested in doing the right thing. Maybe he knew you'd have the courage to do more than talk about it."

Maggie shook her head and sat on a corner of the desk. "I don't understand why Rx would want to hide the fact that the compound you were developing for a herpes drug also happened to treat a neglected tropical disease. Montgomery is a neglected tropical disease crusader."

Zartar laughed bitterly. "Don't be so naïve, Maggie Mae. The discovery would've let Montgomery enjoy some serious ego masturbation, but once management started crunching numbers, it was all over. The analysts started throwing around words like 'financial viability.' Pharmaceuticals love creating drugs that are small variations on the successes they already have. The new ones don't even have to work better than the previous iterations, just better than a placebo."

Zartar took a sip from her drink. "It's a money game. Roselyn talks about how much it costs to bring a drug to market, but the truth is, our marketing budget is higher than the R&D budget. We're not trying to save the world. We're trying to make money. Rx knew they'd get way more for a herpes drug marketed to wealthy Americans than the cure for a tropical disease that would be donated to the poor. The herpes drug wasn't even where the real money was. Another researcher, who shall remain nameless, discovered that the compound had skin-firming properties. *That's* what was next in the Rx queue. Forget curing disease. What this world needs is Baby Boomers with taut skin."

"That's sick."

"That's 'strategic resource development.'"

Maggie shook her head. "Even so, I don't get why you would go along with it. Why would you agree to cover up a treatment of such a horrific disease? You saw the slides at Professor Sharma's presentation. You know what Ghana necrosis does."

"Yes I know," Zartar snapped, her olive skin reddening. "You think I wanted to keep this a secret? They *made* me bury the report."

Maggie felt the pinprick of adrenaline on her scalp. "Who's 'they'?" Ethan had the report. Was he a "they," or was he part of the resistance?

"Who do you think?" Zartar said. "The king of all theys: the Montgomerys—especially junior."

"He leaned on you?" Maggie asked.

Zartar dragged her fingers through her hair, yanking out artfully curled spirals. "He tried to. When that didn't work, he leaned on my brother. He figured out which Narcotics Anonymous meetings Ari attended. Chatted him up over cold coffee in cheap Styrofoam cups, got him to trust him. Then Miles gave Ari a tiny white pill that knocked him off the wagon he'd worked so hard to get on. Miles cornered me in the parking lot. He told me what he'd done, that I needed to 'get with the program' or he'd expose Ari's drug use to his new boss and get him fired."

"That's horrible. What happened?"

Zartar took one last sip, then threw the can into a small recycling bin under her desk. "What happened was I told Miles to go screw himself and went and told his daddy. The old man was the main architect of the cover-up, but he wanted to keep everything strictly PG because of the upcoming IPO. His plan was to bribe me or give me shitty assignments until I complied. He had no idea Miles went maverick and decided to do things his way. Senior was suitably horrified when I told him. I made some threats and he promised to rein Miles in, but it just made things worse."

"Worse?"

Zartar's voice broke. She took a shuddering breath, and the façade of confidence, the persona of the office badass, cracked. Zartar burst into tears. "Miles hired some muscle to rough Ari up. They broke his jaw and two of his fingers by the time they got around to calling me at the gala."

Suddenly Maggie remembered. The phone call at the gala. Zartar throwing her phone to the floor where it splintered into tiny plastic shrapnel. Maggie felt the color drain from her face.

Zartar wiped her eyes on the shoulder of her lab coat. "The guy on the phone said they'd keep hurting him unless I did what they wanted. Ari was in the background, screaming, begging them to stop. Even when I said I'd do whatever they wanted, they kept hurting him. Ari kept screaming."

"So you did what they wanted," Maggie said. She reached toward Zartar to put a hand on her shoulder. Then put it back down to her side.

"You bet your sweet ass I did," she said, sniffing loudly. She grabbed a tissue from a box decorated with purple butterflies and dabbed her nose and eyes. "Once I realized Miles was a sadist, I had to go along. Problem was, that power trip was just a preview of coming attractions. They started turning up the pressure, making me do other things."

"What things?" She thought about Zartar leaving—or almost leaving—with Ethan and the report in his bag. "Who else is involved? Who else knows about the treatment?"

Zartar shook her head. "Doesn't matter. The point is, the shoe's on the other foot now. That little scene you saw with me and Miles marked the end of an era. That's the last time I'm going to bow to that bastard." She wadded the tissue and chucked it into the trash.

"You're going to blow the whistle?" Maggie asked.

"Whistles aren't what I like to blow, Maggie Mae." She stood and fluffed her hair. "Rx is cooking up something new, and I'm going to start stirring shit into it." Her eyes blazed with anger and resolve. "I can't tell you what I have up my sleeve until I have a few more things in place, but you'll find out soon, I promise."

"But what—who—?" Maggie's stammered questions rushed together, but Zartar was already on her feet. She watched as her friend strode out of her cubicle and down the hall, leaving Maggie shell-shocked and confused.

A lump grew in Maggie's throat, then traveled down to her stomach where it sat like a poisoned seed ready to germinate. Questions pushed their way to the front of Maggie's brain, unearthing the fears and possibilities that had been interred beneath ignorance and denial.

Was Ethan involved? What did he know? Who else was wrapped in the secret's tentacles? What lengths would they go to keep the secrets secret—and the secret keepers silent?

Maggie swallowed the growing disquiet that seemed to infect every cell of her body and wandered back to her desk. She put her head on the cool brown laminate.

Maggie's computer pinged. An incoming email.

She lifted her head, dread drumming steadily through her now. Oh, God. What now?

She looked at the Subject line. Empty. She looked at the From line. Empty as well. There was nothing threatening or frightening about the email. It was just...odd.

Curious, Maggie opened the email. Inside was a folder. Maggie double-clicked.

The folder opened matryoshka-like to reveal document after

document of confidential data. Proprietary formulae. Classified analytics. Internal emails between James Montgomery and Roy. Everything that made her look like the mole who had leaked Rx's latest creation to a competitor.

Maggie gaped in horror and clicked frantically to close the document. A clock icon appeared. It was replaced by a bomb that looked like it had come straight out of Wile E. Coyote's most recent Acme purchase.

"No." Maggie said aloud. "No." She pressed control-alt-delete. Nothing. She repeated, hitting the keys harder this time. Her machine was locked up. "Dammit," she said. "Damn, damn, damn."

"What's the problem?" As if by magic, Steve Poole appeared at her elbow.

A perpetual lurker who smelled like cheese and wore his hair in a pompadour, Steve loved his IT position with an almost unhealthy devotion. He seemed to have a sixth sense about computer problems and would often show up before a trouble ticket was issued. He claimed he could read the digital minds of computers, which Maggie thought was handy, if not a bit creepy.

Maggie spun around and met Steve's questioning brown eyes. "Oh, nothing," she laughed, trying to sound light-hearted. She blocked the computer monitor with her body. "Just doing too much too fast and made my computer cranky."

"Let me take a look." Steve pushed his pear-shaped form toward Maggie. Maggie remained seated. Steve ushered her from her seat with a gesture of impatience that looked an awful lot like jazz hands.

Feck.

Steve attacked the keyboard with vigor, the keys vibrating beneath his stumpy fingers. "Hmm," he said. He tapped again, leaned back in Maggie's chair. "I'm not sure what you've done here, but your computer is most unhappy. Most. Unhappy."

"I'm such an idiot. I'll just restart it." Maggie reached for the power switch.

Steve grabbed her hand as if she were about to touch something hot. "Hang on there—" But Maggie was too fast. She flicked the switch and watched the digital image on the monitor collapse like a neutron star. Good.

"Not the best way to restart," he said, "but it shouldn't be a big whoop." Steve played with his patchy, anemic goatee. "I'm guessing it's some kind of virus. I guess you can relate to that, huh? Viruses, I mean." He flashed a broad, self-congratulatory smile at the joke. Maggie smiled back, silently praying he would go back to his salty snack foods and leave her and her computer alone.

Steve stood and stretched, revealing a dimpled abdomen tufted with hair. He reached for the back of the computer. "I'll take it down to IT for a peek-ola."

Panic rose sharply and quickly. "A peek-ola?" Maggie squeaked.

There was no way in hell she wanted Steve taking a peek-ola at her machine with all that incriminating evidence on her desktop. "No," Maggie said too loudly. "I mean, you don't need to bother with that now. You're so busy."

"Oh, it's no trouble. It's helpful for us to know what we're dealing with in case it goes system-wide. My guess? Your machine won't be doing anything but collecting dust today."

Maggie's mouth hung open. Steve sidled closer. "Look, I can see that you're worried about letting go of your computer," he said confidentially. "I get it. Deadlines are deadlines. I'll personally see to it that your computer is put at the head of the line. We'll probably know something first thing in the morning."

"But—"

Steve unplugged her machine and began winding cables. "No need to thank me. Just doing my job." Steve hoisted the computer onto his paunch, which he used like a dolly.

Maggie opened her mouth, but no sound came out. Maggie watched as her future disappeared down the hall.

Chapter 25

"Oh, it can't be that bad," Constantine said into Maggie's phone.

"Oh, it is."

Maggie had gone outside for some fresh air. Instead she got stagnant, waterlogged air carrying fumes from a small fleet of Rx trucks idling near the loading ramp. She rubbed a hand over her face. "We're talking about private email conversations and classified drug data—*top* top secret stuff—on my computer."

"Tell them the truth: someone emailed it to you. Viruses happen."

"You know what I think? I think a virus was deliberately sent to make me look bad, especially now that I know Rx is in the middle of a conspiracy."

She brought Constantine up to speed on what Zartar told her about the Ghana necrosis treatment and cover-up.

"Wow. Nice company you work for, Mags. But didn't you *just* talk with Zartar about this, like, minutes ago? I mean, even if this were some weird trap or something to get you into trouble, it would take time to develop and deploy. It couldn't be a reaction from a conversation you just had."

Maggie considered this. "Yeah, but I seem to have been making enemies here for a while."

She thought about telling Constantine about Miles's near-attack and the botched sexual harassment report to Roy. She couldn't bring herself to do it. Instead she said, "Besides, I don't think Zartar would say anything about me, even if she did decide to take a stand against the Rx establishment. She's like the big sister version of a mama bear.

She's not going to do anything that would get me into trouble. Besides, Miles knew I overheard his argument with her. For all I know, he's already added two and two."

"But there's no way he came up with four, then reacted *that* fast."

Maggie sighed. "I guess you're right. But I'd better get back to work. The last thing I need is someone thinking I've now gone AWOL."

"Let me know what happens, 'kay, Mags? I'll be sending good vibes your way."

"Thanks, Gus. I will."

Maggie spent the next two hours in the lab. After splashing her face with water in the ladies' room and pouring herself a half-cup of bark-colored coffee, she headed to her cubicle.

Maggie's desk phone was ringing when she arrived. She answered in the steadiest voice she could muster.

"Maggie? This is Roy." His baritone boomed through the phone.

Maggie felt like someone was stepping on her throat. "Yes, Roy. How are you?"

Big pause. "Well, not too good, actually. I got a call from IT a few minutes ago. Seems they found something on your computer that sent up a whole mess of red flags."

Maggie closed her eyes. "Really?" So much for her computer collecting dust before IT got to it.

"Yes, really. Classified files, emails, memos, notes, all found on your computer's desktop. That's very interesting, don't you think?"

"Roy, I—"

"Montgomery's ready to bust an artery over this. He's in meetings for the rest of the day, but he wants to see you first thing in the morning. I hope all of this is some mistake. See you at seven fifteen tomorrow."

Roy clanged his receiver into its cradle. She replaced her own quietly.

In her mind, she could see her father in his recliner, sipping Bushmills from a plastic soda glass swiped from the restaurant's kitchen.

She felt his future ebbing away along with her own.

*   *   *

The alarm sounded at six o'clock the next morning, but Maggie had been awake since four thirty. She stared at the ceiling, her eyes following the fine cracks that formed at the corners of the room. Architectural smile lines, as she thought of them.

The anxiety that had festered in her belly since the night before was gone, replaced by a feeling of leadenness that anchored her to the bed. After several minutes, and with every ounce of energy she had, Maggie sat up, swung her legs over the bed and moved toward the closet.

She selected a coral silk blouse and linen skirt, then studied her reflection in the mirror. The skin beneath her eyes was purple-blue and her auburn hair was lank as it clung to the back of her neck. But Maggie's green eyes blazed with challenge. *Hit me with your best shot, Rx.*

They were waiting for her when she arrived. She knocked on Montgomery's door and was commanded to enter. "Ms. O'Malley," James Montgomery boomed from behind his obscenely large desk. "Please have a seat."

Jon Baumgartner moved his crutch out of the way and gestured to the seat next to him. He moved slowly, almost painfully. It didn't seem to be a shadow of the polio, which sometimes slowed his movements. This morning his face was marred by exhaustion and worry. Maggie cast a sidelong look at Jon, wondering if he'd indeed left the file on her desk as Zartar suggested, then slid beside him onto a hard-backed chair with a tufted fabric seat depicting a classic fox and hounds motif.

I know how you feel, she wanted to say to the fox.

Roy stood at Montgomery's side, looking more henchmanly than fatherly. Miles, ever the cliché, flexed a rubber stress-relief ball.

Was he playing the devoted son? Assistant to the executioner? Both?

Ethan leaned against a bookcase. His mouth was turned down, his face waxy and pale. He looked as if he was going to be sick. Maggie could feel him staring at her, trying to catch her eye. She looked away. She couldn't face him.

"I'd like to go ahead and get started," Maggie said.

Montgomery burst into a thunderclap of hearty laughter. "That's what I like about you, Maggie O'Malley. All business." He leaned forward. "But what I don't like, what I won't *tolerate*, is disloyalty. I won't ask you why you did it, Ms. O'Malley. I won't ask why, through subterfuge and artifice and cunning, you got a hold of confidential information and downloaded it to your computer. I won't ask you because I know. Money. Pure and simple." His accusations came at Maggie like machine-gun fire. "You stole the research data and the private conversations for the sole purpose of selling them to the highest bidder," he continued. "Not that I have a disdain for money, you understand." At this, he leaned back in his chair and stroked his paunch.

"Mr. Montgomery. I know how it looks. Sensitive information that I had no business seeing was found on my computer."

"Damn right it was," Montgomery boomed. "I'm just glad Miles brought it to my attention. He happened to be in IT when Steve Poole brought your machine down."

Miles. He had to be behind this whole thing. In the corner of her eye, Maggie could see Miles puffing up, his back practically arching under the rare strokes his father was giving him. He glanced around the room to make sure people were paying attention to him.

"Be that as it may," Maggie said, "I assure you, I didn't put the information on my computer. The file downloaded itself onto my desktop when I opened an attachment that was emailed to me."

Montgomery looked at her as if she'd sprouted another head. "You're saying it's your computer's fault? Your computer ate your ethics?"

"No," she said firmly. "I'm saying that a virus infected my computer and downloaded the files you found."

"If Rx had a virus, IT would have informed me." Montgomery looked at the other men. "Anyone else catch a virus that made their computer steal corporate secrets?" No one said anything. "I didn't think so."

"I'm not saying it's a company-wide problem," Maggie said, trying to remain calm. "I think the virus was sent to my computer intentionally to make me look bad."

As soon as it was out of her mouth, she knew how it sounded. *Hi,*

I'm paranoid and everyone's out to get me. Want to hear my theories about Lee Harvey Oswald?

"Well, the 'looking bad' part has been an unbridled success, Ms. O'Malley," Montgomery said. "But let's be serious. You're not really suggesting you've been set up, are you?"

Maggie bristled. "All I know is that I opened a document, my computer locked up and these documents downloaded themselves onto my desktop. It seems intentional."

Montgomery waved a hand, swatting her comment as if it were an annoying fly. "Even if your computer was infected with a virus in some sort of *conspiracy* against you..." He paused, smiling. "There's still the small matter of the items that were found in your desk." The smile widened into a grin, a red gash against greasepaint-white skin.

"My desk?" Maggie heard herself say.

Montgomery wheeled his girth away from his desk. He yanked the top drawer open and produced a small black cloth bag with game show panache. He shook the bag.

"A most interesting inventory," he said. He opened the bag and placed the contents on his desk one at a time as if he were doling out Twinkies to fat camp kids. "Let's see here. We have the usual office supplies, lipstick, tampons." Maggie felt her face grow hot. "An alarming amount of over-the-counter medications and this little treasure." He paused and shook the bag. Something clattered inside. "A whole pharmacy's worth of Oxycodone and Valium."

"But those aren't mine," Maggie cried.

"I've got to agree, Mr. Montgomery," Ethan piped in. "I know Ms. O'Malley well, as does Jon." Jon nodded his assent. "This has to be some kind of mistake. These don't belong to her."

Montgomery held up his hand. "It's no mistake that Ms. O'Malley has a reputation for not being shy about self-medicating. By all reports, she's a walking dispensary, popping pills like Tic-Tacs."

"Pepto and Tylenol maybe," Maggie said, "but that's it."

Montgomery grunted. "You're telling me you've never seen these bottles?"

Maggie squared her shoulders. "That's exactly what I'm telling you."

Montgomery continued as if he hadn't heard her. "What interests me is that the drugs bear no patient identification of any kind. Like the kind you might find at a hospital or a lab. Curious, don't you think? In fact, we've had some...inventory irregularities in some of our development areas lately. Missing medication. That kind of thing."

Maggie felt her face grow hot. "Are you suggesting that I stole these drugs from Rx?" she demanded. "That doesn't even make sense. We don't make these medications."

Montgomery laced his hands on his desk. "I'm not suggesting anything, Ms. O'Malley. I'm just sharing my innermost thoughts." He hefted himself from his office chair, which groaned in relief. "I haven't even shown you my favorite item. A veritable *pièce de résistance.*" Montgomery upended the bag. A small leather case tumbled out. Montgomery opened it slowly, delicately, and showed the contents to Maggie: a hypodermic needle.

"That isn't mine, either!" Maggie's voice teetered on the brink of hysteria. She caught Ethan's eye. He looked sick.

"That's what they all say. But heroin is making a comeback."

Miles made a subtle tsk-tsk motion with his fingers.

Maggie shook with anger. She'd never hated anyone before, but by God, she hated Miles. In the ancient, reptilian part of her brain, she imagined bashing his smug face against his father's polished desk, his nose coming away splintered and bloody. He was behind this setup. The virus. The printer. The planted drugs. He was behind it all. He wanted to destroy her the first moment they met. She could feel it in their first handshake, in the grinding of flesh against bone that crushed her fingers against her mother's ring. She wasn't sure why. She was just sure it was true.

"That isn't mine," Maggie repeated. "I'm not a liar, I'm not a spy and I'm not junkie. This is all a setup."

James Montgomery held up a hand. "Oh, right. The conspiracy. I'd almost forgotten."

Maggie opened her mouth, but Roy interrupted with a loud cough. He was wearing his best TV-dad face, the kind Mr. Cleaver would use when Wally or the Beav were caught doing something they shouldn't. "Maggie," he began carefully. "Until we get this all sorted out, we're going to have to ask you to take a...leave of absence."

"A leave of absence?" She could feel her fingernails digging into the palms of her hand, her heart thud heavily in her chest, a boxer ready to be let loose in the ring. "But none of this is true. I've done nothing wrong. It's a big..." She stopped herself, choosing her words carefully. "A big mix-up."

Roy continued as if he hadn't heard her. "You don't need to box anything up. We're keeping everything for—" The unspoken word "evidence" shimmered in the air between them. "For...the time being. Miles here will escort you to your car."

Maggie turned slowly to meet Miles's gaze. His lips disappeared as the shark grin swallowed his face. His eyes were cold beneath his baseball cap. "Let's go," he said.

"But—" Maggie looked around the room, imploring someone, anyone, to stand up for her. To stop the madness, halt this miscarriage of justice.

Jon worried his cane, but looked away. Roy rubbed the back of his neck. Ethan seemed dazed, his mouth half-open, his eyes full of shock, concern and something else Maggie couldn't place.

"Hang on, now," Ethan stammered. "Isn't this a bit extreme?"

Miles rounded on Ethan, "*Extreme?* Putting someone who has unauthorized information on her computer and illicit drugs in her desk on a leave of absence is *extreme?*"

"There's no proof—" Ethan began.

"I'll talk with you about your insubordinate attitude later, Mr. Clark," Montgomery hissed. "Meanwhile, I wish you all the best, Ms. O'Malley. Goodbye and good luck."

Chapter 26

Miles opened the office door. Maggie stood and walked into the hallway with as much dignity as she could muster. Miles grabbed her elbow to guide her along the maze of cubicles and office machines. Maggie tried to shake him off, but his grip tightened, digging into the fabric of her blouse.

"I need to stop by my desk," Maggie said.

Miles smirked. "I'll bet you do," he said. He leaned in. Maggie could feel his hot breath on her ear. "But that's not going to happen."

Maggie wrenched her arm away and hurried toward the elevator, half-running, half-walking. Miles was right on her heels. She did not want to be alone in the elevator with Miles. She looked at the door to the stairwell. Or alone on the stairs with him. A stream of bile pushed into her stomach and up her throat.

"Roselyn, Zartar," she called into the maze of cubicles.

"Shut up," Miles hissed. He'd caught up with her and re-administered his death grip on her bicep.

"Roselyn!" Maggie called louder, keeping her eyes on Miles. "Zartar!"

Roselyn hurried around the corner, followed by Zartar, who was drinking another Diet Mountain Dew. Zartar took in Miles's grip on Maggie's arm, her friend's wide eyes.

"What's up?" Zartar asked. Her voice was calm. Her body language said she was ready for a fight.

"I'm being placed on leave and escorted from the building," Maggie said, again wrenching her arm free. "Can you guys come with me to the parking lot to make sure—" *I don't get chopped up into tiny pieces* "—my car starts?"

The women followed Maggie and Miles and the four rode the elevator to the first floor. Miles stood in front. Zartar stood behind him, making gestures about the size of Miles's penis, how he uses his genitals in his spare time and what she wanted to do to his neck. When they reached the lobby, Miles walked the women to the glass doors, which opened automatically as if awed by his amazingness.

"Goodbye, Maggie," he said. "I don't think you'll be back here, but I'm sure I'll see you...around." His eyes crawled over her body.

"Only in your wet dreams," Zartar hissed. She let loose a stream of Armenian, which Maggie guessed weren't directions to the bus station.

Miles turned to Maggie. "Remember what my dad said, Maggie. Be careful. It's a dangerous world out there." He strode back toward the building, kicking gravel as he went.

"What happened? Why did you get placed on leave?" Roselyn asked when he was out of earshot.

Maggie shook her head and led the women to her car. "'On leave' is code for 'fired.' And I don't even know where to begin. I'm not sure you'll even believe me."

Zartar raised an eyebrow. "Try us."

Maggie summarized yesterday's IT fiasco and the morning's scene in Montgomery's office.

Roselyn put her hand to her heart, which was hidden behind a rust-colored polyester vest. "They can't just get rid of you like this. What are you going to do? What can we do?"

"I don't know," Maggie admitted. "But when I do, you'll be the first to hear."

"One thing you need to do is be careful," Zartar said. She looked at Maggie hard. "There are a lot of bad people out there."

Maggie reached out and grabbed Zartar's hand, then pulled her in for a hug. Zartar squeezed her tightly, then broke away. "Don't worry about me," Maggie said.

"Who's worrying?" Zartar reached into her lab coat, pulled out a pair of oversized sunglasses and put them on. "I'm just trying to avoid having to bail your sorry ass out."

Roselyn gave Maggie a small, shy hug. "I'm sure it's just a misunderstanding. You'll be back here in no time. I'll see if I can help clean out your desk and get everything boxed up for you."

"In alphabetical order?" Maggie asked with a wan smile, knowing Rx would let her do no such thing.

"Unless you want it by color and function."

Maggie gave her another hug, then opened the door, slid onto the bench seat and started the engine. She cranked down the window. "See you ladies soon," she called as she pulled slowly away. "That's a promise."

Zartar clicked her heels together and gave Maggie a regal salute. It was something Ethan would've done. The thought made her heart ache. She managed a small smile and waved.

Maggie took a side street and drove aimlessly for a few minutes, then pulled over in front of a small white bungalow at the end of a cul-de-sac. She rescued her phone from the bottom of her purse and called Constantine.

"What's your vector, Victor?" Constantine quoted from *Airplane!*

Maggie could feel her throat closing up. *Don't. Don't get emotional. Don't lose control. Don't think about Pop and the restaurant and your career and...*

"Maggie?"

"Constantine." Maggie's voice cracked.

"Maggie? Are you all right?" He sounded alarmed.

Maggie swallowed hard and dug the nail of her forefinger into the cuticle of her thumb. A woman in her eighties, a dead ringer for an old saddle, or with enough moisturizer, the Marlboro Man, stared at Maggie from a flower bed near the driveway. "I'm fine," Maggie choked out.

"Really? Because you pretty much sound like the opposite of fine."

"I'm okay. Upset, but okay. I just got fired. Or placed on leave. Whatever."

"Shit. Over that virus that unloaded all that stuff on your computer?"

"That was part of it."

"Part of it? What was the rest of it? I thought you were a pharmaceutical superstar like Beaker from the Muppet Show. What was so bad they had to fire you?"

Maggie massaged her eyelids. "The drugs they found in my desk."

"What?"

"A large stash of prescription medications. Plus a nice little heroin starter kit. All of which makes me look like a drug-using, secret-stealing, corporate-spying junkie. Not exactly promotion material."

"Double shit."

"You're telling me." She watched the woman hack at the flower bed and pull weeds with the fervor of one eradicating an alien species.

"You think the whole thing's a setup because you know about the treatment for whatever-it's-called? There's also the stuff you stole out of Ethan's man-purse. He has to know it's gone and that you were around when it disappeared."

"Ethan doesn't have anything to do with this."

"Right," he scoffed. "Because you know him so well."

Maggie felt her cheeks grow hot. She opened her mouth to retort when call waiting beeped. It was Ethan.

"Call you back," she told Constantine, then clicked over. "Ethan?"

"Are you all right?" Ethan sounded frantic with worry.

"I'm fine. Mad, but fine."

"When I saw Miles grab your arm to escort you out of the building..." He exhaled loudly. "I thought I was going to lose my mind. Miles didn't..." A pause. "You're sure you're okay?"

"I'm *fine*. Zartar and Roselyn walked me to my car. Miles was his usual assface self, but that was it."

"Maggie, things have gotten so...God, I don't know. The computer files. The drugs in your desk..."

"I'm not a corporate mole, and those drugs aren't mine," Maggie said tightly.

"I know, I know. It's all so...*dammit*." The line went quiet for a moment. "Don't worry. I'll find out what's going on and put a stop to it. I'll talk to you tomorrow."

He cut the connection. Maggie hugged the phone to her chest. She imagined Ethan marching into Montgomery's office, asserting her innocence, demanding she immediately be reinstated. She pictured her in his arms, sheltered, protected, listening as he explained the report in his messenger bag, his meeting with Zartar, his plan to help bring the GN cure to light...

The reverie was interrupted by the *Rockford Files* ring of her phone.

"What gives?" Constantine said. "You call me with the waterworks on, then hang up on me?"

"Sorry. It was Ethan, and I really needed to talk with him."

"What did our Boy Wonder have to say?"

Maggie clenched her teeth. "God, Constantine, what is your problem with Ethan?"

"No problem," Constantine said. "Other than I don't trust him as far as I can throw him. And you've seen me throw stuff. We're talking feet. Maybe inches."

"What do you mean you don't trust him? You don't even know him."

"And you do? Come on, Maggie. You've gone out with the guy, what, twice? And on one of those dates you discovered that he stole a secret file from your desk. I'd wager he's also hiding intermittent flossing habits and a Howard Dean bumper sticker. Plus, he's management, and management is probably involved in the GN cover-up and God knows what else. Face it, Maggie, you don't really know him. And you see only what you want to see: that he's rich, powerful and handsome."

Maggie balled her hand into a fist and hit the steering wheel. She could feel the gardener watching her. "This is what you think of me? That I'm so shallow that all I care about are his money, power and looks?"

"And his rugby trophies. I'm sure he has some scattered artfully around his office."

Maggie's temper flared. "You know what? Forget it. I know Ethan, you don't. So don't worry about him, or me, for that matter. I can take care of myself." She was holding the phone so hard her fingers cramped. "I've gotta go. I'll talk to you later."

Maggie dropped the phone in her lap and burst into tears. She sat crying in her car until the elderly woman had freed her flowerbeds from botanical insurgents. The shadows grew tall and gangly.

Maggie wiped her eyes, popped open the glove box, liberated a bottle of ibuprofen and swallowed two pills without water. She closed her eyes. Remembered Montgomery's accusations of drug abuse. Saw the hypodermic needle in her mind's eye. With a sigh, Maggie started her car and pulled into the lane, unsure where she should go.

Her apartment was the most obvious choice. She made her way there slowly, her mind buzzing with the words of their argument, her heart aching over the pain she'd caused and the hurt she felt.

She parked on the street and dragged herself to the door, bone weary and heartsick. She'd lick her wounds, fall into bed, decide what to do about her failing career and her broken friendship tomorrow. Everything would look better in the morning. At least, she hoped it would.

Maggie took the key from her pocket and raised it to the door, her eyes bleary from fatigue and tears.

That's when she started screaming.

Chapter 27

The doorknob was wet and sticky. Maggie snatched her hand away and wiped her fingers on her pants, a terrible habit Fiona never cured. Then she saw the hamster.

The small rodent hung over the peephole, obscuring the tiny glass. It had been impaled with a screwdriver, mating the animal not only to her door, but also to a glossy 8x10 photo of herself, running alone on a wooded trail. It was the same photograph that accompanied the craigslist ad promoting her supposed escort services.

Blood was trickling down the door. Not much, but more than zero, which was what Maggie considered the appropriate amount of blood on her front door.

Maggie fought to bring her terror under control. Her entire body shook as she stood at the door, staring at the carcass dangling from its makeshift kabob skewer. The animal looked like Miss Vanilla. But it couldn't be. Miss V. had been in Constantine's pocket just that morning. Or was that the day before? Or the day before that?

Maggie tried to remember the last time she'd seen Miss Vanilla. She shook her head, trying to clear it. She couldn't remember.

The blood from the doorknob dripped from her hand onto the porch, staining the entrance with blobs of red that flattened and smeared. She stumbled down the stairs, grabbed a handful of tall grass beside the porch, pressed it against the doorknob and turned as she twisted the key in the lock. It opened and she staggered inside, slamming the bolt into place.

Maggie ran to the bathroom, half-sobbing, half-whimpering. She bumped the faucet on with an elbow and scrubbed the blood from her hands with soap and scalding-hot water. She washed until her own skin nearly started bleeding, then toweled off on a soft cloth she typically reserved for drying the Studebaker.

Still shaking, Maggie went to the kitchen and retrieved a plastic grocery bag and a pair of dishwashing gloves. She walked to the door and peered through the peephole. Maggie squinted hard, trying to see around the shadow of the impaled animal. Nothing but the sun's halfhearted light filtered through. She held her breath, waiting, sure that he was there, waiting as well.

Five minutes crawled by. Then two more. *Put your big girl panties on*, she told herself. But she couldn't make her hand close around the door's handle and turn. She yanked a large black umbrella off the entrance coat rack and felt its heft. Not a baseball bat, but better than nothing.

Maggie opened the door a crack. Silence beckoned with the promise of nothing and no one. She opened the door wider. More silence. She stepped out and looked at the hamster hanging on the door like a macabre doorknocker. She wrenched the screwdriver free and the animal fell into the open grocery bag she held beneath it. She examined the animal briefly. It was smaller than Miss Vanilla and darker. It wasn't her.

The photo of her jogging, now smeared with blood and gristle, still stuck to the door. Maggie pried it off and stuffed it into the bag, considering for a moment that she might be tampering with evidence of her own future murder. She shivered, tied the plastic bag shut and went inside.

She was considering where and how to dispose of the animal when her phone pinged merrily in her pocket.

The reminder app.

Her stomach cramped, a fresh burst of acid streaming into it. She tried to swallow. It felt as if she'd been sucking cotton balls. She extracted the phone and looked at the screen.

Zartar's face, lovely and dark and mysterious, gazed back.

Chapter 28

Maggie felt as if someone had yanked the earth out from beneath her feet. Her knees buckled and she slid to the floor. "No," she moaned. "Please, God, no." Her mind's eye saw the digitized faces of Elsa, Carson and Mia. The newspaper articles intoning the details of their deaths.

Run over. Entombed in a car. Stabbed in the street.

She clicked the app.

MEETING REMINDER

TIME: 12:15 p.m.

The time on Maggie's phone read 12:10.

Maggie exited the app and frantically scrolled through her contacts.

Come on. Come on. Why do you have to be at the end of the alphabet? Zartar's magic digits finally appeared and Maggie clicked to call.

She waited three rings. Four. Six. Then Zartar's voicemail clicked on, greeting her with a friendly, slightly pornographic invitation to leave a name and number.

She was talking before the beep ended. "Zartar, it's Maggie. Call me as soon as you get this message. It's urgent. I mean it, Zartar. Call me now."

Maggie's heartbeat had tripled. Each beat seemed to urge her to action. *Do something. Do something. Do something.*

She scrolled through her contacts again, landing on Constantine. Voicemail, this time with Constantine impersonating Jack Nicholson. "You can't handle the voicemail!" his recorded voice shouted.

Dammit. She hung up, in too much of a hurry to leave a message. He was probably mad enough to avoid listening to her voicemail. Maggie tried Ethan. No answer. She hung up.

Finally, she called Roselyn. "It's Maggie. Do you know where Zartar is? I really need to talk with her."

"Zartar? She left work right after you did. I'm not sure where she went. She said something about a meeting. She seemed pretty uptight about the whole thing. Like she wasn't supposed to say but also wanted me to know what it was. Classic Zartar."

"Who was she meeting? Where?"

"I'm not sure. Like I said, she was pretty secretive about it. She did say she needed to run home first. Not sure that helps."

"Rozzie, give me Zartar's address."

"Can't you just look it—"

"Now, Roselyn. Please."

Maggie waited in agony as Roselyn looked it up, then read it slowly, as if performing the announcer voiceover for a commercial advertising hearing aids. Maggie thanked her and hung up the phone.

She dialed Constantine's cell again as she started the Studebaker and slammed it into gear. Panic built inside her like a wild animal scrambling to get out. She waited for the beep. This time she'd leave the damn voicemail.

"It's me," Maggie paused, gathering her thoughts. "Something very bad is about to happen. Or has already happened. I need you to call me. Right away. Please. I need you."

Maggie sped to Zartar's neighborhood nestled in the city's next great place. Local clothiers, organic food carts and hipster galleries sprouted like weeds between the cracks of tumbledown houses and dilapidated office buildings. Old churned beneath new in a boiling architectural mulch that made Maggie feel like she was walking into a Tim Burton movie.

Zartar's apartment was smack dab in the middle, a trendy little flat on the trendiest block. Maggie parked and tried Zartar's phone again. When she got no answer, she got out of her car and locked it. She reached into her purse, suddenly wishing she had a gun or a knife, and pulled out a half of a piece of gum. Right. She'd freshen the murderer's breath. Disgusted, she crammed it back in her bag.

She walked up the stairs to Zartar's second-floor apartment and stopped in front of a door guarded by twin statues of naked men holding baskets of plastic fruit at groin level. She rapped sharply on the door. Then pressed the buzzer.

Somehow, she knew there'd be no approaching footsteps. No "just a sec." No curse words on the other side of the door as Zartar arranged her kimono and prepared her complaints.

Maggie tried the door handle. It turned easily. She pushed the door open. The light in every room in the apartment seemed to be illuminated.

"Zartar?" she called softly. "Zartar, it's Maggie. Can I come in?" Maggie's heart pounded sickly in her chest, and Maggie hoped she'd be able to hear her friend over the blood that roared through her ears.

Maggie stole through Zartar's living room. Chintz pillows in chartreuse and persimmon reclined on a heavy Persian rug. An oak coffee table bedecked with more plastic fruit surrounded by a moat of fun-size candy bar wrappers stood in the center of the room.

It was like the Ropers' apartment from *Three's Company* had bred with a World Market sale circular.

Maggie paused by a giant faux fig tree. She smelled something. Something hot, acrid and metallic.

She moved like a sleepwalker from the living room into the kitchen. On the stove, a saucepan of hardboiled eggs had boiled over and burned down to a shallow pool of water which was now cementing the overcooked eggs to the bottom of the pan. Maggie flicked off the stove and surveyed the kitchen. A jar of mayonnaise. A plate of toast. A small puddle of something sticky oozing down the Formica.

Maggie bent to examine it. The smell, more pungent than before, assaulted her nostrils. *Blood.*

Maggie whirled around, her heart pounding so hard she thought it would explode. Blood was everywhere. A smear on the cabinet. A spatter on the chandelier. Thick globs on the floor leading down the hall.

She pressed nine and one on her phone, her index finger hovering over the final one, then followed the globs down the hall to a small pink powder room.

The door was ajar. Maggie stood at the threshold for a moment, straining to hear the evil that lay in wait on the other side. Then pushed gently against the rose-painted wood.

The door swung wide, exposing a bathroom replete with volumizing hair products, makeup and a fuzzy toilet seat cover. Zartar's lifeless body lay in the center of the tiny room, her head haloed by a pool of blood.

A sound something like a moan escaped Maggie's lips.

She fell to her knees, the phone skipping across beige tile. She turned Zartar over and felt for a pulse. Her skin was cool and still, the arterial echo of her heart silenced.

Zartar stared blindly at the ceiling, her mouth gaping in an endless scream. Her left temple had been crushed, leaving a caldera ringed by bone and the indentation of something heavy and jagged. Zartar's peasant blouse bloomed with crimson fleurettes that turned the white shirt into a riotous floral print. A trinity of stab wounds in Zartar's chest gaped accusingly. A gash at her throat where the point of a knife could be used to control and coerce wept quietly onto the floor.

"Zartar." Maggie's voice broke in a choked sob. "Oh, God, Zartar, I'm so sorry. I'm so sorry I didn't get here in time. I'm sorry I was too late. I'm sorry. I'm sorry. Oh, God, I'm sorry." The mindless apologies poured out of her like a prayer. She rocked back and forth, holding her friend's head, and the prayer became a low, wordless keening.

Panic took hold, tearing through her mind. She had to get out. She had to get away. She had to escape the blood and the bone and the smell boring into her brain.

Maggie fumbled for her phone, dropped it again. It bounced against the commode and next to Zartar's body. She snatched the phone from beside her friend's leg and crab-walked backward towards the door, her stomach lurching with terror. She became entangled in one of Zartar's bathrobes hanging on the back of the door. Maggie slapped the silky kimono from her skin as if it were a venomous snake, then found her feet and fled for the door. "I'm sorry, Zartar." She sobbed as she took one final look at the motionless form on the floor. "I will stop them. I will make them pay."

Chapter 29

Maggie ran into the hall, knocking a scarf-festooned lamp onto the coffee table, which shattered into a thousand tiny pieces. She kept running, not bothering to shut the front door as she bolted from the apartment. She looked over her shoulder, silently bidding Zartar one final anguished goodbye as she tore down the stairs and raced over the narrow walkway—and right into the spindly form of a middle-aged man.

She took in his shock of dark hair, his hunched frame, skin so white it brought to mind albino spiders that spend their whole lives beneath rocks. His shirt was embroidered with *Ivanovich, Manager*.

"Hey," he said irritably, bouncing back a bit from the impact. "Watch where you're going."

"Sorry," Maggie muttered, the latest in her endless litany of apologies. She pushed around him and ran toward her car. She chanced a glance his way as she unlocked her car. He was watching her from the sidewalk, scrawny arms folded across a narrow chest.

Maggie flung open her door and clambered inside. She cranked the key, threw the gearshift into first and stood on the gas pedal, steering with her knee as she entered the final digits to complete 911.

"911, what's your emergency?" the dispatcher said. Maggie's throat felt as if it were swelling shut. She took a great, gasping breath, struggling against lightheadedness. "Your emergency?" the dispatcher asked again, more sharply this time.

"There's been a mur...a woman is hurt," Maggie cried into the phone.

She was suddenly unsure whether Zartar was really dead. Maggie was no doctor. Maybe there had been a pulse. Slow, weak. Easily missed.

"What are the injuries?"

Maggie gulped, trying to squelch her sobs and the scream that seemed to build somewhere inside her. "She's been stabbed," Maggie finally managed as she turned the Studebaker onto an old county highway. "She's bleeding. Oh, God. So much blood. Please hurry."

"Your name?"

Faces swam before Maggie. Elsa. Carson. Mia. Zartar. She could feel the horror bubbling up again. "She's at 1914 Westview, apartment number five."

She hung up and dialed Constantine. Straight to voicemail. When it beeped for her to leave a message, her voice was a strangled gasp. "Gus. Call me. It's—"

The yelp of a siren cut off Maggie mid-sentence. She peered into her rearview mirror. Red and blue lights rotated atop an unmarked patrol car.

What?

Maggie pressed the End button and dropped the phone onto her lap. She pulled the Studebaker onto the shoulder.

Why was she being pulled over?

She couldn't think clearly. She felt as if she'd been cleaved in two, her sane, rational self trying to shout through an ocean of murky water to her bewildered self, which was floating away.

Suddenly she remembered the apartment manager she'd run into as she fled Zartar's home. He could have seen her leave Zartar's apartment. He could have known what she'd done—or what he thought she'd done, guilt radiating off her like the stench of death.

Maggie checked her rearview mirror again. The patrol car, a nondescript Crown Victoria, had pulled in right behind her, nearly touching her bumper. The interior of the police car was partially illuminated, silhouetting the man inside as he spoke into his radio.

Maggie dragged her nose across the back of her hand. She detected the scent of something acrid and recoiled. She looked down at her hand. It was sticky, still smeared with Zartar's blood.

Zartar's silent scream, her missing skull, crowded into Maggie's mind. Adrenaline pumped into her bloodstream. The shaking returned.

She reached into her purse and rooted around until her hand closed around a small plastic packet. She pulled it out, dispensed three Handi Wipes and began scrubbing the skin.

The rap of a flashlight against her window made her jump. She slowly rolled down the window.

The officer put his hand on the door and leaned into the window. His face was flat and broad, marked by a red mustache that looked like it had been placed there during a game of Pin the Facial Hair on the Cop. He was young, twenty-four, twenty-five tops, and he frowned as if to make himself look older, more in charge. "Do you know why I pulled you over?" he asked.

"No," Maggie said. Her voice sounded funny, high and breathless, even to her. "Was I speeding?"

The man looked at her sharply. He waited expectantly, as if giving her time to come up with the right answer. Maggie aimed for a pleasant smile and said nothing.

The cop considered her for a moment, then jerked his head toward the phone that lay dormant in her lap. "Cell phone. Against the law to dial and drive."

Right. The phone.

"Plus your headlight's out," the cop continued. "Imagine it's hard to find for a car like this. What is this, a Rambler?"

"Studebaker." Maggie relaxed a little. Car talk. A good sign. "1960. I restored it with my dad."

The cop gave a low whistle. "It's a beaut, I'll say that. But I still gotta cite you." He shrugged an apology. "Sworn to uphold the law and all that."

A burst of static blasted through his radio, followed by a garbled voice Maggie couldn't understand. The officer, J. Nehl, according to his name tag, pressed the button on a transmitter cuffed to his shoulder. He furrowed his brow and looked at Maggie. "Say again?" he said. More garbled messages. A glance at Maggie. "Affirmative." J. Nehl held up his hand at Maggie as if he were instructing obedience school. "Stay here."

J. Nehl trotted back to his car, the sound of boots on asphalt ricocheting off sleeping hills. Maggie watched in the rearview mirror as the cop dropped onto his seat and worked a small computer on his dash. Nehl looked up at Maggie's car. Then back down at his dash. He picked up his radio again.

Outside her car, traffic continued to stream by, the drivers blind to anything but the asphalt artery that pulsed with the cars before them.

Panic sparked anew in Maggie's chest. A snarl of panicked thoughts flooded her mind.

He knows. They're telling him who I am and how I was the last person to see Zartar. That I ran from her apartment, my hand covered in her blood. That I know too much about Mia Rennick's last, violent moments. They'll say I killed her. Them. Then they'll lock me away. If whoever killed Mia and Zartar don't get to me first.

Maggie reached forward to touch the key in the car's ignition. It wasn't just the key to start the car. It was the key to a few more hours of freedom. Of hope.

She depressed the clutch, wincing at the squeak it emitted, wondering if he would hear it and guess her intentions. Then in one seamless motion, she turned the key, shifted the car into gear and slammed her foot onto the accelerator.

The Studebaker leapt from the shoulder of the highway, tires chirping as they tried to gain purchase. The car veered into the path of a speeding SUV. Maggie swerved, missing the SUV, but cutting off a sedan helmed by an old man. A chorus of horn blares rose from the cars around her, but Maggie was too busy mapping out her escape to care.

She saw the patrol car blast from the shoulder and barge into traffic. The rotating lights bored into the blackness of night and Maggie watched with horror as the car darted from lane to lane in search of its prey. The siren was on now, an angry, plaintive howl, and traffic slowed and pulled over, a red sea of taillights parting to let the patrol car—a veritable Officer Moses—through.

Maggie spotted a motor home ahead. Its blinker was on, signaling a desire to pull over for the long arm of the law, but faster, nimbler cars continued to speed by, preventing the lumbering hulk from easing to the right. Maggie accelerated. She pulled ahead of the motor home, then changed lanes until she was driving beside it in the right lane.

The driver of the motor home, capped by a red hat emblazoned with "Explore America" frowned at her. He waved his hand impatiently for her to move on. Maggie waved back. The man's frown deepened. He hunched his shoulders and turned his attention back to the road ahead.

The police siren grew louder, building to a crescendo of electronic dismay, then began to fade. Maggie craned her neck. The patrol car had passed her and was weaving through traffic, its lights red like streamers through now-vacant lanes.

Rivulets of sweat streaked down her temples and beneath her arms. She spotted a 7-Eleven and pulled into the lot. She parked in the shadows alongside the building, her car nearly invisible to both motorists and passersby, and killed the engine.

Maggie took a deep breath. And then another. She felt a sudden, urgent need to move her bowels. She closed her eyes and waited, hoping the feeling would pass.

Laughter erupted outside her open window. Maggie started and looked over her shoulder. Three teenage boys taunted each other as they walked toward the building, undoubtedly hoping to fuel the evening's festivities with Slurpees and PBR and God knew what else.

Maggie gazed into the flat light of the 7-Eleven window and considered her options. Obviously she couldn't call the police. Or go home. Or go to work. She could call Constantine again, but she'd already left two voicemails that he hadn't returned. Maybe he'd never call back. They'd both said some terrible things. Maggie wasn't sure where the line between terrible and unforgivable was inked in a friendship's invisible contract.

The phone rang. She answered without checking the caller ID.

"Maggie?"

"Gus. Oh, God, Gus." Maggie bit the inside of her cheek and jabbed her fingernail into her cuticle, an old trick to control her emotions. "She's dead," she said. Her voice cracked on "dead."

"*What?* Who's dead?"

The grief Maggie had kept at bay oozed out of her like something foul and poisonous.

"Zartar," she croaked. "Zartar's dead. He got her. He killed her. I found her in her apartment." Maggie's throat ached as she tried to choke back the sobs. Hot tears streamed down her cheeks.

"Maggie! Maggie!" Constantine shouted over her keening. "What happened? Tell me what happened!"

Maggie swallowed again and again, trying to stop the hitching that came with every breath. She found her voice, broken, like the rest of her. "I got a reminder with Zartar's picture. I got to her apartment as soon as I could, but I was too late. I found her in the bathroom. She had been..." Blood. Bone. Body. "She'd been murdered, Constantine. Stabbed. Beaten. Broken."

He fell silent as he processed the horror of Zartar's murder. "What did the cops say? Could they—"

"I didn't talk to the cops. I had to get out of there."

Maggie could hear the hysteria creeping into her voice. She could feel herself losing control. And for the first time in her life, she felt like letting go. Loosing the dark emotions that scuttled in the corners of her mind and letting herself sink into the oblivion of feelings unfettered by thought or intention.

But she couldn't. She had to think. To act. To find Zartar's killer and end this.

Maggie fought the undertow of helplessness and fear. She pushed away the images that slunk from her memory. She squeezed her eyes shut, swallowed hard and told Constantine about the animal impaled on the door, the murder scene, her frenzied 911 call and her panicked flight from the policeman who'd pulled her over.

"I'm so sorry, Mags," Constantine said when she had finished.

"Me, too." Grief sat in her chest like a rib spreader, pulling apart her heart. "And I'm sorry about...you know...earlier. What I said."

"Me, too," he said softly.

Maggie stared into the night, feeling unmoored in the blackness. "What now? My friend has been murdered. I've run from the police. I'm no closer to finding out who's behind the appointment reminders and the murders—or how to stop them."

Dread, familiar as a lover, caressed the back of her neck. Then she did something she had once sworn she'd never do but found herself doing more and more.

She asked for help.

*   *   *

The moon had just appeared at the horizon when Maggie arrived at Constantine's apartment, propped up by distant billboards that seemed to sag beneath its yellowed, bloated mass. Maggie slipped out of the Studebaker, eased the car door shut, then crept up the walk, shivering under the blanket of darkening cobalt overhead.

She didn't remember the drive there. She wound through the streets of the city on autopilot, her mind bobbing between anger and fear, images of death and loss on auto-repeat.

Constantine opened the door before she even had a chance to knock. He smiled at her, eyes cinching up into his trademark half-moons. She felt her eyes tear up. She had cried more in the past few days than she had since she was twelve. Maybe the stoppers hadn't just come loose but disappeared.

Constantine drew her into his arms for a hug. "I'm so glad you're here," he said. She melted against his worn shirt, then pulled back, batting the newborn tears at the edge of her lashes.

Constantine swept his hand toward the interior of the apartment with an extravagant flourish. "I present to you," Constantine said dramatically, "Chez Papadopoulos, swinging bachelor pad, cool hangout and part-time safe house."

Maggie stepped onto the chipped parquet of the foyer. The small living room smelled of damp towels and a carpet invisibly tagged by the previous owner's dog. A small TV blared from the kitchenette. Empty pizza boxes and a small cluster of beer bottles stood unabashed in the corner.

Constantine nodded, following her gaze. "I know, right?" He grabbed her hand and pulled her farther into the apartment. "Come in, come in," he said as he closed and bolted the door. "First of all, are you okay?"

"I'm okay," Maggie said. "Or at least on the way to okay."

"No more reminders? No strange cars following you?"

Maggie shook her head. "I turned off my phone. I was afraid the police would track my location. Detective Nyberg called right after I talked to you." She looked at him. "I let it go to voicemail."

Constantine nodded, his expression suggesting he agreed that was sensible. He gently pulled Maggie toward his couch. She sank down onto the couch's blue denim cushions, remembering how excited he was when he found it at a garage sale.

He looked into her eyes, his own filled with concern as he searched her face. "You're sure you're okay? I mean, really, really sure? I'll make coffee. I know I always feel better with a few grams of caffeine coursing through my veins."

He was rambling. Her anxiety, Zartar's murder, the catalog of reminders and victims had infected him, too. He rose, paced in front of the denim couch, then strode the few paces to his RV-sized kitchen. "I've got rotgut and rotspleen. Preference?"

Maggie flopped against the rough blue fabric and rubbed her temples. "Surprise me."

She could feel one of her headaches coming on, the kind she had always suspected stemmed from a tumor spreading its roots into the hills and valleys of her gray matter. She massaged her skull harder, then stretched out on the denim couch.

"I've got work tomorrow," Constantine called from the kitchen, "but I can take a long lunch. We can do some research. Go visit the workplaces of the people from your phone. We can also go see Travis at Reincarnated Phones, maybe even visit the police station. I don't think you have anything to worry about with the cops. I mean, you were at the crime scene, end of story. They'll just want to get your impressions and move on." Constantine emerged with two steaming cups. "Here we go. Rotgut for me, rotspleen for you."

His words barely registered as Maggie fell into a deep sleep.

Chapter 30

The Post was an island of prosperity in a sea of hopelessness. White, shiny and grand, it looked like a plantation house amid sharecropper cabins.

Maggie had taken the city bus to *The Post* after spending the morning alone with her thoughts. And Constantine's collection of sci-fi fan fiction. She couldn't just sit and wait for something to happen. She had to do something. Anything. So she left Constantine's apartment and headed for the anonymity of public transit in case there was a BOLO for her Studebaker.

The bus dropped her near a parking lot across from the great building. An overpowering odor emanated from the little sliver of alley that separated the crowded lot from *The Post*. Maggie covered her nose with her hand. Maybe Zartar was right about despair having a smell.

Maggie walked quickly, pulling her hair off her sweat-slicked neck as she moved. The heat wave had become obstinate, refusing to relinquish its hold on the city despite the predictions of weathermen who wielded satellite images like meteorological divining rods. Even in the best of neighborhoods, fetid air seemed to bake in the city's nether regions.

Maggie walked into *The Post*'s air-conditioned lobby. It was deserted. Dimmed spotlights frowned down at her from a ceiling seamed with acoustical tiles. A water cooler adjacent to the wide oak-veneered reception belched.

She rang a bell on the reception desk. Waited. No one appeared. She plucked two Kleenex from the floral dispenser and blotted her neck, her cleavage and under her arms.

"Can I help you?"

The voice came from behind her head, low and sonorous like a sonic boom. The man stood in the doorway of the men's room, filling it, folds of flesh that had once been muscle encased in the faded blue of a well-worn rent-a-cop uniform. He crossed his arms under a name tag that read LESTER and glared. Maggie could see a copy of *People* magazine tucked into his pants pocket.

"Oh," Maggie said, yanking the Kleenex from her armpits. "I didn't see anyone." She stuffed the Kleenex in her purse. "I thought the building had been abandoned. Or maybe taken over by brain-eating zombies lying in wait for their next victim."

She chuckled. The security guard recrossed his arms.

Maggie paused to find the right lie. "I'm interning for Elsa Henderson."

"Elsa Henderson?" The man rolled the name around on his tongue as if it were a foreign object someone had slipped into his onion dip. "Elsa Henderson is dead. Killed in a hit-and-run. Didn't nobody call you?"

"No. Nobody called."

The guard grunted. "Well. She's gone. Guess the job is, too."

Maggie looked down. "Killed? How terrible. I imagine she left a family. Plus a lot of loose ends here at work, too." She glanced at the guard's face. "Stories she was working on. That kind of thing."

The big man grunted louder. "I wouldn't know."

"I wonder if Ms. Henderson's work got turned over to another reporter. Maybe I could talk to someone...?"

Lester narrowed his eyes. "You're talking to me, aren't you?"

"Of course, of course," she stammered. "I mean, someone who might know what Ms. Henderson had been working on and, um, if I can still get the job."

"New positions are posted with HR, down the hall. Not sure if there are any more internships."

"Okay, I'll check that out. I'd really love to help with anything Ms. Henderson had been working on. It seemed like she always had something new and exciting lined up."

Lester strode toward Maggie, turned into the corral that encircled the reception desk and sat down heavily. He looked at her impassively. "Ask for Denise in HR. She's the one who handles new hires."

Maggie's shoulders slumped. "Okay. Thanks." She opened her mouth to ask about Elsa's boss, then clamped it shut. Lester the guard had begun working the *People* crossword. In pen. How courageous.

Maggie walked through the double glass doors and around the building, digging in her pocket for her phone. She'd call Constantine, give him an update, apologize for not waiting for him to join her and—

She barreled into a man partially concealed by the building's noontime shadows.

"Oh my God," Maggie said. "I'm so sorry. Are you all right?"

The man smiled, three rotting dental stumps poking through puffy red gums. He wore a set of old Walkman headphones, holding the end of its cord in his right hand as if it were a microphone. "Oh yeaaah," he sang into the headphone's plug, moving his head in time with imaginary music.

Maggie stepped to the side to bypass him. "Excuse me," she said. He imitated her move. She stepped to the other side. He did the same.

"What do you want?"

She had compassion for those who suffered from mental illness. She had done an internship in a mental hospital and knew what a prison the mind could be. But she was not in the mood to dance the two-step with this guy.

"You're looking for that lady what got herself killed," he said slyly. "I heard you talking to Big Les." His eyes gleamed, a kid with a secret he was dying to tell. His voice dropped to a stage whisper. "It wasn't no accident, neither. It was murder."

He had Maggie's attention. "You know she was murdered?"

The man held the headphone plug at his mouth and spoke into it as if it were a Dictaphone. "I saw it."

"You saw it?" Maggie couldn't believe her luck.

He dropped the headphone cord and moved closer to Maggie. "I saw it happen *before* it happened." Spittle sprayed from between his teeth, showering the air between them.

Maggie began to push past him, annoyance supplanting manners. She'd had enough. "You're out of your mind."

"Ain't it grand?" He flashed a lopsided grin, then fingered the circle of Barbie doll heads that rested against his collarbone in a grotesque necklace. "'Course, doesn't mean my eyes don't work.

Doesn't mean I didn't spy him *spying* on her. Especially when she talked to us."

She stopped. "Who's 'us'?"

He gestured expansively at the cardboard shantytown that had sprouted in the shadow of the WPA-era *Post* building. "*Us* us. She used to pretend we were invisible, like they all do. Then she started chatting up some of the regulars."

"Did she talk to you?"

"She tried, sure. But I know a spying spy when I see one. This whole newspaper thing is a cover for a government project." He picked up Malibu Barbie's head from his necklace and began chewing it thoughtfully. "But the lady got some people to talk."

"What did she get them to talk about?" Maggie asked.

"Whatever they wanted. Orpheus. Obi-Wan Kenobi. How to make a radish rosette." He cackled. "Before she come along, a lot of them would talk to the ones in white. The angels who told them they'd chase out the incubus and the succubus and exterminate the bugs that crawl under your skin and in your brain." He shrugged. "And maybe they did do the exterminations. But there was always a price to pay."

"A price?"

He released Malibu Barbie from between rotten incisors and whispered into his Walkman jack. "Folks would get what they want. Demon removal. Brain pollen removal. Then they'd *get disappeared*." He nodded. "At first I thought he was part of the telepathy war, because there was talk of men in government-issue clothes driving government-issue vans. And some of them are a little…" He tapped the side of his head. "You know." Maggie nodded solemnly. "But I seen 'em. I seen 'em get in the van and go to the rotting place where staying isn't an option, it's a law. Like gravity." He cackled again, delighted at his joke. Spittle flew again.

"And then I saw the Watcher looking at her while she talked to us. He was like an animated stick figure, that one. There but not there. And I could see what he was thinking because words flashed across his face like those neon bar signs. And I knew. I *knew*. Elsa the government spy lady was going to get disappeared, too." His eyelids drooped to half-staff. "He watched. He waited. Then he made sure he'd quiet her mind like he had the others."

Maggie felt like her stomach was being dragged to her knees. "Do you know who he was?" she asked. "Would you recognize him or his van or car or whatever?"

He swiped a grimy sleeve against his nose and poked at his eyes. Then brightened. "I took a picture."

"Really?" Was it possible that she'd find Elsa's killer so easily? Would she see the face of the killer who'd eliminated the lives of those who had graced her appointment reminder?

"Yeah, it's a mental picture. You can email me at Al@telepathywar.gov.edu.net.com and I'll send it to you."

Maggie kept her face neutral. "Got it, thanks." Suddenly, she had an idea. "Would it be okay if I showed you a few pictures of my own?" She got out her phone, accessed the appointment app and brought up Carson Parks' photo. She turned the phone toward the man. "Do you know this guy?"

"Carson? Sure, everyone knows him. Works at the shelter. 'Course, it's just a front for money laundering."

Maggie nodded as if she agreed completely. "Did you ever see Carson with Elsa Henderson, the newspaper lady?"

"I know her name," he said irritably, "and yes, the twain did meet. I saw them together on more than one o-casion." He said it as if it were two words.

Maggie swiped the phone again. Mia's face appeared. "What about her?"

He grabbed the phone, and Maggie resisted the urge to snatch it back. "No, I'd remember this one if I'd seen her. Bet she has nice titties. You don't have a picture of her titties, do you?"

"Uh, no. Sorry."

His mouth collapsed in a sunken pout.

"Can you think of anything else?" Maggie asked. "About Elsa Henderson or the man who watched—"

"Killed."

"Right, *killed* her?"

"Nope. But I can tell you where the real Harry Potter lives."

"Maybe some other time. I really appreciate you talking to me, Mr..."

"Al. You can call me Al. Like in that Paul Simon song."

"Al, then. Would it be all right if I came back and talked with you some more?"

"Sure. Just bring some teriyaki jerky." He spoke into the headphone jack. "And try to keep yourself alive."

"I'll do my best on both counts," Maggie said.

Chapter 31

It was four thirty when Constantine got home.

"Beware of Greeks bearing gifts," he said as he nudged open the door with a knee. "Unless those gifts involve takeout from Levitz's Deli."

He wound his way to the coffee table, plastic key ring in his teeth, plastic bags in his hands. He set the bags down and began removing white cylinders, which he placed in front of Maggie. "They were out of that chicken thing you like, so I got meatloaf. You do like loaf-shaped meats, right? If not, I could form it into something more pleasing. Like a butterfly."

"I'm pro-loaf," Maggie said, sitting up. "Not to mention pro-macaroni salad." She plucked a plastic fork from the tabletop. "May I?"

"Please."

Constantine watched as she attacked the food. "Sorry I couldn't make it for lunch—or return your call. Putting out fires all day. But I'm home somewhat earlyish for our various and sundry fieldtrips. I'm thinking we start with phone victim one, maybe take a jaunt to where she worked."

Maggie choked on her macaroni salad and shook her head.

"Don't tell me you forgot about our sleuthing date," he said. "You Sherlock. Me Watson. I brought a magnifying glass and an English accent and everything."

"Aw, damn it."

"Okay, okay, I don't have to do the accent."

Maggie picked up the two-liter Dr. Pepper Constantine had brought from the deli and chugged, then started coughing again from the carbonation. "Constantine, I'm so sorry," she finally managed. "I couldn't stand just hanging around here all day so I went down to *The Post*."

"Alone? Without me? I thought I was supposed to play comic relief. Tell you how brilliant you are and point out obvious clues."

"Ugh. I'm sorry, Gus. I had to get out of here, so I caught the bus and headed downtown."

Constantine plunked down beside her and gave her a sideways hug. "No worries." He cut a slab of meatloaf with a plastic knife and put it on a paper plate. "Just tell me what kind of breakthroughs your solo, non-Watson-including investigation yielded."

"Well, there was a security guard who was basically the newspaper's bouncer. He wouldn't tell me anything about Elsa Henderson, other than she was dead. But there was this homeless guy who'd overheard me talking to the guard. He had a lot to say."

"About world affairs?" Constantine said with his mouth full.

"More like stories about some guy stalking Elsa who was spending a lot of time hanging with the homeless."

"'Hanging with the Homeless.' Sounds like a new sitcom."

"Can you be serious for a moment? Please?"

Constantine performed a deep Carnac the Magnificent bow. "Your wish is my command."

Maggie cleared her throat. "This homeless guy I talked to—Al—was sure that the man who stalked Elsa had also killed her. He also mentioned something about the homeless 'paying a price' for trusting guys in government clothes and government vans to exorcise their demons. It all sounds pretty ominous, no?"

Constantine took a gulp from the two-liter bottle. "Was he wearing a tinfoil hat at the time?"

"Oh, he was definitely nuts, but something about this story had the ring of truth. And he recognized a photo of Carson Parks and said he'd seen him with Elsa. There's something here."

Maggie stirred her macaroni salad, her appetite suddenly withering.

Constantine put his plate down and looked at her. He bounced to his feet, grabbed her hands and pulled her up with him. He spun her around the tiny room. "What next, Sherlock?" he said in a terrible English accent designed to brighten her mood. "Visit Reincarnated

Phones to see if Travis can tell us anything about who owned your demonic device? A trip to Mia's office? A jaunt to the homeless shelter?"

He stopped spinning and Maggie smiled in spite of herself. She understood using humor as a defense mechanism. She had often brought it out of her own secret stash of sublimations and suppressions. Sometimes it even worked.

She grew serious again, straightened up and looked him square in the eye. "Yes. To all three."

They started with Reincarnated Phones, which was situated at the end of a strip mall next to a nail salon, health supplement store and Starbucks. Maggie and Constantine ducked beneath the Christmas lights and Chinese lanterns that festooned the store's turquoise door and walked in, an overhead bell obediently announcing their arrival.

A man emerged from the back like the Wizard of Oz. He focused on Maggie, staring at her with small rodent eyes, squinting as if unaccustomed to the brilliance of the front room.

"Can I help you?" he said, donning his affable sales guy face.

Constantine rounded Maggie and thrust his hand out. "Hey, Travis. My man."

They performed a series of awkward, half-missed fist bumps. Then Constantine extended his arms in Vanna White fashion toward Maggie. "I want you to meet my friend, Maggie."

"Yes, we met on the phone," Maggie said coolly.

Surprise registered on the man's face. He covered it by stroking a nonexistent beard. "Right, right. The problem with the wipe. Like I said, we've got some sweet new models, but I got the impression you're not interested in switching. What I *can* do is completely wipe this phone. Give it a top-to-bottom scrubbing. Make it good as new."

Maggie crossed her arms. "I don't want you to wipe my phone again. I want to know who owned it before I did."

Travis was already shaking his head, long brown curls sproinging against the collar of his shirt. "I'd like to. I really would. It's just that—"

"Company policy," Constantine interrupted. "I heard." He stepped closer, placed his hands on the low orange counter in front of him. "But we go back, man. Way back." Travis's eyes shifted away, trying to deny the past. "I'm not just here to ask a favor. I'm here because I'm worried about you."

Travis's eyes snapped to Constantine's face. His mouth formed a perfect circle. "What do you mean?"

Constantine looked at Travis as if he felt sorry for him. He lowered his voice. "The thing is, the guy who had this phone, well, he's been doing some bad things."

Constantine took his wallet from his back pocket, opened it and flicked out a business card onto the counter.

Travis leaned forward to read. "Joe Hurley, FBI?"

Constantine made a *play it cool* gesture. "Cybercrime division. I've been doing some consulting with him on this phone case."

Joe Hurley? Who the hell was Joe Hurley? Maggie looked at him, marveling at the sociopathic ease with which Constantine lied.

Travis stared at Constantine, a penlight trying to penetrate fog. "Are you messing with me?"

"Just tell me what you know about the guy who used to have this phone, and I'll make sure my friends keep you out of it."

Travis eyed him suspiciously, then wiped his nose on the inside of a *Me for President* t-shirt that promised cake and hookers for everyone. "I didn't do anything wrong," he said.

"I'm sure you didn't. Tell us what you know, and we'll get out of your very lustrous hair."

Travis picked at a small scab on his chin. "I didn't do anything wrong," he repeated, looking toward the curtained area at the back of the store and lowering his voice. "I mean, maybe I exaggerate sometimes to get a sale. If someone comes in for a repair and I think he has dough, I'll upsell him one of my already repaired models, even though I know I'll fix and sell the old one. The guy gets a great new phone, and I keep an old, totally fixable phone out of the landfill. Win-win, right?"

Constantine nodded as if Travis were a paragon of social consciousness. "And that's what happened to the previous owner of Maggie's phone?"

Maggie placed the phone on the counter to jog the details loose.

"I remember because I was happy I'd upsold the guy. I thought he was just your garden-variety mealy-mouthed loser, but he turned out to be a total asshole." He looked at Maggie. "Pardon my French." Maggie smiled sweetly. "He came in only a couple of hours before you did. Phone had a broken screen. I told him the repair would be expensive, but that I had a new latest-greatest model and wouldn't he prefer that instead.

"Well, the guy totally lost it. Said he wanted his phone back, that it was very important, he *needed* it. Yeah, like I don't hear that a million times a day. Anyways, I reassured him we could transfer all his contacts and shit to his new phone, and that I'd wipe his old one. I gave him back the SIM card, which seemed to give him some kind of boner. He was happy to have a replacement phone and all his data squared away. Bada bing, bada boom. That was the last I saw of him."

"Do you have his name? Maybe on a work order?" Maggie asked.

"Yes, I have a work order," he scoffed. "What kind of operation do you think we run around here? I'll go get it."

Travis disappeared behind the curtain, Oz returning to his magic machine. Maggie and Constantine waited. Constantine picked up a brochure that advertised shop services and prices, folded it and put it in the front pocket of his jeans. "Just in case I need my phone repaired," he said.

Maggie rolled her eyes. Travis strode back into the room, yellow paper held aloft like an Olympic torch. "See? Knew I could put my hand right on it. I run a tight ship here."

"Except for when you forget to wipe people's phones," Maggie pointed out.

"I did wipe it." He sniffed. "Just, you know, not all the way. Here's the guy's work order." He let the paper fall from his fingers. It floated to the counter like a giant leaf.

Maggie picked it up. She groaned. "Ugh. Just a company name. MediPrixe. And no phone number or address." She mumbled something about tight ship.

"Can I help it if people don't follow directions?" He sniffed again, gave his nose another wipe on the inside of his shirt.

Constantine took the work order from Maggie. He creased it and put it into his breast pocket, then patted it significantly. "I'll need to keep this. Evidence."

Travis blanched. "Oh, right."

Constantine made as if to leave, then turned back. "Before we go, maybe you could take a look at the phone, see what information you can extract."

Travis narrowed his eyes. "Can't your cybercrime guys do that?"

Constantine rolled his eyes. "Yes, but this way I get to report that you were cooperative. You *do* want to be cooperative, don't you?"

Travis sputtered about already being cooperative. When Constantine said nothing, he sighed, then extended his hand. "Fine. Let me see it."

Maggie handed it over.

Travis began swiping the keys. After several minutes, he put the phone on the counter. "I was able to find a partial log of incoming and outgoing calls, a bunch of spam emails and a text."

He slid the phone to Maggie. She scrolled through emails advertising hair restoration, weight loss and work-at-home opportunities, then clicked the messaging icon.

Dolores has been taken care of, it read.

Maggie's arms erupted in gooseflesh. She turned the phone toward Constantine. He read, then mouthed "Dolores?"

She shook her head and shrugged. She turned to Travis. "Can you tell who this text was sent to?"

"Nope. Number's blocked." He scrolled. "But there is a number that shows up a few times. Not the only number dialed or received, naturally. Just all I'm able to recover."

He handed the phone to Maggie. She glanced at Constantine, who nodded. She pushed the CALL button.

A woman's voice answered. "Capital Ideas, may I help you?"

"Um, yes," Maggie said, startled, "what are your hours?"

"Monday through Friday until five thirty."

Maggie concentrated on sounding normal. "Great, thanks." Maggie hung up and looked at Constantine with wide eyes.

He wrinkled his brow quizzically, then frowned at Travis. "Travis, I guess that's all we need from you for now." He walked to the door and flung it open, the bell jingling loudly. "Oh, by the way," he said over his shoulder. "Don't leave town. You know, in case we need to contact you."

Travis nodded enthusiastically. "No problem. No problem at all." Constantine and Maggie walked through the door. "Come again!" he called after them.

Chapter 32

"And the award for the best impersonation of a federal agent goes to…" Maggie said when they were far enough away from Reincarnated Phones.

"I wasn't impersonating," Constantine said. "I was *suggesting*. I said a few things, flashed a business card. He filled in the rest. Fortunately, I still had the guy's business card from my interview at the FBI."

They jogged across the street. Constantine unlocked the Datsun and they climbed inside. "I'm guessing you don't know who Dolores is?" he said.

Maggie buckled herself in the lap belt. "Nope, unless it's a nickname for Mia or Elsa."

Constantine started the engine then stared into space. "My gut says Dolores is someone we don't know. Someone who was '*taken care of*' before."

"Before what?"

"Before you got the phone. It had a life before you came along."

Maggie gaped at him. "This whole hit list thing could have been going on for weeks before I got the phone. Months. Longer. Maybe Elsa wasn't the first victim."

Maggie felt the familiar churn of her stomach. She gripped the side of her seat. A muscle in her jaw twitched. She put her finger on it and pressed.

"Let's get back to what we know," Constantine said, pulling into traffic. "The number Travis came up with was familiar, right? The look on your face sure said it was."

Maggie nodded. Yes. Something tangible. Good. "The number was for Capital Ideas."

Constantine looked at her blankly, shook his head.

"The name of the brokerage firm where Mia worked."

He stared. "Really?"

"Yep. Which means whoever owned this phone knew Mia. Like Travis said, it's not the only number called or received, but it's something."

"Maybe a big something," Constantine said.

They drove in silence as strip malls gave way to the city's downtown, which was populated by glossy wine bars, tony department stores and coffee shops catering to those who preferred their organic half-caf lattes in Italian porcelain mugs hand-painted by monks.

"Here's what we know," Maggie said. "Whoever owned this phone knew Mia Rennick well enough to call her. He also 'took care of' someone unknown named Dolores and, if we believe what's on the form, worked for or with a company called MediPrixe."

"Hmm...sounds medical-y. Ever heard of them?"

Maggie got out her phone. "Not until now. Let's see what Dr. Google says." She pressed, scrolled, repeated. "There's got to be something about MediPrixe that will help us find the previous owner. Employee list. Contact info. Something."

She grew quiet, thumbing through digital pages.

"Here we go. MediPrixe...dedicated to blah, blah, committed to yadda, yadda." She paused, digesting the text. "Looks like they're a pharmaceutical." She looked at Constantine. He raised a brow. "That's a bit cozy. Anyway...it was founded five years ago by Maxwell Simmons, who according to the bio, was a gentleman and a scholar. Emphasis on 'was' because Mr. Simmons is dead."

"He's *dead*?"

"The whole page is basically a memorial. There's a handy 'request information' form, but no email address or phone number, just a physical address, which I'll bet is a post office box." Maggie tapped the phone against her cheek. "Guess we'll have to look it up on the business registry." She sighed. "So much for progress."

Constantine pulled up in front of his apartment. He rounded to her side of the car and put an arm around her as they climbed the steps.

"Don't worry, Mags. We'll figure it out. I'll whip up something I call Spam Surprise for dinner while you chase down MediPrixe info on my shiny new internet connection."

He unlocked the door, disappeared into his bedroom and emerged, laptop in hand. "For your interwebbing pleasure."

She sat on the couch, opened the laptop's lid and pressed the power button. The machine hummed, whirred, then emitted an alarming string of grinding thumps. Maggie looked at Constantine.

He waved a hand. "It always sounds like it's trying to eat itself," he said. "Here, let me see that." He plopped down beside her, turned the laptop toward himself and attacked the keyboard with flying fingers. "There. It's all yours."

He disappeared into the kitchenette. Maggie began combing the internet.

MediPrixe's digital footprint was small. Size one small. Beyond the company website, Maggie found little else other than un-updated social media properties, a few CVs posted by former employees on job sites and an old article penned by one of the company's researchers.

Undeterred, she checked the state website to find out who owned the corporation. She pointed, clicked. And groaned.

"What?" Constantine called from the kitchen. "Are you smelling my cooking already?"

"Ugh. No. The business registry site is down. I can't find anything about MediPrixe. Yet another dead end."

Constantine emerged with two steaming plates and sat beside her. "No worries. I'm sure it'll be up and running tomorrow. Besides, we have other leads to chase, no? Mia's workplace, Carson's shelter. Et cetera, et cetera."

Maggie shrugged. "I guess." She took the plate Constantine offered and peered under her stack of browned meat squares with a fork. "Is that...?"

"Yep," he said with his mouth full. "Mashed potatoes from a box. That's the surprise."

Maggie watched him eat, then shoved a forkful into her own mouth. It was surprisingly good.

"Let's take our mind off all this badness, shall we?" He picked up an ancient remote and pointed it at a small tube TV. A picture flickered into view, stabilized.

He frowned. "Hang on. What's this?" He jabbed the volume button. The speakers sounded tinny and overmodulated.

"Thank you, Brett," a woman in a cherry red pantsuit said to the camera. "The search for answers in the murder of an Eastside woman continues as this quiet yet vibrant neighborhood grieves the loss of one of its own."

Maggie squinted at the screen, which was embellished with a giant yellow banner that shrieked "Eastside Murder." She noted with alarm that the reporter was standing in front of Zartar's apartment building. The camera panned to a pair of transvestites who simultaneously sobbed and vamped for the lens.

"The police are hoping to question this woman"—Maggie's work ID badge photo flashed up on the screen—"Magnolia O'Malley, who fled the scene of the crime and a subsequent traffic stop."

Maggie breathed in sharply. The images on the screen swam in front of her, the reporter's undulating voice hollow and muffled as if it were coming from inside a deep well. Maggie gripped the denim fabric of the couch to steady herself. The reporter consulted her notes. "The women reportedly worked together at a pharmaceutical company, Rxcellance. According to an anonymous source, Ms. O'Malley was terminated from her position shortly before Ms. Nazarian's death. This source also told us that Ms. O'Malley disappeared with nearly $100,000 from a charity fund she managed on behalf of Rxcellance. Police urge anyone with information to call the tip line. Brett, back to you."

Constantine punched the power button on the remote and the newswoman and her stiff bobbed hair collapsed into a tiny bright line in the center of the screen. Maggie's breathing had become ragged. Her vision narrowed, vignetted around the edges like she was looking through a pay telescope at a distant landmark.

Put in another quarter. Watch your life disintegrate.

Maggie buried her face in her hands. Light and dark blobs popped behind her eyelids. "God, I am such an idiot. I should've stayed at Zartar's, I should've stayed until the cops came so I could explain what I found. What I saw. What I know."

"You were scared," Constantine said gently. "You were in shock. Besides, you called the police when this whole thing started, then tried to tell the detective what was going on when you got that video. It's not like you're trying to get away with something."

"Tell that to Candace Mullen and the Channel 12 News team," she said. She felt her old friend nausea return. "Not only am I the last person to have seen Zartar alive, I've been painted as a drug-using embezzler who bilked a charity out of 100k."

Maggie placed her plate on the coffee table, stood and walked to the window. The darkening sky was a bruise of purple and blue. "I should've known that Montgomery had a reason for asking me to administer Rx's NTD foundation. I was so flattered that he noticed me. I felt special. *Chosen*. But it was all a setup, a game." Maggie ripped at the cuticle on her thumb with her teeth. "Now no one will believe me. No one will listen to my conspiracy theory about hidden cures, corporate blackmail or a phone that shows who's next to die."

Constantine rubbed his neck. "Can they make it stick? The embezzlement charge, I mean?"

"Probably. I made deposits into a special account. I assumed everything was legit. I was so eager to please, to prove that I was a superstar, I didn't ask any questions. I just made the deposits and turned in the slips to Montgomery." She groaned. "How could I have been so blind?"

"It's not your fault, Mags. You didn't know. The account was probably manipulated by Montgomery or Miles from the moment you stepped up to the plate. And I'm sure one of them is the 'unnamed source' mentioned in the news clip."

"Even if there's no way to prove anything, as far as the police and the press are concerned, I'm a drug-addled, thieving murderer who evaded the cops."

She sagged against the wall, overwhelmed by all that had happened and all that was surely to come. Then she jerked to attention. "Oh, no."

"What?"

"Pop. He watches the news like it's his job. He probably saw Candace Mullen string me up on live TV and is worried sick."

She grabbed her cell and powered it up, something she hadn't done since she'd found Zartar. She watched *CSI*, knew about triangulation. If the cops wanted to find her, all she had to do was leave her phone on. But now it was a risk she was willing to take. Maggie dialed voicemail, input her security code and waited. Three messages, the first from her father.

"Maggie?" Jack O'Malley barked into the phone. "I don't know what the hell is going on, but I just got a phone call from some woman at the TV station. Something about you being in trouble. I'm sure it's a bunch of BS. Damn liberals always making—" Maggie held the phone away from her ear as he ranted about the media. Jack took a long, wheezing breath. The storm blowing over. "Give me a call, will you?" He recited his phone number as if she'd never heard it before.

Feck.

Maggie advanced to the next voicemail. Nyberg. She skipped the message without listening to it.

The last message was from Fiona.

"Hello, dear." She spoke with the measured calm of someone on the verge of a breakdown. "I'm wondering if you can tell me where your father is. He got what you young people call a 'wild hair' and decided to go see you in Collinsburg. I suppose he went to your apartment. But that was hours ago. Could you call me when you get this? Please, honey."

Maggie closed the voicemail app. She sat down hard on the couch and dropped her head into her hands. "Oh, God," she groaned. "My dad got a call from that newswoman and decided to come see me in person to find out what's going on. But Fiona hasn't heard from him. She's worried. She was trying to sound casual, but she's afraid. I could hear it in her voice." Maggie lifted up her head and looked at Constantine. A new worry, bright and hot, began to burn in her mind. "What if they got him, Gus? What if whoever is killing these people decided to come looking for me and found Pop? They could take him. Use him. Hurt him." She thought about Zartar's brother. She balled her hands into fists.

Constantine grabbed one of her fists, gently eased it open and put his big hand in hers. "He probably went to your apartment, saw you weren't there and decided to hit the pub for a pint. He's okay, Mags. Everything's going to be okay."

"Even if Pop is at the pub, 'okay' isn't going to happen unless we do something." Her voice was louder than she had intended.

"Like what?" Constantine asked.

Maggie's phone rang. She and Constantine jumped. She fumbled to look at the screen, answered.

"Pop?" she blurted into the phone.

"Maggie, thank God I got you. Where the hell are you? I went to that damn apartment of yours, but no one's there. Do you know what time it is? And what's this about a murder? Are you in some kind of trouble?"

Maggie took a breath and steadied her voice. "I'm fine, Pop. I just—" she paused. "I'm at a conference in Springfield for work."

Her father grunted. "Conference? So all this about the police wanting to talk to you is BS?"

"Just a misunderstanding, Pop. They have me confused with someone else."

The line went quiet as Jack considered this. "You're sure? Everything's okay?"

"Everything's fine. I'll get it all straightened out when I get back to town. How's everything at O'Malley's?"

It was a conversational punt, a verbal Hail Mary pass designed to direct Jack's attention elsewhere.

It worked.

"Restaurant's actually doing pretty well. I didn't want to worry you, but we'd had some rough months. We're in the black now. Guess things picked up without my noticing. Last night was the best we've had in...well, I don't know when."

"That's great, Pop." And she meant it. He didn't know about her contributions to keep the restaurant afloat and the bank at bay. Now it seemed people were discovering O'Malley's unusual charms on their own. Luck? Divine intervention? Maggie would take either.

"You'll call me when you're back in town? Let me know you got everything worked out?"

"Absolutely."

Her father mollified and her conscience soothed, Maggie hung up and turned her phone off.

At least something was going well. At least her father was safe.

Chapter 33

Breakfast was Pop-Tarts and more rotspleen from Constantine's overworked coffeepot. He decided to play hooky from work so they could get an early start on their day.

"What did you tell them when you called in?" Maggie asked.

"I told them I had a raging case of scurvy. Or maybe it was syphilis. I can't remember. Ready to hit the road?"

"Just as soon as I put on my disguise." Maggie plopped a wide-brimmed hat on her head and pulled on oversized sunglasses. "I found these in the trunk of the Studebaker."

Constantine gave her a thumbs-up. "No one will recognize you, Mrs. Howell, especially since we're not on Gilligan's island."

"Let's get this three-hour tour started."

The Datsun put them in front of a high-rise of steel and glass just as rush hour began in earnest. Constantine craned his neck to take in the city's latest monument to greed. "Nice," he mused, "in an *I've-got-mine-screw-you* kind of way."

Constantine parked in front of the building, killed the engine and reached into his shirt pocket. He produced a nose-wriggling, whisker-twitching Miss Vanilla.

Maggie rolled her eyes. "You're not seriously thinking of taking her inside, are you?"

"It'll sell the Richie Rich look. Hamsters are the new Chihuahuas."

Maggie was already shaking her head. "No, Gus. This is a place of business, not Miss Percy's Pedantic Petting Zoo."

"As impressed as I am by your alliteration and intrigued by the idea that there's a Miss Percy with a petting zoo, I really need to take her. It's too hot to leave her in the car."

Maggie regarded Miss Vanilla, who looked as if she was trying very hard to be generally adorable. Despite the stripper name and the fact that she peed in Maggie's hand, Maggie had always secretly loved the hamster for softening the edges of Constantine's grief when his beloved dog had died. After fearing Miss Vanilla had been impaled to her door and lost forever, she loved her all the more. "I don't understand why you brought her in the first place, but fine, bring her. But make sure she stays in your pocket."

"It's only her favorite place to be."

Maggie walked ahead of Constantine, pressing her lips together to redistribute her lipstick. "Do we have a script for this little adventure?" she asked.

He paused with his hand on the handle of a glass door adorned with the words *Capital Ideas*. "Script? Who needs a script? Just follow my lead."

"I think I've seen this movie before, and I don't like how it ends," Maggie muttered.

Constantine opened the door and they stepped into a plush lobby that looked as if it had been copied and pasted from a Pottery Barn catalog. Constantine elbowed Maggie and jutted his chin in the direction of a steamer trunk-style coffee table. "Aye, matey, I'll wager there be pieces of eight within."

She turned to shush him when a receptionist appeared behind a counter. Her face was small, nearly elfin, punctuated by frosted pink lips and eyes a shade of blue that only comes from Bausch and Lomb. A snug tank top and three-quarter-length yellow cardigan stretched across generous breasts. Mutton dressed as lamb, as Fiona would say. A placard on her desk announced her as Sylvia Marchesi.

"Hello," Sylvia said. Her voice was low and husky. "How may we help you?"

Constantine tripped over himself to extend his hand. "Hi, we're the Millers." Maggie performed an inner eye roll, annoyed and amazed that he used such an obvious movie reference. "We don't have an appointment, but a friend referred us to Mia Rennick. And since the wife and I were in the neighborhood—" Constantine put his arm around Maggie's waist, pulled her close. "—we thought, what the hell? Let's drop in and see where she tells us to park our money."

The receptionist's pink mouth went flaccid, caving in at the corners.

"I'm so sorry," she said, "but Ms. Rennick passed away. Janice McAffee has taken over her accounts. Let me buzz her."

"Passed away?" Constantine gasped. "What happened?"

"She was killed in a mugging," Sylvia half-whispered, as though the cause of death might be contagious.

"I'm so sorry to hear that," Maggie said, self-consciously touching her hat. "I'm sure she'll be missed."

Sylvia Marchesi neatened the papers on her desk.

Maggie and Constantine exchanged a look. "Yep, a lot of people will sure miss Mia," Maggie said again. She shook her head sadly. "Her friends and family must be devastated."

Sylvia began putting the now-neatened paper into piles. "Ms. Rennick didn't have much in the way of family."

Maggie clucked sympathetically. "What a loss for her friends, then."

Sylvia straightened her piles.

Maggie looked over the top of her sunglasses. "It's not a loss for her friends?"

Sylvia shrugged. "She didn't have many friends."

"Why not?"

Sylvia picked up the handset. "Let me call Ms. McAfee for you."

"You weren't friends with Mia?" Constantine asked.

Sylvia pursed her lips. "We were coworkers. Mia wasn't really the friendly type."

Constantine nodded chummily. "That's what I heard. The friend who recommended her said she was a financial whiz, but a bit of a bitch."

"Honey!" Maggie hit Constantine on the arm with a brochure about annuities. "You're being rude."

Constantine gave a rakish grin. "Sorry. Just repeating what I heard. I can't remember the details. Something about the other girls being jealous of her and..."

"That's a laugh." Sylvia replaced the handset a bit harder than necessary.

"Pardon?" Maggie said.

"It's just that no one was jealous of Mia. Mia was jealous of everyone else."

"What do you mean?" Maggie asked.

Sylvia crossed her arms over a silicone-enhanced bosom. "Okay, maybe not jealous. More like covetous. If she saw something she wanted, she'd take it, no matter who had it first. A parking place. The corner office. A boyfriend."

"She had a reputation for stealing other girls' boyfriends?" Constantine asked.

Sylvia put on a prim smile. "I'm sorry. I shouldn't have said that. Please have a seat and—"

"I worked with someone like that once," Maggie blurted. "Back in college, when I hostessed at TGI Fridays. My boyfriend was a waiter and we were practically engaged. Then this bar waitress who thought she was so hot waltzed in, and the next thing I knew, *they* were going out." Maggie swiped a finger beneath her sunglasses as if brushing away a tear. "Is that what happened to you, Sylvia? Did Mia waltz in and steal your boyfriend?"

"No." Sylvia shook her head. Tears began streaming down her face. The head shakes turned to nods. "Okay, yes. I don't know why I'm trying to protect her, why I'm trying to protect *him*. Everyone knew about it." Maggie yanked a tissue from the floral box on the treasure chest and handed it to Sylvia. "This is so embarrassing," she said, dabbing her eyes.

"The only one who should have been embarrassed is Mia."

Sylvia blew her nose. "I guess you're right. It was like a game with her. She saw Reed and decided she had to have him. He was handsome, smart. But not smart enough to realize he was just a rung on the ladder. She was clever, though, I'll give her that. Right before she died she said..." Sylvia stopped. "I shouldn't be saying all this. I'm being so unprofessional."

Maggie shook her head. "No, no. You're being honest, and that is so refreshing. Isn't it, honey?"

She looked at Constantine, who nodded vigorously. "Very refreshing."

"Get it all out, Sylvia," Maggie said. "It's all part of the healing process."

"You really think so?"

"Absolutely."

Sylvia perked up, sadness turning into delight over the chance to have an audience.

"Okay, well..." She adjusted her top. "Mia told me she had a big payday coming."

"A payday?" Constantine asked.

Sylvia shrugged. "Something to do with a guy who worked for a fancy pharmaceutical—the same pharmaceutical Mia was working with on an IPO, as a matter of fact."

"Interesting," Maggie said as casually as she could.

"That's what I thought. Then the romance with Mr. Pharmaceutical went south. No surprise considering the guy was a total creep. Always flexing his muscles, getting in your space. I got the feeling he liked to push women around." She ran a finger underneath each eye then checked it for mascara runoff. "Maybe that's why Mia dumped him. His bank account measured up, but maybe the rest of him didn't. And I'm not just talking about his personality." She caught Constantine's eye and gave him a wink.

Constantine opened his mouth but didn't say anything.

"When did she and her, um, gentleman friend break up?" Maggie asked.

Sylvia thought for a moment. "A few weeks ago? Maybe longer? But losing the boyfriend didn't seem to mean losing out. She'd come in with something new to show off nearly every day. Jewelry. Handbags. Clothing. Expensive brands, too. Someone was showering her with gifts, and it wasn't my Reed. She'd dropped Reed as soon as she realized his idea of a getaway was camping in a Winnebago, not cruising in the Bahamas. 'Course, I didn't take him back. Once burned, twice shy, I always say."

"Definitely," Maggie said. She turned toward Constantine, then back to Sylvia. "Well, we've taken up enough of your time. And we're running late for another appointment."

"Sorry, didn't mean to talk your ear off." Sylvia picked up the handset one again. "I'll buzz Ms. McAffee right now."

"That's okay," Constantine said. "We really do have to go." He selected a business card from the assembly line of holders on the counter. "We'll call her when we're back from Barcelona. We're just dashing over for a quick holiday."

Sylvia smiled warmly and sing-songed, "Have a nice day!" as Constantine held the door for Maggie.

They stepped from the air-conditioned oasis of Capital Ideas into the sweltering heat of early evening.

"Nicely done, Meryl Streep," Constantine said as they walked toward the car. "I especially liked the bit about your philandering boyfriend."

"What can I say? I was inspired by your performance as the FBI agent. Besides, I figured she'd be more willing to talk if she thought we had something in common."

"Well, I did pave the way with my implication that she was jealous. Sounds like Mia the star financial planner was good at making enemies."

"And good at advancing her own self-interests," Maggie said. "Did you catch the part about her pharmaceutical boyfriend?"

Constantine unlocked the car and they climbed in. "Think it's your pal Miles?"

Maggie pulled off her hat. "The guy works for the same pharmaceutical Capital Ideas was handling the IPO for, and he's a meathead who likes to push women around. Sounds like a fair guess."

"He sounds like the charmer you described."

Maggie felt an involuntary shiver snake up her spine. "He's worse than I described."

"Meaning?"

Maggie hugged her legs but said nothing.

"Mags?"

She shrugged and looked out the window. "Nothing. He's just bad news."

Constantine inserted the key into the ignition, but didn't turn it. He twisted his body to look at her full on. He waited.

Maggie sighed in resignation.

"Okay, I had a problem with Miles."

Constantine frowned. "What kind of problem?"

"It's no big deal," she said. She cleared her throat. "Miles just tried to..."

Maggie swallowed the lump that was growing like a cancer in her throat. She would not get emotional. She wouldn't.

Constantine reached over and touched her shoulder. "Mags?"

Maggie shook her head, and the tears streamed down her cheeks. She slapped them away. It was weak. Ridiculous. "He tried to...he almost attacked me," she finally said.

Constantine squeezed her shoulder. "Why didn't you tell me?"

She wiped her nose on the back of her hand. "I didn't tell you because *nothing happened*. Ethan came by and stopped him. Or prevented him from starting. Whatever."

Constantine withdrew his hand from her shoulder and placed it back on the steering wheel. "Ethan?"

Maggie nodded. "He made Miles go away. Not that I couldn't have done it myself. Anyway, nothing happened, so I didn't mention it. I didn't want to worry you."

Constantine turned the key. The car coughed to life. "I thought we told each other everything. I'm your best friend. Or has that title gone to someone else?"

She clenched her teeth. "Of course not." She could feel her frustration rising right along with her guilt. Why did Constantine have to make such a big deal out of Ethan? Why hadn't she told Constantine what had happened? There was plenty of blame to go around. None of it helped. None of it made her feel better. She inhaled deeply, tried to find her calm. "I'm sorry, Gus. I should have told you. I just..." She stopped, the words slipping away. "Everything has been so confusing lately. And complicated. And weird."

Constantine looked over at her. His face softened. He reached over and squeezed her hand. "Especially weird." He looked out the window. "I'm sorry, too. We seem to be saying that a lot lately."

He put the car in gear and pulled out of the parking lot. They rode in silence for several moments, then Constantine asked: "Could Miles have had something to do with Mia's death?"

"Miles is a jerk, but that doesn't make him a murderer."

"It might if the circumstances were right. Mia is handling his daddy's IPO. What if Mr. Macho wanted to flex his importance, show her what a big man he is at work and told her too much?"

Maggie nodded slowly. "Maybe the pillow talk gets too heavy,

Miles spills the beans about something at work, then decides to kill Mia so she can't talk."

"Or maybe Mia tries to play Miles as well as the market and uses what she knows to her advantage."

"Blackmail?" Maggie asked.

"The ultimate retirement plan. You heard the receptionist. No boyfriend, but the jewelry, handbags and clothes kept right on coming."

"So what's the secret?" Maggie asked. "What's so big, so bad, it's worth killing for?"

Constantine exhaled loudly. "That's the sixty-four-dollar question. The only way to find out is to find the previous owner of your phone. Or figure out how all the victims are connected. I mean, we know Elsa and Carson knew each other and that Mia Rennick was connected to Rx and Miles. And we're pretty sure Rx and Miles were up to something naughty. Are the others connected to Rx, Miles or Mia? That's what I want to know."

"So far, the search for the previous owner has net us a big fat zero. And I don't know how far we're getting trying to connect the victims. Nothing's clear yet."

Constantine raised an eyebrow. "The good news is we're not done trying."

Chapter 34

New Horizons Recovery & Shelter was a half-mile away from Capital Ideas. Housed in a converted Lutheran church, the exterior still had an ecclesiastical quality. Neat brick face. Gothic arch windows. Sky-kissing steeple. But the shelter looked uncomfortable, as if it were wearing a costume. As if hope and salvation were merely dress-up ideas.

Maggie and Constantine pulled open a heavy wooden door carved with scenes from the Old Testament and strode into a large room pebbled with round tables. Men, women and children huddled over plastic trays, mechanically shoveling colorless food into their unsmiling mouths.

A girl of about five or six stared at them intently, her arm protectively encircling a filthy stuffed pig. She kissed her pig, burying her face in the matted pink fur, then peeked at Maggie over the pig's ears. Maggie doffed her hat, lowered her sunglasses and gave her a small wave. The girl gave a sidelong glance at her mother. Satisfied that her mother was too occupied with a slice of margarine-coated white bread to notice, she waved quickly before hiding behind the pig's ears and cramming one of its worn feet into her mouth.

"Hello?"

Maggie jumped at the voice at her shoulder. She turned to a see a small older woman looking at her. "Can I help you?"

Maggie replaced her hat and smiled. "I'm Maggie and this is my friend, Constantine."

"I'm Joyce." The woman wiped her hand on the front of her apron and extended it. "Are you here to volunteer? New volunteers usually start on Wednesdays since that's typically our slowest day and I have more time to train them. Although we don't have many slow days anymore, so I guess one day's as good as another." She looked at them expectantly, her large eyes brown and watery like silt-bottom ponds stirred by a storm. When she blinked, they disappeared into the white landscape of her age-worn skin.

"Actually, we're not here to volunteer—at least not today," Constantine said. "We're hoping you can give us some information."

Joyce furrowed a brow already plowed low by time and worry. "What kind of information?"

"We understand Carson Parks used to work here?" Maggie asked.

The woman's eyes softened. "Oh, Carson. What a wonderful, wonderful young man. Yes, he worked here for several years, as a matter of fact. Unfortunately..." Her voice trailed off.

"We understand he passed away," Maggie said gently. "I'm so sorry for your loss."

Joyce sniffed. "You know, it still doesn't seem real. One day, we're working together. The next day, he's gone. Seems like that's been happening a lot these days."

"What do you mean?" Maggie asked.

Her hands fluttered. She clasped them together as if trying to corral them. "Oh, I'm just being silly. It just seems like some of my favorite people aren't around anymore."

"Like who?" Maggie prompted.

Joyce's hands took flight again. She stuffed them in her pockets. "Like I said, I'm just being silly." When neither Maggie nor Constantine said anything, she sighed. "But it's not just me. Carson noticed, too. People have been disappearing."

"But isn't there a lot of turnover here?" Constantine asked. "I would imagine your population is pretty...well, transient...for lack of a better word. Wouldn't it be typical for people to move on?"

"You'd be surprised," Joy said. "For temporary housing, it's permanent for a lot of folks. We've had people stay with us for years. Believe it or not, this is the only home some kids have ever known."

Maggie felt her cheeks flush with the unexpected shame over having enough. Enough food. Enough shelter. Enough of everything she needed. She cleared her throat. "But you noticed some residents disappearing?"

Joyce nodded. "Yes. I'm not talking about 'moving on.' I'm talking about outright vanishing. They'd go out for a smoke and just never come back. At first I thought they were going to other shelters or maybe getting lucky finding a job. When Gladys disappeared, I knew something was wrong."

Maggie and Constantine waited for Joyce to fill the empty air.

"Gladys is—was—this sweet little old gal who couldn't quite get the hang of life. Carson would help her with her medication and connect her with social services. She'd be fine for a while, live out on her own. Then she'd decide that avoiding wheat or drinking dandelion tea would accomplish the same thing as her medication, and she'd wander away. A few days later, she'd be back, confused and lost." Joyce closed her eyes. "Then one day, she tells me she's going to go for a walk and boom! She's gone. A week went by, then two. It gave me a bad feeling. I knew she'd never leave without her treasures."

"Treasures?" Constantine asked.

Joyce twisted the corner of her apron.

"An old Tupperware box that held everything she owned: a pair of red shoes, a few photographs, a pretty cut-glass candy dish. It wasn't much, but it was everything to her. She looked after it like it was her baby. I called the other shelters, the police, the hospitals—you know, thinking she was hurt or something. No one had seen her. Then I started walking the streets to see if I could find her myself." Joyce shook her head. "She was gone. Gone-*gone*. It was like she'd never existed."

"When was this?" Constantine asked.

Joyce thought a moment. "A few months ago, more or less."

"And she wasn't the only one who disappeared?" Maggie asked.

"Like I said, at first I didn't think much of it. I guess part of me hoped our regulars had found better lives. But after Gladys, I knew. Something or someone was making them vanish. I know that sounds crazy. But it was just a feeling. Over and over, they'd just disappear. The police weren't interested. No one seemed to care. Well, not nobody. Me and Carson, we cared."

"Did a man named Al ever come here?" Maggie asked. "Tall? Brown hair? Wears a necklace made of Barbie-doll heads."

Joyce nodded. "Just a couple of nights ago. He's not a regular by any means, but he'll wander in if he can't get enough to eat on the street."

"Did he stay the night?" Maggie asked.

"He said he was going to. He picked out a cot and everything." Joyce walked toward a curtain that separated the dining hall from the dormitory and parted the lank fabric. "Right over there, in the corner. He always wants his back against the wall. Lots of them do."

Maggie poked her head through the curtain's opening. The room, floored with worn vinyl, was a city all its own. Neat avenues of beds intersected alleys of sleeping bags. Coat racks scraped an interior sky painted with high-gloss enamel. Here, Collinsburg's invisible men, women and children, shoved between society's psychic cracks and mental blind spots, found shelter and refuge.

The evening was early, but many of the beds were already occupied, its residents cocooned inside the memory-blunting embrace of sleep. Some fit the mold of what Maggie envisioned when she heard the word "homeless." Most looked like faded, hollowed-out versions of the people she knew.

"We pretty much run at capacity 24/7 now," Joyce said. "Poverty has become an epidemic."

Maggie looked at her shoes, then back at the sea of cots. She stepped back and let the curtain fall. She turned toward Joyce. "Is it strange that Al didn't stay the night?"

"A little. He went out for his 'constitutional,' as he called it, and didn't come back." She frowned. "I didn't think much of it 'til just now since he's not a regular."

"He'll probably be back tonight," Maggie assured her. "Did you and Carson ever talk about the homeless disappearing from the streets?"

"Yeah, like I said, we both noticed. We both tried talking to the police, social services. Neither of us could get any traction. Most people only care about the homeless when they're in the way. Then he started talking to that newspaper woman."

Maggie pulled her phone out of her pocket. She scrolled to Elsa Henderson's obituary photograph, which she'd saved to her phone's gallery, and handed her mobile to Joyce. "Her?"

Joyce squinted at the picture. "I think so. I only saw her once, waiting in front of the shelter. He told me they were working on an article about what was happening. He hoped it would make a difference." She looked over at the curtain, now obscuring all who lay behind it. "But how do you make people care when the invisible vanishes?"

Chapter 35

Maggie and Constantine emerged from the shelter and stood blinking against the sun's glare.

"Well, that was interesting," Constantine said. "Completely depressing, but interesting. Now we know Carson and Elsa were working on a newspaper article about disappearing homeless people, and your pal Al might be one of those disappearing people. But what does that have to do with Mia and Miles and Ghana necrosis—and perhaps more importantly, you and your phone?"

"I'm not sure, but I say we go back to *The Post* and see if Al's there. If he is, maybe he'll have more to tell us about his disappearing friends and where he's been hiding himself."

"Sounds like a plan."

Constantine nosed the Datsun through the crowded streets of downtown Collinsburg, then pulled into the same parking lot Maggie had used when she'd visited *The Post*. They got out of the car and gazed across the lot at the hulking monolith. The light, soft and diffused as it filtered through the perma-smog, had turned *The Post*'s exterior into a rust color that reminded Maggie of dried blood.

"Where does Mr. Tinfoil live?" Constantine asked, jabbing down the locks and shutting his door.

"Just look for a guy with a Walkman and an appetite for doll hair."

As they approached *The Post*, Maggie peered into an adjacent alleyway furnished with garbage cans and broken pallets. She motioned Constantine to join her, and they made their way down the alley.

While the street fronting *The Post* was newly paved, crisp, the asphalt that lined the alley was brittle, crumbling beneath their feet like the broken dreams of the backstreet residents. "Al?" Maggie called as they walked. "Al?"

A few of the people living on the street, their faces creased by sun, dirt and the scythe of time, turned toward her like sunflowers following the sun. Satisfied Maggie and Constantine were neither threat nor opportunity, they turned away.

Maggie and Constantine walked the entire length of the alley. No Al.

They circled back to the front of the building and mounted gravestone-smooth stairs to the entrance.

Maggie hesitated at the door. "Maybe you should stay out here."

"You're worried I'm going to blow your cover?"

"I wouldn't want this fabulous disguise to be for nothing."

"Fine. I'll wait out here. Maybe make a new friend. That guy who chiseled his teeth into points looks friendly."

Maggie opened the door and walked toward the reception desk. Lester the security guard had been replaced by a male receptionist with a bad perm and a small, pinched face. He looked up from the book he'd half-hidden under the desk. "Can I help you?" he asked.

"Yes, I was here the other day, and when I left there was an odd man outside."

The man pursed tiny lips. "You'll have to be more specific."

"He sang into his headphone plug?" Maggie prompted. "Doll heads around his neck? He said his name was Al."

The man nodded primly. "Ah, Al. We have 'No Loitering' signs all around the exterior of the building, but do you think it does any good?" He didn't wait for her to answer. "No, it does not. They're always there, with their hands out and their 'Anything helps' signs. I don't know why they just don't go somewhere else."

"Maybe because they have nowhere else to go?" Maggie suggested.

The man waved his arms. He couldn't be bothered with little things like other people's misery. "What do you want with Al? Did he pester you? I swear, the guys on the security team are so—"

"No, no, he didn't bother me," Maggie said. "I just wanted to talk to him."

Suspicion crawled across his face. "Why?"

"I wanted to ask him a few questions about the other homeless people around here."

A light bulb in the recesses of the man's brain flickered to life. He gave the secret handshake of nods. "Oh, right," he said confidentially. "You're doing a story like Miss Henderson's. You're the new girl, right? I heard they just hired someone."

Maggie touched her sunglasses and gave a dazzling smile. "That's me."

"Why didn't you say so? We could have fast-forwarded through all that other stuff. I'm Sam, by the way."

Maggie thrust her hand over the desk. "Claire." She'd always wanted to be a Claire.

They shook. "Well." Sam sighed. "I don't know exactly what Miss Henderson was writing, but I know it was big. She always gave me a wink when she came in from interviewing...*them*." He jerked his head toward the tide of homeless people that buffeted against the building and frowned. "Like she'd gotten something good. It'd be nice if all that hard work wasn't for nothing. She was a nice lady."

"She was," Maggie agreed.

"I'm sure they'll get you all looped in about Miss Henderson." He gestured toward the elevator, the "upstairs" where the news was created and curated. "Sorry I can't help you with Al. He hasn't been around the past day or so, which is sort of strange. He's not usually the wandering-away type." He gave her a meaningful look. "Unfortunately."

"If you see him, would you mind giving me a call?" Maggie fished out a Post-it note from her purse, scribbled down her fake name and phone number and affixed it to the counter. "I, um, don't have my business cards yet."

Sam gave her a "tell me about it" look, then stuck the Post-it to his computer monitor. "No prob. Happy to help."

Maggie strode through the double glass doors.

"Well?" Constantine asked.

"Well, you can count Al among the missing homeless. And I now have double confirmation of the article Elsa and Carson were working on."

She brought him up to speed as they walked to the car.

"So we have Mia connected to Rxcellance and Elsa and Carson connected to each other," Constantine said, counting on his fingers. "But we don't know if Mia knew Elsa or Carson. Or if Elsa and Carson had any connection to Rx."

"Not yet. But we are connecting some dots." Maggie frowned. "Which is good. As long as no new dots show up."

Chapter 36

Turned out scurvy had some very serious side effects, namely serious overtime at work.

While Constantine was fake-recuperating from his faux illness, servers had crashed and mayhem was made. A phone call resulted in a deluge of pleas, a smattering of rants, promises of doughnuts and a few vague threats.

The stages of IT grief.

"Crap," he said, tossing his phone onto the denim couch.

"What?" Maggie asked. "Why does your face look like that?"

"Because I have to go into work."

Maggie felt her throat grow tight. "Tonight?"

Constantine nodded. He stripped off his shirt and walked into his bedroom. He reemerged pulling on a red and gold jersey that read Gryffindor on the front and Potter on the back. "Sorry, Mags. Duty calls. Or in this case, doody. The whole network has gone to shit, and I guess I'm up for shoveling after having the day off. If you consider a sick day a day off."

"You do realize you weren't *actually* sick, right?"

Constantine scoffed. "Yeah, but that's not the point. They want me there 'right friggin' now' in the very eloquent words of my boss." He looked at her. "You going to be okay?"

Maggie affixed her best fake smile. "Why wouldn't I be?"

He shrugged. "No reason, other than, you know, your friend being murdered and being wanted by the police and stuff."

Maggie could feel Constantine looking at her closely. She uncrossed her arms, then crossed them again. She tucked a lock of hair behind her ear. "What?"

"I love..." He hesitated. "I love having you here."

"Yeah?"

He put his hand on her back. His skin was warm through her thin cotton tank top. "Yeah. You're my favorite person in the whole wide world outside of Jessica Alba, for all the obvious reasons. And I'm glad I'm here to protect you with my sharp wit and crucial survival skills, like when to use a semicolon."

He drew her into a hug. Maggie closed her eyes. Constantine smelled like clean sheets, cheap soap and corn chips. She could feel his scratchy beard on her forehead and imagined his thick lashes closed around his dark brown eyes. His straight chin. His muscled arms pulling his shirt over his bare chest.

Maggie squirmed out of the hug and gave herself a mental slap across the face. What was the matter with her?

"I love being here, too. And not just because of the ready access to Ding Dongs. Now, go on. Go save the world from computer problems. I'll be fine."

He squinted like he was trying to read her mind. "You're sure?"

Maggie rolled her eyes. "I'm a big girl, Gus. I can take care of myself."

"I shouldn't be too long. Meanwhile..." His arms swept the room. "Make yourself at home. Mi rat hole es su rat hole."

"I appreciate that."

Maggie helped him gather his things, then pushed him out the door. She locked the deadbolt, then leaned against the chipped beige paint.

Time for a distraction.

She busied herself with making the apartment more habitable, or at least less likely to be condemned by the health department. She washed dishes. She wiped counters. She recycled, carpet-swept, stacked piles and even dusted with an old t-shirt she found balled up under the sink.

She surveyed her handiwork. "Worthless," she said to the empty room.

Sure, the apartment looked better, but what had she really accomplished? Was she any closer to finding out who had owned her phone? How Elsa, Carson and Mia were connected? What role Rx played? Who had murdered the first new friend she'd had in ten years? Maggie sank onto the couch, an unspoken *no* to her questions resounding in her ears. She closed her eyes. Thoughts thrummed through her brain, then through her blood.

Do something. Do something. Do something.

A familiar beat. One that compelled her to move.

She rose. Paced. Fished her phone out of her pocket. Caressed its blank face.

She could call Roselyn, ask her if Zartar had told her anything, find out if she knew about Rx's corporate shenanigans. But Maggie hadn't heard from Roselyn since she'd been fired (and been accused of embezzlement...and become a person of interest in Zartar's murder...and...and...and). Roselyn was probably hiding under her bed.

She hadn't talked to Ethan since she'd been fired from Rx. Since he'd promised he'd work on her behalf to restore her good standing. Since she'd been branded a crook and a possible murderess. She wondered what he thought of her. She wondered *if* he thought of her.

On impulse, she powered up the phone and dialed his number. Voicemail. Fine. Probably meant to be. The providence of phones.

Yet the urge to talk with Ethan didn't dissipate. It intensified. She suddenly felt compelled to set the record straight, to—if she was completely honest with herself—make sure he still liked her. Despite the turmoil and the danger and the heartache of the past few days, she wanted, no *needed*, the approbation of the man she liked a little too much a little too soon.

She decided she had to see Ethan, to talk with him in person. He could provide inside information, she reasoned, tell her what was going on at Rx, help her fill in the blanks of her life which was starting to feel like a crazy Mad Lib. Noun: death. Verb: run for your life.

Maggie grabbed her keys off Constantine's coffee table and headed for the door. The truth was out there. With Ethan's help, she was going to go find it.

Chapter 37

Maggie knew the Studebaker wasn't exactly low profile. If she was being watched, the vintage car was sure to give her away. But the freedom it afforded was too appealing, and she missed feeling in control, even if it was only which gear to select.

Still, she knew she had to be careful. Camouflaged by night rather than a hat and sunglasses, she parked behind a grove of trees down the street from Ethan's and approached his house on foot.

From the drive, she could see that the house was dark save for a smattering of twinkle lights that adorned an ornamental potted plant by the door. She approached the door and knocked softly. No response. Maggie closed her eyes and listened. She could hear the soft sighs of distant traffic but nothing else. She reached into her pocket and produced her phone. She dialed Ethan's home number, which went unanswered. Then his cell number. No answer. No ring from inside the house. He wasn't home. She'd have to wait.

Maggie plunked down in front of the door. She shoved her phone back into her pocket and put her hands in her lap. Stared into the night. It seemed to stare right back.

She wriggled against the door as if trying to disappear into the wood. She felt exposed. Vulnerable. In danger. Waiting in the open for Ethan was starting to feel like a bad idea.

Maybe she should wait in his house for him. He wouldn't mind. In fact, he'd probably insist on it.

Maggie tried the door handle. Locked. She reached under the welcome mat, palpating the pavers in search of a key. Nothing.

She considered a terracotta planter stuffed with a pink-lipped hibiscus. She tipped it, felt beneath, then restored it to its upright position and moved her hand inside the earth-clotted rim. Maggie's fingertips brushed against something hard and small. She grasped the object and exhumed it. A key.

Maggie wiped the key on her shorts, then inserted it into the front door's lock. She turned the key. The door swung open.

Maggie winced, half-expecting the bleat of an alarm to attack her ears and batter the night's still air. But there was nothing except the sound of blood rushing through her ears. Maggie stepped inside and carefully closed the door. "Ethan?" she whispered. "Ethan, are you here?"

She wasn't sure why she called his name. Even less sure why she whispered.

She walked through the foyer, moving past the chair where she'd waited for Ethan to get out of the shower. Past the kitchen where they'd drunk wine. Past the couch she'd leaned on when Ethan kissed her.

She found herself in Ethan's home office and surveyed her surroundings. An oversized desk with massive morgue-like drawers held court. She plunked into the chair that sat imperiously before it and waited.

Minutes crept by. She raised and lowered the chair. She spun around like when she was a kid.

She stopped mid-spin. Something had caught her eye.

A silver-hued picture frame, facedown on the desk.

Curious, Maggie reached for the frame. Her fingers hovered over its black velvet back as questions fired inside her brain. Why had it been turned over? What was on the other side? Had it toppled accidentally or been purposely placed? Would it be wrong to turn it over, to take a tiny peek?

The answer to this last one was clear. It was wrong to let herself into Ethan's house, even more wrong to snoop through his things. But Maggie didn't care. She had to know.

Maggie turned the frame over. Ethan, dressed in a blue suit and red-striped power tie, grinned back, his handsome face animated in a candid, mid-laugh shot. He was in the center of a three-person group hug, one arm slung casually over the shoulder of a man, the other around the sequined waist of a woman.

Maggie squinted. The man beside Ethan was Miles, who looked more human and less roidy than usual.

The woman was Mia Rennick.

Maggie's mouth went dry. Ethan knew Mia. Was friends with her. Was friends with Miles, for God's sake.

Her mind rewound to Ethan's denial that he knew Mia. To his suggestion that he despised Miles. To the GN file in his bag. To his secret meeting with Zartar.

It was all so clear. She'd been so stupid. Ethan had been lying almost since the moment she'd met him.

Maggie's intestines cramped, sending a wave of pressure through her abdomen. She felt sick. Sick with grief over the loss of her friend. Sick with betrayal. Sick with fear that she'd very possibly wandered into the lion's den.

She now knew that Ethan couldn't be trusted. She wondered what other secrets he'd been keeping.

She reached for the desk drawer. Then stopped herself. She should have brought gloves. Isn't what they did in the countless movies she watched? She looked despairingly at her traitorous fingerprints. She considered dish gloves from the kitchen. Too cumbersome. Too slippery. Too ridiculous. She decided to leave her hands naked. The chances of anyone fingerprinting Ethan's home was remote, and it wasn't like hers were on file. She'd have to just go for it.

Maggie took a breath and eased open the top right drawer. It was so big she half-expected to see a toe tag instead of the usual cache of pens, paperclips and stamps in the enormous compartment. She rifled through the assortment of office odds and ends. She found nothing.

She reached her hand farther into the drawer's gaping maw, clutched the flotsam within and pulled. She came up with a few sheets of scrap paper and some address labels.

Maggie returned the items to the drawer and closed it. She eased open the remaining desk drawers and gingerly picked her way through garbage masquerading as mail. Nothing interesting.

She surveyed the room, then turned her attention to the computer, the modern-day filing cabinet.

She wiggled the computer mouse that crouched atop an Rxcellance mouse pad and awakened the computer. She scanned the computer's desktop. Where to begin? She double-clicked the Outlook icon.

Ethan's email opened to reveal an electronic cornfield, rows and rows of folders in which nearly anything could hide. Maggie clicked the folder labeled Rx. It opened, revealing a dozen more folders inside. One stood out immediately.

MAGGIE

The words seemed to leap at her from the screen. She pointed, clicked. An hourglass appeared. She felt like Dorothy in the Wicked Witch's lair. Cue the flying monkeys.

Finally, the folder opened. At the top of the email history, illuminated in the blue-white light of the monitor, was an email containing the digital Trojan horse that had infected her work computer.

His betrayal had gone beyond the pilfered GN file, his denial he knew Mia Rennick, his covert friendship with Miles. He set her up to look like the company mole. He had stood by, his face drawn by false confusion and manufactured concern, while James Montgomery crucified her.

The depth of his deceit ripped through Maggie like a bullet.

She buried her head in her hands. Why did he do it? Why had he trampled the relationship that seemed to be growing between them?

The answer forced its way past Maggie's denial, glimmering in the half-light of Ethan's study.

There was nothing between them. He didn't care for her. He didn't want her. He was just using her, and she had been so hungry for the attention of this handsome, successful, charming man, she ignored every red flag and turned a blind eye to every warning sign.

Was she that desperate to shrug off the mantle of nerdy bookishness that had relegated her to science fair maven instead of homecoming queen? Was she that determined to become desirable girlfriend rather than smart and funny gal pal? Or was she simply blinded by the possibility of love—or, at the very least, infatuation?

Maggie was pretty sure she knew the answer, but didn't have time to psychoanalyze herself. The point was Ethan wanted her out of Rx, plain and simple. She needed to know why.

Maybe it was because Zartar had told her about Ghana necrosis.

Or maybe it was because Zartar was on the brink of telling her more.

Maggie skimmed the other email folders for more evidence. She found nothing else and quickly guided the cursor to the computer's hard drive. She was sure it was the burial ground of Ethan's deepest secrets.

Maggie found a folder titled GHANA NECROSIS saved to the computer's hard drive. She opened it. Inside it contained scores of files.

The data swam in front of her. She knew it was important, perhaps the key to all that was going on. But she couldn't go over it here. She'd already spent far too long in Ethan's house. She needed time to review, space to digest.

She'd have to take it with her.

Maggie looked around the office. On a built-in bookcase, sandwiched between a framed diploma from Columbia and a rugby trophy (damn it, Constantine had been right about that, too) stood a lonely pile of electronic media storage devices. A single thumb drive roosted atop a nest of CDs.

Maggie grabbed the thumb drive and pushed it roughly into the machine. Her fingers tap-danced across the keyboard as she copied the folder's contents—memos, reports, photographs—onto the portable storage device.

Maggie had just opened a file titled PROTOCOL when she heard the jangle of keys at the front door. Had the computer keys been loud enough to mask a car pulling into the driveway? Adrenaline shot through her nervous system. She held her breath, right hand frozen in mid-click, and listened.

Outside, keys dropped onto the porch. Ethan swore under his breath.

Maggie imagined Ethan outside the front door, stooping, scooping up his keys, fumbling for the lock. She knew he was almost inside.

Fifty steps and a handful of seconds separated Maggie from the man who betrayed her. From the man who could be planning to end her.

Maggie began frantically copying the contents of the Ghana necrosis and Protocol folders onto the thumb drive, praying the computer wouldn't decide to bomb and drag her into its digital collateral damage.

Hurry! her mind screamed. *He's coming!*

The status bar moved like honey on a winter morning. Maggie wanted to pound on the machine, to implore it to go faster. *Faster!* But she sat quiet as a stone, listening. Waiting.

The sound of key grating against lock floated to the office. Then the *whoosh-click-clunk* of a door opening, closing. Locking.

Hard-soled shoes beat across polished wood floors, harmony to the keyboard melody that still echoed in her head. House keys jangled as they hit the entry table.

Maggie dragged her eyes from the office door to the computer screen. The status bar had vanished, signaling that the transfer was complete. Maggie yanked out the thumb drive and clicked the Microsoft Windows icon. She selected Sleep and held her breath, silently urging the machine to execute the task without a jaunty electronic jingle. Silence.

God bless Bill Gates.

Maggie crept to the window, twisted its lock open and pushed. It stuck. She pushed again. Something in her shoulder tore. The window remained unmoved.

Biting her lip against the pain, Maggie squatted low and repositioned her body to improve her leverage. She pushed hard, using her back against the frame.

The window inched upward then suddenly gave way, shooting to the top of the casing.

Maggie clamped her hands to her mouth to stifle a yelp and stood motionless, trying to gauge how much noise the window had made. Straining to hear the heavy footfalls that she was sure would approach the door.

Yet Ethan didn't come charging in to inspect the source of the noise. No alarms howled. No attack dogs came charging in. The hall was silent and empty. Maybe the movement had been more felt than heard. Or perhaps Ethan was too engrossed in reviewing recipes from *Bon Appétit* to hear anything above the turn of each glossy page as he considered what to prepare for dinner.

Maggie put one leg through the window, ducked, brought the other leg through. She began to close the window when she saw Ethan's old lanyard hanging on a drawer pull.

The lanyard was a vestige from his pre-managerial days. Like the pizzeria's first dollar, framed and displayed proudly above Pop's ancient cash register, it was a reminder of where he had started and how far he had come.

Maggie wondered if the ID card still worked as a passkey. She decided she'd have to find out. She scrambled back through the window and reached for the shiny plastic rectangle dangling on the drawer pull. She had the sensation that she was a fish being lured by something shiny, something tantalizing, and would soon be reeled in.

Surely he'd miss his passkey. Surely he'd notice its absence and look for other signs of disarray, of intrusion. The desk. The computer.

Yet Ethan hadn't missed the folder Maggie had plucked from his bag. And the ID hanging from the desk was old, outdated. He didn't need it anymore. Perhaps he wouldn't notice its absence. It was a chance she had to take.

Maggie grabbed the lanyard and hung it around her neck like an Olympic medal. Maggie O'Malley takes the gold in Burglary.

From the kitchen, Ethan's enormous refrigerator door closed with an authoritative click. The light strains of Dvorak and the clatter of pots and pans sailed down the hall.

Then a new sound.

The bicycle bell of her phone slicing the silence.

Maggie flinched, whacking her hand on the top of the drawer. She yanked her hand back as if bitten by some unseen animal and crushed the phone's volume key in one deft maneuver. She froze, her nervous system in overdrive, and strained to hear if she'd been detected. She heard only her own breathing, ragged and uneven. Eaten away by fear.

She listened again for Ethan's imminent arrival, the moment she'd be caught. Or worse.

She knew she should run, put as much distance between her and Ethan as possible, but she was rooted to the spot by tendrils of fear that seemed to bind her to the floor.

Her heart ripped in her chest as she considered Ethan down the hall and the phone in her hand.

Bicycle bell = reminder app = next victim

Maggie turned the phone's screen to face her, fear and dread coming in twin waves. *Please no. Please no more. Please not Roselyn.*

She was shaking so hard she couldn't control her hand and had to try multiple times to swipe the display into life. Finally, a photo appeared. She peered into the face of the secondhand phone.

Her own face, fresh and full of hope on her first day of work, gazed back.

Chapter 38

Maggie clutched the lanyard at her neck and slithered back through the window. She ran down the drive, frantically clicking the reminder for the date and time as her feet threatened to tangle beneath her.

Nothing.

Maggie kept running, willing her legs to move fluidly, reliably, as if she were just on another jog. She was nearly to the Studebaker when her phone vibrated. She started, nearly skidding on the gravel and into a street sign. She swallowed and looked at the display, certain it was the face of the unknown killer calling to confirm her appointment with death.

Hi, I'm your personally assigned murderer. I just wanted to be sure I could reach you.

Instead Constantine's photograph filled the screen.

Maggie answered, the words tumbling out before Constantine could say hello. "I'm next on the list. I'm next to die."

"Mags, what are you talking about?"

"The reminder. I just got another one. It's me. My face was on the reminder app."

A stunned silence hung between them.

"You're on the reminder app?"

Maggie clenched her teeth, biting back the sob that was building in her throat. "Yes. I'm next to die. To be run over or bludgeoned or carved into tiny pieces."

"Easy, Maggie. We don't know that—"

"Of course we do," she snapped. "We know exactly what happens to people who appear on this app. They die. More specifically, they're *murdered.*"

"Where are you?" he asked, his voice thin and high with worry.

"I'm at Ethan's."

A pause. "Ethan's?"

She closed her eyes. "It's a long story. The point is Ethan was friends with Mia. He knew about the Ghana necrosis treatment. He's helping Rx hide another secret. And the virus that got me fired came from his computer."

"Holy…" Constantine breathed. "I'm so sorry, Mags."

"You're not going to gloat that you were right about Ethan?" she asked softly. "Say 'I told you so' and tell me about your superior ability to judge character? He even played rugby."

"I know how you felt about him. How much you must be hurting. I would never want to add to that."

Love and gratitude and shame swelled inside Maggie. A symphony of emotion. Basket Case in D Minor. "Thank you," she whispered.

"Are you driving the Studebaker?"

She nodded, knowing he couldn't see her yet somehow certain he could sense her doing so. "I didn't think the bus went out here, and I wanted the freedom of having my car. But I was careful."

"Come home, Mags. Come home now."

Maggie sped to Constantine's. Every shadow was someone following. Every sound, the whoosh before a crowbar struck or a blade plunged.

By the time she knocked on Constantine's door, her skin was shiny with perspiration.

He opened the door and she dashed inside, bolted the door. She had begun shaking uncontrollably. She felt like she was going to be sick. The words came rushing out, jumbling together, running over each other. "They're going to kill me. They're going to find me and they're going to kill me, just like they did the others."

He folded her into a hug. "That's not going to happen."

"No?" She shook him off and paced the room, combing her fingers through her hair, mashing it into a bun, letting it fall again. "Am I luckier than Elsa Henderson? Smarter than Carson? Better than Zartar? What makes me so special?"

"What makes you special? Everything, for starters. And for specifics: what you know and what you're about to know. So let's prove that whole knowledge-is-power thing, find out what they've done and figure out how we're going to stop them."

Maggie reached into her pocket and pulled out the thumb drive. "Let's start here."

They sat. Constantine booted up his laptop, inserted the drive then angled the machine toward Maggie. She opened the Ghana necrosis file. They scanned the text in silence. "Not much here I didn't already know from Zartar," she said.

Constantine nodded. "Same conspiracy, different day."

"Let's see if we have any luck here." She closed the file and opened the folder titled PROTOCOL. She read silently. Soon, she was engrossed, opening folder after folder, scrolling through page after page, the skin tenting between her eyes as she frowned in concentration

"I know that look," Constantine said. "You found something."

She nodded. "I did. But it's complicated."

"Then talk slow."

She took a deep breath. "Well, in a nutshell, when new chemical entities—NCEs, for short—show promising activity against a certain biological target, researchers begin trials to assess stuff like the toxicity, pharmokinetics and metabolism of the NCE. They start using isolated cells, then move to experimental animals. If everything looks good at the preclinical testing stage, the data is submitted to the FDA. If the feds think it looks good, an application for the NCE to become an 'investigational new drug' is approved, and clinical trials on humans begin."

"Okay, talk faster. I know all that."

"Then you probably also know these tests are conducted according to a predetermined protocol."

"Right," he answered. "To make sure the guinea pigs—I mean the *trial participants*—are not exposed to health risks and that the studies are scientifically valid."

Maggie nodded. "Exactly. A protocol outlines who may participate in the trial, the schedule of tests, procedures and medications, how the participants' health will be monitored and how the data will be collected, analyzed and shown to be a success. Or not, as the case may be. And most of them, by the way, aren't." She grabbed a pillow from the couch and hugged it. "Out of ten thousand NCEs, only, say, ten will make it to human clinical trials. And of those, only a fraction will make it to market."

Constantine pantomimed a rapper counting out from his fat stacks of cash. "Sounds spendy."

"It is. Which is why companies like Rx prefer to create variations on already successful drugs. And why the new herpes drug that also treats Ghana necrosis will only see the light of day as a *new-and-maybe-improved* herpes med. Or even more likely, as a skin-firming agent."

"That's nuts."

"That's business, as Zartar would say. And she'd be right." A lump pushed its way into Maggie's throat as she thought about her friend. The tough girl who took Maggie under her Bedazzled wing, doling out lipstick and clothes and advice like a surrogate sister to a motherless child. "The truth is, despite efforts to eradicate NTDs and instituting so-called 'orphan drug' initiatives, poverty is a disease that's easy to ignore. I'm starting to think the GN treatment isn't what Rx is so desperate to hide."

"Then what?"

Maggie tapped the keyboard and scrolled. "According to these documents, a universal flu vaccine. People poo-poo the flu, but it kills tens of thousands every year—in the United States alone. A vaccine that stopped multiple strains year after year would be—"

"The next best thing to a cure for cancer. Or close to it."

Maggie felt a pang, a momentary twinge that always struck when she thought of cancer. Like amputees who felt phantom pain or sensation in limbs lost to war or disease or accident, Maggie would always hurt a little, bleed a little, where her mother had been excised from her life.

"This must be what Montgomery senior was hinting at when he announced the IPO to the staff. He said there was a new miracle under development, something that would eliminate a disease and save lives."

Constantine disappeared into the kitchen and returned with two cups. He handed her one.

"Wouldn't a vaccine like that be a good thing?"

"A truly universal flu vaccine would be great—revolutionary, even. In time, it has the potential to save millions worldwide. But something's not right. A lot of somethings. Check this out."

Constantine scanned the document on-screen and shrugged. "Looks like an electronic invoice for a vendor." He squinted at the machine. "A research organization to do some work on contract."

"Did you notice the name of the vendor?"

Constantine's eyes fell to the bottom of the page. "Holy shit. MediPrixe."

"There's more."

"I love more."

Maggie closed the document and opened three more. She scrolled as Constantine looked on.

"There's tons of data here about the vaccine under development, and everything seems pretty buttoned up until you get to the trial protocol." She jumped to a new page. "The trial began in Mexico, then was halted and moved to a new site with no explanation."

"Can't be the first time that's happened."

"No," Maggie admitted. "And it's not necessarily the kiss of death if a trial is put on hold or moved to a new location, especially if it's a multisite trial. But there's no indication of why the trial was stopped and moved. And there's not one iota of data from the trial itself."

"Strange. You said it was conducted in Mexico?"

"Yeah. I'm not sure where. Let's see..." She scanned the document, then froze. "Gus, the trial took place in Dolores Hidalgo."

Chapter 39

Constantine's face clouded over as he worked to connect the name with files stored in his memory bank. "Dolores Hidalgo?" The clouds broke. "As in 'Dolores has been taken care of'?"

"It has to be. Dolores isn't a person. It's a place. The remnant text Travis found must be related to this test site. Something went wrong with the trial in Dolores Hidalgo, and they pulled the plug. 'Took care of it.'"

"Think this is the fan-hitting shit Zartar hinted at?"

Maggie grabbed her phone. "I don't know, but I'm going to try to find out. You see if you can find out any more online. I'll call Dan."

"Ah, yes. Mr. FDA. I guess if anyone has any outside insights, it'd be him."

Constantine steered the laptop toward himself. Maggie walked into Constantine's tiny kitchen and dialed, praying Dan didn't watch the news or hear about her alleged involvement in Zartar's death. Dan answered on the sixth ring.

"Hope I didn't catch you at a bad time," Maggie said.

Dan laughed, sounding totally normal. She guessed he didn't watch the news. No surprise there. He didn't seem to pay attention to anything outside the lab or his office. "It's never a bad time to hear from my favorite prodigy. How goes it at ye olde new job?"

Maggie put on her breeziest voice. "It's good." *I was set up to look like a company mole, had drugs planted in my desk, got fired and found one of my coworkers murdered.* "Yep, real, real good. But I have another little mystery I thought you could help me solve."

"Absolutely. How can I help?"

She toyed with a kitchen towel imprinted with a *Doctor Who* TARDIS. "Do you know anything about Rx using a company called MediPrixe as a contractor for clinical trials?"

There was a pause as he considered this. "I can't say I've ever heard of a 'MediPrixe.' Or of Rx using trial contractors, for that matter. Why do you ask?"

Maggie sighed and let the ragged towel fall from her fingertips. "Oh, I came across an old vaccine trial that MediPrixe administered. It looks like the trial was never completed at its location in Mexico, and I can't find any actual data about the trial itself. I don't know if the data was misplaced, if the trial failed and moved or if the NCE made its way to the FDA and got stalled there. I'm hoping you can fill in the blanks. It's related to a new discovery I'm working on. Seems like anyone who knows anything is out of the office."

Out of the office. Dead. Tomato. Tomahto.

"Honestly, none of that sounds familiar. But the FDA is a big beast, so that's no big surprise. Do you have a New Drug Application number?"

"No. My information is a little...spotty."

"No worries," Dan said jovially. "I'll see what I can do and call you if I find anything. You're at work today?"

"I'm actually not at the office today. If you could call my cell that would be great."

"Will do, mildew. Talk soon."

Maggie thanked him and hung up. She was grateful for his time, but couldn't help feeling deflated. It was another dead end. She walked into the living room and plunked down beside Constantine. "He didn't know anything about it. Hadn't heard of MediPrixe, didn't know about an Rx vaccine trial that was abandoned. He said he'd look into it, though. Hopefully he'll find something useful before it's—"

She couldn't bring herself to say "too late," but the unsaid was already gaining power. She'd been so preoccupied by the possibility of finding answers in Ethan's files that she'd been able to avoid what the phone's app had foretold. She'd put it into the basement where all the other things she hid from herself lived. Now she felt it stir. Growing hungry.

"Aw, don't look so glum, chum," Constantine said. "I struck gold on my internet mining expedition while you were talking to Professor Pastel."

Maggie hopped onto her knees, threw her arms around Constantine's neck and planted a kiss on his cheek. "Constantine, you beautiful genius, you. Tell me everything."

Constantine looked at the floor and rubbed the back of his neck, which glowed red. "Well, don't get too excited. I haven't filled in all of the details yet."

As Constantine turned the laptop toward Maggie, a soft thud sounded from outside the window.

Maggie's heart jumped. She looked at Constantine. He raised his eyebrows. Another thump, something loud and heavy against the house, vibrated through Maggie. Maggie felt her eyes grow wide and her pulse quicken. Had she allowed herself to be followed? Had she been so careless that she had put both herself and Constantine in harm's way? She opened her mouth to say something and emitted a raspy squeaking sound like a bicycle tire losing air.

Constantine put his forefinger to his lips. He slid to the floor and crawled across the stained carpet toward the window. He crouched beside the painted wooden frame, then slid the curtain away from the window just enough to expose a sliver of glass. He peered outside.

He turned toward Maggie with one eyebrow raised.

"What is it?" she whispered.

"Probably the neighbor's dog," he whispered back. He hitched his thumb toward the door, signing that he'd go check it out.

Maggie felt her heart jump again. Her whole body flinched as if she'd been jumpstarted by a defibrillator. "Constantine, no," she hissed. She shook her head emphatically.

"Shhh," he whispered back. "You don't want Fido to hear you. He's hated me since I moved in, probably because I peed on his tree." He sprung to his feet. "I'll be right back."

Maggie watched Constantine ease the door closed behind him. She stared at it, wondering what was on the other side. Was it really the neighbor's dog, nosing through trash left to decay during the sanitation strike? Or was it a ruse, a ploy to lure Constantine out into the open so he could be eliminated as a barrier to the killer's next target?

Constantine's sneakered feet whispered down the stairs. She

murmured a silent prayer, the thousandth she'd said since Zartar's murder, promising reform, piety—anything—for Constantine's safe return.

The minutes ticked by. Maggie slid the curtains to peer outside. Nothing moved but the tops of the trees, which swayed to the silent music of the wind. She sat back down and chewed her lip.

Moments later, the knob turned. Maggie held her breath. A dribble of sweat snaked down her back. The killer had found her. He'd followed her, bided his time, then lured Constantine out into the night so she'd be alone, vulnerable, trapped.

She tensed, ready to run or hide or fight back. The door swung wide. Constantine traipsed in humming "Goodnight, Ladies."

Maggie released the breath she was holding.

"It was Fido. Guess someone had put some questionable chicken into the trash. He thought he'd won the jackpot." He pulled off his shoes and socks and jumped onto the couch beside Maggie. "Did you read what I had on-screen?"

"No, I was too busy worrying about you."

"Moi?" Surprise touched his eyes. "Really? Well, don't. Worrying about *you* is my job."

His eyes held hers for a moment, then dropped to the laptop, a fringe of black lashes like crescents on his cheekbones. She was sure he was blushing again.

"Back to Dolores Hidalgo," he said. "The short story is that MediPrixe went to Dolores with lots of money and even more swagger. They opened shop in one of the local clinics and told the residents they wanted to help them live longer, healthier lives and help them stave off dangerous flu strains—indefinitely."

"Wow. Nice job, Sherlock." She grabbed a handful of peanuts from the Spock-shaped bowl on the coffee table and eased back against the cushions, a facsimile of relaxation manufactured to convince herself she was fine. That everything was going to be fine. "What happened?"

"A little thing called informed consent."

"Ooh."

"And a bigger thing called people dying."

"Oh, no."

"Oh, yes," Constantine said. "I think this part of the program calls for fortification."

He walked to the kitchenette, pulled out a bottle of Irish whiskey from the cupboard and poured it, and his signature rotgut coffee, into mugs. He returned and placed the mugs on the coffee table. "At first MediPrixe could say, 'Old Gramps was too frail and elderly. That's why he kicked off.' But then it got harder to explain when Mom died and then little brother."

"Oh my God." Maggie's head hurt even more as she tried to assimilate the information. Entire families destroyed by the very thing that was supposed to save them. "What did they die from?"

"Besides the natural causes they told the families? Pneumonia."

"And people kept participating in the study? Kept...*dying*?"

"It took some time for people to make the connection. There were assurances from the company that the deaths were coincidental or bad luck. When that stopped working, the incentives began. Money to locals for participating. Bribes to government officials for looking the other way." He grabbed his mug, slurped the Irish coffee, then stared into the cup for a few moments before returning it to the coffee table. "Finally, the wrong person died: the wife of the mayor. And that, as they say, was the end of that."

"What happened?"

Constantine laced his fingers behind his head. "MediPrixe was escorted out of town by the local 'peacekeepers,' armed to the teeth and mad as hell. MediPrixe paid them off, lucky to get their crew out alive."

Maggie shook her head. "Sounds bad." The power of understatement. The whole thing sickened and infuriated her. "And you got all of this off the internet? In just a few minutes?"

"Most of it from local news stories, plus a few from blog entries. I was an Evelyn Woods speed-reading graduate."

"But why would MediPrixe, and Rx, for that matter, engage in such obviously illegal conduct in order to test this vaccine? I don't know anything about MediPrixe, but Rx is on the brink of an IPO. Why would they take these kinds of risks?"

"Money? Not very original, but very popular. Maybe they didn't want to spend a lot to test it, or lose their shirts if the vaccine turned out to be unsafe."

Maggie sighed. "I guess. The truth is that it's getting harder and harder to find participants for some of these trials. The pool is small and, depending on what the study is for, can become even smaller when we add in demographics, combinations of disease characteristics, et cetera. If we're talking Phase II trials, they'd need hundreds of people. Sometimes the greatest barrier to completing the study is the shortage of human subjects."

Maggie grabbed her mug and took a swig. "So MediPrixe and Rx banked on a lack of informed consent to conduct a clinical trial on the cheap. A problem came to light, and they tried to come up with a solution. But things went south in Dolores and they couldn't continue there. So they moved."

Constantine raised his eyebrows. "Where?"

"Somewhere they could continue to fly under the radar. Right in plain sight."

Chapter 40

Constantine looked at her, waiting. "More under the radar than Dolores Hidalgo, Mexico?"

"You found out what happened on the internet, didn't you?"

"Well, yeah, but I'm a genius. A *beautiful* genius."

"What if they decided it was easier to hide behind *who* they were testing rather than where?"

"Okay, you lost me."

Maggie felt her breath quicken, the tickle-prickle of hair rising on the back of her neck as an idea flowered in her mind. "What if they selected a group of people that wasn't exactly credible—not only because of economic status, but because they're branded as erratic—even crazy?"

Constantine polished off his Irish coffee and walked into the kitchenette. Maggie followed him. He opened the refrigerator and placed packages of deli ham and Swiss cheese, a loaf of Wonder bread and a jar of Miracle Whip on the counter, then looked at her quizzically. "I assume you're *not* talking about Congress?"

"I'm talking about the homeless. More specifically, homeless people suffering from severe, untreated mental illness." She opened the bag of Wonder, took out four slices and began slathering the bread with the slightly gelatinous condiment. "Think about it. Rx could keep their eye on the trials, make adjustments as needed in the lab. And not have to worry about anyone—or anyone *sane*—complaining about violating their rights."

Constantine shook his head. "I dunno, Mags. The Dolores Hildago testing sounded a little *Constant Gardener*-y. This sounds impossible."

"Not at all. And it wouldn't be the first time this kind of thing has happened. I took an ethics in pharmaceuticals class from Dan in college. It covered all kinds of stuff: laws governing the industry, treatment of patients. And unethical practices in the past."

"The dark ages of pharmaceuticals?" Constantine stacked the ham and Swiss over the Miracle Whip and handed Maggie a sandwich.

"Yeah, only it wasn't exactly in medieval times. Playing fast and loose with informed consent still happens. A few years ago, a pharmaceutical needed a human trial for approval for a new antibiotic. They went to a small African village and set up a tent near a medical station where doctors were treating people for cholera. The pharmaceutical got two hundred kids to participate in the trial without consent of any kind on a drug that had shown problems in animal testing." She turned and faced Constantine. "Some kids died. Others suffered brain damage."

Constantine gave a low whistle. "Nice business you're in, Mags."

"That's the exception, not the rule. But there's more. As late as the 1990s, people suffering from mental illness were forced to take part in drug trials. Many of them were in prison. Some were in institutions. Most were also poor and minorities. These practices were later condemned as immoral and inhumane, and laws were put in place to protect trial participants. But as the African village debacle shows, not everyone plays by the rules."

Constantine took a giant bite of his sandwich. "So you're thinking Rx goes abroad to play fast and loose with testing protocols. When the good people of Dolores Hidalgo realize the potential cure was worse than the actual disease, Rx moves on to a new group to exploit."

"Exactly," she said with her mouth half-full. "Rx wouldn't have to worry about pesky details like informed consent or ethical practices. They could steamroll, intimidate, fool or cajole their new subjects into participating."

"But not everyone who is homeless suffers from mental illness," Constantine pointed out.

"True," Maggie replied. "And only a small portion of those with mental illness have delusions or hallucinations or thought disorders. But..." She licked a glob of mayo from the corner of her mouth. "Nearly 25 percent of those who are homeless do have acute, untreated mental illness, including psychotic disorders. It's a vulnerable group, ripe for exploitation. I mean, who are the authorities going to believe: the homeless guy convinced that the FBI installed a camera in his cardboard TV, or the stuffed shirts at your friendly, neighborhood pharmaceutical?"

"It is the perfect setup," Constantine admitted. "No limits. No questions. No autopsies if the test subjects die. No one to believe them if they don't."

Maggie wiped her hands on her shorts. "And it fits with Joyce's disappearing residents, Al's account of people being lured away never to be seen again, even what that strange old woman at Carson's funeral said."

"The one you had the nice chat with?"

"I realized the shirt I wore to the funeral had an Rx logo embroidered on the pocket. She must have seen that, and it set her off."

Constantine chewed, considering that. He set his plate on the counter and folded his arms across his chest. "So we have ties with Elsa, Carson, Al, the homeless shelters and the former Miss America from Carson's funeral," Constantine said. "How does Mia fit in?"

"Mia knew the Montgomerys professionally and Miles personally. My guess is that Miles told Mia about the flu vaccine they were developing in order to inflate the company's value."

"Classic 'pump and dump' IPO scheme," Constantine said with his mouth full.

"Never heard of it, but okay. I think Mia found out the vaccine had problems. She figured Rx would want to bury the damning data before the IPO. And voila: a blackmailer is born."

"Guess Rx didn't count on Miles not being able to keep his mouth—or his pants—zipped."

"Or on anyone noticing this invisible population vanishing," Maggie said. She picked at her thumbnail. "Once Rx got wind of Elsa's and Carson's story, they made sure they'd never tell."

"So Rx put Elsa's, Carson's and Mia's last days on the calendar and sent reminders to a hit man to ensure they'd meet with death. So to speak."

"Looks like it," Maggie said.

"So who sent the video of Mia's murder to me? And why?"

Constantine stared at the sink. Silent. Thinking. "I'm not sure, but my money's still on the cloud. The more pressing question is what we should do next. I mean, other than reporting Rx to the Better Business Bureau."

Maggie grabbed an old Burger King plastic cup from the counter, filled it from the tap, took a drink, then tossed it into the sink. The plastic landed with a loud clunk in the stainless steel basin. "I know what we do next. We pay them a visit."

Chapter 41

"Do you want to get the straightjacket or should I?"

"Okay, maybe it's a little nuts. But so is waiting around for someone to kill you."

"A little nuts? Try a lot. You'll be walking into the lion's den, and I don't think you'll have Daniel's luck. In fact—"

"You have a better idea?" Maggie looked at Constantine. She could see herself reflected in the liquid chocolate of his eyes: arms across her chest, pointed chin thrust upward. A challenge.

Constantine was quiet a moment, then shook his head. "No, no. Just checking. I think it sounds quite sensible. Although we could wait. I forgot to mention the previous owner of your phone clicked through that fake email we set up."

"What? Why didn't you tell me?"

"I got kind of distracted by the threat to your life. Anyway, the IP address he was using is allocated to a local internet service provider, which happens to employ a very good friend of mine. He's going to do some digital digging and let me know who the IP address belongs to. All we have to do is wait."

"We don't have the luxury of waiting." She walked to the back of the kitchen, where a key rack shaped like a zombie's hand perched above a tiny microwave. She plucked the keys from the zombie's middle finger and dropped them into Constantine's hand. "Let's roll."

Constantine parked a block away from Rx beneath a willow that seemed to suckle the earth with its sagging branches. They walked silently to the Rx complex, hoping for nonchalance but feeling ridiculously conspicuous in the head-to-toe black they'd picked up at a sporting goods store.

The gate to the Rx entrance was locked with an electronic arm that looked more suitable for an Eastern European military base than an American corporation. Fortunately, it wasn't hard to squeeze by. Maggie slipped beside the metal arm. "The gate's really just a suggestion," she whispered to Constantine.

"I've heard you say the same thing about stoplights," he hissed back.

Maggie waved him on. He gave an "okay already" wave back and jogged to join her. Maggie walked toward the main building, head held high and with an air of *I Belong Here* accented with a dash of *Don't Screw With Me or I'll Have Your Job.* Constantine walked behind her, eyes scanning for the security guard Maggie said patrolled the grounds after dark.

No one stopped them. Two minutes after they'd stepped on hallowed pharmaceutical ground, Maggie and Constantine beeped themselves into the employee entrance using the ID keycard Maggie had stolen from Ethan's study.

The door whispered closed behind them. Constantine stuffed his hands into his pockets and looked around. "Nice. Like a mausoleum, except not as cheerful."

Refrigerated under the blast of air conditioning and devoid of the heat of humanity, the walls of Rx HQ had grown icy. There was no sound other than the low but insistent hum of crucial equipment kept alive by electronic life support.

Maggie's nose wrinkled. The smell of antiseptic, so familiar, so clean, now seemed deceitful, designed to conceal the smell of putrefaction. She breathed through her mouth.

They walked noiselessly down the hall, new rubber-soled shoes— 50 percent off at the sporting goods store—gliding over polished institutional flooring. They reached the hall's terminus and took the stairs to the second floor.

The laboratories branched off the main corridor, capillaries fed by the arterial flow of workers streaming in to deliver rich, oxygenated ideas. Maggie bypassed the lab where she had worked and led Constantine to a set of three doors at the end of the hall. She gave

Constantine a look that said *cross your fingers* and swiped Ethan's ID card adjacent to the door of the lab where his team conducted their research.

The lights on the electric lock danced a conga line of green, then blinked twice. There was a metallic click and Maggie pushed the door open. She wriggled her eyebrows at Constantine. "And that's how it's done," she whispered.

They stepped inside. The room was empty. Walls and floors free of adornment. Counters naked save for a single computer and a knot of cables where a squadron of electronics used to stand.

"I'm no expert, but shouldn't there be more, you know, stuff here?" Constantine asked.

She opened cupboards at random. "I don't get it," she said. "This is the lab where Ethan's team has worked for years. Now it looks like it's never even been used."

"The great clean-out?"

Maggie nodded. "I guess. Maybe they got paranoid and moved everything. Seems like overkill, doesn't it?"

"Things got too hot, so they decided to move the kitchen. Or at least hide it."

Maggie put her hands on her hips and surveyed the vacant room. "You can't make a whole lab just disappear," she said.

"Like you can't make homeless people disappear?"

Their eyes met. Maggie nodded. "In both cases, gone isn't really gone. It's...moved. Hidden. Buried." Maggie looked at Ethan's ID badge, turning it over in her hand as she thought. His adorably crooked teeth suddenly seemed less adorable. "Let's keep looking."

Maggie swished out through the lab door and down the hall. Constantine trailed behind her, his eyes taking in the photos, the art, the aura of money and power. She opened the door of her own lab. Satisfied it was intact, she moved on to the next one and the next. All seemed untouched, normal. Not an item out of place.

She paused in the hallway, then gestured for Constantine to follow. She pointed to a windowless door. A white sign with crisp black lettering announced "Employee Locker Room."

"They sent the lab equipment out for calisthenics?" Constantine whispered.

"Maybe they stashed the evidence in their lockers."

"What, like a centrifuge and a couple hundred beakers?"

"Okay, so I don't know where all the lab equipment went. But I think we should at least look for something incriminating. I don't know, maybe an internal report or a memo or a thumb drive or—"

"—a signed confession?" Constantine finished.

"Stop being so negative. We're already here. We might as well look around."

Maggie pushed the door open and the motion-activated lights flickered to life. The room smelled musty and damp, still-moist showers facing off against a sizeable knoll of sweaty clothes in the Lost & Forsaken pile.

Maggie trailed a finger along the bank of high schoolesque lockers, some postered with women straddling items that looked vaguely automotive, others defaced by inspirational posters that urged passersby to PERSERVERE or act with CONVICTION.

Her hand paused at the locker labeled CLARK. Ethan's locker.

Maggie felt a pang. She wondered if it would ever go away, if the pain of betrayal, of embarrassment, would fade into the background, there but dulled like the grief for her mother. The truth was, it didn't matter. She'd probably die before her broken heart began knitting itself whole again.

She glanced at Constantine. He gave an almost imperceptible nod, his face expressionless. There was no lock. Maggie lifted the locker's mechanism and pulled the door open.

The locker contained everything Maggie feared and dreaded. Which was to say, absolutely nothing useful.

The locker's contents consisted of two lab coats (size L), moldering gym clothes, an elaborate grooming kit that contained jojoba-infused cleansers and ampules of wrinkle-reducing moisturizer and several thick pharmaceutical journals. It was a Sunday-best locker, dressed to impress. Did that mean it was hiding something?

Maggie patted down the locker's interior, flipped through the journals and rifled through the lab coats' pockets. Still nothing. She closed the locker quietly, wordlessly, feeling at once disappointed and strangely elated. Maybe Ethan wasn't bad after all. Maybe the computer virus and the protocol files were some mistake.

Maggie shook her head, trying to dislodge the seductive voice of denial that whispered somewhere deep inside her brain. *Don't be stupid*, she told herself. *It's not a mistake. Ethan is one of the "They," a soldier for Rx. Maybe even its general.*

Maggie sighed and motioned Constantine onward. They continued down the line of lockers. MCGEE. PATTERSON. MORGAN. DUPUIS.

Finally, they came to MONTGOMERY.

It was bolted with a keyed padlock. Great. Maggie groaned and slumped against the locker.

Constantine produced a paperclip from his pocket. He broke it in two, folded each half into an L and held it aloft for Maggie's inspection.

She shrugged. "What?"

"Prepare to be amazed." Maggie gave him a look. "A trick I learned during summer camp while bunking with Joey Tuscano. See, one half becomes the pick, the other, a torsion wrench. Pretty easy on a cheapo lock like this."

Maggie put her hand on a hip and cocked her head. "And you just happened to have a paperclip in your pocket?"

He turned one half of the paperclip clockwise as he jiggled the other half rapidly. The lock sprang open, and he pulled it off and opened the locker door. "Never leave home without one."

Maggie was duly impressed—and surprised. She gave him a silent round of applause.

Inside the locker, she found a cheap blue tie, a tailored lab coat bearing the name M. Montgomery in fussy script, a black overcoat, a Mary Poppins umbrella and a bottle of men's cologne—the cologne that seemed to hang in her nostrils when she was alone at night. As with Ethan's locker, there was nothing notable or damning.

She moved the items aside. Crouched in the back of the locker was a red nylon duffle bag.

Maggie hauled the bag out of the locker, placed it on the wooden bench before them and unzipped it with an eagerness usually reserved for trousers on prom night.

The bag disgorged its contents with alarming speed, as if it couldn't wait to vomit up what had been stuffed inside. Green latex gloves, handcuffs, rope and a black leather whip shimmered slickly beneath the room's harsh bulbs. A clatter of keys sprawled drunkenly at the bottom of the bag. Bile climbed up Maggie's throat. She wondered if the paraphernalia was meant for her.

"This must be how he spends his coffee breaks," Constantine said.

"I wonder how many of his playmates are willing participants. And I don't even want to think about what the gloves are for." She thrust her hand into the red gym bag and swatted about blindly, her hand batting aside the handcuffs and whip in search of her prey. Her fingers closed around the keys. She grasped them and wrested them free. She thought it was probably the only item in the bag that wouldn't fluoresce under Luminol.

She dangled the key ring. "I think I know what these go to. Come on."

They took the stairs to the basement in hungry strides, leaping onto landings, sweaty hands squeaking on railings. Maggie moved quickly, surely, operating under an emotional autopilot that let her cruise at an altitude of semi-sanity. She'd deal with everything—the murders, the accusations, the betrayals—later. Now all she wanted was enough ammo to bring Rx down.

In two minutes, they were there: the door where Zartar had inadvertently led Maggie during a company party that seemed to have taken place a lifetime ago. The room Maggie suspected was the birthplace of conspiracies, the romper room where lies were coddled, then reared to grow big and strong.

Maggie inserted a key from Montgomery's key ring into the lock. It jammed. So did the next one. And the next.

"Seriously?" Constantine said.

Maggie waved him to be quiet and went to try another key. Then she heard something on the other side of the door.

Maggie put her ear to the thin cold metal. She could hear the whir of the air conditioner. The rhythmic click of machinery. And something else.

Voices.

"Someone's in there," she mouthed.

"Who?" he mouthed back.

Maggie shrugged, then slowly backed the last key on the ring out of the lock, mentally cringing at how loud her previous attempts must have been and amazed they hadn't roused attention. She knew they should leave. They weren't just in a compromising situation. They were trespassing. But there was a chance they could learn something by listening. They'd only stay for a moment, utterly and perfectly quiet. Ready to leave the moment they heard chairs squeak against the floor and feet begin to stir.

Maggie leaned against the cold door again. Constantine did the same.

"This is totally out of control," a gruff male voice said. A giant gray shark leapt into her mind.

James Montgomery? The voice sounded too young. Miles? Maybe. It had a sneering, predatory quality that brought to mind clammy fingers and the flat doll's eyes of a shark.

"It's not out of control," the other voice replied. "I'm working on the problem. Be patient." Pleading. Wheedling. Maggie recognized this voice, too, but couldn't place it.

She closed her eyes, trying to draw out some memory, some connection. The canvas of her mind remained blank.

"Be patient?" the first voice boomed. "My patience ended when Maggie O'Malley started putting her nose where it didn't belong. How do you explain her finding out about our little secret? Zartar only knew bits and pieces. You didn't let something slip, did you?"

The voice replied. Unintelligible behind the door. Sounds of denial and hurt reproach bleeding through.

"Your excuses bore me. Find Maggie O'Malley. Then eliminate her."

Chapter 42

Maggie backed away from the door. Her heart felt like it was going to explode from her chest. She staggered back down the hall and toward the stairs.

Her fingers raked against the rough surface of the naked concrete wall as she reached to steady herself on the railing. In some distant part of her mind, she noticed that her pinky nail had broken.

Constantine was beside her. Saying something. Soothing.

But she didn't feel the desperation she'd felt earlier, fear slicing through her until rationality was shred into ribbons.

No, she felt pissed off.

Maybe it was temporary. Maybe the fear would come thundering back. But for now she brimmed with anger and resolve. They had taken her security. Her friend. Her reputation and future. She sure as hell wouldn't let them take her life.

Maggie looked at the keys in her hand, her attention lighting on one capped with black rubber. A tiny key toupee.

Constantine looked at it, too. "Car key?"

She nodded. "That's what I was thinking." She remembered the woman from Carson's funeral and her wild rant about white vans bearing the mark of transformation. "It has to belong to one of Rx's company vehicles. Come on."

They jogged up the stairs, condensation springing from the concrete pores of the walls beside them. They reached the ground floor landing, then sprinted down the hall, past the breakroom, past the cafeteria, past the supply closets, through a small room skirted by hibernating janitorial equipment. They reached a large, heavy door. Maggie waved Ethan's ID badge at an illuminated security panel beside it.

Beep. Swish. Kerplunk. They were in the garage.

Maggie hit the light switch and the overhead lights blipped on, revealing a fleet of five white vans. They dashed to each vehicle, flinging open the doors to search for evidence they could tuck in their pockets and spirit away to the authorities. To safety. To freedom.

The first two vans were empty. The third was filled with fast food wrappers and invoices.

The fourth van was locked. Maggie looked at Constantine, who performed his signature eyebrow crook. She took the black-topped key and slid it into the door lock. Locks on all doors popped open. Constantine slid the large side door wide. The inside of the van was murky, lit only by a single dome light.

Maggie hoisted herself onto the running board and waited for her eyes to adjust. Shapes in bas-relief sharpened, became visible. She gaped.

Within the sterile interior of the innocuous white van was a portable hospital cot, an assortment of vials and an empty IV bag that hung flaccidly from its metal tree.

Constantine saw the look on her face and climbed up beside her. His head swiveled as he took in the scene, eyes landing on the cot's leather restraint straps. "Frankenstein's lab on wheels?"

"I don't think it's that good," Maggie said as she scrambled inside the van. "Looks like they were conducting trials in this little van of horrors."

The van and all it represented disgusted her. She thought of all those who were duped into the trials or held against their will. Confused. Afraid. Some eventually dead.

The one bright spot? The van was a treasure trove of evidence.

Maggie picked up a small unlabeled glass bottle to examine it. Instantly, a siren began wailing.

For a brief, brain-addled moment Maggie thought the bottle she'd picked up was attached to an invisible alarm. Then reality dawned.

Ethan's ID badge.

Maybe he'd realized it was missing. Maybe he had been alerted that it was used to access the building. Maybe he had followed them. Whatever the case, he'd raised the alarm, which was now howling incessantly in her ears.

Maggie scrambled to the van door and looked out the window at the alarm panel embedded on the opposite wall. UNAUTHORIZED ACCESS, it accused. Lights flashed overhead, seeming to pulse DANGER with every flash of the strobe.

"This might be a good time to leave," Constantine yelled over the din.

Maggie looked around the mobile laboratory for evidence to take with them. Notebooks. File folders. Vials. Yes. Yes. And yes, please.

She grabbed a company-issue knapsack from the van floor and began stuffing whatever she could inside, wincing as the alarm clanged painfully in her ears. Despite the air-conditioned room, sweat trickled down the small of her back, tracing an icy arc that felt like the fingers of a dead man's hand.

Constantine dangled the van's keys in front of her eyes. "I know you're trying to abscond with proof of a conspiracy and all, but what do you say we turn this van into a getaway car? That way we can take the evidence and live."

Maggie nodded and slammed the van door shut. "Let's go."

They both dove into the front seat, Constantine on the driver's side. He inserted the key into the ignition and waited.

Maggie looked over at him. "Let's go," she urged.

"I have to wait for the glow plugs."

"The what?"

Constantine held up a hand. A light on the dash blinked off and Constantine cranked the engine. He crushed the accelerator pedal and the van coughed from its parking space toward the garage's large overhead door.

"Why aren't we going faster? Do I need to wind this thing up?"

"Diesels don't just get up and go when they're cold, you know." He pressed the button of the garage door opener, which was clipped to the visor. The garage door yawned open, moonlight spilling onto the floors.

Constantine nosed the van toward the gaping doorway. Ethan jumped in front of the vehicle, waving his arms like a traffic cop on meth. Maggie gasped.

Ethan shielded his eyes from the van's probing light, blinking and searching to discern the vehicle's occupants. "Maggie?" Ethan shouted. "Maggie, stop."

Ethan lunged toward the car. Maggie shrieked, a strangled burp cut short by her own hand.

"Maggie!" Ethan shouted again. "Stop. Stop!" He grabbed for the handle on Maggie's door. Missed. Swiped again.

"Go, Gus, go!"

Constantine jammed his foot onto the accelerator with even more force and the van lurched forward. Ethan's hand landed on the handle. He stumbled beside the van, trying to yank the door open.

Maggie slammed the lock down. Ethan's eyes, still half-blinded by the headlights, rolled in his eye sockets, which were rimmed an angry red. His mouth turned down in a grimace, which grew longer and deeper with every pull of the handle.

"Get us out of here," Maggie said.

The van shuddered. The engine engaged the axle, axle engaged wheels, and the van sped out of the garage, leaving Ethan sprawled on the oil-stained ground.

Maggie stared at him in her rearview mirror. He had scrambled to his hands and knees. He stared after them, his eyes drilling across the widening distance, piercing into hers.

Maggie flopped against the van's gray leatherette seat. The aftershocks of adrenaline rolled through her body, sparking tremors in every nerve.

Constantine's head flicked her way. "Are you hurt?" No response. He reached over the gray peninsula of the van's center console and squeezed her hand. "Maggie?"

Maggie shook her head. "I'm fine," she said finally. She looked out the window. Hooded street lights marked their passage, tiny flying saucers suspended on tall metal stalks. "It's just...everything. Zartar. The police. The reminders. Ethan." She cast a sidelong glance to gauge his reaction. He looked straight ahead. "I guess part of me kept hoping I was wrong about him," she said more to herself than him. "That everything would end up being a misunderstanding. I don't know why I liked him. I guess I liked that someone like him would pay attention to someone like me."

Constantine swung his head around and looked at her incredulously. "Someone like you?" He gave her hand another squeeze. "You mean someone amazing? Someone who's beautiful and smart and funny and knows all the lines from *Vacation*? Don't sell yourself short, Mags. You are the most incredible woman I've ever known."

Maggie looked at him, surprised by the passion in his voice. She opened her mouth to reply, but he interrupted.

"I'm thinking this might be a good time to call the police," Constantine said.

Maggie set her jaw. "Absolutely not."

"But isn't that why we gathered all of that evidence and risked our lives? Or was that just for funsies?"

"Yes. I mean no. I mean..." Maggie closed her eyes. "Yes, we need evidence, but I don't think we should go to the police. I'm a suspect in Zartar's murder—and possibly Mia Rennick's."

"You're not a suspect. More like a person of interest." He said it as if this were an inconsequential annoyance.

Maggie shook her head vehemently. "They'll arrest me or detain me, giving Miles and God knows who else time to bury the evidence. Then they'll start all over again, testing and killing, while I rot in some cell."

Constantine sat quietly for a moment. "Okay. What about this: we go back to my place, comb through the van, figure out what kind of evidence we have, then go to the press."

Maggie shook her head again. "No good. Ethan saw you. He must have. He'll find out where you live and come looking for us before we can match up Conspiracy A with Evidence B. A guy like that has resources, and he won't stop until he gets what he wants."

"You know, I'm really getting tired of that guy spoiling our fun." He drove in silence, his mouth set in a hard line. "If we can't go to your place or mine, let's go to your dad's. Ethan doesn't know your dad." He paused. "Or did you take him home to meet the family?"

"No," she shot back, knowing she sounded defensive. "I didn't take Ethan home. But it's not like Pop's hard to find." She pictured Pop changing out the parmesan shakers, bad guys lying in wait outside the restaurant.

Maggie watched the city bump along outside her window, the gray and brown lumps of buildings nestling the dawn sky as the sun's first rays tentatively reached across the land. A new day. Another chance. "I have an idea," she said at last.

Chapter 43

"You're sure?" Constantine looked at Maggie, the skin between his eyes creasing with worry.

Maggie put her hand on his, nearly overcome with the desire to trace the length of it with her finger. To feel the bramble of his hair against her hand. "Absolutely," she said. "Drop me off at the corner."

She stuffed a small black backpack with notebooks and vials from the back of the van. "I have some of Rx's data and a sample of whatever the hell they're pumping into people. Not to mention a damn good backstory of what's been going on. If anyone knows what to do, it's Dan."

Constantine nodded and eased the van into the right lane. "Seems like a smart choice. Actually, it seems like the only choice. I'll let you out, then go play decoy."

She turned her phone on. "I'll call you after I talk with Dan. What are you going to do while I'm in there?"

Constantine shrugged. "I don't know. The usual. Grab a cup of coffee. Try not to get killed."

Maggie looked at his profile, felt something stir in her stomach. "Be careful, okay? Don't die or anything stupid like that."

"No, no, never," he replied in one of their favorite *Fletch* quotes.

At the intersection, the stoplight climbed from green to amber to red. Maggie grabbed her bag and leaned over, her lips brushing against Constantine's perpetual five o'clock shadow.

He turned to look at her. He leaned in. Maggie felt her pulse accelerate, her heart beating not in response to the anxiety that had become her constant companion, but to the rhythm of a song she didn't realize she'd always known. A shared life. A oneness that was more than emotional twinhood. Maggie closed her eyes. Constantine placed his hand on the side of her face and drew her lips to his, setting off a spark that blazed through her.

The angry honk of a horn jolted them apart. Maggie looked at Constantine, her eyes seeing him and new possibilities for the first time. "See you on the flip side," she said.

Then she was gone.

Maggie tried to look as normal as possible as she approached the reception desk. She realized that was pretty unlikely given it was before six in the morning, her mascara had liquefied into two cesspools beneath her eyes and her now sweat-stained black ensemble made her look like a backpack-wearing ninja with a glandular problem. She wondered if her hat-and-sunglasses disguise would have been better. It was a close call.

She took a deep breath to calm her nerves and push the strangeness—the wonderfulness—of Constantine's kiss from her mind. What was that all about? A heightened emotional response to danger? A side effect of adrenaline? Or something that had been there all along, simmering below the surface, at the corner of her consciousness?

She'd deal with those questions later. Now, she was on a mission. She placed her arms on the counter of the reception desk.

The security guard, a young woman who was all angles and frowns and keys, glared at her. "Yes?"

Maggie smoothed the wisps of hair that had escaped from her ponytail and cleared her throat. "I'm here to see Dr. Wilson." She had used her most confident, imperious voice, the one in which she imagined herself in a smoking jacket and ascot à la *The Thin Man*'s Nick Charles.

"It's 5:50 a.m.," the woman snapped. "Business hours are eight a.m. to five p.m."

Maggie gave a toothy pageant smile. "I know it's early," she said. "But I just spoke with Dan on the phone. He's here, and he said he'd meet with me. I just need to be buzzed in."

Maggie had indeed spoken with Dan minutes before on his cell phone. She could tell he was surprised to hear from her so early and was taken aback when she pushed to meet with him in person. But ever the gentleman, he'd agreed to meet. He was on his way into the office to prepare for an early meeting anyway, he had told her, and always had time for her, especially when she so urgently needed to see him.

Maggie upped the amperage on her smile, going for full Miss America. The woman made a show of sighing, then consulted her directory. She dialed, arching a brow at Maggie. "Dr. Wilson?" the woman bleated into the phone. "There's someone here to see you. She says you're expecting her?"

This last sentence delivered with absolute certainty of the opposite. She says she's the queen's secret half-sister? She says there's no such thing as gravity? She says Piers Morgan would make a pleasant dinner companion?

A pause. The woman listened. Her angles seemed to sharpen. "Okay." She sighed with an air of suffering. "I'll send her up." She let the receiver fall into its cradle and thrust a pen at Maggie. "You'll need to sign in. And take one of these guest passes."

Maggie dutifully complied. The guard returned the ballpoint to its holder and watched Maggie lick her fingers, then smooth her eyebrows. "Do I know you?" the guard asked as Maggie continued her feline-inspired grooming routine. "You look familiar."

Maggie's pulse jumped. Of course she looked familiar. Her face was all over the news. Disguised or not, she couldn't believe she wasn't spotted earlier at *The Post* or the homeless shelter or on the street. Maggie shouldered her bag and smiled again, hoping her face wasn't as red as it felt. "I get that a lot," she said.

Maggie walked past the desk and into the lobby. The building seemed deserted except for the cleaning crew, who were busy spraying, wiping and polishing the floors and tabletops of the waiting area.

Maggie rode the elevator to the fourth floor and walked the squat hallway to Dan's office. She knocked softly on the door.

A muffled "Come in," sounded from the other side.

Maggie opened the door and walked into a small, windowless office. There, standing in pink and blue plaid pants and a violet shirt was her mentor, an oasis of calm in Maggie's wasteland of turmoil.

"Dan." Maggie ran to him and hugged him in an uncle-niece embrace.

He hugged her back, then put her at arm's length, taking in her ruined makeup and sweaty clothes. "Hey, hey," he said softly, awkwardly patting her shoulder. "Are you all right? You look like you've been through the wringer."

Maggie squeezed his hand and sank into a chair, mid-tone veneer on mid-tone particleboard. She smiled weakly, trying to be brave, affecting calm. "I've had better days," she said.

"I was glad you called. I mean, it was early, and my wife hates to have her beauty sleep disturbed." He smiled weakly and sat heavily in his own chair. "But I've been worried sick. I just saw the news. They make you out like you're some kind of..."

"Murderer? Drug addict?" Maggie looked at her hands, wincing at the tiny crescent moons her fingernails had tattooed on her palms, the cuticles she'd ripped to shreds. "None of it's true. The lies, the accusations, the crazy news stories, it's all part of what's going on at Rx."

Dan's eyebrows jumped like they were on tiny pneumatic lifts. "Rxcellance? Is this about your phone call? Your question about—what was it—Pharma-something?"

"MediPrixe." She was annoyed he'd already forgotten her request to look into the company. Seeing your friend murdered and trying to escape your own seemingly inevitable death could make anyone peevish. "Yes. I mean, that's part of it. Did you find anything out?"

Dan leaned against the desk and stroked his chin pensively, channeling the professor he used to be. "Not really, no. I looked back at some Rxcellance filings, but I didn't see anything about MediPrixe and certainly nothing out of the ordinary. I did discover an early application for a flu vaccine, which was abandoned a few months later. That's not exactly unusual, you know. Pharmaceuticals start trials, find problems, move on."

Dan shook his head. "I guess I don't understand what any of this has to do with any of what's going on at Rxcellance. Other than the fact that you seem to be having problems over there." He leaned back in this chair and steepled his fingers. "It's all highly...unusual. These cloak-and-dagger phone calls you keep making to me, missing money from the foundation you were supposed to be administering..."

Maggie could practically see the ellipses hanging in the air. Pride and indignation clawed against her lacquer of calm. "You mean the money Rx claims I embezzled? It's not true, Dan. They're lying to cover up what they've done. What they're doing. Because they know I'm on to them. They know I know their secrets."

Maggie knew she sounded crazy, padded-room crazy, but she had to make him understand. She had to get him on her side, to get his help, before it was too late.

"That's why I called you," she said. She leaned forward in her chair, hands reaching across the desk in supplication. "I need your help. Everyone I've put my trust in has betrayed me. I don't know where else to turn."

Dan stretched out a hand and placed it over Maggie's and squeezed. "I'm glad you came to me," he said.

Maggie's phone chirped. A text message. The sound sliced the companionable silence between them. She felt her cheeks flame in embarrassment. She smiled an *I'll-get-that-later* smile. The phone chirped again. Her cheeks grew impossibly hot.

"Just a sec," she said sheepishly. She looked at the screen. A text from Constantine. It had to be important for him to interrupt. She swiped to read.

Mags, don't go in there. Dan's in on it. The email address, the phone—they're registered to Dan. GET OUT NOW.

Maggie stared at the words, trying to understand.

The emails they were trying to trace had come from Dan.

He had owned the phone before her.

None of it made sense. She looked at Dan. She felt her mouth grow lax, fall open in surprise.

Dan read her face and snatched the phone out of her hand. He read the text silently, his mouth twisting into something hollow.

"I..." It was all she could say. Her mind stopped working, stopped reasoning, tumbled and turned as it fell down a rabbit's hole from what is to what should never be. The artifact of a Led Zeppelin song thundered through her mind, Robert Plant's plaintive wails fighting to be heard above the jackhammer of her heart.

Then it came to her. The company gala. His appearance in the Rx breakroom. The voice behind a closed-door meeting with Mia Rennick. The voice promising to snuff out her life.

The office seemed to grow hotter. Maggie's stomach dropped. The glands near her ears fired a warning shot. *Oh, God, please don't let me puke.*

"I...um..." Maggie stammered stupidly. It was like her voice belonged to someone else. "This used to be your phone?"

Dan caressed the face of his old phone with his thumb, his fingers swiping the text away. "Yes, yes it was. I was told this phone was unrepairable. And yet here it is." He dropped the phone on the desk, watching it bounce on the rubber blotter. "This is a very interesting development, indeed."

He walked to the door, his paunchy, poofy, professorial veneer dissolving into something hard and cold. He gently turned the lock. Maggie flinched.

"But it does explain why you started looking into the deaths of all those inconvenient meddlers. Evidently, my orders to kill were being delivered to my old phone as well as my new one?"

Maggie nodded stupidly. "It wasn't completely wiped," she said hollowly. "Your old phone was still receiving information from the cloud. Meeting reminders. And later, a video."

Surprise registered in Dan's eyes. "Technology. To direct my actions. To prove my mettle. And now to bite me in the ass. Ironic, isn't it?"

He crossed the room and perched a buttock on the edge of his desk. "You know, I do feel bad about all of this." Dan looked pained, regretful, a parent about to dole out punishment to an incorrigible child. *This will hurt me a lot more than it hurts you.* "I should have put a stop to you working at Rxcellance when I ran into you at the party before all this—" He waved his hands around. "All of this got so out of hand. But I didn't. I couldn't. You were the brightest student I ever had. You could have done amazing things at Rx, things that could have bettered the human condition and changed the world. All that shit." He laughed an explosive little "Ha!"

He rose and circled around to the back of Maggie's chair. He put his hands on the chair back. His hot breath fell on her neck, every puff molesting her hair follicles. "I thought you'd be a reflection on me, my tutelage and my example," he continued softly. "A feather in my cap. I had no idea you'd be the fly in my ointment. You were always so nice, so compliant. I thought you'd be a good girl and mind your own business."

Maggie sat paralyzed as her mind struggled to process this new information and her changing situation. She knew she had to stay calm. Keep him talking. Wasn't that what they always did in the movies? Didn't the murderers always soliloquy themselves right into jail, their explanations and assertions creating a nifty little gap into which the hero could insert a daring rescue? All she needed were some great one-liners and an exit strategy, and she'd be Bruce Willis in *Die Hard.*

Maggie's eyes scanned the desk for something to use as a weapon. She spied a basket of paperclips and a deck of plastic label flags. *Right. I'll organize him to death.*

"You're in on Rx's conspiracy?" she asked, her voice steadier than she felt.

"I invented the conspiracy," he spat. "It was my brainchild, my fast track to the big payout. That greedy, sophomoric Montgomery bastard saw dollar signs and hopped on board. Then promptly took over." He smiled. It was not a pleasant look. "He had the money, the power and the leverage, especially after I set everything in motion. Once I sullied my hands, I was under his thumb. So I did his bidding. It wasn't so bad. I was used to playing the dutiful public servant. I didn't even mind the wet work when things went south." The smile broadened. "It allowed me to explore my darker side."

Maggie felt a fresh rush of acid flood her stomach. "Don't pretend this was your first walk down the unethical aisle. You took your thirty pieces of silver and betrayed the trust of your office long before this. How did it start? Rx incentivizing you to give their subpar drugs the rubber stamp treatment?"

Dan sniffed and flicked an imaginary speck of dust from his shirt. "I'd hardly be the only one. Used to be that drug makers would bury bad news in a five-hundred-page report, and we'd look the other way. Then we started getting paid to grease the approval skids."

"The PDUFA," Maggie said dully.

Dan looked pleased that she'd been paying attention, had played the part of devoted pupil. "Those fat fees were all at the organizational level. Not enough to filter down to the people actually doing the work.

So I started taking personal contributions to accelerate approvals. Suddenly, I'm doing quite well by not being so...picky. Then I got a new boss, a Mr. Goody Two-Shoes who liked to do things by the book. He didn't seem to care that I had bills to pay, a lifestyle to keep, a wife to satisfy." He fingered a gold-colored picture frame from which his wife smiled. "He was always hovering over me to make sure everything was aboveboard, that we were acting as bastions of public safety. He made things difficult, but not impossible. So I upped the ante for an even bigger win with Rxcellance."

"Mexico," Maggie said.

Dan hugged himself in delight. "You never fail to impress. Yes, Ms. O'Malley, Mexico. Where bonuses like human rights aren't all the rage like they are here. Such a shame we had to pull the plug."

"If you were working for MediPrixe, which was working for Rx," Maggie said slowly, "what role did Maxwell Simmons play?

"Simmons played dead," Dan said, fingering a pencil on his desk. "The founder of MediPrixe was a ghost, a name on a form I stole from a dead colleague. I figured he wouldn't be needing it anymore. The rest was easy. Fill out some forms, invent a digital profile and poof, you're a corporation."

Maggie nodded, the pieces of the puzzle falling into place. "You thought Rx's new vaccine sounded like a sure thing. You created MediPrixe and hired subcontractors south of the border to run the trial. But then you ran into a snag. Pneumonia."

Dan released the pencil and straightened the cuffs on his Easter egg-hued shirt. Bored. Distant. Ready to move on. He looked at his nails.

Disgust threaded its way through Maggie's body like a living thing. She couldn't decide if she wanted to scream or cry. "Didn't it sicken you knowing you were giving those people something that could cause pneumonia?"

Dan looked at her with mild, amused surprise. "Of course not," he said. "We were counting on it."

Chapter 44

They wanted the vaccine to *cause* pneumonia?

Before Maggie could make sense of what Dan said, his hands were at her throat.

Instinct drove her hands to his and she began clawing, her feet kicking as she tried to scramble backward and away from the pain. Evidently, he was done soliloquizing.

The chair toppled. Maggie crashed to the floor, pulling Dan on top of her. His grip tightened. Something flashed through his eyes as his fingers clenched. Satisfaction. Pleasure.

Maggie's vision dulled around the edges, blurring the office like a distant, televised memory. She stopped fighting for her life and instead fought for self-control. She forced herself to focus on self-defense, to remember the training she'd sought out after a rash of rapes erupted on campus during her junior year.

Maggie stopped flailing. She took her thumbs and dug them into Dan's eyes. His hands flew to his face. She brought her knee squarely to his crotch. He heaved forward and fell off her and onto the floor.

Maggie grabbed her phone from Dan's desk and ran for the door. Her fingers, jittery with fear and adrenaline, fumbled with the lock. The lock turned. She turned the door knob. It slipped from hands slicked with sweat. She tried again, bearing down on the metal, focusing on grasping and turning the knob. The door opened. She bolted from the room.

Maggie heard him coming behind her. A sick *swoosh-thunk, swoosh-thunk* as he limped from his office and into the stubby hallway. Like Jack chasing Danny in *The Shining*.

The groin shot had hurt him, but it wasn't enough to stop him.

Maggie glanced over her shoulder. Dan was portly, out of shape, yet somehow continued to gain on her, his face contorted into a mask of murderous determination as he took each lumbering step. Maybe if she'd taken an Advil after she'd hurt her shoulder at Ethan's she'd feel more spry. Or maybe if she'd been getting uninterrupted sleep, good nutrition. None of that mattered now. She needed to move.

Maggie skidded to a stop in front of the elevator and lunged at the call button. She hit the down button repeatedly with the palm of her hand, knowing it might confuse the elevator's computer but unable to stop herself.

Dan was a few steps away, swoosh-thunking toward her in his foppish golf wear. The elevator light was illuminated. Maggie could hear the metallic grind of the car slowly ascending to her floor. There was no indicator showing the elevator's progress. Was it at the second floor? Third? Maggie pounded on the elevator button again. *Come on.*

Dan grew closer. She could almost feel waves of rage coming off him. Maggie tore herself away from the elevator and ran to the stairwell door.

She grasped the handle and yanked. The door wouldn't budge. She pulled again. It was locked. She felt irrational outrage tear through her. That was a safety hazard. Stairways should be accessible in the event of a fire. Maggie pulled again and again, futility colliding with desperation. It held fast.

Dan had picked up speed, his listing walk taking on a new spring as he closed in. In another moment, he'd be there. Hands at her throat. Splitting her head like a piñata to release a gruesome prize.

Maggie again changed course and ran down the hall, trying doors at random. Locked. Locked. Locked. Locked. *Feck.* The panic came on fast, its tiny red claws digging into her spine, crawling into her brain where it would erase all reason in one electrifying stroke.

"Help," she called out. "Help me!"

Downstairs she could hear the cleaning crew's vacuums and floor polishers humming. No one could hear her over the equipment's whirring motors.

The last door on the right was topped by the kind of glass Maggie associated with TV detectives' doors. The ladies' room. She tried the handle.

Unlocked. Thank God.

Maggie shouldered her way inside, threw the narrow lock closed and slammed her body against the door. She fumbled for her phone, swiping and stabbing buttons to initiate a call.

The door crashed into her back, knocking the phone from her hand. Maggie watched it skip across the floor like a stone over a pond. Dan hurtled his body against the door again and Maggie heard the snap of wood cracking against its hinges. She whimpered, looking around for something to defend herself with, heels digging in to keep the door closed and the wolf at bay.

And then he was in. On top of her. Pushing her to the ground, her knapsack mashed between her body and the hard tile. She wondered how the vials in the pack were faring, worried the evidence would spill, be lost forever.

He pinned her hands to the side of her head with his knees, his patella grinding against her flesh. "Gotcha," he said with a grin. She stared at him, still trying to comprehend how her beloved professor had become a sick parody of a monster. Was he a monster all along, hiding behind the mask of his profession, his role as affable, bumbling, nerdy professor?

Maggie writhed beneath him. Dan fumbled in his pocket and produced a knife. He pointed it at Maggie's eye and she froze. Dan jingled through his pocket like a father digging for pocket money for a Fudgsicle from the ice cream truck. He extracted a small rectangular black bag. He opened it with his teeth. A syringe, a vial and a rag bounced out.

Dan uncapped the vial with his teeth. He placed the vial on the floor and filled the syringe with his free hand. "Should've done this back in my office. Much tidier. But you're a slippery one. Just like Mia Rennick. She was handy with the IPO, then proved most troublesome when she wanted more than her fare share." He tapped the side of the syringe. "Heroin. Not the good stuff, though." He wrinkled his nose. "Probably cut with bleach and who knows what else. It'll be no surprise when they find you with a needle in your arm and smack in your bloodstream. All those drugs found in your desk. The stealing. Suspicion of murder. With so much hopelessness and remorse, it would be a wonder if you *didn't* kill yourself by accident—or by design.

Not that the cops will be looking too closely. They're busy with the strike, and it's not like you're their best friend."

"You won't get away with this. People know I'm here. I signed in downstairs. I have a pass."

Dan laughed. "Oh you have a pass? A *pass*? Then I guess I can't kill you." He moved his face closer to hers. "Don't be stupid, Maggie. I'll wait until the cleaning crew is done and drag your body out the back door. It's early. No one's here. Then I'll return your pass and sign you out during the shift change. No one will remember you. You'll be a distant signature on a page destined for shredding."

"Wait!" she screamed. "You don't have to do this!"

He held the knife against her throat with one hand and palpated the inside of her elbow with the other. "Yes, I do," he said calmly. "You know I do. I have to eliminate witnesses. Or don't you watch the movies?"

Then he raised his arm and plunged the needle into her vein.

Chapter 45

Pain seared through Maggie's arm. She bucked and flailed, determined to stop Dan from pushing the syringe's plunger and forcing its lethal cocktail into her bloodstream. He held onto her just as her rodeo boyfriend had held onto his bronco for the required eight seconds. One. Two. Three. She could feel her arms tire, lactic acid burning through fatigued muscles. Four. Five.

The door of the ladies' room flew open. Ethan, wild-eyed and breathless and sweaty, filled the doorway.

Dan looked up. "Ah, Mr. Clark. You're early. You can help me with the clean-up." He gave Ethan an appraising look. "I hope that's not a problem?"

A shadow crossed Ethan's face, turning his eyes black and unreadable. A strange smile sprang to his lips. It crawled slowly across his face. "Not at all."

Ethan crouched next to Dan, eyes fixed on Maggie. She tried to scream, to plead, but only strangled sobs came out. Ethan's eyes, turgid, bottomless, inscrutable, locked with hers as she struggled against the encroaching blackness of unconsciousness. Her strength bled away. There was no more fight in her. She tried to summon a fresh burst of adrenaline, of will. The leaden certainty of her death rendered her muscles useless. She steeled herself, bidding her father, Fiona and Constantine a silent goodbye.

Then Ethan's fingers closed around the syringe protruding from Maggie's flesh, plucked it out and drove it into Dan's neck.

It was Dan's turn to scream. Then gurgle. His hands grasped for the hypodermic as wet, useless sounds escaped his mouth. But Ethan held the needle fast, pushing the plunger with his thumb until the liquid was gone.

Maggie rolled away as the men continued to struggle, an obscene parody of Friday night WWF. Dan slashed with his knife, slicing through the air, dicing against tile, as if demonstrating the latest in late-night TV cutlery. Ethan bashed Dan's head against the floor, stunning the older man.

Dan began thrashing, the drug that had been injected into his bloodstream finally taking effect. Then he went still, the needle protruding from his neck, knife nestled against his leg like a child's cherished blanket.

Ethan grabbed the knife and rounded on Maggie.

She shrank against the base of a stall door. "Please, Ethan," she whimpered. "Please don't."

Ethan walked heavily toward her. A red line materialized through the breast pocket of his white button-down, then spread and ran. Blood. Dan's knife had found its mark after all.

Ethan dropped heavily to his knees and extended his hand. Dan's knife tumbled from his fingers.

"Get out of here," he said huskily. "Now."

Maggie hesitated. "I thought..."

Ethan pitched sideways and dropped heavily into a sitting position. His head lolled against the doorjamb of the bathroom stall. "I know. I wouldn't trust me, either."

Indignation swelled inside Maggie. "You participate in these...these *atrocities*...then murder one of your brothers in arms, *then* expect me to buy your good guy act?"

"The only atrocity I was involved in was the Ghana necrosis cover-up. And I did save your life."

Maggie laughed bitterly. "After you tried to frame me."

Ethan didn't say anything for a moment, then: "The cover-up was my contribution to the bottom line. My first step up the corporate escalator, especially when I found the drug's skin-firming properties." He laughed, put his hand to his side. Winced. "Then Zartar told me her suspicions about the flu vaccine. Her theory about breaches in protocol, in morality. She started snooping after what happened with her brother, looking for any bargaining chip she could find. At first I thought she was trying to play some kind of angle. I knew she was pissed about being coerced into hiding the GN cure, over threats to her family. But science experiments on unwilling participants? It seemed—"

"Impossible?" Maggie finished, using Constantine's word.

He nodded. "Then I started looking around, sniffing in places I wasn't supposed to. Turned out she was right." Ethan flopped onto his uninjured side, pulling his knees toward his chest. "Once I knew the score, I gave her everything I'd dug up on the vaccine and the trials. She was already fired up about Ghana necrosis. I figured I'd let her fight the good fight."

"So you let her put her career, her *life* on the line while you sat safely in the shadows, telling yourself you were doing the right thing." She was shaking now.

"I did want to do the right thing," he said, his voice going sulky. "But I didn't want to flush my career down the toilet. I thought she could blow the whistle, end the whole thing."

"Well, you did manage to end something: Zartar's life."

Pain that had nothing to do with his injuries shot across Ethan's face. "I know," he said softly. He closed his eyes. "I made mistakes, Maggie. Big ones. I thought I could control things. Handle the situation. Maybe even come out smelling like a rose. I didn't know anyone was going to die."

Maggie's jaw worked as she tried to hold back tears. "Zartar wasn't the only one who died. There was a social worker. A reporter. Mia Rennick, a friend of yours. Don't deny it. I saw her picture in your home office."

"She was a friend of Miles and a financial advisor to James Montgomery. I knew her because of the Rx IPO."

"And because you were friends with Miles. He was in that picture, too."

Ethan sagged. "Miles and I used to be friends. A long time ago, before I knew what he was. Mia's murder was my first hint that Zartar was right. By then, it was too late."

"It was too late the second you started lying. Then you kept right on lying. Deceiving everyone. Yourself. Me. Making me think you cared about me when all you wanted was to protect yourself and keep Rx's money machine running."

Ethan reached for her hand. Maggie yanked it away. "I did care about you. I do." Maggie turned away. "I know you don't believe me, and I don't blame you. There's only one person who's at fault for that."

Ethan reached for her hand again, his fingers cold and white. "I tried to warn you in the Rx garage, when you and Constantine were in the van. They're coming for you, Maggie. And they'll keep coming until they're satisfied that you can't say anything. Go to the police. Stop them before it's too late."

Maggie's fingers danced over the keys of her phone as she raced down the stairs and out of the FDA building. She told 911 where to find Ethan, guilt tugging at her conscience despite Ethan's insistence that she go, despite all that he had done. Then she disconnected and began thumbing her way to Constantine's number.

A hand closed roughly around her arm. The smell of sickly sweet cologne assaulted her nose. She spun around expecting to see Miles.

James Montgomery stood there.

"Maggie," he said cheerfully. "A little bird told me you'd be here."

Maggie blinked. "Mr. Montgomery?" What was he doing here? Why was he wearing Miles's cologne? Did they share toiletries? Why was she even thinking about that?

He gripped her arm more tightly and pulled her close to him. "Hey," she said, trying to shake off Montgomery's arm. "What are you doing?"

"Now, now," he said, a smile spreading across his face. "Don't be like that. We have things to discuss."

His smile broadened. *You're gonna need a bigger boat.*

He grabbed the phone from her hand, dropped it to the ground and crushed it beneath a designer oxford. Italian leather as executioner.

Maggie twisted her arm, struggled to break free. Montgomery's grip tightened, fingers penetrating flesh. Maggie cried out in pain. "It must be terrible to be so weak." James shook his head sadly. "Miles is weak, too. Not physically. Mentally. Socially. Doesn't know how to handle things. Women. His temper. That little gift he left on your door was a prime example."

"Little gift?" Maggie heard herself say.

"The hamster," he said impatiently. "Not what I would have done. None of it was. His little campaign to intimidate you—to punish you for brushing him off—was childish. Following you. Printing things from your computer. Posting your number on craigslist. All of it was so reckless."

"He did all that—and you knew about it?" Maggie asked hollowly.

"The moron told me." he said wearily. "He was so proud of himself, like when he told Mia all about the vaccine. He got involved with her beyond a professional capacity. Idiot." He shifted his gaze to somewhere in the middle distance. Remembering. "The only idea that was actually worth a damn was convincing Ethan to infect your computer and plant those drugs. That almost made up for all his other screw-ups. Almost."

He jerked her closer. He was incredibly strong for a man his age.

Maggie squirmed. He twisted her wrist and Maggie felt a snap. Not bone. She'd broken her tibia when she was eight and she knew what that felt like. This was something else. Soft tissue. Ligament, tendon, maybe.

Pain rocketed up her arm, kissed the pain already growing in her hurt shoulder. Her vision tunneled, started to turn black. She fought her way above the agony, the blackness.

"His biggest mistake was letting Dan do his dirty work. I thought Miles would be good at it, like it even. He was clearly a budding sociopath." He rolled his shoulders. "He convinced me Dan was the better man for the job. But Dan failed. Dan let you get away." He shook his head. "I guess listening to Miles was *my* biggest mistake."

Maggie bit back the pain. Her eyes scanned the shallow stairs leading up to the FDA building, the sidewalks that skirted its perimeter. There were a few people out, a jogger, a dog walker, a newspaper boy on a bike. All were already wilted in the early morning humidity. All were too far away to summon. "You were behind everything," she said more to herself than Montgomery. "Behind the trials. Behind the murders. Pulling the strings to make Dan dance."

"Who else? It's not like my son was good for anything."

She had been so sure it was Miles. She knew the senior Montgomery had some involvement, had participated in the lies and cover-ups, but figured Miles had orchestrated—if not participated in—the violence. Yet another misjudgment.

"Yes, Dan was a disappointment. Couldn't seem to make you go away." He turned his eyes on Maggie. Appraising. Taking her measure. "Maybe he likes you too much. Maybe he warned you that you were next on the chopping block, told you to scamper off into the woods and hide, like the huntsman to Snow White. Strange, since by all accounts old Danno ended up enjoying his little side job as a hit man. But you know what they say. You want something done right..." He smiled.

"You're not going to get away with this," she said for the second time that day. "Too many people know."

"Nobody important knows," he hissed. He yanked Maggie's arm, and she collided against him. Fresh pain surged through her and for a moment, the world fell away.

Tires squealed. Montgomery looked up, eyes squinting behind bifocals. Maggie followed his line of sight. A van sporting photographs of hair-helmeted news anchors and "WXYZ—*Your* News Source!" rounded the corner and screeched to a stop at the curb in front of them.

The van door sprung open and a woman leapt forth like Athena from the head of Zeus. She was on them in seconds. She fluffed her hair, glanced at the cameraman and rotated her finger, signaling him to roll. "You're James Montgomery, aren't you? The president of Rxcellance?"

She thrust a microphone in his face. Montgomery released Maggie's arm as if it were made of lava and put on his politician's smile. He turned up the charm to eleven. "Yes, I am," he said loudly, pride tingeing each word.

The woman looked at Maggie, who was staring at her wide-eyed. "And you're Maggie O'Malley."

She put the microphone beneath Maggie's nose. Maggie simply nodded.

The woman turned toward the camera. "I'm Candace Mullen from Channel 12 News, and I'm here because of a tip I received about Rxcellance." Her voice was deep but melodious with an almost singsong variation in pitch and volume.

A small crowd had gathered in front of the FDA building,

materializing as if from thin air. Where were they when Maggie needed help? Maggie took in their blue uniforms and printed signs. They weren't the early morning exercisers she had seen earlier. They were protesters.

Attracted to news cameras like magpies to anything shiny, the group formed a semicircle behind the news crew, waiting to peck at sound bites as they fell from the mouths of interviewees, wondering what could have supplanted their exploits in a city they'd held hostage for a month.

Maggie's eyes swept over the crowd. A man waved wildly. She squinted. It was Constantine. He gave a huge thumbs-up, then made a show of patting himself on the back. She tentatively waved back.

"A tip about Rxcellance?" Montgomery said indignantly. "There's no story about Rxcellance. If you're looking for news, here's Maggie O'Malley." He pointed at her accusingly. "She stole from our company's charity and most likely killed one of our employees."

A murmur surged through the crowd like the wave at a high school football game.

"He's lying," Maggie said. Her voice was steady. Confident. Belying the growing desperation she felt within. "He's lying to cover up what he's done, what he's still doing."

"And what is that?" Candace asked, pushing the microphone beneath Maggie's nose.

Maggie took her battered arm and tucked it next to her body like a broken wing. "Rxcellance is using homeless people as guinea pigs to test a drug designed to cause pneumonia."

Montgomery chortled good-naturedly. "Homeless guinea pigs? A drug designed to *cause* pneumonia?" He opened his arms wide in an appeal to the growing crowd. "Why would we do that?"

"Because Rxcellance holds the patent for the country's leading pneumonia medication."

Veins bulged in Montgomery's neck. It looked like someone was making balloon animals beneath the surface of his skin. "That's ludicrous. Yes, we're developing a new flu vaccine, a universal vaccine that will work on all strains for years." He flashed the politician's smile to show what good news this was. "But it's totally safe. It's not designed to do anything but alleviate human suffering." He paused, looking up to the sky in a show of male sensitivity. "We follow strict protocols in all of our studies and do everything we can to ensure the well-being of our participants—including getting informed consent and ensuring the drugs we're testing are safe."

Maggie flung her knapsack from her back and held it high with her good arm, making sure the Rx logo was visible. She dropped the bag to the ground and wrenched it open with one hand. The crowd gasped, fearful of what she'd pull from the depths of its black nylon folds.

Maggie's fingers clasped a small vial. She jerked it free from the pack, dove back in for a hypodermic needle, then dropped the black bag to the ground. She held the vial, which also sported the Rx logo, and the needle high. "This," she said loudly, "is a sample of the drug that Rxcellance has been giving to unsuspecting homeless people."

Maggie snapped the cap off the syringe and drove the needle into the vial, which she had placed between her knees. The crowd flinched. She set down the vial and turned to Montgomery. "If your new vaccine is so safe, why don't you give it a test drive? Right here. Right now."

Montgomery leaned away from the needle, almost losing his balance. "I don't have anything to prove to you."

"What's the matter?" she asked. "Are you scared?"

Montgomery regained his stance, leaned in, veins pulsing wildly at his neck and temple. It looked like the balloon animals were having an orgy under his skin. He fought for self-control. "I'm...not...scared," he said between clenched teeth.

"How do you talk without moving your mouth like that?" Constantine called out from the crowd. "I love ventriloquism."

The growing throng laughed. Montgomery glowered, forgetting his politician's demeanor. He didn't move.

"Is there a reason you're reluctant to try your own vaccine, Mr. Montgomery?" Candace Mullen asked. The crowd leaned in.

"No," he snapped. "I—" His voice faded away.

Everyone waited. A dog barked. Someone coughed. Candace folded her arms. Maggie could hear the growing hum of traffic in the distance. Rush hour ramping up.

"This is slander," Montgomery growled. "These accusations are the product of a warped mind."

"Who are you calling warped?" squawked a male voice from the crowd.

Commotion erupted behind the news crew. People stepped aside. A wiry man with electrified hair pushed his way through the horde. The man grabbed a Barbie head from around his neck and stroked its hair between his fingers. "I wouldn't let her inject me, either, pal," Al said in a stage whisper to Montgomery. "That shit'll kill you."

Chapter 46

Constantine watched with slack-jawed amazement as Maggie attacked her four-egg omelet. "Near-death experiences don't affect your appetite, do they?"

Maggie gulped her coffee and stuffed a corner of jam-slathered toast into her mouth. "Hey, a girl's gotta eat. Besides, I'm pretty sure running from a homicidal maniac, holding an impromptu press conference and bringing down a billion-dollar corporation burned several thousand calories. Good job on the news conference, by the way."

Constantine wiped his mouth and leaned back. "I figured Candace Mullen would want an exclusive on the Maggie O'Malley, murderess at large story. Plus having a shot at breaking the biggest scandal of the year. Little did I know I'd led you to the den of a wolf in pastel pants."

Maggie shook her head. "It was so weird. It was like Dan was an entirely different person. Either he changed, or he had me fooled all along."

"Greed does bad things to people."

"Finding Al was a nice touch, too. How did you manage that?"

"Accidentally. Like all the awesome stuff I do." Maggie raised her eyebrows, waiting for a real answer. "After I dropped you at Dan's building, I headed to the news studio to tell Candace Mullen about Dolores Hidalgo, the drug trials on the homeless, the murders, everything. Trial by media, and all that. On the way back to the FDA, I spotted a doll necklace attached to a weird-looking dude. I pulled over. He was freaked out because I was in an Rx van, and he'd evidently just escaped from an Rx van, which is a whole different story. After he calmed down and stopped throwing headless Barbies at me, we had a nice chat. Then I got a message from my friend that the email address we sent the fake spam to was registered to Dan. I texted you, contacted the news crew, then headed back to the FDA with Al. And the rest, as they say, is history."

"You did good, Gus. Real good."

Constantine bowed. "My only desire is to serve you. Well, that and eat more bacon. You can never have too much bacon." He put two pieces of bacon into his mouth to demonstrate. "What's next for Rx?" he asked, crunching loudly.

"Bankruptcy, I expect. There's no way Rx can weather this kind of storm. There will be an investigation, a trial. I'll be called to testify and they'll probably give Ethan immunity to do the same." She paused, remembering their last moments at the FDA building. "He's lucky to be alive. Too bad he ruined his life. I'm seeing long prison sentences for the star players and a funeral no one will attend for Dan." She pictured Dan's wife taking the news of his death, crying into her Hermès hankie, running to check his life insurance policy.

"All to profit from pneumonia."

"Despite what Dan said, I think it originally started as an unintended side effect. At first Rx tried to fix the problem. Then they realized its financial upside. So they decided to hone it, control it, *amplify* it, using those unable to give consent or defend themselves as test subjects. What better way to create demand than to develop a vaccine that causes a disease the company happens to have the corner on treating? The flu can develop into pneumonia, especially for the at-risk populations who'd get the vaccines. The pneumonia would look like a consequence of the illness rather than a side effect of the vaccine. Even if some people discovered the vaccine caused pneumonia, Rx figured the profits would outweigh the costs of the lawsuits."

"Like the car manufacturers with faulty parts."

Maggie nodded. "How'd the police show up so soon after the big showdown between James and Al? Did you call them?"

Constantine wiped his mouth on a napkin. "They finally triangulated the location of your phone. You were a person of interest, remember?"

"Oh. Right."

Constantine summoned the waitress for the check. "So

Montgomery was the head of the operation. I'd pegged Miles for playing the heavy. Sounded like he was blossoming into bad guyhood."

Maggie poured coffee from the table's carafe into her cup, sipped, added sugar and cream. "Miles played his part, advanced his father's plan where he could, tormented me for fun when it suited him. But Montgomery senior was really pulling the strings. Dan was the perfect puppet—and henchman. Smart. Seemingly benign. Driven by avarice. Looking back, I wonder if the ethics class he taught helped inspire their awful plan."

"Maybe he figured if big pharma had gotten away with unauthorized testing on the poor or mentally ill before, it could be done again."

They looked at each other for a moment.

"Oh," Constantine said. "I have something for you." He reached into his pocket. "Or should I say 'someone'?"

He opened his hand. Miss Vanilla wriggled her nose at Maggie.

"Miss Vanilla!" She extended her hand and Constantine plopped the rodent onto her palm. "I'm actually glad to see you."

"*Actually* glad?" Constantine said.

"Shhh...We're bonding." Maggie stroked Miss Vanilla's triangular head. The animal closed her eyes. "Look. She didn't even pee on me. It must be true love."

"Oh, it's love all right," Constantine said, his eyes on hers. "It always has been."

Maggie felt herself grow hot, imagined the red tide of blush washing across her face.

"Miss Vanilla and I were wondering if you'd like to go to a movie tonight. And by 'Miss Vanilla and I' I mean 'I' and by 'movie' I mean 'something terrible at the local multiplex that we can make fun of for years to come.'"

Maggie looked at Constantine, at the lips she'd kissed that were now caught between his teeth. She felt her strange self-consciousness fade away. "Constantine Papadopoulos, are you asking me out on a date?"

"No. Well, maybe a little. Like a small date. A date-ette, really."

Maggie passed Miss Vanilla back to Constantine and grasped his free hand. "I'd like that," she said softly. "I'd like that a lot. I just need to visit an urgent care on the way." She indicated her injured arm. "Assess the damage."

He brought her hand to his face and brushed her knuckles against his lips. "Absolutely. Then I'll help nurse you back to health."

The waitress placed the bill on the table. Constantine grabbed it, slurped the last of his coffee and rose. "I've got this. And it's not because I'm being boyfriendy or anything. I want to see if they have any kids' coloring menus at the register." He made his way to the front of the restaurant.

Maggie slid out from the vinyl booth and raked her hair behind an ear with her fingers. The sound of a bicycle bell chimed from her pocket.

Not again.

Maggie fished out her phone, dread returning like muscle memory. She was no different than Pavlov's dogs. The bell rang. Her stomach clenched.

Maggie gave the phone CPR with the swipe of an index finger, and it came to life, displaying the next meeting on the app's appointment reminder.

James Montgomery's face loomed from the phone's tiny screen.

Evidently the puppeteer had a puppeteer. And another killer waiting in the wings.

She knew she should try to find out who was behind the text, try to stop whatever was next for Montgomery Senior and likely Montgomery Junior.

But she couldn't muster the energy to care. The bell had tolled for Rxcellance and its conspirators. She imagined it would be the last time she heard its peal on her phone.

"Nice knowing you, Mr. Montgomery," she whispered. Then she switched the phone off and stuffed it back into her pocket. She was going to take Travis's advice and get a new phone. She was ready for a new beginning all around.

She stood and joined Constantine at the cash register. He paid. They linked arms. Then the two walked out of the diner into a dawn washed clean by unexpected rain.

Author's Note

Ghana necrosis is fictitious, but the neglected tropical diseases that inspired its cultivation are all too real. Ghana necrosis grew in the petri dish of my mind during the development of this book, presenting itself as both literary vehicle and illustrative example of the viral, parasitic and bacterial diseases that affect those already afflicted by poverty. Neglected tropical diseases live up to their name, persisting in the world's most marginalized conflict-ridden communities, sickening more than one billion people worldwide. To learn more about NTDs and find out how you can help, visit end.org.

KATHLEEN VALENTI

When Kathleen Valenti isn't writing page-turning mysteries that combine humor and suspense, she works as a nationally award-winning advertising copywriter. *Protocol* is her debut novel and the first of the Maggie O'Malley mystery series. Kathleen lives in Oregon with her family where she pretends to enjoy running.

**The Maggie O'Malley Mystery Series
by Kathleen Valenti**

PROTOCOL (#1)

Henery Press Mystery Books

And finally, before you go...
Here are a few other mysteries
you might enjoy:

TELL ME NO LIES

Lynn Chandler Willis

An Ava Logan Mystery (#1)

Ava Logan, single mother and small business owner, lives deep in the heart of the Appalachian Mountains, where poverty and pride reign. As publisher of the town newspaper, she's busy balancing election season stories and a rash of ginseng thieves.

And then the story gets personal. After her friend is murdered, Ava digs for the truth all the while juggling her two teenage children, her friend's orphaned toddler, and her own muddied past. Faced with threats against those closest to her, Ava must find the killer before she, or someone she loves, ends up dead.

Available at booksellers nationwide and online

Visit www.henerypress.com for details

SHADOW OF DOUBT

Nancy Cole Silverman

A Carol Childs Mystery (#1)

When a top Hollywood Agent is found poisoned in the bathtub of her home suspicion quickly turns to one of her two nieces. But Carol Childs, a reporter for a local talk radio station doesn't believe it. The suspect is her neighbor and friend, and also her primary source for insider industry news. When a media frenzy pits one niece against the other—and the body count starts to rise—Carol knows she must save her friend from being tried in courts of public opinion.

But even the most seasoned reporter can be surprised, and when a Hollywood psychic shows up in Carol's studio one night and warns her there will be more deaths, things take an unexpected turn. Suddenly nobody is above suspicion. Carol must challenge both her friendship and the facts, and the only thing she knows for certain is the killer is still out there and the closer she gets to the truth, the more danger she's in.

Available at booksellers nationwide and online

Visit www.henerypress.com for details

CIRCLE OF INFLUENCE

Annette Dashofy

A Zoe Chambers Mystery (#1)

Zoe Chambers, paramedic and deputy coroner in rural Pennsylvania's tight-knit Vance Township, has been privy to a number of local secrets over the years, some of them her own. But secrets become explosive when a dead body is found in the Township Board President's abandoned car.

As a January blizzard rages, Zoe and Police Chief Pete Adams launch a desperate search for the killer, even if it means uncovering secrets that could not only destroy Zoe and Pete, but also those closest to them.

Available at booksellers nationwide and online

Visit www.henerypress.com for details

IN IT FOR THE MONEY

David Burnsworth

A Blu Carraway Mystery (#1)

Lowcountry Private Investigator Blu Carraway needs a new client. He's broke and the tax man is coming for his little slice of paradise. But not everyone appreciates his skills. Some call him a loose cannon. Others say he's a liability. All the ex-Desert Storm Ranger knows is his phone hasn't rung in quite a while. Of course, that could be because it was cut off due to delinquent payments.

Lucky for him, a client does show up at his doorstep—a distraught mother with a wayward son. She's rich and her boy's in danger. Sounds like just the case for Blu. Except nothing about the case is as it seems. The jigsaw pieces—a ransom note, a beat-up minivan, dead strippers, and a missing briefcase filled with money and cocaine—do not make a complete puzzle. The first real case for Blu Carraway Investigations in three years goes off the rails. And that's the way he prefers it to be.

Available at booksellers nationwide and online

Visit www.henerypress.com for details

3 1531 00461 4100

CPSIA information can be obtained
at www.ICGtesting.com
Printed in the USA
LVOW13s1955280917
550415LV00011B/687/P

9 781635 112399